SHOW SOME RESPECT

"Agent, you will address your comments to me," the Admiral said. "And show some respect. I won't warn you twice."

"Admiral, have you read Imperial Edict 97?" I asked.

"I have."

"Do you understand it?"

"You are impertinent. You are activated as a Quarantine Agent to advise us."

"Sergeant-Major, have you read Imperial Edict 97?" I said.

"Yes, sir."

The Admiral interrupted. "Agent, you will stand silent."

I ignored him. "Sergeant-Major, tell me what it says."

"It requires assistance," he hesitated and restated: "Unlimited assistance, to the holders of specific documents, without regard to rank, privilege, station, protocol, or security. Holders are the equivalent of the Emperor himself."

"Am I a holder under the edict?"

"Yes, sir, you are."

The Admiral intervened. "My patience is at an end. Security, take that man off the bridge."

I spoke to the Sergeant-Major directly. "Shoot the Admiral."

AGENT OF THE IMPERIUM

MARC MILLER

Copyright © 2015 by Marc Miller

A Baen Book

Baen Publishing Enterprises
P.O. Box 1403
Riverdale, NY 10471
www.baen.com

ISBN: 978-1-9821-2580-6

Cover art by Alan Pollack

First Baen printing, November 2020
First Baen mass market printing, December 2021

Distributed by Simon & Schuster
1230 Avenue of the Americas
New York, NY 10020

Library of Congress Control Number: 2020036504

Printed in the United States of America

10 9 8 7 6 5 4 3 2 1

To my mother, who was the first Enna.

The GALAXY

Core

Rift
Arm

Charted Space

◄ Spinward • Trailing ►

KiloParsecs

1
2
3
4
5
6
7
8
9
10

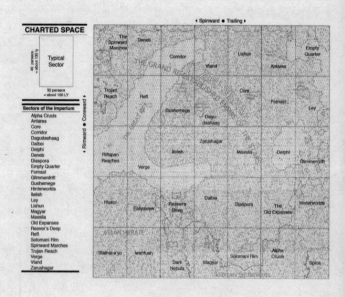

CHARTED SPACE

Typical Sector

40 parsecs = about 130 ly

32 parsecs = about 100 LY

Sectors of the Imperium

Alpha Crucis
Antares
Core
Corridor
Dagudashaag
Daibei
Delphi
Deneb
Diaspora
Empty Quarter
Fornast
Glimmerdrift
Gushemege
Hinterworlds
Ilelish
Ley
Lishun
Magyar
Massilia
Old Expanses
Reaver's Deep
Reft
Solomani Rim
Spinward Marches
Trojan Reach
Verge
Vland
Zarushagar

◄ Spinward ● Trailing ►

◄ Rimward ● Coreward ►

The Spinward Marches
Deneb
Corridor
Vland
Lishun
Antares
Empty Quarter
Trojan Reach
Reft
Gushemege
Daigu-dashaag
Core
Fornast
Ley
Riftspan Reaches
Ilelish
Zarushagar
Massilia
Delphi
Glimmerdrift
Verge
Htakoi
Eallyalsiyw
Reaver's Deep
Daibei
Diaspora
The Old Expanses
Hinterworlds
Stahai-a'yo
Iwahfuah
Dark Nebula
Magyar
Solomani Rim
Alpha Crucis
Spica

THE GRAND REEF
ZIRU SIRKA
ESTABLISHED LIMIT
THE SPLIT
THE GREAT RIFT
ASLAN HIERATE
Solomani Sphere-plots

CONTENTS

THE WORLDS OF THE IMPERIUM

The worlds of the Imperium (as well as those beyond its borders) are identified by location, name, and a brief recapitulation of their physical and social characteristics in the standard format:

> Sect xxyy WorldName StSAHPGL-T Rem1 Rem2
>   Rem3
> Core 2118 Capital A586A98-D Hi Cx

Sect is the four-letter sector name abbreviation, xxyy is the starchart locational coordinates, and WorldName is the common label applied to the MainWorld (the most significant world) in the stellar system at this location.

St is the Starport type, S is World Size, A is a code for Atmosphere, and H is the rough percentage (in tens) of surface covered with water (or perhaps fluids).

P is sophont population as a power of 10, G is the code for government type from a standard list, and L is the code for the local legal system on a permissive-oppressive spectrum.

T is a code for commonly available technology on a standard scale.

Rem1 and others are remarks identifying commonly encountered trade classifications and world characteristics. Ri is a Rich World; Ag is Agricultural; In is Industrial; Po is Poor; Cp, Cs, and Cx are Capitals. The thoroughness of the remarks listed varies.

High Population Worlds (billions or more) are traditionally named on charts in ALL CAPS.

Values greater than 9 are represented by hexadecimal numbers (A=10, B=11, through F=15). When required, correspondingly higher values use successive letters of the Anglic alphabet (but omit I or O to avoid confusion).

Decode:

Core 2118 Capital A586A98-D Hi Cx

Capital is a medium-sized planet (the 5) with a dense atmosphere of standard gas mixture, and seas covering 60% of its surface (the 6). It has a population in the tens of billions (the A, which represents 10, so population is 10^{10}), governed by an impersonal bureaucracy with strict laws abridging personal freedoms in order to reduce conflicts. Available technology is among the best the Imperium has to offer (the D, which represents 13). The initial A is the starport; the best available. Remarks indicate the world is High Population, the Imperial Capital.

The chart locations of most (but not all) worlds can be referenced at the comprehensive online Traveller Map site.

THE IMPERIAL CALENDAR

Holiday	Wonday	Tuday	Thirday	Forday	Fiday	Sixday	Senday	Wonday	Tuday	Thirday	Forday	Fiday	Sixday	Senday
1	2	3	4	5	6	7	8	9	10	11	12	13	14	15
	16	17	18	19	20	21	22	23	24	25	26	27	28	29
	30	31	32	33	34	35	36	37	38	39	40	41	42	43
	44	45	46	47	48	49	50	51	52	53	54	55	56	57
	58	59	60	61	62	63	64	65	66	67	68	69	70	71
	72	73	74	75	76	77	78	79	80	81	82	83	84	85
	86	87	88	89	90	91	92	93	94	95	96	97	98	99
	100	101	102	103	104	105	106	107	108	109	110	111	112	113
	114	115	116	117	118	119	120	121	122	123	124	125	126	127
	128	129	130	131	132	133	134	135	136	137	138	139	140	141
	142	143	144	145	146	147	148	149	150	151	152	153	154	155
	156	157	158	159	160	161	162	163	164	165	166	167	168	169
	170	171	172	173	174	175	176	177	178	179	180	181	182	183
	184	185	186	187	188	189	190	191	192	193	194	195	196	197
	196	197	198	199	200	201	202	203	204	205	206	207	208	209
	212	213	214	215	216	217	218	219	220	221	222	223	224	225
	226	227	228	229	230	231	232	233	234	235	236	237	238	239
	240	241	242	243	244	245	246	247	248	249	250	251	252	253
	254	255	256	257	258	259	260	261	262	263	264	265	266	267
	268	269	270	271	272	273	274	275	276	277	278	279	280	281
	282	283	284	285	286	287	288	289	290	291	292	293	294	295
	296	297	298	299	300	301	302	303	304	305	306	307	308	309
	310	311	312	313	314	315	316	317	318	319	320	321	322	323
	324	325	326	326	327	328	329	330	331	332	333	334	335	336
	338	339	340	341	342	343	344	345	346	347	348	349	350	351
	352	353	354	355	356	357	358	359	360	361	362	363	364	365
	1day	2day	3day	4day	5day	6day	7day	1day	2day	3day	4day	5day	6day	7day

THE IMPERIAL CALENDAR

The empire, variously called *Ziru Sirkaa*, the Re-Established Grand Empire of the Stars, the Third Imperium, the Imperium, the Empire, or simply the empire, was re-established as the interstellar community in this particular region emerged from the thousand-year Long Night.

The Imperial Calendar takes as its reference point the day and year in which the Imperium was declared: the first day of Year Zero. Dates are expressed as a three-digit day followed by a three-digit year: The Imperium was declared on 001-000. The day is often omitted in a year reference: Anguistus became eighth Emperor in 326.

Dates before the Year Zero are negatives: The First Imperium fell in -2204; Cleon Zhunastu was born in -57.

For finer detail, time on a 24-hour clock may be prefixed followed by a space. 0000 001-000 is beginning midnight of the first day of the calendar. 0800 045-123 is the eighth hour of a specific morning. 2000 045-123 is the twentieth hour of the same day. Subtract 12 to convert to traditional clock time. Local star- or sun-oriented times may vary.

IMPERIAL EDICT 97

This Executive Order is the enabling act for the activities of Imperial Agents and the use of Imperial Warrants. Unusually obscure for such a wide-ranging and powerful edict, it is nonetheless on file at all Imperial installations. The edict text runs to 34 pages plus encrypted appendices. Much of it is pure legalese; when distilled down, it is extremely direct—assist designated holders without reservation.

Imperial Edict 97 requires unlimited assistance to the holders of specific documents, written, oral, or electronic, without regard to rank, privilege, station, protocol, or security. Holders are the equivalent of the Emperor himself.

Holders may be designated Agents, or may be empowered through an imperially signed Warrant.

Imperial Star Marines are the designated implementers of the Edict: trained in its terms and instructed to obey a holder's orders "even if it's stupid, or suicidal, or without explanation."

THE RULES

Agent Standing Orders (Executive Summary)

*Rule 1. You speak with the voice of the Emperor.
Brook no resistance.*

*Rule 2. Millions of lives depend on your actions;
you may need to spend some of them in
the process.*

*Rule 3. You act through your team; build it (quickly)
by whatever means available.*

*Rule 4. Your team is your greatest asset: use them;
depend on them.*

*Rule 5. You hold the ability to punish and reward;
do both.*

Rule 6. Right action requires intelligence.

AGENT OF THE IMPERIUM

MAARUUR

It is important to establish dominance
immediately upon awakening.
The first ten minutes are crucial.
—Quarantine Manual

109-350
Aboard BB *Ikaniil* Orbiting
Core 0707 Maaruur B694987-9 Hi In Sa Tu
I was awake, my eyes still closed, standing rather than reclining, and so I knew this must be the start of a new activation. The wave of disorientation passed, and I opened my eyes.

Before me was an expansive bridge, the transpex allowing me to see the curve of a world below. Twenty or so officers and spacers all stood at a respectful distance, waiting for me to begin, wondering what I was going to do.

"Who here is senior?"

"I am, Admiral Gonchan. We have . . ."

"Who is the senior marine?"

"Me. Sergeant-Major Joslin."

"Come here." Joslin took a few steps forward.

"I need a mirror."

Joslin turned and directed, "Dinsha, run to your locker and bring us a mirror." One of the marines dashed off.

"Show me your comm."

The screen was unfamiliar to me. "Activate it."

I now took it and selected a familiar double eye icon and felt it click. As this happened, I spoke to the group in general. "Who is the briefer?"

"I am, Commander Arlian Huffler, Sensops."

"Please stay your briefing until I am ready. It will be a moment."

I now examined the unfamiliar image: a young, reasonably handsome Naval officer. Brown eyes, brown hair. Tall. A strange line to his chin, perhaps Cassildan? No, not tall enough. No matter. The pips on his collar said I was a Naval sublieutenant.

I returned the comm to the Sergeant-Major. "Thank you."

The admiral now spoke, his tone betraying his impatience. "We have activated you so that you may advise us on our current situation. Commander Huffler, you may begin."

While he conveyed impatience, I suppressed my own feelings of annoyance.

As a realtime image of the world below appeared on the screen, the briefer began conveying information. "Maaruur, Core Sector oh seven oh seven. Maaruur is a cold, medium-sized far satellite on the outer fringe of the habitable zone, with a diameter of 9,880 kilometers and a circumference of 31,030 kilometers. It has a dense atmosphere with a tainted, exotic gas mixture and a pressure of 200 kilopascals at . . ."

I interrupted. "Skip the planetology and fast forward to the statement of danger."

The screen changed to a display in a standard format as the briefer continued his narrative, essentially reading and elaborating on screen text. The headline was Danger-10. Someone, or some committee, or some computer, had evaluated this problem as potentially reaching the whole of the world below. There followed a less-than-brief statement of the problem: a mass of grey text in small type. The image confirmed what the briefer was saying in far too many words.

"Now show the statement of the threat." The new screen was headlined Threat-6, perhaps a hundred thousand actors, apparently very determined, parasites of some sort. Codes said they were confined to the northern continent, with some reports of presence elsewhere.

There was an obscure code appended to the report: the parasite hijacked the host's consciousness and intelligence. They were able to act in concert. Even one or two on a ship out of the system would be disastrous. How could anyone not see the depth of the danger?

"Show the Risk Assessment." The screen changed again: three numbers 4, 4, and 0 adding to a larger 8. They were all subjective: how probable, how severe, how imminent the Danger was. The action point was usually 9 or 10.

Images changed and the briefer droned on about resources, activating protocols for containment, provisions for contingencies, anticipated exceptions, and a timeline for completion.

From the corner of my eye, I saw the marine appear

at the entrance to the bridge, genuflect perfunctorily at the captain's chair and step forward to the Sergeant Major with a mirror, who took it and passed it to me.

I motioned to the briefer. "Pause please."

The reflection confirmed what I had seen on the comm, and I moved it around to see more detail at different angles.

"Why am I in this specific host?" I was curious why he—I—was a junior lieutenant.

The admiral spoke. "You overlay Sublieutenant Patel. Our report to sector generated an internal interim requirement to activate Quarantine."

"How many volunteered?"

"Patel."

"Anyone else?"

"I didn't think we needed more than one volunteer."

"Have you stopped traffic in and out of system? On and off world?"

"There isn't a need yet. We're monitoring traffic."

"Admiral, is there some reason you have not yet shut this system down?"

"The threat is contained on the northern continent. You were activated as a precaution. We have the situation in hand."

I unconsciously raised my hand in a pause gesture and turned my attention to Joslin.

"Sergeant-Major, do you know me? Personally?"

"Casually, sir."

"Who am I?"

"Sir, you are Sublieutenant Patel. Supply officer. You've been here for about five months. Sir."

"Am I any good?"

"Sir?"

"Your experience with Patel: is he any good?"

"Average. Good at PT and sports. A little slower than some at assertiveness."

"I need a sidearm. Make that two, one non-lethal. Are these your men?"

"A couple are women, sir."

"Yes. Arm them lethal-non-lethal as well. You are under my command. I also need a flight jacket. Make it say Agent on the back over the Imperial Seal."

"Yes, sir." The Sergeant-Major turned and gestured to several troopers.

"Agent, you will address your comments to me. And show some respect. I recognize that you may be momentarily disoriented, but I won't warn you twice."

"Admiral, have you read Imperial Edict 97?"

"I have."

"Do you understand it?"

"Certainly."

"Tell me, in a sentence, what it says."

"You are impertinent. You are activated as a Quarantine Agent to advise us on our current Danger and Threat levels."

"Sergeant-Major, have you read Imperial Edict 97?"

"Yes, sir."

The Admiral interrupted. "Agent, you will stand silent."

I ignored him.

"Sergeant-Major, do you understand it?"

"Certainly."

"Tell me what it says."

Joslin recited rote. "It requires assistance," he hesitated and restated, "unlimited assistance, to the holders of specific documents, written, oral, or electronic, without regard to rank, privilege, station, protocol, or security. Holders are the equivalent of the Emperor himself."

"Am I a holder under the edict?"

"Yes, sir you are."

Two marines stepped forward with a jacket and a weapons belt with two holsters. "The rough red handle is lethal, sir; the yellow smooth is non-lethal."

I took the flight jacket, looked at the back to check the markings. It said AGENT in thick black marker; I had sometimes seen it spelled AJENT. I reached to my collar and removed my rank pips, then put on the jacket. The weapons belt strapped on easily.

"Are the recorders on?" A nod from Sergeant-Major said they were.

"Who is Captain?"

"This is my ship; I am Captain Argent."

"Suspend all traffic. No lift-offs. No landings. Divert incoming traffic to the outer system at the very least. Allow no jumps for any ship that has been on-planet in the past seven days."

The Admiral intervened. "My patience is at an end. Security, take that man off the bridge." And then "Patel, whoever you are, you will be silent."

I spoke to the Sergeant-Major directly. "Shoot him."

"Sir?"

"In the knee. Shut him up."

We all heard one shot. The Admiral dropped to the deck, howling, spewing a variety of ill-chosen words.

I raised my voice for all to hear. "I am Agent Patel of the Quarantine. I act under Imperial Edict 97. Imminence is advanced to Now. This situation has escalated to Risk-14. Comms, call up the Edict File and make sure it's recording. Captain, get started on my orders. Sergeant-Major, take the Admiral to his quarters."

* * *

An hour later, I visited the Admiral in his suite. The Sergeant-Major dismissed the medic tending to the wounded leg.

"Get out! Get out!"

Calmly, ignoring the outburst, "Admiral, why did you select Sublieutenant Patel?"

"What? You shot me. I'll have your head."

"Answer my question."

"You're crazy. This is impossible! Intolerable!"

"Do I need to kneecap your other?"

"Sergeant-Major. Do something."

But he didn't.

Deliberately. "Answer. My. Question," with a hand on the red grip of my lethal option.

"You. Patel was available. The crisis already needed every available resource, and then in the middle of it all, the stupid computer required we activate a Quarantine wafer. It gave a list of wafer-slots, and I picked you. Patel."

"You have no wafer-slots on your staff?"

"I needed them for the crisis. We could do without a supply officer for a week; your petty officer can handle things."

"Your staff gave no objections?"

"My staff does not object to clearly logical conclusions."

"Do you have a wafer jack?"

"Certainly not."

"I see."

I turned to leave and spoke to the air, "Fit him with a wafer jack."

***

Admiral, now Agent, Gonchan, stood on the bridge before his staff. Stiffly; his leg still healing.

"I am Agent Gonchan of the Quarantine. I act under Imperial Edict 97. Let's get to work."

034-336
Core 2118 Capital A586A98-D Hi Cx

I worked in an obscure office in the Ministry of State. After a basic education and a fairly ordinary university degree, I spent a term in the Imperial Star Marines. That may sound romantic, and it certainly sounds active, but in reality, it was mundanely bureaucratic. My comrades wear their battle scars proudly and they display their particular badges of service that tell those who recognize them that Enn fought in the Assault on Greer, or that Ank served with the Emperor's Own Imperial Guard.

If I had such a badge; if there were such a badge, it would say that I served at the scheduling desk of Imperial Reaction Force Zalaa deciding which regiment would interact with what world at when point in time. I learned valuable lessons that have served me all of my life, but they are not the stuff of stories that entertain friends.

As my term of service neared its end, one of the offices

with which I worked invited me to interview. Although initially I had dreams of travel with one of the megacorporations, in the end I received rather few offers in response to my inquiries, and so I visited with the Office of Appeals at the Imperial Quarantine Agency. They liked my answers to their questions; they confirmed I was suitable because they had direct access to all of my Marine service records; they offered me a job doing much what I had been doing in the Marines, albeit with more money.

At the time, the Quarantine was a semi-autonomous force within the Imperial Navy. Fully a tenth of the Navy's fighting ships carried the mission modifier Q: crewed by Quarantine officers, trained in Quarantine doctrine and policy, and dedicated to protecting the Empire from the strange and deadly threats that the universe creates from time to time.

It became clear to me that the Navy disliked the Quarantine for reasons too many to list. From the inside, I heard the justifications for Quarantine's existence and structure, and I adopted them as my own, partly because they made sense, partly because they supported the existence of my own employment, and partly because I never looked deeper into the controversy.

The Office of Appeals, my particular assignment, was an obscure component of the far larger Quarantine Agency. Once a world was Quarantined, many interests arose: business, noble, economic, political, family, ancestral, moral, civil, scientific, cultural. All of those concerned registered their objections or affirmations, to be heard by an agency magistrate who had the theoretical power to change the designation. The process took years, decades, even centuries. Appeals covered not only current designations, but also labels applied long long ago.

A smooth-running bureaucracy needs an institutional memory to ensure its decisions are both correct and consistent. It fell to me to maintain that memory, some of it in the computer, some of it in my brain. I spent my entire adult life dedicated to my particular part of the overall whole.

I began as a lowly clerk and steadily climbed the bureaucratic ladder: senior clerk, supervisor, senior supervisor, assistant manager, manager, senior manager, and ultimately Assistant Director for Appeals, reporting to the Director himself. Since the Director changed with the whims of the faction currently in power, I was effectively in charge of my own petty empire. I enjoyed my life, and my job. I was good at it. I could even say that I loved it.

It all changed in an instant.

At my annual physical, the doctor told me I had incurable, terminal cerebral degeneration. I would be dead within five years. There was no hope. This was an area of medical science for which there had been little progress made and little knowledge gained. He said I had time to get my affairs in order, plenty of time, actually. I could expect a good year or two, and then an inevitable decline.

When I arrived at work the next day, my console showed a new meeting flag: The Director himself wanted to see me later that day.

* * *

The Quarantine Agency has a bifurcated control structure. The ships in the fleet are commanded by Quarantine officers with a rank structure parallel to the Imperial Navy: Lieutenants, Commanders, Captains, and Admirals. The titles are the same; the loyalties merely reach the Emperor along slightly different paths. The administrative structure, on the other hand, consisted of several Offices: Personnel, Research, Training, Appeals, plus a few others.

The current Director of the Quarantine Agency was Lord Nam Aankhuga, Count Mishaar, a tall red-haired politician installed as Director when the Orange Party became ascendant in the Moot some six years before.

As his assistant ushered me in, the Count rose and offered me a seat, at the same time telling me how sorry he was to hear of my diagnosis and prognosis. After some awkward comments, he came to his agenda item.

* * *

"Jonathan.

"The downturn is taking its toll on the economy." He paused. I was sure at that moment that they were going to cast me aside without a thought and he saw that in my face.

"No. Jonathan. Your retirement is secure; your support package is substantial. You have no worries, except, of course, for your prognosis.

"This is something different." He called up a display with some graphic quantity charts and started to explain them.

"The capital ship hulls of the fleet are nearing the end of their design life. Our quarantine ships are doing only little better." He explained that the tension between the Navy and the Quarantine had come to a head; that a ship-building budget that would stoke the economy was being considered; that powerful political figures did not see the need for devoting a tenth of the fleet to Q-mission ships.

"Their solution is simple, so they say: make all ships Navy; in Quarantine emergencies give temporary situational command to a designated Quarantine officer with full authority to do anything required. The Emperor, Anguistus himself, backs this plan."

As part of me listened to this disclosure of the inner policy workings of the Imperial bureaucracy, I wondered why I was being told these details even as my tenure with the agency was coming to an end.

The Count continued with a few more comments, and then made his proposal.

"Jonathan, you know as much about this agency as anyone. You know our procedures, our policies. You know how important the right decisions are. You know the devastation that can follow a wrong decision. More than that, you have seen the right decisions being made; the wrong decisions being avoided.

"We have a process that can capture all of that knowledge and use it to enable our Quarantine Agents in the field under this new scheme."

He leaned forward, "We can capture your personality and implant it temporarily in a naval officer to manage quarantine emergencies. With all your knowledge and experience, it is a better solution than training officers for a situation they may never face.

"But, there is a problem.

"The scanning is destructive. You will die during the process."

110-350
Aboard BB *Ikaniil* Orbiting
Core 0707 Maaruur B694987-9 Hi In Sa Tu

Time was important, the operation needed to start even as I scheduled planning sessions. I called up console imagery myself because I knew what I wanted to know; it took less than minutes. I turned to the assembled staff officers.

"Intel."

"Yes, Agent."

"Go over the details of this world."

He tapped his controller and the screen in front of me brightened. Titles appeared, "Maaruur Core 0707 B694987-9." The officer decoded it aloud, "Moderate size, tainted dense atmosphere, less than average water. Billions of people, bureaucratic government, reasonable law, comfortable tech, although it lags the mainstream." He tapped again and a new screen appeared. These codes were denser, "8 billion people, a third are mostly Vilani dating from the Third Millennium. The rest are indigenes: Shingans. Bilateral bipeds about as far from the Human template as they can get. Hairy exoskeletons. Graspers instead of hands.

"It's an industrial world; that explains some of the taint in the atmosphere. Satellite of a gas giant. Cold, a lot of the terrain is marked tundral, thus short growing seasons. Apparently much of the food comes from vats."

"Wait." I had a habit of raising my hand to pause an interaction. "Personnel."

"Yes, Agent." This was an older Human woman.

"Do we have any Shingans, or Maaruurans with us?"

"No, Agent."

I was relieved; one less issue to deal with. Back to Intel.

"Get me a census of who is on the Highport."

I work by heuristics: close enough without spending a lot of time on it. Barring problems, my ships could get anywhere in the system in a day. They can get started crafting kinetics in a day. The kinetics can start hitting in a day.

"Operations?"

A tall Cassildan (that description is redundant, they are all tall) responded. "Yes, Agent."

"Put three of the capitals in equidistant stationary orbit. Dispatch the other two as siege engines to the planetoid belt. Get some pickets there at high speed to help locate what they will need." A pause for breath. "Put marines in place on the Highport control center. Am I being redundant? I want this world on interdict. No one, nothing in or out. Cut comms and links. How long?"

"Yes, sir. Interdict is already in place. Four hours for the Highport operation."

"Come back to me before you execute." My knee hurt. There was a stab of pain.

"Medical. Get me a pain pill." I didn't wait for a reply. "Logistics."

"Yes, Agent."

"The siege engines will start building kinetics tomorrow. Are they properly stocked? Tell me the foreseeables."

"The critical path constricts on flash chips. Everything else can be lasered and makered. They did an exercise last season with excellent results. The chip stockpile is full; that's just a commodity. We have more than enough."

"Confirm all that and come back to me with specific numbers."

I turned to the Captain. It was time for some semblance of social connection. "Captain, you have an excellent crew. Everything I see is competent. I commend you." Since I was speaking with the voice of the Emperor, I hoped this would keep him in check.

"Thank you, sir. My duty is to serve the Empire." What else could he say?

I talked to various officers until Operations and Personnel came back. Sensor protocols. Competencies. Exception responses. Morale. Notifications to sector flag.

"Agent." Personnel waited for me to respond.

"Yes?"

"Highport has thirteen hundred personnel. Half are transients, passengers, crew. The rest are staff, clerks, functionaries."

"How many are Shingans?"

She looked down. "A third." She didn't see where I was going, and I had to ask gender proportion. "Seventy-thirty." That was consistent with the sophont gender census.

"What ships are in port?"

"Just four. Not counting us, of course. A Jumpliner. Three traders."

I touched a nearby console and asked it for similar

worlds nearby. It showed graphics which I tapped. 1901 Zaniin had room. 2624 Idas was a hellworld, so no. 0302 Khaam was close, empty, and similar; it could actually use some people.

"Tell the marines that I want every Maaruuran," my mouth twisted on the word, "Shingan, Human, whatever, on that jumpliner and bound for Khaam. Brook no questions, but use non-lethal force. I don't think they are going to understand. Set up a resettlement program for them.

"Activate any reservists over there and bring them on board here. Load everyone else on the traders and get them out of the system. Make that penultimate priority." Priority and security classifications use the same scale: Ultimate (Last), Penultimate (Last but one), Antepenultimate (Last but two), and Preantepenultimate (Last but three), and Propreanteppenult (Last but four). In practice, the terms after Penultimate are technical terms within the bureaucracy; they devolve into Ante, Pre, and Pro. Ultimate priority would have authorized lethal force; I didn't want to lose any of them.

"Yes, Agent."

"Operations? Can the marines handle all that? Are you ready?"

"Yes, Agent."

"Then execute." I turned to my next task.

Scrubbing a world takes a lot of planning, a lot of work, a lot of attention to detail. I delegated to the captain the positioning of the ships and the details of the attack. Some of the rest I delegated to my other self: Patel. I assigned tasks and responsibilities to others as well; no one person could do all that had to be done. It would be three days before the true scrubbing began, but we started immediately. We tilted Highport out of orbit to impact the largest city. The dreadnoughts emped the world from three sides, repeatedly. Civilization below evaporated.

What few comms survived the emps called frantically and repeatedly. There was an instant information vacuum: were we pirates? invaders? rebels? anarchists? luddites? sociops? usurpers? No one below knew and we stood silent. Several ships tried to boost to orbit; we knocked them back. A couple of feeble grav carriers tried as well; their efforts to climb out of the gravity well would take them hours and we blasted them. It was a gift.

Our siege engines reached the belt ahead of schedule and started work immediately. The ships extended their rail guns and prepared for a long campaign.

They harvested FeNi chunks, peeled them of their outer husks, then sliced them into manageable pieces. Lasers engraved them with textures to help them plunge through atmosphere.

Makers processed the shucks into thrusters that they spot welded into place.

In a last step, crew swarmed over the newborn kinetics and inserted their brains: flash-programed chips that knew where and when to strike. Then they launched.

Streams of thousands followed pre-determined paths. Some looped far afield to arrive later; others proceeded more directly.

We had divided Maaruur arbitrarily into thirty thousand cells: map locations a hundred kilometers across. Ten waves of three thousand kinetics were supposed to be sufficient to sterilize the world. The first wave was probably enough to kill everyone; the rest were just insurance.

The first wave arrived at the end of day four. The impacts were designed to overlap. For that first wave at least, we had to watch. We couldn't not.

The brownish globe that was Maaruur hung before us, bright in sunlight, part cloaked in shadow. Sensops was a droning background narration as we watched. The kinetics had six-digit names; she gave up reciting the entire string and gave us one- or two-digit identifiers. "Four-four to impact. Now. Set Seven approaching. Group One impacting now." A bloom of bright, then another, then a dozen, then a hundred flared in the planet's night, a neatly drawn line from pole to pole. We knew without asking that the ground beneath was burning beyond recognition; that impacts were crushing everything on the surface and then fracking the bedrock; that winds and blasts were destroying all in their paths.

Scattered other impacts shattered the perfection of the flowing glowing line as stragglers hit their targets and special mission nukes seasoned the air.

Comms' job was to monitor. She listened to multiple pleading transmissions from below, shifting in no particular order from anger, to bargaining, to despair, and even to acceptance. I moved to her console and put my hand on her shoulder. "Turn that off. You don't need to listen anymore."

One of the specialty cooks, a tripod with striped skin and booming voice, collapsed. Personnel said it was unusually sensitive to emotions; the death throes overwhelmed it, even at 50,000 kilometers. A later update told me it died.

Over the next two days, there were scattered impacts: specialty target strikes where sensors saw life or movement or emissions in various spectra. We launched ten waves of kinetics total: we hit every possible location on the world, some twice, some three times. Special targeting boiled parts of the seas and sloshed hundred-meter waves across shorelines. Strikes hit fault lines and shook the continents to their very foundations: no subsurface structures could possibly survive those quakes. Repeated drops awakened volcanoes from their slumber and they spewed out angry ash that turned the skies blacker yet.

My remaining sleeps dwindled to a handful as our mission moved toward its natural end. Some of our ships would remain here for decades. I wouldn't be here to see it. I would be dead again.

I addressed the ships' crews: I told them that they had served the empire well and that the Emperor himself would know of their service and dedication. I told them that by their service they had saved a trillion lives and that I was proud of them. Some were moved by my words; I could see the tears in their eyes.

I admit that I felt a similar pride. The Emperor had chosen me to do his will, and I had again proven myself competent. I went to sleep that night satisfied.

090-336
Core 2118 Capital A586A98-D Hi Cx

I arranged for my own funeral. My wife was already dead, my children long-gone. I had few friends; I had poured myself into my work.

For reasons I accepted but did not fully understand, my family had rejected the commonplace full cremation and adopted the custom of sampling: we, that is, my family, could point to specific stone crypts that held pieces of us going back six generations. It was a source of continuity, of comfort to us, to me. When I was dead, I would have a place with my ancestors.

Keeping a whole body, however, was nonsense. Too big. Bulky. A sample was enough: humility and family tradition dictated that it be the least significant digit of my non-dominant hand.

I arranged for a monument in the Bilanidin—that was our name before we anglicized it to Bland—family memorial section in rural Intell. The stele was black granite with swirls of grey, standing as twice as tall as I, as wide as I. I eschewed any decoration; there was no one to appreciate it. Incised on its base was my name in both Anglic and Vilani:

Jonathan Bland
301-277 / 102-336
Chonadon Bilanidin

My sample, my left little finger, suitably preserved for the ages, was to be deposited in a sept carved under the stele's base.

THE RULES

Agent Standing Orders (Executive Summary)

Rule 1. You speak with the voice of the Emperor.
  Brook no resistance.
Rule 2. Millions of lives depend on your actions;
  you may need to spend some of them in
  the process.
Rule 3. You act through your team; build it
  (quickly) by whatever means available.
Rule 4. Your team is your greatest asset: use
  them; depend on them.
Rule 5. You hold the ability to punish and reward;
  do both.

060-336
Core 2118 Capital A586A98-D Hi Cx

We five agent personalities were trained at a secure facility some ten kilometers beneath the surface of Capital. We already had the skills and expertise; aptitude tests and rigorous screening had winnowed down more than two million potentials in the bureaucratic workforce to several thousand, then several hundred, then dozens, and finally us.

Not that the analysis of the others was wasted. The process identified people with very high levels of skill in specific areas: obscure technical fields that took years of study and experience to master; bureaucratic domains that depended on an intimate knowledge of regulations and rules created over the course of centuries; even interpersonal skills that many people seem incapable of developing. For pure skill and expertise, there are other harvesting methods. Those identified as the best-of-the-best were non-destructively scanned. Their extreme skill sets were distilled onto standardized wafers without the associated personalities and distributed widely throughout the bureaucracy and the various uniformed services and armed forces.

The ship drive set enables an unskilled technician to diagnose and repair (with suitable tools and parts) the most complex of starship drives. Similar sets support vehicles, weapons, flyers, various of the hard sciences, and to a lesser extent, the soft sciences.

Skill alone, of course, is never enough; the user needs an appropriate level of supporting intelligence or education. A thesaurus function may propose alternate wording; it takes intelligence to make the right choice from among many options.

Using pure skill wafers is a balancing act: they provide great power, but at potentially great risk. The first question students ask is, "Why not just give us all wafers instead of making us slog through all this material?" In the first blush of wafer implementation, the technology had proponents who advocated just that. Fit users with wafer jacks after a rudimentary (and cheap) education and achieve a well-trained, efficient, and effective work force for an overall lower net cost.

The problem is that wafer use naturally challenges the essential functions of the brain: the conflict between long-established neuron channels and the transient new knowledge has a small, but significant and cumulative, risk of permanent damage. Several decades previous, there had been entire sheltered-care communities for those permanently impaired by skill wafer overuse.

On the other hand, a starship with a crippled jump system, stranded between the stars, is often willing to risk the sanity of its drive technician if a thousand passengers and megacredits of cargo will make it to their destination.

But I digress.

We were trained not in skill use, but in basic principles. Our collective assignment was to use our own expertise in combination with a broad grant of power and authority to protect the empire. Academic experts and the project leaders drafted specific guidance; we five gave our own feedback and some of it was incorporated into the final text. Admiral and Warlord helped craft Rule 3. Negotiator suggested details for Rule 5.

The text of this particular section runs five thousand words, complete with an elenctic method question-and-answer tutorial and a variety of hypothetical examples. All of it was distilled into the less than a hundred words of the Agent Standing Orders. We spent two full days in exercises, discussions, and arguments. Our instructor made us memorize the Executive Summary until we could recite it by rote.

The entire section was then classified Ultimate and attached as an encrypted appendix to our enabling regulations. We five, anywhere, could always consult it with our override codes. Not that, after those sessions, we would ever need to.

* * *

In my previous life, I was a bureaucrat: a functionary. I thrived on making things happen within a system. I couldn't necessarily predict what would happen next, but I could and did strive for order. I established my own particular order.

When I awake, I feel a momentary wash of disorientation. So, I just stand there, eyes closed, and I steady myself as I gradually mesh back into the world.

I call out, "Who here is senior?" The answer tells me something about the situation; any answer tells me something.

I call out, "Who is the briefer?" They activated me; there must be a reason. It follows that someone will be prepared to tell me the situation and the problem.

The routine has a purpose of its own: it's the start of building my Rule 3 team, with just a touch of Rule 1 authority.

ARCANUM

Anguistus' ascent to the Iridium Throne was a long time coming. He was born in the first year of his mother's reign and the public immediately took him to their collective hearts: Prince Angin waved to the court from his mother's lap; crowds of chroniclers followed his every move from birth to adolescence to adulthood. He visited many worlds as mother Porfiria's proxy. His storybook wedding to Margaret of Delphi was celebrated for months after as news and images made their way to the borders of the Empire. Billions grieved with him and his bride when their firstborn died after only a precious few months.

Public opinion turned against him when he and Margaret parted ways and he took up a very public life of dissolution and extravagance. Public approval returned when he gave up those ways, reconciled with Margaret, and their second child Martin III was born. The public grieved again when Margaret died soon after.

At age 45, Angin was given substantial responsibilities in the Moot: promoting the Armed Forces as the guardians of Imperial stability and peace.

After a lifetime of cycles of trial and triumph, Prince

Angin finally reached his ultimate destiny when his
mother died. He was 80.

333-402
Aboard BKF *Kobokoon* Above
Dene 2126 Arcanum B434866-5 Ph

I stood on the bridge of the flagship of the Deneb
Fleet. Elements had been patrolling the system since the
first reports and now, six weeks later, the fleet strike
squadron was present in force.

I had been activated earlier today. The briefer, a
professor of planetology, sounded scared as he spoke.
Maybe it was the threat level; maybe he thought that I just
killed people randomly.

We were in orbit above Arcanum, a poor world with a
lot of people crowded into cities and towns within a few
hundred kilometers of its coastlines, the interiors of its six
continents impenetrable forest. The planet had no known
indigenes, just Humans.

We could see the problem from here. As the world
rotated below us, a silver dome a thousand kilometers
across rose to near world orbit. Arcanum looked out-of-
balance, like it should wobble as it turned. A few fast
communications satellites had already bumped into the
dome. Smashed into it.

It was a stasis globe. The shiny surface was the clue: it
reflected all incoming energy. The interior was frozen in
a moment of time some six weeks ago. We've met people
who can make stasis globes; they wouldn't sell us their
machines and we found we couldn't take them—or steal
them. I am sure someone tried. The problem with stasis

is that we can't turn it off; its extinction date is inextricably set when it's created. If a specific globe is set to end in seventy-four years, nothing (nothing we know of) will turn it off sooner.

Our sensors located the epicenter: a mining site in a coastal mountain range. The effect had a radius. At a thousand-kilometer diameter, we could gauge the hypocenter as about 100 kilometers below planetary surface: deep inside the mines. We had historical information, but now deep radar couldn't penetrate the field to tell us anything more.

The planetary government sent us the mining permits and documentation, but they denied there was any clandestine activity at the site—as if the leaders would even know.

There had been a few deaths: people catastrophically sliced when the globe went on. Some were lucky and only lost limbs; one person lost his nose.

We worked on the evaluations and data analysis for a full day and quit only when fatigue made us too weary to function. I set a renewed meeting for tomorrow. As the meeting broke up, an officer approached me.

"Sir. Agent." Agent was the correct form of address. I looked at him.

"Lieutenant Gilcrest, Agent. I am a reservist; and I just happen to be assigned to the fleet this month shadowing the intelligence officer. Can I share with you some thoughts?"

"Why is this not part of the formal briefing?"

"I am not part of the formal structure here, just a

reservist. My job, to quote someone higher up, is to 'shut up and listen.' I have been, but that doesn't stop me from thinking."

I was skeptical. "Why is your insight so much different from the others?"

"Ah, that's the point, Agent." He pointed to a badge on his uniform, a small silver cluster with a stylized triangle. "I am psi-qualified; I've been to the Psi Service institute. In world surface life, I am a socialization counsellor in an adolescent school. I use psi in my work; we have found that there are psi approaches that help normalize outlier students."

Fringe science, I thought. Hard, if not impossible, to disprove, or to prove; it flourished at the edges of real science. I was surprised that the Navy even had a Psi Service; I wasn't surprised that no one would listen to him. Resisting a temptation to dismiss him abruptly, I invited him to a late meal before I quit for the night.

Gilcrest told a good story; perhaps he had also been to persuasion school. His neighborhood youth co-ordinator took an interest in him; exposed him to a variety of experiences. He found that he was interested in the sciences of the mind. He took several remote learning sequences, even went away for a semester to an intense immersion experience. He ended up with a Second Stage certificate of completion from the local Psionics Institute on Thengin.

I asked if he could read minds. He laughed. "They classify what I do as empathy. I can sort of sense what people are thinking or more usually feeling, even from a distance."

"And I am thinking what?"

"There's a surface skepticism. I don't blame you. But there's also a genuine interest; you want to solve this problem." Anyone could make that up.

"Oh, and there's something deeper that doesn't quite parse. It's like there's another part of you, flailing in a pit of pitch. I don't understand what that means at all."

I had not thought of where my host went when I took over. I thought he was just dormant. I pressed on.

"So, tell me your insight about Arcanum."

"When we pass close to the globe, it feels like they are still there."

We talked for a while; I listened to his opinions and noted his comm code.

* * *

We all met the next day on the bridge. Their consensus was that we should scrub the world before this effect spread. Not that that made a lot of sense: the effect wasn't spreading; nukes won't affect stasis, neither would kinetics, nor emps, nor high energy projectors. It wasn't like we could hide that thing, if we scrubbed the whole world, turned the atmosphere opaque black with dust, it would still be a silver bulb rising 300 kilometers above the clouds.

Scrub this world, they said. I wasn't convinced.

They located a mining engineer who had worked at the site; sent out of system on a consulting assignment and only now returned after some eight months. I expected a Human male; I saw before me a Newt. Newts aren't mining engineers: they are co-ordinators and list makers.

"Tell me who you are."

His voice squeaked. "Good day, Agent. I am Supervisor

Patha, Tafa Patha. Of ThreeMinCo; we are a division of Naasirka."

"Are you aware of the situation below?"

"In part; I have not been formally instructed."

I asked the professor to repeat the latest iteration of his briefing. I signaled and someone brought Patha refreshments and a wet cloth. When the presentation was complete, Patha spoke.

"It appears that the hypocenter is at the Seng level of the mine, the deepest part. The other levels produce heavy metals; we process the ore in a facility near the surface. The site is unusually rich in elements that we cannot easily find in the planetoid belt.

"The Seng level," he stopped, thinking through his words. "The Seng level is seeded with debris from a very old impact. We recover the pieces and ship them offworld for research."

This cleared things up. Three hundred thousand years ago, the Ancients had fought a wide-ranging interstellar war amongst themselves, shattering worlds, destroying stars, destroying their own civilization in the process. Some of their technology was literally unimaginable. This was an Ancient artifact.

I jumped to that conclusion. "So, the Seng level dates to about 300,000 years ago? The Ancient era?"

"No, Agent. It is ten times that old. Three million years."

I wiggled my fingers in battle language and the Marines started clearing the bridge.

I kept the key staff only: a few officers. I asked Gilcrest to stay as well.

* * *

I now felt it necessary to reconfirm basic information.
"Has anyone touched that field?"

"Several people lost limbs, Agent."

"Has anyone touched that field recently?"

"No, Agent."

I sent the marines on a mission. An assault lander
dropped through atmosphere in minutes; they were
adjacent to the field within two hours. I watched through
a drone.

At touching range, the field was a flat vertical mirror
extending from the ground to the sky. It was hard to see;
the optics were tricky. It was a very good mirror.

334-402
Dene 2126 Arcanum B434866-5 Ph

Imperial Star Marine Captain Iileen Vump was
philosophical. Long ago, she had observed that most
Marines survived their enlistment and went home with a
few medals and a small pension. She wasn't foolhardy, but
she followed the Marine slogan: Obey. Here she was next
to something that killed people; she hoped it wouldn't kill
her. She had her instructions and she was smart enough
not to do some of the tasks herself.

The first task was to touch the field. She told a marine
to take off his gauntlet and touch it.

A stasis field reflects all energy and is impenetrable to
matter. It should be neutral; not hot, not cold.

The assigned marine reached slowly forward,
extended a finger, and touched the surface. "Nothing,
sir. It's solid."

"Touch harder."

He leaned into it, palm flat to the mirror. It flexed slightly and he let out a yelp. He pulled his hand away, surface burned. Stasis fields don't do that.

* * *

The observing drone told everyone to step back. There followed a new set of instructions.

A flat surface pressed against the field with a force slightly greater than local gravity penetrated slightly. Temperature probes showed no observable heat effect.

A long rod could be forced, with some effort, into the field. They succeeded in pushing a rod all the way in using another rod. They succeeded in fishing around with a grapple and retrieving it. They pushed in a sensor package and retrieved it: it came out inoperative, the circuits fried. They ran a series of other tests in response to instructions from above. Several of them seemed to echo the recruits' lament: stupid, suicidal, and certainly without explanation, but like good marines, they obeyed.

Then they pushed a sensor package in, and the rod came out empty, except for a scrap of packing board scrawled with a short phrase: "Help Us."

Fleet sent down a full-scale assault team with logistics train later that day and they worked through the night.

101-336
Core 2118 Capital A586A98-D Hi Cx

I met the emperor himself. In his private chambers. I was giddy.

He touched me with his hand and made me a Knight of the Emperor's Guard, with my name recorded forever in the *Galidumlar Dadaga*: The Great Imperial Archive; the records that are never erased.

He spoke knowledgeably about our entire project and of his dream that it would protect the empire. He expressed appreciation for both my sacrifice and my contribution.

His words burned in my memory as he spoke. I have recalled them many times.

"Jonathan. Your knowledge is a great asset; the safety of the Empire itself depends on your wise use of that asset.

"The core of your mission is to save lives. You will speak with my voice, and I expect that all will obey. Serve the Empire wisely."

The personality harvesting process began the next day. I remember nothing after that.

335-402
Aboard BKF *Kobokoon* above
Dene 2126 Arcanum B434866-5 Ph

On the bridge the next day, we reviewed their findings. Later someone would write a report, probably classified Ultimate, which would make its way to Capital, never to be read again. For today, we needed to decide on the answers.

I led the discussion.

"Feedback and contradict, as necessary.

"First, do we know who wrote the note?"

"They haven't answered."

"Let me know as soon as you know.

"Moving on,

"This isn't a stasis field. It stops energy,"

Someone spoke up, "Because it reflects light, heat, EM, just about everything they tried."

"But it doesn't stop matter,"

Someone else, "It just slows it down, strips away energy above a certain level."

Another, "Just above the local force of gravity."

"So, we can shove things through slowly, but the marines tried a shot and the ricochet dented someone's chestplate."

"Electronics are fried when they go through. Or when they come out. We weren't sure which. Probably both."

"That marine's hand was burned. What was that?"

"Not really burned; it's more complex than that. The surface layer of skin cells went into the field and didn't come out."

The discussion continued. After several more circuits fried, and various photon, fluidic, magnetic, and gravitic systems failed, someone tried a mechanical sensor: a clockwork thing that responded to sound and pressure. It came back with some readings engraved on soft metal. The anomaly was that time moved faster within the field: 60 seconds out here was 247 seconds in there. One of the Newts hypothesized that the outside-inside time elapsed rate was the square root of 17, or maybe the cube root of 73. Four minutes inside to one minute outside.

Those inside were already 24 weeks older than us.

One of the techs rigged up a mechanical linkage between terminals inside and outside. Things went quicker after that. There was a small group of people who needed help. We could send through some foods.

Candles; mechanical igniters. Did I mention that it was dark? That their personal respirator batteries were wearing down? That there was nothing we could do?

The time came to decide.

Not only was scrubbing not required, it was ill-advised. There was too much that we did not know about this artifact: Who made it? How? When? Are there others? Are there others outside of the current field? Whatever could create a fast-time field? Is it useful? Useless? Dangerous?

I declared a Red Zone. Interdicted by naval patrols. No one could visit this world; no one could leave this world. The risk that someone would find another one of these devices was too great.

Cutting off almost a billion people from interstellar commerce was an inconvenience; some of those below might object. So might several off-world corporations with holdings on Arcanum. No matter. I already knew how the appeals process worked. It would be years before the matter came before the appeals magistrate on Capital; decades, even centuries, before there would be a contrary decision.

This time I hadn't killed a hundred million people. Did it matter?

THE DAKHASERI

"Look, up there! Each of those lights is a soul! Some are your ancestors, rewarded for their virtue and allowed to watch us down here. Some are your unborn children, learning from our example how to live. Teach your children-to-be well; make your ancestors proud. They watch us constantly and regret the errors they made in life."

Dakhaseri. Literally, *The Audience of Stars* [Vilani]. The ancient story of meritorious souls allowed to watch the unfolding events of the world. Their discussions (and their futile attempts to intervene) are the basis of many Vilani myths and legends.

I stood with my eyes closed, drinking in what was around me: strangeness, a slight breeze, and a murmuring of voices. I spoke, "Who here is senior?"

And I was startled with a hand at my elbow. "Jonathan, come on! The seats will all be taken!" I opened my eyes.

To my left, and to my right, as far as I could see, were rows and rows of spectators, talking, looking, chatting, watching, gesturing, commenting on a vast field below.

Our sky was steel grey and the crowd itself extended far into the surrounding mist.

My mother, youthful as I remembered her, bounced with excitement. She grabbed my hand and led me to some vacant seats. "Arlene is having her baby today!"

The young man seated to my left interjected, "I can hardly wait!" then touched my arm and said, "Hi, I'm Jonathan too!"

I saw, more in my mind's eye than before us, my great-granddaughter Arlene surrounded by her husband, two midwives, and their two pre-teen children. The excitement was infectious, for them, and for us watching. The objective part of me noticed that other small groups seemed to be watching other scenes, each oblivious to all else.

Abruptly, the baby appeared; my mother let out a peep of excitement; my peripheral vision noticed that the seat to my left was now vacant.

They gave the newborn to Arlene and she held him in the first moments of mother–son bonding. "We'll call him Jonathan."

302-410
Aboard CB *Stalwart* Above
Empt 2230 Daruka C574648-5 Ag Ni

I awoke to a chatter of voices: sensops journaling their readings aloud, a pilot narrating his control actions, a spacer repeating readings from the maneuver drives; all the common verbalizations of a functioning starship bridge.

"Silence!" came from an authoritative voice, and there was silence. I opened my eyes.

"Who here is senior?"

"I am Commander Avila. Commanding INS *Stalwart*."
I could see him in the Captain's chair.

"And who is my briefer?"

"I am as well. There is no prepared briefing. I'll just
tell you.

"Captain Usuti, not present, returned from a planetside
call on the local Baron an hour ago ranting about this
world and insisting that it be scrubbed. He was
communicating from the gig as soon as it lifted, giving
preparatory directives, he expected us to start when he
arrived. I countermanded the instructions and had the
captain tranqed on arrival. It took two shots."

"Then I activated you." And dodged the responsibility.
I had questions.

"Where is Usuti now?"

"In his quarters, sedated."

I turned to the Marine sergeant standing off to the side.
"Bring me a flight jacket. Mark the back with Agent above
the Imperial symbol ... and a lethal sidearm.

"Send two marines to the Captain's quarters to ensure
that he continues to be restrained."

To the command staff in general, "Who else was aboard
the gig from the surface? Where are they now?"

"Yes, sir. Wait one." I didn't want to wait at all, so I
moved on to my next question.

"Tell me about this world."

Avila pointed to an officer who rattled off what his
screen told him, "Daruka, 2230 in the Empty Quarter.
C574648-5."

I didn't have the tables memorized. I know that a six

in that position meant millions of people. The seven
meant breathable atmosphere. The final five meant
relatively low tech. That was enough. "Thank you."

A Marine reentered the bridge, kind of nodded to the
Captain's chair and headed toward me with a jacket and
weapons belt. At the same time, an alert sounded in one
of the consoles. Two seconds later, a second alert sounded
at a different console. I spent the time donning the jacket
and buckling the weapons belt. By the time I was ready,
there were competing voices reporting.

"The Captain is not in his . . ."

"The gig crew was a pilot and three spacers: they
are . . ."

Another alarm sounded. "Drives reports a power fault
in three, two . . ."

It was my turn, "Silence!" and there was quiet. Then
the lights went out.

* * *

For a moment, we were lit only by the glow of Daruka
through the transpex. Then the emergency backups
brought up a standard level of illumination.

I always have trouble just observing, so I started asking
the questions to which I needed answers.

"Where is the Captain?"

A spacer at a console spoke up tentatively, "Agent?"

"Just tell us; don't stand on protocol."

"He is not in his suite. The Marines checked and
reported."

"Find out where he is. Interrupt me when you know.

"What happened with the power? Who narrated that
report?"

A rating spoke, "I did, sir. The second engineer was reporting status when the telltales went wild."

"Find out why. Tell me when you know.

"You, what's your name?"

"Lieutenant Nuzhint, sir."

"Yes. Find out where the gig pilot and crew are.

"Lock us down at the bulkheads. Let's find out what's going on."

"Agent, the Captain is in the Drive Room. He just told the Engineer to shut down power."

"Can you override him?"

The deck started to hum beneath my feet. The grav plates quit. Those quick enough grabbed handholds to steady themselves; a few started to float, only to be steadied by their companions.

I pulled myself toward a console pair and its crew persons.

To the first, "Prepare to transfer total control to this console." He objected that it would need authorizations; I waved him silent.

I looked at the console for today's date and made some mental adjustments. "Calculate five-two-one to the four-one-third power. Show me the first ten digits."

The first interrupted, "It's locked; it needs an override."

I reached over and touched numbers quickly. "There. Now lock down everywhere. Disable all consoles until they get the clear from me here. Start with your neighbors. And get gravity back. But warn us first."

I swam toward the Captain's chair. "Commander, I now have command." He was out of it before I arrived.

It was uncomfortable. Wider than I expected, deeper. My expectations had misled me. "Commander?"

"Agent?"

"Is Captain Usuti Human?"

* * *

Non-Human crew was not unusual; I had just assumed there were none, or that they had marginal positions.

The Captain, the gig crew, and the pilot were all Plexxans. Near enough to Human, two legs, two arms, a head, but with a strange metabolism, and an added awareness sense that saw fields and auras that Humans can't.

"Who else is Plexxan?"

Commander Avila volunteered, "Half the drive techs. A few gunners. Maybe twenty total."

"Who else is non-Human?"

"One of the Gunners is a Vargr. No one else."

I wanted to think, but there didn't seem to be time. Console operators began verbalizing their reports as their panels reawakened. I was missing something that I needed to know.

"You," I pointed to a sensop, "Tell me the second screen details of this world."

He started listing seemingly random details: An Agricultural World with some cultural inefficiencies that tamped down technology, an anomalous rating on the cultural strangeness scale, a Plexxan noble and a significant Plexxan population.

"Find out what happened with the Captain when he was down below."

* * *

I wanted to see for myself. I instructed a tech to give me passage through locked bulkheads. Then I gave the bridge back to Avila and told two marines to follow me. Actually, I had one lead to the drive compartment.

They insisted on advancing with drawn weapons and seemed to work efficiently together. In less than five minutes we were before the massive blast doors that separated the main corridor from the complex of drive mechanisms.

The first marine moved me aside, out of any line of fire, and then cautiously touched a panel to force it open. The large doors slid aside. Ten bodies, Plexxans, lay before us. From shelter, I called out: "Weapons down. Come out!"

From within, "I am unarmed. Drive Tech Jickson. I am coming."

"Me too! Spacer Voss."

As they exited, the marines made them lay on the deck to be searched. "Is there anyone else?"

"No, sir. Just the Captain there and those techs." He pointed to the bodies.

I moved closer, and as I did, one of them moved. The marine on my left shot it twice and it stopped moving. Carefully, my companions poked the remaining bodies, but they failed to react.

I addressed the drive tech, "Where are the other Plexxans?"

"These are them. All of them."

"What happened?"

Voss gave a brief narrative, telling how the Captain appeared and gestured wildly as the Plexxans in the compartment gathered around him. They all gestured back and then scattered to their consoles and started shutting power down.

In the middle of it all I stopped. This all made no sense. It was like a detective story without any clues. I had no understanding at all of what was happening. Voss's narrative continued in the background until I interrupted.

To the lead marine, "Take us back to the bridge." I had been violating Rule 4. It was not my task to investigate; there were others to handle that.

As I re-entered the bridge, I was greeted by a cacophony as several spacers each spoke with vital information; it was impossible to understand them all at once. I raised an arm for silence.

"We don't have a complete understanding of events here."

I looked at the clerk closest to me, "What is my surname?"

"Noranda. Lieutenant Inch Noranda. Sir."

"I am Agent Noranda of the Quarantine. My authority is Imperial Edict 97. I speak with the voice of the Emperor himself.

"This system is provisionally Zone Red. No one leaves the world below. Ultimate priority. Implement that now.

"Full communications lockdown. Confirm everything through me first.

"Tell me immediately of any activity below."

* * *

In the days that followed, reports and sensors confirmed that Plexxans on the world below now behaved in a range from peculiar to insane. We dedicated almost all our resources to determining why, and we were universally unsuccessful. We eliminated contagion and environmental elements almost immediately. The crew worked tirelessly to find answers, and they came up empty.

Shortly before my time expired, the first reinforcement ships arrived; their resources were also insufficient to puzzle out the cause of this crisis. In time, perhaps someone would know root causes and perhaps general cures. Then again, there are some questions for which we can never find answers.

COREWARD OF THE IMPERIUM

The essential strategy of the early Empire was expansion. The fallow worlds of the Long Night were ready for re-contact and redevelopment: waiting only for the proper seed and season. Alas, the few dozens of worlds that Cleon the First ruled faced a formidable challenge in reabsorbing the ten thousand worlds that were once the First Empire.

When the Long Night fell, worlds naturally fell back on their native energy sources: animal power, fossil fuels, renewables. High tech worlds embraced the risks of fission systems; still higher tech depended on fusion. Neither fission nor fusion was portable; installations were the size of villages and every city required at least one.

Cleon's secret was FusionPlus: a radical paradigm shift that provided cheap portable energy. It took some sparks of genius, imagination, and craziness to even pursue the concept. When it was perfected in -20, it revolutionized the dozen worlds of the Sylean Federation. Vehicles could run essentially forever on cups of water. Houses could disconnect from the grid. Factories could locate near resources rather than near energy. Power became too cheap to meter and did not require a distribution network.

Productivity skyrocketed; prosperity arrived and seemed to never want to leave (except, of course, for the energy and power grid companies). It was this booming economy that created the Third Imperium and its expansionist policies.

Yet even this economic powerhouse could not reabsorb the ten thousand worlds of the old empire in a few dozen years. Power vacuums and rival empires seemed inevitable, and every rival that arose would constrict future growth. It was Cleon's business genius that solved the problem.

Cleon would gift some trader a hold full of fusion modules and send him out into the Wilds. The trader would ultimately arrive at a ripe world with a hold full of modules. He sold perhaps a few; he gave away a few more, but ultimately, the strategy was to lease them: for oaths of fealty. Cleon's gift included a makershop with templates that could make more and a monopoly on free power. After a few years, the trader and his family were at the top of the local power pyramid.

In a century, or two, when the expanding empire finally reached this booming system, Cleon's markers for his gift came due: the trader's family now owed fealty to the Empire.

There were always some who thought just taking the modules would be easier. It would have been stupid not to prepare for such an eventuality. Deep within every FusionPlus were multiple layers of concealed encrypted control systems: they determined efficiency, they prevented misuse, they could trigger early shutdown, or even explosive self-destructs. Many a powerful family knew that the key to its power was the secret control codes for its makershop and its output.

320-434
Aboard ISS *Talon* orbiting
Caes 0914 Beauniture C8858??-4 Ga Ph

I awoke to the common sounds of a starship bridge. I had heard them many times before and they were a comfort, a familiarity.

"Who here is senior?"

"Captain Tryan, ISS *Talon*."

A scout service ship? "And who is the briefer?"

"I will handle that as well." The voice conveyed self-assurance.

I opened my eyes to see a variety of officers busy at their consoles. Outside the transpex at some distance hung the bright half of a planet against the stars. "Very well."

The captain began without supporting images. This *Talon* was eight years out on a twenty-year mission coreward of the Imperial borders, generally to chart new systems, contact new cultures, and increase the empire's knowledge of uncharted space. We were 800 parsecs, a little over twenty sector-lengths, beyond the border. Few, if any, ships ventured this far for any reason. Prudent minds at Capital apparently thought someone should.

"By the way," he interjected. "The system activated you as an exception. There is no urgent situation. We have time to talk and discuss. Let's adjourn to the captain's suite?"

"Certainly." I was always on the alert for problems, but I genuinely sensed nothing amiss. As we left the bridge, the captain spoke proudly of this ship: a 40,000 ton cruiser of the newest design. This must be part of the new ship-building scheme Lord Aankhuga had discussed.

"We left the Empire in 426. We've been away for eight years; we don't expect to be back for another twelve. We're dedicating essentially all of our service careers to this one mission: to scout out threats to the empire in this direction.

"We're a community: a mix of compatible sophonts and genders; a proportion of dedicated pairs; even provision for youth education. We have a small population of children, the oldest just turned seven."

In Tryan's quarters, we settled into comfortable chairs and he continued. Occasionally, we were interrupted by Marines with refreshments.

This ship could jump five parsecs—sixteen light-years—at a time. Several jumps back, a chance encounter with a local trader mentioned a Human-settled world and *Talon's* course was diverted for a visit.

"By the trader's report, this was supposed to be a thriving Human world with a billion people and rudimentary interstellar trade. When we arrived, yesterday, we found a smoking ruin. Self-inflicted, no less. Two years ago, the locals basically went crazy: no fewer than three nuclear wars, cities sacked by rioting mobs, luddites, berserkers, craziness run rampant. There are a few enclaves of sanity in remote regions, and now we see the first steps of a recovery.

"And they supposedly knew what was coming. They had warning, but just couldn't do anything about it."

"Warning?"

"Bear with me, please. They trade with other worlds, mostly coreward from here. Those worlds experienced the same thing. There's a wave, literally a wave of insanity emanating from the core. It's about a month thick: it starts low, rises in intensity to peak at the half-point, and then subsides. Leaving in its wake a world where about half the people have gone crazy. Some of them recover; a lot don't. Not just people either, animals, fish, trees, plants all act irrationally."

"And how does a plant act irrationally?"

"Plants less so than animals, but vegetation sprouts out of season, leaves grow erratically, grasses grow in quick spurts and then turn winter-brown.

"This world had almost two billion people ten years ago; now it is down to a third. Some died from craziness ... most died from wars and technological failure that the craziness produced. A decade ago, this world had jump drive and sophisticated computers; today, it can barely handle steam power. Almost the entire infrastructure has been destroyed."

As he slowed down, I asked some questions.

"These are Humans? from where?"

"We aren't certain. We don't think they are Ancient castoffs. They seem to have been here about four thousand years."

"Which makes them, what? First Empire refugees?"

"Yes, probably. The records we looked at aren't clear. The local language has hints of Vilani, but there are vowel shifts."

"So tell me your concerns, Captain? What needs to be done here?"

He focused on two:

* * *

What potential does this world have, as it recovers, to threaten the Empire?

What is this Wave of Craziness?

I agreed. We talked for quite a while, laying plans.

* * *

The next day, on the bridge, we put our discussions into action. I announced to all, "I am Agent Insul of the Quarantine acting under Edict 97. Let's get started."

I addressed the Marine officer in charge of ship's troops. "Force Commander. Sensops has identified a library with substantial historical information as well as records of the Craziness. I need it harvested. Your orders have been sent to your comm." The Captain and I had crafted them last night, re-evaluated them this morning, and agreed they should be issued.

I addressed our Engineer. "We need a duplicate makershop for delivery planetside. How long?" He estimated a week and I accepted.

I addressed Comms, "We need a meeting with the top, five? Yes, five leaders. On a neutral field. In two weeks. Set that up." He asked about criteria and I suggested power base and population. I told him there was a memo with more information.

I could have done this all by memo, but it helped that everyone saw what everyone else was doing. The captain looked on approvingly.

340-434
Caes 0914 Beauniture C8858??-4 Ga Ph

We met on a dry lake bed, flat with visibility to the

horizon. All five invited leaders received separate instructions on arrival times; they were assigned distinct preparation areas and they converged from different directions.

We emplaced fabric sun shelters at the five points of a pentagon, centered on our assault lander. I sat in the shadow of the lander and waited as ground vehicles approached, kicking up clouds of dust. Each expedition with its protectors and advisors arrived to its own designated point to be greeted by a single spacer in Imperial colors.

Our reception for them was a demonstration of power. With atmospheric temperature above 40, the air under the shelters was a comfortable 20. Coolers held refreshments. Displays showed views of the other shelters and of our central assault lander; those in each shelter could see where everyone else was and what they were doing. Other displays ran loops discussing in broad terms how a makershop worked and how a portable fusion module worked. It all consumed huge amounts of power. It was meant to make an impression.

At the appointed time, the five leaders were announced by their titles and names and escorted to their audience with me. I greeted them warmly while a translator provided meaning to my words.

Several lander excursions had visited local populations and researched greeting and hospitality customs, and I now was well-versed. Impressions are always important. On the other hand, their names were long and cumbersome: I called them One through Five, and the translator would spew out "Lord and Master Anilainty Fendlkinly" or "First of Equals Thint Inantian Napp" as appropriate.

Once the five were seated, I stood before them and made our proposal. It was patterned on the expansionist policies of the first-century Empire. We had a gift of a dozen FusionPlus modules for each of the attending leaders. They had already seen their power output demonstrated. We promised there would be more.

Our price was simple: all would swear fealty to the Empire and the Emperor. One of them would become ascendent and receive a makershop that would create more modules: enough to fuel the recovery of this world and propel it to greater heights than ever before.

I insisted on an immediate response. I allowed no discussion: I had already ranked them by power and population, and proposed that One, the leader of the Eastern Region of the Primary Continent be ascendant. He accepted. The others acquiesced.

We moved immediately to the oaths of fealty.

A voice in my ear analyzed the five: "They don't like him; they don't trust him. Three seems to be leading the discussion and getting the consensus." I tapped a silent acknowledgement on a communicator stud.

One of my spacers stepped forward and administered the oath in three languages: Anglic, Vilani, and the local tongue.

As he finished, a marine stepped forward. We had rehearsed this. He was a body linguist; he had instructions that his evaluation would be public rather than whispered, whatever the result. We hoped for loyalty; we were prepared for not. In the local tongue, "He lies. His oath is false."

I shot him. He fell. I kicked his body off the raised platform myself. The retainers and entourage in the sun shelters watched in horror, and with a bit of fascination. None made a move.

I made a short speech about how the Empire requires honor and loyalty above all else. That oaths are what bind us in common purpose. That false oaths are worse than death, and they inevitably bring death.

I called up Three (the translator said, "Honored Leader Flinge Baralaso") and proposed that he be ascendant. He accepted, although a bit nervously. The oath was again administered, and my body linguist spoke after, "He speaks truth." The other three leaders swore subordinate oaths. I dismissed them to their sun shelters.

There were details to be handled now: now-dead One's people were told that he had violated protocol. Later, his replacement could swear fealty to Three. Control codes were distributed. Module deliveries were arranged.

My job was done.

345-434
Aboard ISS *Talon* orbiting
Caes 0914 Beauniture C8858??-4 Ga Ph

Captain Tryan and I sat in his suite and discussed our month's work. Tryan asked, "Do you think they will expand to touch the Empire? Do you think the Empire will expand to touch them?"

I mused no. "The distance is too great. We'll probably never see them again. But they will become a powerhouse in this sector; others will have to defer to them; and since they owe theoretical fealty to the Empire, we rise in everyone's estimation."

"So, we have an outpost far beyond our borders. Do we send emissaries to them? Is that even practical?"

"I am more concerned about the Craziness. Does it do this every time? To everyone? What happens when it reaches the Empire?"

"In eight hundred years? That's a long time from now."

"Long time or not, it will get there eventually. When you return, I've marked the relevant files for forwarding to Quarantine. The library the Marines harvested should go to the Archive on Vland."

Over the next several days, I analyzed and researched what I could about this world and this region. On my last evening before I evaporated, I ruminated on this particular experience.

I had only killed one person.

EPIPHANY

Once upon a time, my second father and I visited a windswept shore and he told me of the marvels of the worlds. The wind whipped our faces and I felt very grown up as I told him what I knew of cities and continents and seas while he listened very, very intently. We ate our pre-packaged lunches and then, for some reason, he, or I, or we together decided to send a message to some unknown reader in a far-off land. We thought hard about what we should say and decided on simplicity itself: "Do good in the world." I scrawled it in my childish hand and tucked it into our empty drink container. Out on the breakwater as far as we could venture, we waited until the wind was just right, and then I flung that capsule as hard as my little arm could. I wondered if anyone would ever read it.

132-440
aboard BF *Extreme* orbiting
Verg 3202 Kutubba C563875-8 Ph

The briefing started with the basics: an image of an inverted triangle labeled Process with its vertices marked strategy, tactics, intelligence. The next image provided foundational data: the world below us was in Verge sector.

Lieutenant Harka talked us through the codes, "Just to make sure we are on the same channel." Rudimentary starport, and thus infrequently visited and with very little trade. A small world with a thin atmosphere chemically tainted enough that filter masks were necessary for Humans. About a third of the world surface was seas, less than normal, less than optimal. Billions of sophonts: given the atmospheric taint, most of them were indigenes. Governed by a representative democracy, theoretically at least. That many people meant there had to be a relatively large bureaucracy. The legal system was unobtrusive, which meant that a lot of people carried self-defense items, or clustered in self-protective sub-communities. Finally, technology was fairly sophisticated. That implied, in light of the lack of starport facilities, that this world was not especially interested in off-world affairs.

I noted and appreciated the briefer's editorializing, expanding the single-digit codes with their logical consequences; she was indeed helpful in making sure we were on the same channel.

She moved to the Danger statement. "Danger is potential harm: we evaluate it at 10, extending to the entire world, but not beyond. Threat—the source of the Danger—is regional, actually it's one of the seas, we evaluate it at 8. The other seas are shallow; this Sea of Adesh is extremely deep and accesses core volcanic processes. That brings us to the Risk statement."

A new image appeared: a large numeral 11 flanked by three smaller numbers 5, 6, 0. "Probability, if events continue, is almost certain." The five flashed. "Severity, again, if events continue, will be total destruction of the current social and government structure." The six flashed. "When? Months, maybe even a couple years." The zero flashed.

I interrupted. "Destruction? Is that deaths?"

"No, not necessarily. It's on the next graphic." Which appeared. "Our evaluation predicts volcanic activity will essentially vaporize the Sea of Adesh. That has trade and transport consequences, but they are overwhelmed by the probable atmospheric changes: massive environmental and climate change over a short period of time; crop failures; health issues. This world faces immense challenges within the next year and they will last for centuries."

A new image appeared; I saw predictive animations of murky skies, storms, and flooding. Catastrophic winter. It all seemed fairly straight-forward. "Is there an action plan?"

"No, Agent. Any proaction would work more chaos than letting nature take its course. There are some educational measures we can implement. Our recommendation is to apply an Amber Zone advisory on the system and provide what support we can. There is no way to evacuate billions of people. There are some problems that just cannot be fixed."

"Thank you." I agreed. People would die; fortunes would be lost and won, but that happens anyway. There was no sense that the threat reached beyond this system, or potentially affected the Empire. Rule 2 didn't really apply here.

But with that conclusion, a stray and irrelevant thought came to me. "Lieutenant, please go back to your first image." A succession of flashes brought us to the original triangle. "Tell me about this foundation."

"Yes, Agent. Strategy is our ultimate plan of action (or in this case, inaction). Tactics is our means of achieving our strategy. We invert the triangle to show that all plans are balanced on good Intelligence. I try to show this graphic first in presentations in order to direct our thoughts toward well-reasoned action."

My mind raced. She stood there as I surrendered myself to thought. It wasn't that I purposely ignored her; I was compelled by an epiphany. I felt both used and empowered. The feeling passed in what felt like an instant, but I realized that those around me were waiting nervously.

"Thank you, Lieutenant." I turned to the squadron commander. "Thank you, Commodore. This is an excellent evaluation and I concur. Please arrange for a series of meetings with your staff over the next three watches; I want to take what steps we can to minimize upheaval and consequences." I dismissed them but asked the briefer to remain.

We were now alone in the vast briefing chamber. I quizzed the briefer on mundane facts and concepts. Tell me the current date? 132-440. Who now sits on the Iridium Throne? Martin the Third. How fared the Empire? We grow; we have peace. What party was in ascendence? A coalition of Reds and Oranges: The Centrists and the Statists. What was the latest technological advance she could think of? Some improvement in laser turretry. What was the current social trend within her experience? She liked the current realism-based musical theater, which surprised me because that was popular when I was a boy. As I gathered this information and processed it, I also examined my epiphany.

I was chosen, selected, created to protect the empire. Our training and instructions, our standing orders were all established to direct us to right action. Activate my personality, tell me the facts and the situation, and I applied my expertise to make a decision. When it was over, I returned to my genie bottle wafer until the next crisis.

Her graphic pointed out that without information, without intelligence, I would become increasingly detached from the mainstream of society. My very mission required more. I created for myself Rule 6: Right action requires intelligence. I would be alive for another four weeks; I had the time to start the intelligence gathering process.

* * *

We classified the Kutubba system Amber. The label would propagate through the trade lanes; travellers and merchants would be warned that this world faced upheaval; that there was a personal risk attached to visiting. Visitors were rare in any case, but now the data banks would warn the unwary. In a year or two, the label would reach Capital and become truly official. In a few centuries, someone would re-examine the situation and might, or might not, change the warning back to Green.

My meetings with staff directed a compilation of reference data on dealing with climate change, weather-related catastrophes, and social unrest. The petabytes of information in a variety of accessible formats would be distributed widely and would probably save, over centuries, millions of lives.

I next spent a day reviewing recent historical information. I asked for a census of ships in the system. I interspersed these requests with discussions of Kutubba and projections of the catastrophes it could expect. I arranged for the Emperor's noble to visit us in orbit; we gave him a thorough briefing. We did everything possible.

135-460
aboard BF *Extreme* orbiting
Verg 3202 Kutubba C563875-8 Ph

"Run a personnel screen for me."

"Yes, Agent. What criteria?"

"Let's do it here. Bring up the file overview. Naval officers. Pilot-skilled. Liaison-qualified."

"There are eight."

"Start at the top. Display it."

"Gustav. Lieutenant."

I looked at the text on the screen without commenting. Human. Female. "Skip ahead."

"Trenchans. Sublieutenant."

The personnel file showed a Plexxan. "Skip ahead."

"Cobalt. Sublieutenant. MCG awarded for the Action at Achenaar."

Human. Male. Ah, no wafer jack. "Skip ahead."

"Ten. Lieutenant. Liaison-certified."

This one had exceptional marks. I saw the wafer-jack notation, good. Gender was trans male. Mental pause. How do the hormones work; or the genes? Would this be a male wafer in female? Best not to take chances. "Skip ahead."

"Shuginsa. Sublieutenant. Exceptional pilot rating."

Human. Male. Wafer jack. "Select that one. Have him assigned as my aide."

"What about the others?"

"No need."

160-460
aboard BF *Extreme* orbiting
Verg 3202 Kutubba C563875-8 Ph

Sublieutenant Enn Shuginsa was a capable aide. He was attentive; he understood his place. He ensured that I had nutritious meals with enjoyable tastes. He learned my preferences in music and found pleasant, relaxing melodies to support planning sessions. He gatekept without overstepping. He learned how I operated and worked to complement my methods. I wished he could accompany me into the future.

For my part, I conversationally engaged him in idle moments. I discovered his likes: his passion for his career, for learning. He enjoyed history and the lessons it taught he was especially fascinated with the many Human minor races.

As my days dwindled down, I needed to act.

"Enn, join me. Close the door."

"Sir?"

I was prepared. I simply needed to cover some preliminaries. "I have appreciated your assistance to me over the past weeks. You have done an excellent job of support. I thank you sincerely."

"Sir, I thank you for the opportunity for this experience."

"My time here is drawing to a close.

"The Angin wafer which holds my personality is a special technology. It only works in a specific host once; after that, the host builds an immunity. It malfunctions in non-males, or in non-Humans. My personality in this host will fade in the next few days. Which is fine. The crisis here is relatively low grade and is being handled competently.

"On the other hand, I need to make a report to Quarantine headquarters. Personally. I am sending you to Capital with my wafer. When you get there, you will be my host so I can make the report." Rule 1.

"I have prepared orders." I pointed to a package on the table. "You are promoted to Lieutenant. Congratulations."

He started to speak, and I waved him silent. "There's more. You are assigned command of the fleet corvette *Ukaammur*. Proceed directly to Capital. These orders assign you to the Quarantine Agency in their Appeals Office. Once there, and in place, your instructions govern using my wafer."

These particular instructions were in writing rather than electronic, the safer thus from prying sensors.

"I want you to understand that I make this assignment because I value and appreciate the work you have done for me, and because I have great confidence in your abilities." And to myself, I thought, because you are Human, male, and have a wafer jack. "You will go far in the service."

I removed my wafer from its niche and included it in the package of orders. It records my personality in real time and so I have no memory of my activities thereafter.

THE JOURNEY TO CAPITAL

Maybe you have a wafer jack: then you know how it works. Hold the skill wafer to the niche in the nape of your neck and you can feel the magnets pull. There is just the slightest wobble in your thought processes, but other than that, if you aren't really thinking, then you feel nothing special, and that's normal.

It's when you're thinking that it matters. The skills kick in and suddenly that gibberish of equations in front of you makes sense. You aren't any smarter, but you suddenly understand what the symbols and the characters mean and how they interact. Taking the wafer out is like closing a door: you know that you knew just a minute before, but no longer.

The warnings say, "Don't leave the wafer in place for more than 30 days. Take breaks. Monitor for non-standard reactions or behaviors." Too many people ignore them and end up on restoratives. Worse: they develop an immunity to wafers which either stop working or provide nonsense skills. I once knew a clerk who worked an entire shift finding that the solution to every equation was 1 (or -1, he knew there were two roots to the equation) and never caught on.

* * *

The Angin Wafer is different. Hold it to the nape of your neck and you feel the magnets pull. There is the slightest wobble in your thought processes, and suddenly:

You are somewhere else, in a different position, in a different place, in different clothes. When you check the time it's four weeks later. You, whoever you were in the interim, have done things that will gradually unfold to you, maybe. He used your body and your voice and your name, but it certainly wasn't you. If you are lucky, the use wasn't major, and things return to normal. For some, it was major, and they transfer you to someplace new, where no one remembers that other you or knows what that other you did.

281-461
Aboard AF *Ukaammur* Above
Core 1424 Khusgarlu B652AEE-B Hi Po

Ukaammur's displaced captain had not been happy, but the service is not about making people happy.

Now-Lieutenant Shuginsa's journey, commanding one of the fleet's routine couriers, covered 97 parsecs in just about 58 weeks: a week in jump, a week insystem refueling, a week in jump, another week insystem refueling. There was an element of tourism: seeing new systems and strange worlds. Shuginsa had instructed the astrogator to include Ilelish—the homeworld of the Suerrat—on their itinerary if it did not affect total travel time. Several weeks out, it had become apparent that the travel controls in the aftermath of the Ilelish Revolt would make a casual visit ill-advised. Shuginsa was disappointed, but philosophical, perhaps another time.

Now the ship was almost to its destination.

297-461
Aboard AF *Ukaammur* Above
Core 1822 Holex A200353-C Lo Va

Lieutenant Shuginsa's astrogator strictly followed standard procedures in the final stages of their journey to Capital. At Holex, a rock ball of a world significant only because it had a naval base on the edge of the Identification Zone, they received time-stamped authorization codes and strict compliance procedures.

The final jump itself was uneventful; breakout was almost dead on time, followed by immediate instructions to maneuver to a holding area and then slow movement to the naval base annex of the Highport above Capital.

ANASHAKILA

I opened my eyes to the stadium and its expanse of people as far as I could see. Somehow, I knew that they extended beyond as far as I could see, well into the grey haze. I felt contrary today and I turned my attention not to the events before us and instead to the upper levels of the audience.

I ascended stairs, a seeming infinity of flights, until I reached a concourse, itself overhung by another infinity of stadium tiers. I knew no one, recognizing only the presence of Humans and Vargr and Aslan and others. I had seen such crowds before, in starport terminals, in harvest festivals, at affinity rallies. There were pockets of similar peoples intent on their own destinations, some rushing, some sauntering, a few just standing in place waiting.

I found a transport line: car pods that held a few handfuls each and I randomly boarded one with no real purpose or destination. I watched through its view panels as we passed seas of sophonts ebbing to their own currents.

In that mass of people, I recognized someone, which was a surprise because faces have always meant less to me than identity cards, or uniforms and insignia of rank. More surprising was the look of recognition that the face shot back.

When the pod halted momentarily, I exited and backtracked its route, walking against the stream, forcing myself against their collective flow. There were enough taller than I to make my struggle blind, but then, the flow lessened and in a wider part of the concourse I was suddenly in front of my goal, the chancely recognized face of a Newt. We stopped and considered each other briefly, and then it was he who spoke.

"You are the agent."

In a flash of recognition, I now said, "and you are the mining engineer."

"I am."

There was silence as we stood there, even as we were surrounded by millions. He made an excuse, "I must move on. My *talaa*," and as he said it, I knew in my mind's ear that he referred to an extended family line, "is assembling to observe an important generational accomplishment."

"I understand. But surely there is a reason for this chance encounter."

"Surely," he replied, and he was gone.

233-449
Aboard BB *Courageous* Above
Anta 0204 Anashakila E6748A9-6 Pa Ph Pi

"Excuse me, sir?" This was a young spacer interrupting me.

A Marine moved to hold her back, but I waved him away.

"Yes?"

"I wanted to tell you how glad I am you decided quarantine would work. I'm glad all those people will live." As am I.

"I think my grandmother served with you at Maaruur. She was a comm."

"I remember that action, but I can't say that I remember any specific crew members."

"She came home the next year, back to the farm. She was never the same."

"Tell me about it?" I had time.

"I, of course, didn't know her until years afterwards. To me, she was just my quiet farmer grandmother. She was always gentle. She was always caring and dedicated. I loved going to the farm; my parents run it now. Only after she died did I ask about her service.

"Mother said when she came home, came back to the farm, she stopped selling the livestock. She just let them die of old age. She went vegan. They raised crops, did a lot of gardening. Struggled for a while.

"Mother and I had a long talk when I decided to enlist.

"Grandmother was only in the Navy four years: for her required reserve service. But she came back changed. After a few years, Other Grandmother left her. I read her service record; that she was at Maaruur. That explained a lot."

"Like?"

"She sometimes talked about the spirits that live in the trees and the animals and the sky. About the *Dakhaseri* watching us. She was always trying to appease the spirits.

Sometimes she walked at night in the fields and just screamed.

"I'll follow orders, sir. But I'm glad I'm not going to have these people on my conscience."

There was a hint of something here that I needed to know more about.

"Spacer, I want you to do a project for me. Find the crew manifests for the ships involved at Maaruur. I want to know the post-service status of all involved. A synopsis will be fine to start. Show it to me when you are done." I dismissed her.

234-449
Aboard BB *Courageous* Above
Anta 0204 Anashakila E6748A9-6 Pa Ph Pi

The Sergeant-Major told me to brief the Agent on his sidearms. I took the case to him in the command suite.

"Uh, sir." I was under arms and saluted.

He returned it looking up from a control tablet. "Yes?"

"The Sergeant Major sent you your sidearms."

"Fine. Put them on the table."

"I should really brief you on them."

He put down his work and gave me his full attention. "What are these?"

I opened the case while talking, "This first one is an Ay Snap-13: that's Ay Ess Enn Pee dash 13; that stands for Advanced Snub Pistol, the thirteen is the tech level.

"We call it a staple gun because," I held it out to show him, "it looks like one." I rattled off the standard book information that we all memorized, "It's meant for close stuff, to a maximum of fifty meters. Lightweight: about half a kilo."

He asked, "How much does this thing cost?" while hefting it in his hand.

"Lance Corporal Dinsha lost one three missions ago and it cost him half a year's pay; but lance corporals don't make that much. So maybe a couple thousand credits."

As he hefted it, I showed the control points. "Trigger. Grip safety: it won't fire unless you hold it firmly. Thumb safety: up is on, so swipe it down to make it active."

"The barrel is short, what, ten millimeters?"

"Five, sir. The feed puts the little slivers in place. The battery and coils force them out at half the speed of light."

"Really?" he asked.

"No, sir. That's what we tell recruits. It's about a thousand meters per second."

"Did you know my mandate lets me kill anyone I want?"

I stopped; afraid I had overstepped. "No, sir."

"It's true. But I usually don't kill in groups of less than a hundred, so you're safe.

"What's this other one?"

I decided to just make the presentation and get out of there.

"Sir, this is your non-lethal option. Yellow handle, smooth grip.

"The AshPeeJay dash twelve. It shoots a barbed, self-contained electric thing."

"Thing?"

"Sorry, capsule. A barbed, self-contained electric

capsule that 'inflicts debilitating pain and incapacitating shock' to most targets in the Human size range. It also works against most devices if you hit it right."

"There's ten capsules in the magazine."

I really wanted to be done. "Is there anything else, sir?"

"No, sergeant. Thank you for your briefing."

I saluted and really didn't wait for it to be returned. I also forgot to get the receipt signed. If necessary, I would forfeit half a year's pay.

236-449
Aboard AF *Kadalesh* in the outer system of
Anta 0204 Anashakila E6748A9-6 Pa Ph Pi

With Anashakila interdicted, the squadron set about establishing secure patrols throughout the system. A picket reported an anomaly in a gas giant ring, and because the administrative tasks were well-handled by ship's crew, I traveled with a fast courier to look it over.

"The picket picked this up on routine scans. When sensors said it was not natural, they reported it as an exception, and we were notified."

As I examined the images on a central display screen, I asked natural questions. "Has anyone been up close?"

"No, Agent. We're not sure what they are. The picket captain made his report and left it to us."

"Are they all the same?"

"They sense as similar, two hundred meters across, spherical, density is about four times water, so it's more than just ice, consistent with rock, not enough for FeNi.

"It's not large enough to be spherical by its own gravity, so it has to have been shaped by some process. The picket originally mistook it for a ship. It's big enough to be a *Lioness*."

"Any signals from it?"

"No, Agent. Entirely passive."

"I want to look closer." A gig took us almost to it and we leapt the final gap in suits.

As I drifted closer, I saw that it was an assemblage of smaller puffy sacs, slack balls each roughly spherical— about a double arms-length across—and joined into a mass. I twisted and touched feet first with a thump. Native gravity here was miniscule, perhaps a newton or two. I knew to be careful; an unintentional move could send me drifting away.

The surface was striated with divisions between its many-colored sacs. Here and there, the darkness of a pit, a missing sac. I drifted to one pit, close enough to see that it descended deeper into the interior.

One of my companions cut a sac's membrane and it expelled a glitter of crystals in an expanding cloud. "Metal flakes, sir!"

"Take a sample." I noted that the sacs had different colors and shades. "Are they all the same?"

There followed a series of exhales as several were cut. "No, Agent. This one's a powder. That other one was a gas."

"Take samples."

A now-flaccid gas sac revealed a cavity and below that another layer of sacs. I hauled myself in, and as I did, my foot ruptured a gas sac below; I held tight to the membrane as the exhaling greenish gas rushed past me.

My suitlight showed another layer of sacs below that. I did not want to climb deeper.

I made the leap back to the gig and watched the remainder of the operation on screens from an acceleration couch. After about two hours, we returned to our ship.

***

There were seven of these balls, each as big as a battleship. Tests on samples revealed elemental gases, or solid flakes, or granules. They found no liquids, at least in the outer layers.

In conclusion, I said, "This can't be natural, can it?"

The tech said, "Define natural."

"Not intelligent. This has to be some sort of asteroid miners or ring harvesters who go through the system breaking down minerals into their constituent elements."

"What? With a bio-based technology."

"That makes sense, doesn't it? One of the megacorporations setting up a mining operation with geneered spacers."

"Conceivably. Or some natural species, maybe not even intelligent. Like bees making honey."

The techs created a report. I classified it penultimate and directed it be forwarded to the archives. When I returned to *Courageous*, I ordered the balls be tipped into the gas giant. They were a complication this interdicted system didn't need.

253-449
Aboard BBF *Courageous* Above
Anta 0204 Anashakila E6748A9-6 Pa Ph Pi Pz Amber

"Tell me your findings."

"Agent." Today there was a stiffness, subordinate to superior. "The squadron at Maaruur had six capitals, fourteen others, and a total of 3,442 officers and crew. That was 68 years ago. My Grandmother was not an outlier. Almost all Reservists in the crew left the service as soon as their obligation expired. There were significantly higher rates of suicide, self-harm, charitable behaviors, and depression." There was more, but it all led to the same conclusion.

CAPITAL

Capital (the planet once known as Sylea) is a moderate-sized world with a lot of people, compounded by the fact that a little more than half its surface is water. A lot means eighty billion; moderate-sized means, after subtracting water, about eight billion hectares. A tenth is devoted to food production (long ago, that was two-tenths, but that was long ago): it is impractical (if not impossible) to import food for billions of people. Two-tenths is mountain, canyon, rock, and crag. Another two-tenths is snowlands: both support scattered communities, but certainly no appreciable population density.

Half the land is urban, four billion hectares for 80 billion people: perhaps 20 per hectare, 2,000 per square kilometer.

Terribly crowded, oppressive, single-level urban areas make do with such densities over a few hundred square kilometers. Capital maintains such densities across all its settled lands.

Yet.

For many, Capital is a pleasant environment, an attractive community. High-rise and plunging arcologies house millions in high-density comfort and safety: the masses of the bureaucracy that drive the engines of the empire must live in comfort and safety.

On the other hand, there are the others that are always there: the poor, the disadvantaged, the underendowed, the unmotivated, the disaffected. Strict travel controls (and there are strict travel controls on Capital) cannot completely restrain workers discarded by their employers, or laborers in the shadow economy. Of Capital's eighty billion, some portion probably counted as a tenth survive outside the conventional social structure.

304-462
Core 2118 Capital A586A98-D Hi Cx

After the long journey to Capital, the time had come, and my orders were clear. I wondered what would happen if I just ignored them and reported to my new assignment? Would the Agent ever know? Would I just use this assignment as another step in my career progression? If I become host, what prevents him from some terrible misuse of me, of my body, or my identity? This won't be on his record; what happens accrues not to him but to me.

But the Agent was always cordial, competent, self-assured. He knew what to do and he never abused his power. He treated me with respect, always. Do I just insert the wafer? Does he need to know of the journey? The situation? I suppose a simple message is enough. I would insert the wafer in the morning.

305-462
Core 2118 Capital A586A98-D Hi Cx

I awoke seated, consistent with what I expected. Despite

the disorientation, I opened my eyes and saw a small room, a residence hotel apparently, crowded with a bed, a console, and a door to the fresher. I was certain, because I was on Capital, that this must cost some extraordinary sum. I mused that I had not thought of money for a long time.

Before me was a comm, my comm, with a short text visible:

We are in Intell, on Capital, per your instructions.

I erased it and began.

I made sure I was properly uniformed, checked my destination on the console: walkable combined with public transport. I set out. I dragged a bag with a frictionless bottom; the last time I had done this, the case had had a belly of many small roller wheels. My comm gave me hints and signals and at least once directed me along an unfamiliar route.

I had not been in weather for years. Sheltered walks and subsurface access stations protected me from the snow and the wind, but the experience was both uncomfortable and exhilarating. Nevertheless, after some thirty minutes, I had had enough and was happy to arrive.

My destination was an office tower hundreds of kilometers from the starport and in the opposite direction of the Palace. The building was the same as I remembered, more or less. The neo-classical façade with its ridiculous two-hundred-meter-tall columns appeared to have been cleaned or renewed at least once.

At reception, they did not know what to do with me. I had valid orders assigning me to a position; the control codes and the check digits matched, but there was no local record. They were aware that this sometimes happened: some marquis in another sector gave his favorite sycophant's rising scion a sinecure on Capital, a *pied-a-sylea* so to speak. They thought I was such as that. I did not disabuse them.

I was given an office and a console and told to acquaint myself with their system. I went through the motions in about-an-hour sessions, punctuated by discussions with others to carefully update myself on social norms after more than a century. I made the excuse that I was from the edge of the Great Rift (as indeed my host was, we had talked of his life from time to time), and I was accepted without any real comment. My officemates were always happy to talk of themselves and their interests, and I learned more than they realized.

After a week, I took a break. I arranged the coming week as leave: I was still a naval officer after all. I went to Capital, the city. Strangely, when I had lived here, it never seemed important to visit the icons. I knew what they looked like; I saw them in the distance; I could recognize them, and their names tripped off my tongue: the Palace, the Moot Spire, the grand Plaza of Heroes, Cleon's Tomb, the Imperial Archives, the Central Forest, the Route du Palais, even the Second Empire Monument.

At last, I would see them.

312-462
Core 2118 Capital A586A98-D Hi Cx

I visited the Moot Spire: the very place that the decisions of Empire are made. Technically, I was welcome past the simple barriers that separated the masses from the elite. I was a knight of the empire, one of those elites; my name was recorded in the rolls of those favored by the Emperor. But my host was not, and there was no way that I could even consider crossing those arbitrary boundaries.

I saw the Grand Palace from afar; I peered through its black metal fence rods at the carefully coiffed gardens and its strangely trimmed trees.

I strolled the Plaza of Heroes, conjuring up names of those I had known either before or after my death and asking my comm if they were remembered here: it gave me verbal and visual cues for some. I stood over a brick incised with the name of my Marine comrade Arlane and briefly remembered his life and his death. I touched another brick noting the presence of Patel at the scrubbing of Maaruur. Of others, there was no record. They might be remembered in the other plazas of other heroes on other worlds, but not here.

I visited the Imperial Salons. The exhibit on osmancy was unsatisfying: observing people prepare tastes and conjure smells cannot compare to actually tasting and smelling; it was like a sculpture exhibit one is not allowed to touch. The exhibit of now classic art from the third century resonated with me; I understood those artists' purposes; their reflections of what third-century folk felt. On the other hand, I noticed others around me confused by the same techniques that so spoke to me.

I visited the Museum of History. There was a hierarchy of presentation and naturally the greatest focus was on Emperors and Empresses. They became surrogates for the science, the conquests, the politics, the advancements, and the challenges of each's reign. I knew Porfiria as an image in the news; I had actually met Anguistus, once. I knew little of the Martins, nor of the current Nicholle. Each chamber told me something of the era, reminded me of what I had learned in school, pointed out things I had not then realized, or that time had elevated in importance. I remembered favored sports teams winning championships season after season and all my office mates exhilarated for weeks with the thrill and the pride, but there was little mention of those events here.

I visited the Museum of Sophonts. This was a new structure, built since my demise, reflecting the completion by the Scout Service of its First Survey of the Worlds of the Imperium and its client territories some ten years before. There were major exhibits on the Vargr, the Aslan, and the many variants of Humanity. There was a series of rotating displays on some less common sophonts: those who rejected technology, those restricted by environment or temperament to their own particular planets; those too aggressive to be allowed off their homeworlds. Guided groups of students wandered the halls more-or-less following a docent but more interested in small group social hierarchies than the splendor of independent evolution of intelligent life. I paused at a small display even-handedly presenting the conflicting concepts of the origins of Humanity across many worlds: parallel evolution across a hundred worlds, Vilani origins (my own favored conclusion as my ancestors came from Vland), the Solomani Hypothesis of origins on far-off primitive Terra, the Gashagi garden world concept, and (in consideration of sensitive feelings) presentations on Geonee, Suerrat, and Cassildan origins.

I wandered into a virtual display and pressed buttons randomly to see what came up: images and data on a strange green 4-ped with eyes on stalks and twenty-some fingers on each hand, a hulking nose-horned giant with auxiliary arms folded on its chest, and a strange flattened leather ball that moved by weight-shift rolling. A small group with unusually loud voices entered behind me, and I moved on.

* * *

I took a wrong exit returning from my excursion. The fast transport doors opened, and a rush of people carried me into a waiting area. I was not paying full attention and ended up in a pedestrian mall filled with many small groups of people: diverse as to species, but all at the low end of the economic spectrum.

I was out of place, and I felt it immediately. I could feel eyes watching me.

I stopped to consult my comm; where was I? It told me numbers and names that meant nothing to me. I turned to retrace my steps and found that the transport gates were closed. The comm directed me to a different access portal some minutes away.

"Are you lost?" This growl from the tallest of three Vargr who now blocked my way. He smiled, but a dog smile looks more like a threatening snarl than a friendly greeting. His companions keep their lips closed, but fangs nonetheless protruded.

Part of me imagined myself ripped to shreds by this pack of canines. Others on the street seemed prepared to allow that without interfering.

I knew what to do. With dogs, it's show no fear. Rule

1 works as well. "I am. And I thank you for your question.

"I am Lieutenant Enn Shuginsa, and I have taken a wrong turn. How do I reenter the fast transport?"

The Vargr are motivated by small group dominance. This primary had my attention; his companions would do nothing without his direction. I just needed to dominate him.

He started to make an answer, and I interrupted. "Forgive me. Please tell me your name."

"I am Arrlanroughl." I knew the spelling from the pronunciation: Ar Lan RUFF El. It was in Gvaeg, the most common of their languages.

"Arrlanroughl," I repeated his name properly pronounced, "I appreciate your offer of assistance." He had not offered; I assumed. "Capital is a wonderful place for those who visit; perhaps less wonderful for those who live here. Would you guide me to my transport stop?"

I knew the general direction from my comm. I started walking and assumed he would as well. "Tell me, Arrlanroughl, what do you do?"

There followed a conversation about the transitory jobs that the under people of Capital do: their efforts to live outside the array of standard jobs and avoid violations that would export them in cold sleep to strange and inhospitable worlds. Before that point (and I mean in my former life as well as now), I had been oblivious to anyone but the middle and upper classes.

I enjoyed our conversation. I asked for his comm identifier as we parted, and noted it in mine.

313-462
Core 2118 Capital A586A98-D Hi Cx

There is a classic theme in literature: stories of men, people, sophonts presumed dead who are granted the opportunity to witness their own funerals and hear what those in life felt about someone now passed on. In my various classes I had casually read texts and regurgitated interpretations, but now those thoughts came back to me in a rush as I exited the fast transport line at the necropolis at Intell. I had made my arrangements and would only now after a century finally see them.

I searched with anticipation for our family plot and my memorial.

I had been cheated.

My funerary stele, intended to stand three meters tall, rose barely an arms-length, truncated a third of the way up into a clumsy point. Here it stood a pantographed distorted scale model of itself, cut from inferior stone, rising to my waist, lost among the others. I stooped and thought as I traced the base with a finger, affected by an emotion I rarely felt. The letters of my name were there; the numbers of my time were there, but the pillar itself was squat, unsatisfying. Was this rage? Or just disappointment?

I remembered the functionary with whom I had dealt: Imiirga, an earnest, sincere man who sat with templed fingers, nodding in active listening mode as I outlined my desires for a suitable memorial. We looked at samples of natural stone from traditional quarries. We reviewed a virtual model that we rotated with finger motions, making adjustments until it was perfect. I made the appropriate contingent credit transfers and we parted with an emotional embrace. I remembered that I had left that meeting feeling more positive than I had in days. There was a resolution to issues that had burdened my spirit and I was even some semblance of happy for a time.

I now stood and tapped my comm, asking basic questions about the Imiirga of a hundred years before. The screen told me of someone in that time serving in an appropriate role. He was not of sufficient importance to rate an historical entry, but the genealogical networks placed him properly in the era, with employment and residential confirmations. It told me who his family was, when he died, who carried on his line, where he was interred.

314-462
Core 2118 Capital A586A98-D Hi Cx

I visited his grave the next day: a continent away, in his grand family plot surrounded with the markers of the generations that followed him. He had become an archon, revered by his children's children's children. The center of this family plot was dominated by a sphere of stone two arms' stretches across; its equator incised with a proud epigram from the *Dakhaseri* myth:

> *"Make your ancestors proud; teach your children-to-be well."*

He had left his personal fortune in trust for their educations: the single best choice he could have made to ensure they would have the best of all possible lives, and that they would hold him in the best of all possible memories.

I now labeled my emotion rage: at the cynicism, the dissimulation, the self-service. I had been victimized. I felt momentarily helpless, but only momentarily. I knew the next complete thought in the epigram, and I had near-infinite power. I would make him regret the errors he had made in life.

Baronet Sir Fen Imiirga had built his first fortune in the funerary industry as a confidential advisor. I had seen him in action. It appeared he had accumulated credits from others in the same way: promising post-death arrangements that he provided only half-heartedly. His later life seemed faultless, filled with grand projects accomplished competently and exceeding expectations. Within his small geographic and socio-economic communities, he had been well-respected. The Emperor recognized him at retirement with a Baronetcy, which filled him with pride. He lived a full life and died quietly in his old age, surrounded by family and friends.

But his entire life was built on the frauds of his youth. I would make him pay.

318-462
Core 2118 Capital A586A98-D Hi Cx

From the sea of potential companions in my office, none had expressed the slightest interest in my life. Our conversations touched on office politics, for which I cared little, and personal activities. In the rare events when someone asked me what I had done, even my answer seemed to focus the conversation back to their recreations and interests.

Arrlanroughl's inquiry—Are you lost?—some three days before had then seemed to me an ominous threat, and I now saw it as politeness, interest, even caring. On a whim, I called Arrlanroughl and arranged to meet. I think that my call was unexpected, but after several minutes he agreed that we should join for an evening meal the next day.

319-462
Core 2118 Capital A586A98-D Hi Cx

Arrlanroughl's suggestion had been a small restaurant near where we had first met. I prepared myself by researching the neighborhood, alternative access routes, and even took a virtual tour. The place with a nondescript name—Ella's—provided affordable hand meals in three distinct cuisines: Fast Human, Gvaeg, and Asat.

At the appointed time, I arrived and entered, to be met immediately by the Vargr, alone. I saw his two companions in the distance, but they remained apart. He smiled (and I still half-perceived that as a snarl) and we shook hands. He guided me to a table, and we both examined the bill-of-fare. He narrated our possibilities. "This is the only place around here that captures the taste of Gvaeg cooking, they make their own sauces, so a lot of us like it here." By "us," I understood him to mean his fellow Vargr. "And they have a Newt cook back there that understands their particular cuisine, especially the live-insect garnishes."

The painted menu above the counter listed our choices in wrappers, proteins, options, and garnishes: select one from each column, with an upcharge for additionals.

We made our selections. He chose a crisped bread wrapper around a bone-in beef with a tangy sauce and devoted much of our time gnawing on the bone. I selected a whole grain flatwrap around sliced fowl and a marinated leafy something. I had tried to emulate a selection I remembered, but it didn't quite fit. We also shared a communal bowl of toasted grain.

I was interested in who this Vargr was and how he lived on Capital. He was technically a native, born here to parents who arrived as part of an educational exchange program. When it was complete, they declined to return to their homeworld, and eventually melted into the underground economy.

Arrlanroughl said he made a living doing occasional jobs: deliveries, construction, basic labor. He was a good worker, but such jobs rarely lasted very long. I had the impression that some of the jobs skirted the law, and others were probably outright illegal, but I was polite enough not to probe too deeply.

About midway through our conversation, I realized that his friends at the far side of the diner were simply waiting for us to finish. "Tell your friends to order for themselves, as they wait." He visited with them briefly and returned to say that they appreciated my hospitality.

Our conversation continued for several hours. I was fascinated with this heretofore unseen, for me, aspect of society on Capital. By its end, my eyes were opened in ways that I had not expected.

We parted late in the evening with an agreement to meet in two weeks.

321-462
Core 2118 Capital A586A98-D Hi Cx

In my office, I returned to my job-acquaintance process until I was sure that procedures worked essentially the same as in my time. The value of a stable bureaucracy is that processes are literally timeless.

My immediate supervisor was a political appointee: nominated by someone in power somewhere in the empire. He was happy enough to be here but had little ambition for advancement. Every day at end-of-work, he promptly left to whatever personal pursuit compelled him. He was happy that I took initiative as long as it did not interfere with his own personal time.

I, on the other hand, worked late when I needed to: reviewing procedures, analyzing relative inefficiencies, trying to understand reports from the farther reaches of the empire. One evening, I was alone in the offices and saw my chance to act. There was always a possibility things could go wrong, but I needed to take the risk.

I left my console activated, scanning data in some mindless task while an entertainment flashed on the supplemental screen. I moved to the other side of the office, found a vacant clerk's console, and logged in as a casual user. I calculated the override codes for the day on a side panel and entered them while holding my breath. I knew this would work on naval computers; I was still less sure it would provide access in these offices. But it did.

I spent the next few minutes issuing project orders by checking boxes and appending short phrases. While I was at it, I added some benefits for my host with a suspense date a few months and a few decades in the future. Rule 5. Then I closed up and made my own way home.

***

My next higher superior, Senior Supervisor Len Starpan called me into his office two days later to give me my new job. He started rather abruptly.

"They have instituted an inspection program, who knows where this came from, and you have been assigned." He tapped his screen. "It's all here in the file. Let me know if you have any questions."

All I could say was yes, sir.

My title was now Inspector Unipotentiary of the Quarantine Agency. There were four dreadnoughts insystem, in orbit. I scheduled a surprise inspection for tomorrow.

I started at the Navy Base and my orders preceded and prepared the way for me.

I went alone. I had singleness of purpose. On the other hand, this was new to me. I was accustomed to unquestioned response, and I enjoyed less than that power here. When admirals resisted me, I had them shot; that was probably not my option here.

A cutter awaited me on the tarmac. Once I boarded, it leapt into the sky.

An hour later, the cutter mated with the dreadnought *Sinorak* and I was greeted at the hatch by the Officer of the Deck. We exchanged pleasantries; we were equals. He was, like I, a Lieutenant. I was, like he, armed. He gave a questioning look at that. I smiled.

I showed him my tablet and recited my basic mission. "I believe this is routine, a new program the Agency has come up with." I also needed to relieve his worries. "We are very focused today: I need to see the IT vault and specifically the quarantine wafers. Nothing else. Not a surprise audit. You can tell the captain but don't warn IT, please.

"Oh, I'll need one of your marines to guide me down there."

He was appreciative; told the marine standing nearby to take me to Deck 8. I was on my way.

The IT clerk was surprised. Good. He was flustered. What if his records were not in order? What if his predecessors' records were not in order? Then again, this was new to me too. Rule 1.

"Call up your wafer records." I examined them. Hummed, ticked my tongue. Touched the screen, skipped from screen to screen. None of it mattered, but the records were in good condition. The wafers were all there. I complimented him. Rule 5.

"Now let's look at the wafers themselves." The vault was locked; opening it took a couple minutes. That was a triple fault: he was a rating and knew the codes, he didn't call an officer to supervise; and then it took too long. I ignored it. He knew it.

There were the standard five sets, three of each: Negotiator, Advisor, Warlord, Admiral, and Decider. "Have these been synced?"

"Yes, sir."

"With the other ships?"

"Um, no sir. That takes place during refit."

Which would be every couple decades. I made a mental note on an action plan. Meanwhile, shielded by my body, I substituted my wafer for one of the Deciders. I asked him to run through the sync process. He showed himself capable and completed the task in a handful of minutes. When he was done, I sleight-of-handed my wafer back. I did not, however, re-insert it. That would come later.

* * *

Indeed, later that day, in the quiet of my residence, I took my next risk. I was in uncharted territory. Were the rules that we had been told mere guidances to help us understand? Or did the technicians and their technical writers know more and try to convey it in generalities?

Nothing in our training covered this particular activity. Could I sync a wafer in mid-activation? Would it scramble my thoughts? I had done what I could; my current memories were already synchronized for future uses. The consequences of this fatal experiment would propagate no farther than me and my host.

I re-inserted the wafer, felt it tug at the nape of my neck, and felt a piercing pain in my brain, a ten on a ten scale, accompanied by brightness in my eyes even as they were closed. All was accompanied by a cascade of images and sounds and vibrations and smells. I remembered missions and activations and scrubbings and false alarms that were not there that morning, and just as quickly seemed like they had always been there. I added this particular data point to my experience, along with the resolve that I would not do it again unless absolutely necessary.

331-462
Core 2118 Capital A586A98-D Hi Cx

In my last days, I revisited the clerk's console one evening. This time, I created a series of directives, each encased in a penultimate priority wrapper, validated by single-use override codes, and scheduled to activate over a series of dates. I left them to hatch in the coming month.

A grounds crew visited the Imiirga plot and executed a series of work orders.

A clerk in the Office of Heraldry received a directive and performed the required ministerial acts that gave it the force of the Emperor's will.

A clerk in the Tholar Preservation District coded instructions that warned against any changes to a designated historic section of regional cemetery, but only after the current rehab projects were completed.

A clerk at Imperial Bank noted an exception report identifying a below minimum balance status on specific trust accounts and keyed instructions revoking a series of educational stipends. Formal notifications went out to those affected.

I also arranged for a stipend for the care of my grave.

Ripples of consequences radiated out into the community of now ex-Baronet Sir Fen Imiirga's descendants. Over the next year, students were disenrolled from schools, members in good standing of elite clubs found they were no longer in good standing. Customers, patrons, investors, backers, even friends, were forced to reconsider their relationships based on the newly revealed taint to a formerly honored family line.

333-462
Core 2118 Capital A586A98-D Hi Cx

I met with Arrlanroughl as we had arranged. His two companions again waited across the room. This time, I visited their dining booth and greeted them. "Arrlanroughl and I would like you to choose what you will for dinner. We will be a while." Enough to acknowledge their leader as powerful; enough to establish that I was also powerful.

To Arrlanroughl, I expressed appreciation for the insights he had given me. I reminisced that I had been uncertain of my safety when we had first met. He reminisced that he and his friends had momentarily considered taking my wallet and comm but decided against it on a whim.

"I have a proposal for you. I hope that you will give it due consideration. There is a care-taking position available: a sinecure involving basic maintenance of a gravesite. Grooming of plants, removal of litter, respectful maintenance.

"The position—actually, there are three positions—the position will be advertised in the near future. If you care to apply, these codes will assure your, and your friends', hiring."

I passed over a written card with the details. He expressed polite appreciation and said he would consider it.

"If you accept, please understand that there are responsibilities attached. The duties, while slight, are important and not to be disrespected."

We parted for the evening with me wondering if this would change his life. The cost to the empire would be slight.

335-462
Core 2118 Capital A586A98-D Hi Cx

Lieutenant Enn Shuginsa awoke in virtually the same

place he had vanished. The similarity was enough that he was not sure the wafer had had any effect. His comm even lay in the same place before him, but when he looked, its message was different.

This mission is complete.

The details of your current job assignment are included in the attached memo.

If asked about things you do not know or remember, dissemble: "I am not permitted to discuss that" should be sufficient.

If you ever leave the service, maintain your reservist status, even if as an inactive.

He smiled, remembering his time with the Agent, and inwardly glad that he had survived this assignment. In the next several weeks, he found that he enjoyed his new assignment as Inspector Unipotentiary, and after a year elected to become an inactive reservist and make this his career.

005-463
Core 2118 Capital A586A98-D Hi Cx

"I am sorry," said the managing director of the necropolis, although in truth he was not. "The rehabilitation of the Imiirga plot was conducted in accord with specific directives. The supporting documents are in order, but they have been sealed. You may want to petition the Marquis if you need to review them." As if that effort would bear any fruit, he thought to himself. The fact that the Preservation District had frozen changes after the rehab meant that noble powers were squabbling, and intelligent people did not interfere.

The fact that this family's many-generations-ago archon had recently been dishabilitated was a different signal that confirmed reasonable conjectures. Within a year, the Imiirga plot would be overgrown with weeds.

001-465
Core 2118 Capital A586A98-D Hi Cx

The Empress, like her predecessors, did not notify in advance recipients of the honors she bestowed. She merely published a list; formal notifications would follow in time. Devotees of the nobility subscribed to special notification groups. Higher ranking functionaries made sure that someone or some process monitored the announcements. It fell to sycophants, favor seekers, and just good friends to carry the news to most recipients.

The Empress published her Holiday List of newly named knights and ladies and other minor nobles. There was never an explanation of her choices: The Empress need justify herself to no one.

Inspector Shuginsa was taking advantage of Holiday to sleep in. There would be no work today. But.

Enn's comm dinged repeatedly. From his sleep, he ignored the first three messages, but ultimately gave in and roused to see what was so important.

The first was from an office mate he barely knew: "Holiday List! Congratulations."

There were messages from Senior Supervisor Starpan, from his superior, from a fellow lieutenant he knew from reserve sessions, from the commander of the reserve squadron, from three of the clerks who provided him and others administrative support, and from several people he did not recognize. Each greeting carried some part of the puzzle, which he ultimately assembled in his mind: The Empress had knighted him on the Holiday List.

DEYIS

I could feel around me the comfort of the stadium and I opened my eyes.

Fen Imiirga sat alone in a near vacant section of the stadium, as if contagious and quarantined. Where once he must have sat proudly watching the expanding circles of his descendants, surrounded by his future generations waiting to be born, he was now alone. His children-to-be preferred to sit next to other archons, learning how to live from other, more respectable surnames.

I saw him from a distance, and I saw that he saw me, recognized me. But he did not protest, or speak, or even move.

Before us was the overgrown Imiirga section exactly as I had directed. The stone sphere shattered. Its base engraved with the word CHEAT in great letters. Below that, an exhortation, something Imiirga now wished he had himself said,

> *My progeny: you suffer because of my misdeeds.*
> *Strive to overcome what I could not.*

Perhaps someday they would.

333-501
Aboard BB *Inarik* above
Zaru 0917 Deyis B874777-9 Ag Ri

Abruptly, I again stood with my eyes closed, now in silence, feeling a slight vibration through my feet. I squinted one eye open enough to see the ship lighting and a gathered assembly of crew.

With it closed again, I spoke, "Who here is senior?"

"You are."

This was a good start. At least the basic formalities were in place.

"After me, who?"

"Admiral Slintern commands the squadron."

"Who is the briefer?"

"I am. Commander Slee."

I at last opened my eyes to the broad expanse of the diplomatic reception deck of an *Inarik*-class battle. I had been on similar ships before.

"You may begin." Images flashed on the projection screen as the briefer established that we were concerned with a backwater world brought into the empire in the second century and then more-or-less ignored. Its 94 million inhabitants were about half Humans; the other half were indigenes with a strange caste-gender structure, many arms and many legs, and a dedication to their rural ways. The Humans made their livings buying gathered agriculturals from the natives, processing them, and shipping them to other worlds that seemed to like them.

The current image showed a threat evaluation sufficient to activate me. A local parasite had made the transition from locals to Humans in an unexpected way: it activated endorphins to produce an addicting pleasure that masked a slow, wasting death. Its intersection with Human anatomy made their removal problematic, if not impossible.

The admiral's staff was proud of their action plan: barriers between Humans and locals; careful testing and isolation of those affected; even provision for palliative care. They especially wanted to preserve the historic Second Millennium Karand's Palace. It was clear to me that none of this would work, but that was why the hard decision fell to me and no others.

Perhaps I was missing something, but probably not.

"Thank you Commander Slee. This has been an excellent and informative presentation. You are to be commended.

"Admiral. I would like to meet with your staff by section so that they can brief me specifically on the plan. We should be prepared to act by late tomorrow. Can you please ensure that a preliminary quarantine is in place until we make a final decision? Can you and I and a few of your people dine tonight and discuss this further?" Rule 3.

This was always the hard part. I was the interloper; the unknown; the decision-maker that they wanted to rubber-stamp their action plan. At best, I would nod and approve; at worst, I would require validation, or justification, or budgets, or all-night work sessions. My comments prompted several sighs of relief.

* * *

Meetings that afternoon covered basics. Local forces in the system: a few customs boats; the squadron called in from a naval base some two jumps away, and a few merchants upset that they couldn't pick up their promised goods.

The naval crew was loyal and reasonably well-trained; a staff officer candidly admitted that some were not up to standard, but they were working on it.

The cultural and economic reports showed the indigenes happy to be part of the empire but not especially interested in travelling beyond their own world; the Humans, on the other hand, had strong ties to neighboring systems and a significant number travelled regularly. That data point confirmed my own conclusions.

The penultimate meeting was with the medical staff. They showed slides of the parasites: the size of small beans, or small red pearls. They showed graphs of infection rates trending upwards. They shared optimistic projections of controlled territories. Apparently, they had no psychologists among them.

I mentioned in passing that I would like to talk to security: the leaders of the three watches, the Marine commander (a captain appropriate for this level of force) and the senior non-commissioned officer. We met in the hour before supper.

***

As we sat down, I started with the officer.

"Captain . . . ?"

"Sranti, sir."

"Captain Sranti. Have you read Imperial Edict 97?"

"I have read the summary, sir. I cannot say that I have read the entire text. I have had the training."

"I understand. It is long, legalistic, and complex. Suffice it to say, I have been activated under its provisions and it makes me the ranking authority on this ship, and in this system. You understand that, of course."

"Yes, sir."

"Good. You are to not report the contents of this meeting to anyone without my assent. Not the Admiral. No one."

"Yes, sir."

"Good. We'll leave it at that for the moment."

"Sergeant Major. Have you read Imperial Edict 97?"

"Yes, sir."

"And the implementing regulations?"

"Yes, sir."

"Tell me, in your own words, your understanding about Quarantine Agents. Ignore warrants for the moment."

"Sir, you are the Emperor's Agent, with his total confidence. You speak with his voice. I am to render you every assistance."

"Even if it's stupid? Or suicidal? Or without explanation?"

"Yes, sir."

"Good. Captain, do you understand this situation similarly?"

"Yes, sir."

I turned to the three sergeants, asked them the same, and received the same answers.

"We are now operating under Imperial Edict 97. Share this information with no one. We will meet in the barracks at 0300."

"Meanwhile, I need the following: A flight jacket with the Imperial Sunburst on the back and my surname preceded by the word: Agent, above. What is my surname?"

"Lagash, sir."

"Is he a good man?"

"Good enough. Supply officer. Keeps to himself mostly."

"I also need:

"A chestplate with a frontarm. Make that two; one lethal. Have them ready for me in the barracks.

"Wake tablets. Have them in my stateroom by twenty.

"We're done here. Captain. Send your regrets; you will not attend dinner tonight."

* * *

Dinner in the wardroom was typical of naval formal dining. I sat as the guest of honor at the head of the table. The Admiral at my right was a sparkling conversationalist, although he bridled a bit at not being the center of attention. I took control of the table conversation by emphasizing that I was 16 years out of date. Who was the current emperor? How fared the empire? What was the latest fashion in naval strategy? I got to know, however superficially, the staff officers, the exec, and a few of the department heads. After four hours, I begged off and retired for the night.

But I didn't sleep. I had too much to do, and every sleep I took would bring me closer again to oblivion.

* * *

The barracks meeting went well.

334-501
Aboard BB *Inarik* above
Zaru 0917 Deyis B874777-9 Ag Ri

We met in a side compartment off the hangar deck of *Inarik*: admiral and immediate staff.

"I am Agent Lagash of the Quarantine. I serve under

Imperial Edict 97, which makes me the highest-ranking officer on this ship, in this squadron, in this system, indeed in this sector. My absolute power is confirmed by the silence of everyone present."

I waited several beats just to make sure there were no objections.

"Gather round. I want you all to hear and understand me. We're going to talk, and you should be comfortable as we do.

"Commander Slee. Please give your briefing as you gave it to me."

When it was over, "Thank you Commander.

"I'll be blunt. This scheme is flawed. If any part of it fails, the entire plan fails.

"That world below us is infested with a parasite that makes people happy and then kills them; no quarantine or isolation or barrier can keep that sort of thing in, or people who want it out. This world must be sterilized before it can infect the empire.

"Nothing you will ever do is as important as what we will do in this mission."

We moved to address the assembled crew on the hangar deck. I think the Admiral was surprised.

* * *

We knew we had an agent on board. We had all been buzzing on what he would do. Smith called him a zombie. Trint told a tale of an agent who united a crew into an efficient team with magic words that no one could remember later. They called a mandatory mass assembly for midwatch. They posted marines on each deck; our consoles set to automatic.

No one knew what he would say. No that's not right. The marines did. Every one of them wore gloves.

He wore the body of Lieutenant Lagash. He stood on the platform and addressed us without notes. He began abruptly. I missed most of his first sentence. Most of us did. But no matter. What I heard was enough.

"... of the Quarantine." He paused before this next statement.

"Nothing of value is without cost.

"Our mission is to save literally billions of lives. If we fail, those billions, on dozens of worlds, will die. We cannot let that happen. We will succeed.

"But there is a terrible cost that we face as well.

"The world below is Deyis. It joined the interstellar community in the Fifth Millennium of Star Flight, happy for occasional trade and visitors. It is infested with a parasite that, if loosed on the empire, will utterly destroy it. Our mission, our responsibility is to prevent that. This is not a telenovela. There is no last-minute surprise solution.

"Tomorrow we will scrub Deyis to the bedrock. Tomorrow we will destroy the biomes of Deyis, and with them 90 million sophonts. Make no mistake: they are people. Fathers, mothers, sisters, brothers, sons and daughters, babies. Their lives and their lines will end forever. We have no choice.

"This is not a task we undertake lightly.

"We will push buttons and activate salvos and watch on display screens the terrifying fruits of our labors. We can even congratulate ourselves on a job well done. But years from now, you will wake in the night with nightmare visions of the people we have murdered so effortlessly.

"Trust me. I absolve you of all guilt. The Emperor himself will ratify your actions. But that will not be enough. There will be nightmares and hauntings. The spirits of the dead will cry out to you and you will have no answer."

He paused as his words settled into our minds. After just the right interval, he continued.

"Nothing of value is without cost.

"There must be a cost to us for our actions. We must ourselves taste the pain and the loss that those below will suffer. We must ourselves bear a constant reminder of our participation and know that we ourselves have suffered with them."

This time he sounded like he did not want to continue. But he did.

"Each of you will sacrifice the least digit of your non-dominant hand. Your commanders have bolt cutters and will begin the process now; they will make their sacrifice first. The pain of anticipation will be short-lived; the pain itself is momentary; the loss will stay with you forever as your cost in achieving this mission of great value."

The Admiral interrupted. "This is barbaric! I will not have it!" He stood, towering over the agent in rage. The Agent remained calm; turned to face him fully. He answered in a conversational voice, yet powerful beyond description.

"It is barbaric. We are going to kill ninety million people because we have no other answer.

"Would you *not* kill those below? Would you risk the

very existence of the empire? We have no choice; no alternative; there are no other options."

The Admiral raged on. "This is unnecessary. Our crew, our team, is trained and ready to do its duty. I countermand your order!"

Agent Lagash's fingers twitched in Marine battle language as he simultaneously spoke. "Kill him."

The Admiral dropped, collapsed in an awkward heap, almost before the sounds of the guns could be heard.

To our credit, only a few of us dropped to the deck; the rest stood transfixed by this drama.

Louder now:

"I speak with the voice of the Emperor himself. Strip his rank insignia from his collar and send it to his family with the message that he disobeyed me. Take his finger; I will not allow him to avoid participating in our sacrifice. Then dump his body on the world below."

Turning his attention back to us, the assembled crew.

"Years from now you will understand.

"Begin."

222-514
Delp 0709 Modesta B857400-8 Ni Ga Pa

I hated that agent. He was so calm and arrogant. He expected us to obey him without hesitation, and then literally gave us no choice.

We operated like machines. Targeting. Launching. Monitoring. Runners brought us tasteless meals to eat at our consoles. We slept like the dead; some took pills to avoid the dreams. It took almost a month.

I served in the Navy for another ten years, and I have

come to realize that he did indeed have our best interests at heart. He could have just told us what to do and I agree that I would be having nightmares now because of it.

My lieutenant cut off my finger himself. By the time he got to me, he was no longer apologizing. He just did it; the faster for the med to apply a salve and give me a pain pill. It hurt more than I thought it would; I still shudder to think of the barbarity of it all.

And yet.

I understand today, in a way that words could never have told me then: we were going to do far worse to millions of people. It was right that we should suffer. And for every one that we killed, there were ten, or a hundred, or a thousand that would live and never even know what we had done.

334-501
Aboard BB *Inarik* above
Zaru 0917 Deyis B874777-9 Ag Ri

The little officer scurried forward from the ranks; his tablet cradled in the crook of his arm. He was a Bwap, a Newt, the short, reptilian sophont that seemed to gravitate to obsessive-compulsive tasks like spreadsheets and databases.

His diminutive size made his voice a natural squeak. "Agent Lagash?"

I turned, ready to scowl at an appeal for some special treatment. "Yes? What?"

"I am Lieutenant Commander Epabaa." He held up his hand to show its severed outermost finger. "My digit will regrow. Is that allowed?"

"I suppose that it is."

"But then my shared sacrifice is somehow less than the others?"

"That is also true. Tell me your thoughts?"

"May I give an eye instead?" He proffered his stylus, held it out before him.

I accepted it, turned it in my hands, evaluating its form and texture. Abruptly, I straightened my arm to jab at the reptile's eye. Epabaa recoiled in a reflex action, his hand now covering his face as vitreous oozed through his fingers.

"I apologize, Agent. I had not expected this level of pain."

"I understand. The Emperor appreciates your sacrifice. Have that patched and return to your duties."

"Yes, Agent."

As the Bwap moved away, I extended a hand and supported myself on a console edge. That was harder than I expected.

336-501
Zaru 0917 Deyis B874777-9 Ag Ri

The Goldonan family was only dimly aware of the crisis. Their focus was the farm: the hectares of crop that required constant attention.

Trance was trying to catch that pesky pouncer that was raiding the fowlhouse. The fence didn't do much good; it somehow made it over, or under, or through to find a plump bird, shake it to death in a cloud of feathers and then escape to a pleasant dinner. Here in the dead of night, Trance had his darkvisors on and waited quietly upwind.

Without warning, his visors blanked to safety mode and he pulled them off to middle-of-the-day light. There, just beyond the fence was the pouncer ready to leap. Trance was raising his sandgun when the blastwave hit.

* * *

Filis was worried there was something wrong with her account. She had ordered a replacement translimiter for the drive, had received confirmation, and had spent the last two days almost non-stop getting the foundation brackets ready. Now, on her first real break, she checked and had no messages on the console. None. No weasely marketing notes; no invitations to events; no reminders from the express service. Most of all, no dispatch confirmation from the parts company.

She checked again and it looked like the network was down. That was impossible; how could anyone do anything if the network was down?

She took the long walk toward the open cargo hatch, wondering why it was so bright outside. She reached it just as the blastwave hit, tumbling the ship, and her, end over end across the tarmac. Although the ship did three full rotations, she was dead before the first completed.

* * *

There was a string of slabs targeted on the isolated Sea of Fools; they would vaporize its contents and boil particles of bottom mud into the upper atmosphere, all part of the overall plan to generate global winter for decades to come.

"Something's wrong." The sensop said under her breath as she touched a tab to alert her supervisor. The interaction was silent. The screen was highlighted to show the slabs targeting shore rather than sea. A supplemental screen showed the original target point and its undulating and eddying pattern of surface fish as they darted about, faster than it seemed they should. The supervisor retargeted a backup stream to impact several minutes later. They hit as directed and the exception incident was marked closed.

FIRST EMPIRE KNOWLEDGE

In the First Millennium of Star Flight, the bold, foolhardy Vilani ventured out in their immense starjumpers, huge hulls packed with fuel and drives, marvels of engineering and science.

Looking back, we see those ships as primitive, inefficient, bulky, crude. But to eyes that were accustomed to ships that took generations to travel between the stars, they were marvels! They travelled not at a tenth of the speed of light, not at light speed itself, but a hundred times, almost two hundred times faster than photons. Explorers could visit more than one world in a lifetime and still return to make their reports. Investors could expect profits; scientists could expand their knowledge, and their reputations; the species could expand.

Even better, no one else knew the secret.

The starjumpers visited systems, stars, and worlds. They reached a thousand planets and discovered answers to classic questions of science: they filled to overflowing the data banks of the First Empire.

There was, in those early years, another type of knowledge: the unconfirmed, the incredible, the unbelievable.

Stories of monsters and marvels, strangeness and strangers. These reports were problematic: hard to believe, hard to prove, hard to understand. It was easiest to laugh and then dismiss or ignore them. Who could possibly believe stories of monsters that swarmed in the vacuum of deep space, of worlds where time stood still, of sirens that called men to their dooms, of artificial planetoids in the depths of the outer oort? What reasonable scientist would believe the weird, the occult, the unproven, or the undocumented? More than one scientist was embarrassed to find that supposed fact was really the writings of the deranged, or alien children's morality tales, or startlingly realistic entertainment fictions. This mass of nonsense had a name: the *Niikiik Luur*, literally the words meant the False-Knowledge.

This false knowledge was a source of constant confusion, and to the First Empire the obvious answer was to suppress it. It was systematically removed from the databases; references were tagged unproven or fictional; more than that, they were often scrambled or deliberately corrupted. Over time, over generations, over centuries, this forbidden other knowledge was very thoroughly eradicated. The information networks were all the better for it.

And yet, there are always the few who must be contrary, and some of those contraries had great power and great resources.

***

The Karand's Palace on Nivalia became one such contrary: a secret repository, maintained by its hereditary staff even long after the First Empire fell. The estate was self-sustaining: surrounded by agricultural lands; worked by serfs; managed by a dedicated set of families. Of those, only a few actually knew about the collection, and fewer still saw any real value. Of course, it had no value; its curators were weird mystics with strange ideas and distorted concepts of importance and reality.

011-502
The Naval Base at
Zaru 1410 Sternbach AAA5944-B Fl Hi In Cp

The first ships of the fleet had just arrived insystem in a series of jump flashes as they individually shed energy. Arrivals would continue over the next sixteen hours. The naval base and the starport sensors knew immediately, indeed the arrivals were expected, but to households and businesses and families this was the first hint of homecoming; they started receiving alerts almost immediately. Crews on liberty meant money to be spent, spouses and friends to be reunited, celebrations. Ships in port meant supplies to be sold, services to be rendered, data dumps, database updates. This system would be a busy place for weeks to come.

Slintern House was aflutter with excitement. Servants scurried here and there putting art and accessories in their proper places, adjusting lighting levels, polishing imagined scuffs so that all would be perfect when the Admiral arrived. The Lady Slintern remained in her chambers, primping and preparing herself; there would be a social whirl of receptions and parties and audiences, many dominated by her husband, but many focused on her as the Lady of the house. These were exciting times indeed.

Hours passed with no word, no messages, no alerts to Slintern House, and the Lady began to entertain some slight fret. How unlike the Marquis Slintern not to send some signal or greeting, some indication of the social responsibilities that were coming.

* * *

The coded signals between the flagship and the administration center at the naval base created their own difficulties. Admiral Slintern was more than a ranking naval officer, he was a Marquis; the news could not simply be released.

The naval base had other admirals, and the next in line gladly assumed the mantle of command. Lesser Admiral Tanabula was but a Baronet, although it was clear in his own mind that would change soon. He also knew that with great power comes great responsibility. He could not delegate this particular task.

His black groundcar, preceded and followed by blue security vehicles, drove through the primary gate at Slintern House and stopped precisely at the grand entrance. Footmen opened doors and stood respectfully stiff. The Baronet emerged flanked by officers in grey and officers in white. "Tell the Lady to come here."

No one had time to object. One raced up the grand staircase. Another inquired about refreshments, only to be rebuffed.

After a time, the Lady appeared at the top of the staircase, "How may I help you gentlemen?"

"Come down here. I will not shout my message to you."

* * *

At last, arrogant, even angry, the Lady reached the bottom of the stairs to confront the Baronet. He was enjoying this. She deserved it even more than the Marquis.

He held out the small tray containing the double sunburst insignia that identified an Admiral of the Imperial Navy. He had been careful not to soil his hands by touching it. When she picked it up, he discarded the tray into a corner.

He used no identifier or honorific. The pronoun was sufficient.

"He disobeyed the Emperor. His title and his fiefs are forfeit. Be out of here by dark." Three hours away. Not the traditional morning. By dark. The public would know by then. They would enjoy it; they enjoyed seeing the mighty brought low. Especially the cruel mighty.

She started to ask questions, but he ignored her. He turned to the house manager. "By dark."

Although the Baronet left in his groundcar, the two security vehicles remained. A few minutes before the sunset, a car appeared, and the Lady left with two bags she had to carry herself.

NOVA EVACUATION

I awoke to crowd noises and jostling, and despite my disorientation opened my eyes immediately. Before me were the rows of the stadium, but strangely my back was to the field. I started walking, climbing the shallow risers, swimming against the flow, until I reached the concourse.

At last free of the masses, I stepped to a supportive railing and paused. What caught my eye were a set of broad sliding doors which I recognized as lifts. That immediately implied to me other levels: entrances, offices, exits. I was drawn to it. As I approached, I could not ignore the prominent numeral writ large on its face: 4.

The doors parted as I approached to reveal a large chamber some five double arms-lengths wide and long and two manheights tall. I stepped in, alone, and the doors closed.

They immediately reopened to blackness and I noted that a panel now said 5.

They closed and reopened to an actinic glare that actually hurt my eyes. Light and dark played against me as forms moved beyond those doors. The panel said 6.

They closed again, reopening to a dull red glow and

slow-moving shadows beyond. The doors this time remained open for one of those shapes to enter: some sort of sophont with headless shoulders, a circle of elbowless arms atop a skirt of kneeless legs. Etiquette dictated that we ignore each other, and we did as the doors closed and reopened to the howl of strong cold winds. It exited and the doors reclosed as the panel number changed to 81. I must remember that I started at 4, I thought. I would hate to be lost.

And so, the doors opened to familiar crowds as the panel said 4, and I exited.

091-502
Aboard BKF *Basiiri* Above
Forn 2404 Kulabisha B68799A-9 Ga Hi

I stood in front of the assembled crew: not just the line officers, but nearly every single officer and spacer on board. Consoles had been set on automatic. There was one officer on the bridge, but I had spoken with her, in the presence of the Captain, before everyone else assembled here.

The cargo deck was the only place with physically enough room. After an introduction and a briefing by the Exec, I started.

"That star out there will nova in six months. It will scour the world below of all life. Nothing we can do will stop it.

"This world has a population of 5 billion.

"Do the math:

"A thousand-ton ship can carry about 50 people and 500 tons of cargo.

"Let's stress life support to the break-point: makeshift many-decker cots, doses of calmatives, minimal food, abysmal sanitation. Maybe we can fit 50 people per ton, crowding to the very limit of endurance.

"We can even house some people in unused fuel tankage.

"So, 800 tons of capacity, 50 people per ton, 4,000 people per ship per two weeks. Before the star explodes that ship can save 50,000 people. We need 100,000 ships, each making a dozen runs over six months.

"That will not happen. We can't save them all.

"How many can we save? Let's say we get a hundred ships, maybe a thousand ships, drain the starlanes for this entire sector. That saves one percent of the population. The rest will die. So will the local biomes; animals; plants; culture; goods; precious metals, everything else.

"I have already made a decision that nothing matters but lives. Our mission is to save lives. As many as possible.

"We have 15 million seconds until this star explodes and everyone dies. If we work hard, we may save a hundredth of the population, 50 million people, three people a second.

"But we face a terrible responsibility. Who do we save?

"Who? The best? The brightest? The richest? The average? A cross-section? Who will choose? Who has the right to choose?

"That responsibility lies with me. I must make the choice. Before I speak, you must all accept my decisions, however arbitrary or ill-conceived. You must obey me in this; your oath to the Imperium requires it. Ultimately, the Emperor will ratify my actions and absolve you of any blame or fault. Do as I say. Speak up now, or your silence marks acquiescence.

"Anyone? Speak now."

Silence. No one spoke. No one dared to speak. The responsibility was too daunting. They were all glad that I had the responsibility.

"Fine. We choose as does nature: randomly. Those we encounter we save. Many will die; some will live on a new world to re-establish this society, this species.

"We'll have to kill some to save others; kill those who disrupt the process; kill those who try to take over, or jump the line, or just make trouble, because every one of those problems means delay. Because every second of delay kills three people who could have been saved.

"Your weapons are lethal; your mission is paramount. Every single person you encounter is already dead, except for those you save. If necessary, for the mission kill the others; it is a mercy. They will be dead in six months anyway.

Later, I met with squadron staff.

"I want to relieve the suffering of the rest. We have two strategies: hope, and palliatives.

"Alert the authorities. There is a rescue fleet to arrive at the very last moment, to carry away the loyal functionaries who have so faithfully served us. There will be more than enough hulls to take them and their significant others. Mark it ultimate secret.

"Start a remedy project, modifying the meson gun system defenses. Loose barrage after barrage of calculated fire into the star. Modify and improve the guns, and fire again. Mark this secret penultimate; someone will find out no matter what we do.

"Meanwhile, loosen the rules of society: calmatives; relaxants; entertainments. Release stipends to the poor and give them access to consumer goods. Require only that they be orderly."

I visited every single crew member in the first three days. I repeated the same words in conversation after conversation, and they believed me because they wanted to. "You are doing a good job. The Emperor himself will hear of your work. Thank you."

ENNA PLANT LAGASH
REPORT 1

Video image of a Human woman with dark hair drawn back in a bun; her jaw showing a trace of pudge. Blue eyes focus on the camera lens but shift slightly as they read from prompter notes. She speaks with a meticulous standard Anglic pronunciation. Datestamp: 281-531. Report 1.

This piece rambles: if you are impatient have your console synopsize for an executive summary.

I was an educator.

I worked in a publicly funded school for adolescents, teaching appropriate social roles through an examination of Anglic literature. We read books and graphic novels. We viewed dramas, whether recorded or live, telenovelas, animations, and serials. We engaged in game-playing, ludo, mmo, and even tabletop. We studied wafer entertainments in all their varieties.

My subtext was always an examination of societal roles: how to be a good consumer, a good producer, a responsible citizen, a valuable employee, a compatible partner. We had teaching segments on stewardship of the planet, support of the greater good, and moral principles for social harmony.

I took the seasonal exams along with my students; I strived to improve my scores on a year-to-year basis, both as an example to my students, and because I believed in our society.

I met Rens when he began his job as an administrator at our school, that was on Kanorb. He had just finished his term in the Imperial Navy and came to our world to make his life. We grew to like each other, fell in love, created a marriage partnership, had our allowed two children, raised them to adulthood, and we grew old together.

Four years short of retirement, Rens was diagnosed with terminal, incurable cerebral degeneration. As his faculties diminished, he was forced into an early retirement. As they diminished further, I retired early as well. The counsellor advised euthany, either single or double, but I refused. With our reduced means, I surrendered our many-roomed apartment and moved to a few-roomed apt in one of the arcologies. In exchange for our income streams, we received secure housing, tolerable meals in the communal cafeterias, and even occasional outings.

Rens, although he remained physically strong, had difficulty coping and found solace in an unending series of participation events though his console. I paid the subscription fees through a make-work job staffing a monitoring kiosk. It was the least I could do for my life partner.

For the next three years, our lives were in suspension as we waited for him to die a natural death.

One night, Rens awoke. He normally slept through the night, and so I awoke as well. He moved to the console on the far side of the room and I expected he would start an interactive session. Instead, as I watched, he manipulated the screens and touch pads looking at datapaks, maps, charts, and a variety of information graphics.

He returned to bed perhaps an hour later. "Rens, are you good?"

He responded with a verbal non-word, and after several minutes, he spoke, quietly.

"Did I ever tell you what I did in the Navy?"

He had told me only vaguenesses. On our world, few of us ventured into space, and even fewer returned. Polite company did not speak much of a life in the greater empire; I had never asked, and he had told me little. "Only generally. You said you used a wafer and awoke with no memory of what happened. That you lost a finger. They gave you a promotion, transferred you to a naval base, and that you mustered out soon after."

He started in. "I can tell you what happened. I served on a capital: a big ship that guards the empire. I was only a small cog in a big machine, responsible mostly for supplies that kept people alive and well.

"I was offered a chance to serve the empire. They gave me a wafer and I took it.

"There was a crisis, a system infested with something that, if it got out, would destroy the biomes on dozens of worlds. I controlled an operation, I made decisions, that scrubbed that world. At a cost of many dead, I saved the lives of a thousand times more. Literally, there are billions alive yet today because of that project.

"That wafer put a different personality in my head: a trained expert who knew how to act and what to do in a crisis. After about thirty days, that personality evaporated and Rens' personality re-expressed itself.

"This hasn't happened before. That trained personality has come back. I'm not Rens. I'm him."

I physically shook. I think he thought it fear because he simply waited me out. I'm not sure what it was, but the feeling passed. It wasn't grief; I had felt grief at the loss of my Rens long before. Nevertheless, my eyes were moist, and I dabbed them with my nightblouse. He continued.

"This hasn't happened before. This may last only a day, or a week. Most probably, it will last a month, and then I'll evaporate again. Maybe Rens will come back.

"You have nothing to fear from me. Let's wait and see.

"Meanwhile, I need to make a report."

He swung his feet to the floor and made his way back to the console. There was the final confirmation that he was not my Rens. "Tell me your name?"

"Enna."

It's not like he replaced Rens. Rens wasn't there, hadn't been there for many months. The next day, he said, "Let's try to be normal. Call me Rens. Treat me like I am Rens."

I went about my routine. I cleaned and arranged things, laid out his clothes, showed him where things were. I left him to his own devices while I staffed the monitoring kiosk, and usually returned to find him at the console reading news and history. We enjoyed our meals together despite the lackluster food and prosaic presentation. I told him about our history together and what I knew of this world, and what less that I knew of the universe beyond.

After the second day, he gave me a message capsule. I momentarily thought, "Where did he get that?" but did not say it aloud. He said, "When my personality evaporates, dictate a note about how long I was present, and then send it off. It's all pre-addressed and pre-paid. You just need to give it to the Express Office."

At day thirty-one, after we had gone through our morning routine, he said, "I haven't evaporated." He explained that somehow his personality overlay had re-expressed itself, probably some manifestation of my husband's illness. "I expect to be here for quite a while. I need to travel. I want you to come with me."

"Where?"

"Does it matter?"

"I suppose not." Living here was waiting to die. We could wait to die anywhere.

We left the next day with only the clothes on our backs, a few identity documents, and a book with my library of Anglic literature.

By travel, I thought he meant regional or perhaps continental. The fast transport could get us anywhere on

Kanorb in a few days. We could see the vistas of the Grand Desert, the eternal mists of the Western Islands, maybe even ice floes in the north. We started out across the agricultural region and its endless fields of grain. That night, I immersed myself in a fourth-century Nerstian classic about hope.

The next morning, we arrived at the starport and I panicked. I had never been offworld; I never intended to go offworld; I had not expected that travel meant offworld. He held my hand tightly and said all would be right. I felt for a moment like I still had my Rens with me, and I followed him meekly.

I don't know where he got the money. We lived on sixteen thousand credits a year, our reduced retirement annuities, and we saw almost none of that: it went straight to the arcology. Our disposable balances averaged a couple hundred at any one time and we had an emergency fund of perhaps a thousand.

Our two passages together cost fourteen thousand credits. I don't know where the money came from. Perhaps we would spend some months in debtors' prison before we died.

Space travel seems exciting, and in the beginning it is. The wheeled people mover carried us to a sleek jumpliner on the far side of the field. We went directly to our staterooms and settled in. At the ten-minute announcement, Rens and I made our way to the lounge to watch liftoff on the big screens: they showed forward, aft, down, and even a remote view of us slowly lifting into Kanorb's sky. Over the next ten hours, we cruised to the jump point; the screens showed our receding world; the steward provided commentary and answered questions. He moderated a game in which we used our seat screens to find specific spectral stars, or gas giants, or even other ships in the trade lanes. He awarded prizes in the form of plastic chips redeemable for specialty foods in the buffet line.

We were travelling middle. The stewards fawned over the high passengers who had priority at meals and only they rotated through seatings at the captain's table. We served ourselves at a buffet of tolerable foods, although they were somewhat better than the arcology's fare.

After about half a day, we reached a safe point beyond Kanorb's one-hundred diameter limit and the captain announced jump in ten, nine, eight seconds. At two, the lights dimmed, a tradition on this particular line, and at zero we transitioned to jumpspace. The clock timers reset to zero and started counting immediately. Sometime between 150 and 186 hours we would break out in the Sashrakusha system, two parsecs, almost seven light-years, distant. The purser wandered through the lounges with a pool board, selling ten credit chances on the correct pick for breakout. Rens gave me a coin and I picked my birthday: 166.

We now had a week in jump. The viewports were closed to protect us from the sanity-challenging chaos of jumpspace. Onboard clocks would slowly adjust to Sashrakusha time.

After a day, after our morning meal, after a bout of simple exercise, Rens asked me to teach him Anglic literature. He must have planned this; he produced a book I didn't know he had and asked for me to get him started. In all my years as a teacher, Rens had never asked about literature. I was touched.

The study of Anglic literature is the study of society itself. Writings and entertainments reflect what people, be they the elite or the masses, think and feel. Good literature resonates with them; bad literature fails. What is good in some eras is bad in others, and the converse.

I knew the theories and the curricula, but I would be teaching an educated adult rather than an adolescent. I needed to adjust my approach.

I started with Gilgamesh. We watched a classic video from the second century. He already knew the story, but I enjoyed emphasizing key points, stopping the display, replaying sequences, and noting early events that presaged later resolutions.

He who saw, knew, experienced, understood all
Lived in the temple of the sky god and the love goddess
And wanted to know more.

Rens was more concerned with plot; he wanted to know what happened next, and when it didn't seem logical, he complained or even argued with the screen. He pointed out illogical sequences that I just accepted as story mechanisms.

I, on the other hand, was concerned with character, specifically how each filled roles in society. I sorted characters into their roles: good (or bad) citizens, pleasant (or unpleasant) companions, responsible (or wasteful) stewards. The negative examples were as important to me as the positive.

We had lively discussions: I found Rens could make strong points without alienating me; he found I could argue with both logic and emotion, and I think he was impressed. Time passed swiftly.

* * *

Onboard time had adjusted to strike midnight when the clock timer hit 168. If all went perfectly, we would break out at midnight and arrive at the starport at noon.

As it happened, the hull started rumbling at 2100 ship time, and we broke out at 2219; the timer showed 166.19. Rens smiled and said that was a good omen. I wondered why, but the steward began distributing celebratory beverages and I did not have the chance to ask.

Later, Rens signaled the purser with a wave. "Show him your chip."

I retrieved the 166 and the fellow paid over a demand card with a glowing Cr100 on its face.

The high passengers debarked first; a second mover fetched us, and it lurched across the tarmac buffeted by grey winds and grit. We had only our hand items, and so we stood at the front of the conveyor. Once it mated with the terminal, we stepped through, greeted by a whiff of noxious vapor trapped between the protective doors before they opened.

Sashrakusha Down was a whirl of activity: many people, many sophonts; glaring holos; strange smells. Rens looked around, saw something, and started off. Then he stepped back, took my hand, and said to not let go. We bumped into people, they bumped into us; no one seemed to notice or care. This was so unlike home. Were all starports like this?

Eventually, we stopped in a calm spot outside the rush and I said, "Tell me what we're doing. There's no reason to act without explanation. We are travelling together."

He acknowledged fault. "I am unaccustomed to this. Forgive me; I shall do better." And he did. He narrated the remainder of our walk, pointing out shops that catered to specific sophonts, occupations, even avocations. We stopped at one and he enticed me to spend my winnings on a close-fitting hat with a short bill; he said I was now officially an adventuress and deserved to look the role. I blushed and picked a red one.

We eventually reached massive blast doors uncharacteristic of the remainder of the terminal. Lasered into the steel was a person-sized insignia consisting of upright sword and surrounding wreath. Rens identified it as the seal of the Imperial Navy. "You will need to wait here. It's safe, but don't venture beyond those shops there. Go with no one. If I send someone, he will tell you that I sent for you and will know both your name and mine."

I waited for an hour. Left, bought a drink with energy and electrolytes, looked at some trinkets in a display, and returned. After two hours, Rens appeared and said all was prepared.

I gave him a look, and he stopped. "Oh. Sorry. The Navy has arranged for a ship for us. We are going to Vland. We'll leave later this week. Meanwhile, we'll stay at the TAS Hotel."

Almost a sector away. The homeworld of the Vilani

people. The center of the First Empire. My mind wobbled.

We checked into the hotel, a tall tower defying the corrosive mists of this world: its effort was less than successful; long drools of corrosion stained its façade and the transpex of the room was scratched by windblown grit. All outside was shades of grey: the buildings, the clouds, the sky, the ground, the sea.

Rens noticed and closed the interior shutters. "Ignore all that, we'll be on our way in a few days."

"Rens." I said. "We need to talk. I don't know what is happening. You aren't communicating. Just tell me."

His shoulders slumped slightly. "I understand. I apologize."

He hesitated, clearly thinking through what to say. "We'll be on our ship day after tomorrow. Can details wait until then?"

I agreed.

"Then, let's see what this world has to offer."

We saw a locally staged production of one of Nerst's scripts, the same one on hope that I had just read. I enjoyed it.

We walked the Grand Promenade and saw the only trees that grew on this world.

We peeked into the door of a Vargr bar, but my courage failed me and Rens did not insist. Moments later we saw a fight break out and several dogs thrown into the street.

We strolled a balcony encircling the TAS and watched the sun rise for local morning.

***

The next day I spent in our room; Rens had, considerately, told me he needed to be away making preparations. He warned me not to leave the room; I could order food to be delivered. I obeyed.

He returned late that night, greeted me amiably, and went to sleep almost immediately.

The next morning. "We're ready. Gather your things."

I checked the corners of the room, looked into the compartments, donned my new red adventuress's cap, and followed.

We passed through a warren of tunnels deep beneath the tarmac. I smelled noxious fumes, lubricants, strangenesses. We passed occasional uniformed spacers and technicians; they ignored us. Rens walked like he owned the place. Eventually we reached a shaft, an airlock, a connector, and another airlock. And we were inside a ship. Later I came to see that it was a strange ship, but at the time, all ships were strange to me.

In an alcove, we were greeted by aliens. Sophonts. Tripods with striped skins and booming voices. Rens introduced them and their names washed over me: Boorn, Truul, Flaal, Flink, and others. They acted happy to see me: deferential, eager to please. Perhaps I just did not understand their non-Human ways.

"Boorn will take you to the lounge." I thought that one was Truul. I would have to try harder. "I'll meet you there in a few minutes."

The lounge was utilitarian. Not at all like the jumpliner. As I waited, I saw the ship's nameplate and read its cryptic details:

INS *Argushii*
TF-HA63
Laid Down: 005-414 Vlandian Yard 2
First Flight: 273-414 Vland

Argushii was Vilani for *hidden truths*; sometimes it meant *sacred knowledge*. The word had its origins in ancient myth: the valuable thing early seafarers sought, only to find that it was good will rather than gold.

Rens spoke from behind me, "I picked this one partly because of the name. Our other choices were *bird-that-eats-carrion*, and *dangerous-thoughts*."

"Well chosen. They just gave this to you?"

"It was an auxiliary in long term storage. They weren't using it; I knew some override codes."

"And the crew? They come with the ship?"

"They want to travel to their homeworld. When we get there, they'll muster out and we'll find some replacements.

"Oh, this is for you." He handed me a small silver pin: a many-rayed sun. "This makes you a brevet lieutenant in the Imperial Navy Auxiliary. You outrank everyone but Boorn, and Truul, and me."

He told me I was now the astrogator. It was a formality. Someone else made the first course calculations and we jumped within several hours.

I learned my craft with OJT. Truul knew astrogation and had a gentle style. He explained how to consult the astrogation console, plan a courseline from one system to another, make provision for strange anomalies. During our week in jump, I divided my time between learning astrogation basics and teaching Rens Anglic literature. Time flew.

Truul also schooled me in the finer details of astrogation. He spun stories of early astrogators and the challenges they faced: learning to plan courselines that missed rogue worlds and ice chunks; checking and double-checking for math errors that could strand a ship deep between the stars. He told me that we shuttered our vision ports to protect us from the nightmares that looking at jumpspace could bring. He confided that not everyone suffered from the visions, but it was better to be safe; that he had seen a spacer struck mad when a shutter malfunctioned. His lessons were not lost on me; I saw jumpspace as a terrible force, and my responsibilities were not to be lightly held.

By the time we reached Vland, I was proficient in telling the console how to calculate a course. Good astrogators could calculate with a tablet; great ones could do it in their heads. I ranked probably fair.

Rens became proficient in identifying social traits in literature: the solid characters that prudent people settled down with; the users that gave stories action but were examples of traits in the negative. Like my students before him, he mused aloud about where he fit in the spectrum.

Strangely, our time at Vland was short and unremarkable. We remained in orbit, docked at the highport while Rens and Truul ventured to the surface. They returned the next day and we left immediately.

Our new destination was Othsekuu in Lishun: the tripods' homeworld. It would take us perhaps half a year. I learned more of my new craft.

I instituted a book club; I posted a title on the network just after jump and we discussed it twice, several days later. Rens was enthusiastic, the tripods less so.

Boorn did not understand why Roger did not expose Hester immediately. Truul said he understood, but clearly didn't. Flaal did understand, tried to explain it to Boorn, and eventually decided he didn't understand.

At one point, we could have refueled at the local gas giant, but Rens directed our ship to the mainworld of the system: a deserted globe with varied biomes but neither sophonts nor indigenes.

While the crew maneuvered the maws of huge hoses to the banks of the river, Rens took me to the edge of the purplish forest.

He gave me an ocular overlay: a grey curve that covered my eyes. From within, all appeared the same except for a bluish tinge. All the while, he talked to me in a confident tone.

"Here. This is a Snap-10. You hold it here, like this."

I had never touched a gun in my life.

"Notice this clicking part at the back. It won't work unless you grip tightly. If that isn't pushed down, it won't fire, even if you drop it, or throw it, or bump it.

"This is the front. It shoots out little needles at half the speed of light." He laughed to himself as he said this particular fact.

"When you hold this, with the grip compressed, like this, you see a dot out there somewhere. See? That's where it will hit if you shoot.

"But there's a safety. It's body-fenced. If you point at a person wearing a crew badge, the dot is green. Safe. It won't shoot. Everywhere else, the dot's red. Deadly. Shoot and it kills."

He was gentle as he spoke, "I know you are accustomed to calling an enforcer when you need help: to delegating the protection of your safety to someone else. On our journey, there will be no one else on whom you can depend, not even me. In fact, I will depend on you more than you know.

"This gun is just a tool. You carry it, as I carry mine, because there are forces in the universe that do not care about you, or your health, or your life. They are dedicated to winning the evolutionary battle, and in the process, they will trample everything in their path.

"This tool is an equalizer, our own evolutionary advantage."

I searched my memory of literature and found comforting examples of roles such as this as I felt the Snap-10's weight in my hand.

SAKALIIN

The breeze was bone-chilling, and I shivered as I opened my eyes. The stadium was sparsely attended today. Where normally we were shoulder-to-shoulder with a buzz of conversation, row after row had only one spectator each; in a few places there were clusters of parents and children.

I made my way to the railing: to see through dark clouds to the windswept surface below. It was lifeless. There were occasional signs of once-upon-a-time life: fallen squat trunks of massively strange trees, mats of purplish grasses blown by galeish winds, but all were frozen in time by a lack of eaters and reducers.

One of the parents saw me, said something to his companions, and came in my direction. "This is all that is left of Nivalia." I knew somehow that was his name for Deyis II. "Once, this whole section was filled with our ancestors, our children, and our children's children. Nivalia won't have people again for ten thousand years, if that, if ever. Our ancestors have left in despair. The children have just faded into," he shrugged, "nothing."

Did he know me? Did I know him? He answered my unasked question, "I am Ansha. Your ship made an inquiry

147

about the records at the Karand's Palace. There wasn't
time."

He spoke without emotion, calm, articulate. "Do you
see that small cluster there? My family. We have not yet
given up hope. Those in the front are our grandchildren-
to-be; we talk to them every day about their future and
their responsibilities."

He had a purpose in this appeal, and he went right to it.

"The Karand's Palace has records, physical records: the
Niikiik Luur. They were maintained by the hereditary
staff. Myself. My family. I know that you want that
knowledge."

He did? Did I know that I wanted that knowledge?

"My grandchildren over there are embryos stored in
the vault. They can yet live. On another world, I know, but
they can live. When you recover the starcharts, you can
recover my grandchildren." He paused again. He pleaded,
"Please."

225-530
Aboard BMF *Koliliss* Above
Reft 3029 Sakaliin B857876-A Ga Pa Ph

Ravens pecked my eyes; they deafened me with their
screeching; the stink of their wet feathers offended me.
Their claws raked my shoulders and arms. Every fifth one
was snow white: I know, I counted them to be certain. I
waved my arms and they scattered so I could see, just a bit,
the officers standing on the bridge. I tried to speak, "Who
here is senior?" but their beaks had taken their toll on my
tongue. I tasted blood in the back of my throat; I strained
to hear the answer to my question, but no one spoke. I

strained against the pain and stood straighter, to do my duty despite, but it was too much and there was black.

* * *

Lieutenant Shugili took the wafer casually; he used skillsets all the time and he expected this to be much the same. He was cocky, pleased that the Admiral had chosen him. He didn't understand that his selection meant he was expendable.

They told him to stand over there, by the console. Jamison had seen this before; he whispered to his companion Grent, "It's amazing the transformation that comes over the Agent."

The Lieutenant closed his eyes and pressed the wafer into place. His arm slowly went back to his side, and he just stood there. Suddenly, he crouched and squirmed and flapped his arms scraping his biceps against his face and ears; his entire body twisted in strange ways. He said something no one could quite understand, "Ooo ear ivv veenyur?" and then gagged, choked, spit, braced in a rictus, and then just collapsed as if every bone in his body had dissolved.

Jamison whispered, "That's not supposed to happen," as several marines dashed forward.

The Executive Officer raised his voice, "Something's gone wrong. Take him to the clinic.

"Wait. Retrieve the wafer. Jamison, you're up."

225-530
Aboard BMF *Koliliss* Above
Reft 3029 Sakaliin B857876-A Ga Pa Ph

I awoke to a crew that acknowledged me senior. Before

me was a Commodore with her Lieutenant Commander as briefer. We orbited a world with a high population, a comfortable society, and, through no fault of their own, a rogue AI in its world-spanning network.

The crew had reacted to the threat immediately and appropriately: stopped lift-offs; prohibited landings; cut all communications. The Commodore and her staff had a plan: emp the network to cleanse it of the rogue. I reviewed the briefing and made a few suggestions: a series of timed emps to corner the AI and then ensure it was dead; some gravity drops of printed references to help the locals survive the loss of their networks. There was no point in waiting.

We acted without warning; one moment they were a functioning technology founded on electronics and computers; the next moment they weren't. They lost maybe one percent of population because control systems failed; they would lose another ten percent in the next year. On the other hand, their society would rally and return, newly based on analog controls and mechanical devices. Careful monitoring over the next five generations would make sure the AI wasn't lurking in some dormant circuit or forgotten memory. Eventually the world would return to the interstellar community. But for now, they were quarantined: red zoned, prohibited, forbidden.

I was pleased that we lost as few as we did. It felt strange that I could be pleased to kill only two hundred million people.

I spent the next two days meeting with squadron staff officers. The Personnel Officer needed direction on long-term staffing; these ships would be here for generations, rotating in and out in five-year watches. The Intelligence Officer needed to set up proper monitoring, both electronically and with over-the-ground drone patrols, and all the while making sure they were not contaminated by AI spores. The Operations Officer needed to plot out the details of who did what why when and how; the emp strike was over and the tedious details rose in importance. The Logistics Officer faced supply problems simply because they could not depend on the local system for anything. They took the first steps to establish a farming colony on a nearby world. Medical told me that my wafer had malfunctioned in the previous host: he had been nominally and hormonally male, but genetically female; they expected him to recover. The Civil Affairs Officer needed to plan how to present this crisis to neighboring systems: revealing enough of the danger to keep them away yet avoiding attracting looters and gawkers. Finally, the Information Officer needed to make sure systems were in place to protect against AI breakout and infiltration. I met with him last.

Commander Damurkhede was a manager rather than a tech; he could tell people what to do, but not how. On one particular line item, his assistant volunteered, "Stikky would know how to do that," and they assigned the task to him; we went on. I made mental note to seek Stikky out; we had dinner two nights later.

Stikky was nervous and I tried to put him at ease. Once I got him going, I could hardly stop his babbling. He loved his particular niche in technology, and he was good at it. Although people wanted results, they rarely stopped to listen to him, and they never wanted to hear why some approach was better than another.

On the other hand, although I wanted something, I was also genuinely interested. I had spent my last twenty months of consciousness addressing literally world-shattering crises, and something as mundane as starship information networks was a pleasant diversion. I enjoyed myself and I think Stikky did as well.

230-530
Aboard BMF *Koliliss* Above
Reft 3029 Sakaliin B857876-A Ga Pa Ph

We met again the next day. After some pleasantries, I asked for some help.

"Can you trigger wafer activation for a specific system?"

"Sure. You mean, if the ship enters the Vland system, you want to be activated so you can visit the archives?"

Not exactly, but close enough, I thought, while I said, "Exactly. You understand precisely what I need. But not just this ship, every ship."

"Sure, I can set up an astrofence. I know I can do this ship. It's just a simple instruction file. All I need is the override code." He leaned closer and whispered, "I have the override codes for this ship."

He reverted to a more normal tone. "When ships return to base, they sync with the base network and with each other. Ultimately, the files make it to Depot and propagate through the other fleets as well. Over time, maybe a couple years, everyone is synced with everyone else.

"It just takes override codes. The captain decides what

is safe, or appropriate, to sync with other ships. He periodically reviews stuff and approves it. The safety interlocks look for override codes to assure itself there isn't an unapproved phage, or worm, or—like here—a rogue AI."

"Let's get started then. I want an, astrofence? set up." He said it was no problem and that he would ping me when it was ready. An hour later, my comm pinged.

* * *

With him at his console and me at a tablet, we identified the systems to astrofence: basically, every crisis I had handled; I thought I remembered them all. Now, when a ship entered one of those systems, it would declare a potential crisis and activate my wafer.

"Sure," he said, "that takes care of this ship. But it won't sync without the override."

"I have that."

"Sure, then just key it in, in the red bar at the bottom."

"It will be a minute," I said, "I need to figure it out. What's today's date?"

Long ago, my training included the basic formula for quarantine overrides. Theoretically, they worked anywhere that used the master naval operating system, which would include not just the fleet, but the scout service, naval surface installations, probably a lot of imperial bureaucracies. We, that is our little class of five subjects, made them up and entered the code into the system ourselves. I suppose someone else might know them by now; or maybe they had been deleted at some point between then and now. They were intended to be valid until the turn of the millennium.

Our original code concept was today's three-digit day with leading zeros to the power of today's three-digit year (no need for leading zeros). Make it the other way around if today is even. Take the first ten digits. Then someone commented that an observer might intuitively understand the code if they saw us look up the date, so we added plus 1 to each digit, without carrying. It took me several minutes to confirm the calculation. "Now. I am ready."

Ding. "It confirmed it. This should work."

"By the way," he volunteered, "You know this was relatively easy because there is already an astrofence process subsystem in place."

"Oh?"

"For example, unless we are a Core sector ship, our guns won't work in Core sector. It's an anti-mutiny, no, anti-insurrection precaution."

"That must make the Emperor feel safer."

Stikky said he couldn't imagine the precaution ever being needed.

255-530
Aboard BMF *Koliliss* Above
Reft 3029 Sakaliin B857876-A Ga Pa Ph

"I want to thank you for your help."

"Sure, it's nothing; just my job and . . ."

I interrupted his polite demurral by putting my hand on his shoulder. "Look at me. I am not Jamison. This is his body, but I am not him."

I took his chin firmly in my hand and forced his eyes to look into mine.

"Listen. You have done for me, you have done for the

Emperor himself, a great favor and we appreciate it. But you must never speak of this; you cannot tell anyone.

"Say you understand." I released my grip. "Don't nod. Say yes, you understand."

"Sure, yes. I understand."

"Good."

I held out a beribboned medallion, the service medal that everyone called the XS, the Exemplary Service. Anyone who could put his cap on straight got one after a couple years. Stikky probably had three or four already. He reached to accept it.

I held up my other hand and bid him wait. From my tunic pocket, I withdrew a wafer, showed it to him briefly, inserted it into the suspension ribbon of the medal, and handed it over to him.

"There will come a time, someday, when you are certain that the Emperor himself appreciates your work. On that day when you arrive at your new job, you must use this wafer yourself. There may be danger; there may be reward. You may not understand what is happening. None of that matters. You must not fail me, us.

"Tell me again that you understand."

"Sure. Yes, Agent Jamison. I understand."

"Then you are dismissed."

ENNA PLANT LAGASH
REPORT 2

Video image of a Human woman with dark hair under a red-billed cap decorated with an astrogator's badge pinned on upside down. She conveys a casual confidence. Datestamp: 266-532. Report 2.

I am now an astrogator. Who would have thought?

Upon arrival at Othsekuu, Rens discharged the crew, paying them their accumulated wages and updating their naval records. He insisted that they remain reservists and told them they were valuable components in the Emperor's Navy. They listened with little attention, intent on returning to their homes and old neighborhoods, and anxious to be on their ways.

Argushii hung in orbit as Rens shuttled the Threep to the surface. I was alone literally for the first time in decades, and I busied myself straightening and ordering things. I prepared a meal and when Rens returned, he was pleased.

We discussed our future plans. I asked what we were going to do.

"It's hard for one person to operate a ship this big, but

we can make do with just the two of us for a short while. There's a naval base one system over, and we can probably draft replacements there. But there's no hurry; we can stay here for a couple weeks. There are things to see below: magnificent mountains, beautiful seascapes."

After a few days' work onboard, Rens flew me to the surface in our lander. The first week, we travelled by fast transport through mountains and deserts and forests, enjoying the diverse biomes that the universe creates. Rens talked about beauty and nature and how important they were.

The second week, we touched major cities and I selected dramas and concerts that caught my fancy. I had trouble understanding the complex plots and alien themes that the Threep preferred. Rens was bored and spent much of his time reading his book.

At the end of the week, abruptly, he said we had to return to the ship. I found I was ready; it would be like returning home. As the lander rose back to orbit, Rens showed me the controls and how they worked; how they translated hand and foot motion into flight maneuvers. He let me take them in hand, and I controlled our flight for a few minutes.

Once we had docked and tightened the grapples that held the lander tight to our hull, Rens told me what was going to happen next. "I was hoping for this. That's why we've been waiting. I sent some cordial messages to the Threep, reiterating to them that they would be welcome as crew. It usually happens with spacers: they want to go home, but they never really can."

***

A day later, a dozen tripods crowded the narrow passageway, all eager to enter, to re-enter, their ship. Their booming voices sounded over each other as they all conveyed their regret for their decision.

"It just wasn't the same. Everyone has changed."

"I thought our pod would all be together; about half have just moved on and no one knows where they went."

"Some of the pod still live together, but they all have different jobs. Boont is a vehicle operation instructor; Gaarnd manages a belt shop—with people from a different pod!"

"Niink sells financial instruments: he tried to sell me life insurance that would someday support my retirement, but once the company found out my occupation, the costs tripled. Niink was very disappointed."

"And there aren't any jobs! No one wants to hire an astrogation calculator."

"Or a jump drive technician!"

"There was a job serving cheap meals, but it would barely cover my own eating expenses. Where would I live?"

"Even for a good job, my pay would only be a fourth of what I earn here. How does anyone live?"

"Then I take it that you want to return as our crew?"

"Oh, could we? We admit we have made a mistake. It was nice to visit, but it is impossible to live here. Perhaps we can retire here someday."

"Yes."

"Yes. Yes."

Their booming voices competed to drown each other out.

"Could we?"

Rens hesitated for a moment, but just for a moment. "Certainly. You are the best crew I have ever had. Welcome back."

They crowded even closer.

* * *

Rens educated me about our crew. I had found that, once I became accustomed to their three legs down, three arms up, narrow belted waist physiques, I saw them as people (and in my mind, that equated with Humans) in some sort of costume. I saw (or imagined) Human minds behind those three-eyed faces, Human bodies inside those elastic costumes.

One evening, alone, Rens talked about who they were.

First, he said, their true species name is Threep. It is uncountable. One of them is Threep. Many of them together are Threep. Tripod is technically a pejorative, although its been used for so long that they usually don't take offense.

They have a six-gender structure: there are gender names, but they really don't matter. There's a long evolutionary tale behind it, and even now it's not totally clear. Imagine a circle with the six genders equally spaced around it. Each gender has two partners, and in mating season, they sit next to each other for hours, and eventually each of them becomes gravid with eggs that hatch after about six months. Then there are miniature ones running around. They all grow up together in a pod, which is their family structure.

That's the physical element. Sociologically, and

psychologically, their genders shape their lives. They, pair isn't the word, six up at adolescence to create a group, a sixtet. Someday, that six may produce offspring, but that isn't certain. They have allegiance to their pod, a group of several dozen sixtets, from which some day will come the next generation.

Within a sixtet, with one of each gender, each has a variety of roles. Imperial society has influenced them, and they believe in gender equality, but deep down there are leaders, enablers, workers, thinkers, nurturers, and others. I keep mapping their genders to Human male and female, and that just doesn't seem to work.

But think back to the book club. A good sophontologist with a specialty in Threep could have predicted how each of them would react to *The Scarlet Letter*. They know Human genders, but they map them to their own. So Boorn (a sort-of male) had a typically male reaction. Truul, a worker and essentially neuter, saw Roger's reaction as a neuter as well. Flaal is an enabler: she? it? is always trying to help out the others, explaining, teaching, even stepping in and doing. It's just her nature.

You don't have to internalize much of this. Outwardly, they all want to be treated equally.

The other important part of their nature is their sensory palps. They have eyes, ears (although not very acute), noses, and a general sense of touch. The palps are for their perception sense: they can sense life—the presence of living things—and some level of emotion and thoughts. It's not psionics; they can't read minds. But they are good at sensing what people think about them. You could call one of them a tripod and it wouldn't take

offense because you have a kind heart; some drunk in a
bar might use the same word as a pejorative and it would
probably start a fight.

Or they basically know if the next room is empty: they
can sense if there is someone over there, or not.

* * *

Soon after we left Othsekuu, I was moved to research
Rens' activity in the Navy. I was surprised with what I
found: it seems that he had understated the events,
perhaps to spare me, perhaps to avoid a discussion. The
datapak was revelatory and I brooded over it for much of
the day. We went to bed without Rens noticing, and he
fell fast asleep. Finally, in the middle of the night, I could
stand my inner turmoil no longer.

"Rens? Are you awake?"

He mumbled something I could not quite hear, and I
continued.

"Rens. We need to talk."

His answer told me he was awake, although he still lay
there with his back to mine.

"About what?"

"How could you kill all those people?"

"You have been reading the histories?"

"I looked them up today. Maaruur. Deyis. The others."

"Those are hard reading."

"They are."

He was silent for a while.

"Do you know how autodrivers work?"

"You mean for groundcars?"

"Or flyers. Yes."

"More or less. There's a computer hooked up into the

master grid, plus a set of sensors. It takes you where you want to go. What does this have ..."

"Bear with me.

"There's a classic challenge in the autodriver logic. What if there's a crowd ahead, suddenly, unpredictably? Your car will hit it and kill a dozen people. Or it can swerve aside and only kill one, or just you, the car occupant.

"From your point of view, do you want your car to decide to kill you rather than a crowd of a dozen?"

"Maybe. Yes. Maybe. It depends."

"The people who install that decisionware are the ones who decide who lives and who dies. Someone has to.

"Kanorb is a nice, peaceful world. It doesn't need a navy to protect it. The nearest current threat is a full sector away, probably the Vargr across the imperial border.

"Then again, Maaruur was almost as close. If Maaruur's parasite had gotten loose, two hundred years ago, you would never have been born. Kanorb would be a dead world, along with a thousand other worlds. Maybe not a dead world, but certainly not Human."

"But there must have been a better way. Research. Quarantine. Some cure."

"You are confusing reality with escapist Anglic literature. People want stories that give them answers. Magic answers. Solutions to life's problems. Stories are all about formulating answers to instruct us to live better lives.

"Maaruur was a tragedy. The protagonist was the empire itself; the tragic flaw was the nature of the universe. We can't know everything; we can't save every life; we can't make life fair."

I listened. My heart ached for those millions who died in terror. I said so to Rens, or to this person who was now Rens.

He answered. "For every one of those millions, my heart ached as does yours for a thousand times as many who would also die if I didn't act.

"There was more that I did, of course, but at its core all I did was make a decision, touch a tab, or say a word. Could you do that?"

"Never. It would be just too horrific."

"That's just the point, isn't it? That if you were in that situation, and could save a trillion lives, and more than that in children-to-be, you . . . not just you, but everyone around you . . . would hesitate. In the end, the greatest of tragedies would touch us all because of your fatal flaw. You could not bear the weight of the smaller deed in order to achieve the greater good.

"You asked how could I kill all those people?

"The truer question is how could I not?"

I had not yet fully processed all that he said, but I at least started to understand. I count that night as the beginning of a new time for us. This wasn't Rens; he just looked like him.

Exhausted from this conversation and as I drifted off to sleep, "Tell me your name?"

I called him Jonathan after that.

STIKKY MADE BARON

I was exhausted; why should I even awake? My eyes were closed, but I knew by subtle cues that I was probably in the stadium. I opened them.

This section of seating contained but few people, a cross-section of the intelligent species of the empire, all of them intent on a performance. A traditional drama.

I had known Trallian Nerst. For most of his life, his creative output was associated with video drama, usually under contract for other producers. In mid-life however, his habit of buying a daily lottery chance uncharacteristically paid off with wealth beyond his greatest imagining. He had the funds to do anything he wanted; he chose to produce his true masterwork; his own concept of what drama should do.

He spent the next ten years of his life, supported by every possible assistance, creating The Eighteen, his series of dramas investigating the nine cardinal emotions and their antonyms, building a series of seemingly unrelated characters and situations into a dramatic double climax of Love and Hate.

Four hundred million credits buys almost anything; in this case it even bought quality and acclaim.

Nerst was a proponent of situational drama: classic stories with strong characters interpreted anew in each production by current actors and directors. Roles are recast by era, by culture, and even by sophont. Each script produces archetypal characters involved in universal situations; Nerst's intent was adaptability to any era, any life pursuit, and any motivation.

His classic Minus Seven explores Disappointment as experienced by an ambitious central character interacting with a series of counterpoint situations. I have seen it staged against:

The Vilani Transitional Era, as Shugina struggles against the last functional Ancient battle machines.

The Sylean Grand War epoch, as Adjunct Admiral Tran and his fleet of ironclad oceanships search the seas for the rogue squadron of the traitor Sanaxam.

The Artisan milieu of Lianma, as disgraced Professor Raleo uses vast computing systems to pursue the ultimate particles of matter.

In each, and in many others, the central story remains, interpreted by new actors against new backgrounds to reach new audiences in new ways.

Now before me was Nerst himself (I recognized him), raptly watching a production of Disappointment, commenting on stage business, on the delivery of lines, on inspired pieces of staging.

As the drama drew to a close, I saw him mouth to himself the climactic dying words, "In this life, anticipation is never equaled by the reality. Perhaps in the next."

And then it was over.

238-534
Aboard BB *Kokaasii* Above
Dagu 1640 Lenashuuk A7A8A76-C Fl Hi In

Stikky was not an excellent spacer. He had been up and down the rank ladder several times: promoted because time had passed; demoted because he overslept or failed an inspection. He was, however, an excellent computer tech. He intuitively understood the workings of the Navy's information systems better than any of the officers, indeed, better than anyone on the ship. It was Stikky to whom the other ratings turned when connections failed, or new installations balked, or old devices slowed. More than once, another rating got the credit and a promotion based on something Stikky did.

Yet in all of this, Stikky was content. He enjoyed what he did; he had a continuing parade of devices to puzzle through, install, and confirm as operational. As section officers cycled in, each tried to rehabilitate Stikky as a spacer, soon found that the network suffered, and so learned to leave Stikky alone.

Stikky was the butt of good-natured derision, which he ignored, or didn't notice. It was always good-natured because the network suffered if it wasn't. Today's ribbing was somehow different.

"Stikky! The Captain wants to see you!"

"You're in trouble now! Did you let his link crash?"

Stikky was immune to their comments and ignored

them, until the Lieutenant touched his shoulder firmly, and said, "Stand up. Let's see you. Your tunic has a spot; let's get it changed. The Captain wants you on the bridge."

It took longer than he expected, and the Lieutenant was starting to get nervous.

* * *

Normally, Commander Liment would wait patiently until a break in the routine on the bridge before speaking. Course-keeping for a 200,000-ton behemoth like the *Kokaasii* required the full attention of the pilot consoles, and the Captain disliked interruption. In this case, Liment interrupted anyway.

"Sir!" He stepped forward.

The Captain, irritated, met his eyes, "Speak."

"We have an express from Fleet Command."

This was different. Not a flash; not a coded transmission. An express: a package. A physical package. The Captain turned to his Executive: "You have the bridge," and walked to the exit.

"A piece of paper?"

"Aye, sir. From the Emperor." He added redundantly, "Himself."

The package lay on the table in the wardroom, carefully centered in front of the Captain's place, positioned on a neatly folded cloth. The lid was removed, nestled beneath it. Centered in the container, held immobile by tabs, was a single sheet emblazoned with the many-rayed imperial sunburst, inscribed with the Emperor's will and whim, in Anglic and Vilani, that Ragla Niffield be henceforth and forever, Baron of the Empire. Paper touched by the Emperor himself, his initial inscribed at the bottom.

"So, who is Ragla Niffield?"

"That would be Stikky, sir. Petty Officer Ragla Niffield."

His incredulity showed. "Stikky? Why would the Emperor make Stikky a Baron?"

There was no clear answer.

"He's made him a Baron. He's only a rating. We can't make a Petty Officer a Baron."

"So, commission him. Do whatever it takes. Then Admiral Steen, the Marquis can knight him.

"Then, and only then, we hold the investiture."

* * *

Stikky had never been on the bridge. Even network fixes were performed through access panels. For that matter, he had never actually spoken to the Captain, let alone the Admiral. He was like a beast in a maze, unsure of what to do, afraid of what lay beyond the blind corners ahead. He nervously felt for his tablet but resisted the impulse to look at it.

The Captain returned Stikky's awkward salute, then stepped forward and pointed out a spot for him to stand. At a nod from the Captain, a rating began to recite from a screen.

"The Captain is pleased to announce that by virtue of his inherent powers he hereby presents this commission in the rank of Lieutenant in the Imperial Navy, and with it the responsibilities and authorities of an officer who serves the Empire."

The Captain waited, and finally someone behind him signaled Stikky to salute, which he did. The Captain returned the salute, stepped forward, and touched his collar to attach the insignia of Lieutenant. They shook hands as well. Commander Liment grabbed Stikky's elbow and herded him off the bridge.

"Let's get a proper officer's uniform. Make sure the badges are correct. And service stripes. You have an XS? How many? Lieutenant, yes, you, you're a lieutenant now, is your service record correct? Good. I'll be back in an hour for the next ceremony."

That left Stikky standing in an anteroom surrounded by three clerks and a Chief Petty Officer, all fussing with things that he never concerned himself with. "What just happened?"

"You were just commissioned as an officer in the Emperor's Navy and jumped two more ranks in the blink of an eye. It normally takes ten years to make Lieutenant; you made it in about ten seconds."

"Sure. I noticed that. But why?"

"That, sir, is a different question. The bridge has been buzzing about you ever since the fleet courier arrived. There's a rumor that you are the long lost karand, suddenly identified by genetic analysis. Could you be the Emperor's brother's long-lost orphaned son?"

Stikky shook his head.

"Are you sure? Would you know?"

Stikky shook his head again no.

* * *

In the next hour, the Admiral arrived from the station. He was escorted immediately to the Captain's office suite, ushered past the various clerks and ratings and into the private quarters.

"Welcome, Your Grace. I apologize for the urgency of

our message. I thought, under the circumstances, that we should meet immediately and . . ."

"Certainly, Hulm. Tell me what's going on."

With the Admiral on board, the Captain was no longer lord of all. The sooner the Admiral left, the better. The Captain told his story in as few words as possible.

They had received, out of nowhere, a Barony for Petty Officer Ragla Niffield. They couldn't just hand it over. They had immediately promoted him to a suitable officer rank: Lieutenant. Now he needed to be knighted. That required the Admiral, as Marquis the proper proxy hand-of-the-archduke. Once that was done privately, they could have a proper investiture on the hangar deck.

Could the Admiral please oblige?

The final step was more elaborate. Officers assembled on the hangar deck. Cutlass-armed marines marched forward carrying the sunburst banner of the Imperium to the strains of the *Melody Navale* followed by the Emperor's Anthem.

By that evening, it was finished. The officers gathered in the wardroom for a ceremonial dinner with Sir Ragla, Baron Sima as guest of honor. The next morning, Stikky cleared out his cubicle and took the shuttle to the orbiting starport with his discharge in his pocket and still only a vague idea of where Sima was.

The auxiliary data network on the *Kokaasii* went down ten hours later.

TO SIMA

Sima is an ancient world, settled in the First Millennium of Star Flight by the Vilani pioneers as they reached out along the contorted single jump links of the Vilani Main. Sima, twenty-six jumps out, was an attractive world with a pleasant environment and biomes quickly overwhelmed by imported Vilani crops and livestock. The fact that there were no indigenes simplified the process, and the colonists soon settled into a comfortable existence. Later development of faster jump drives turned Sima into a backwater, self-sufficient and bypassed by mainstream society.

When the First Imperium fell, Sima was assigned a governor by Terra: a naval lieutenant who soon settled into this world's agricultural routine. The Long Night had little effect: far fewer visitors and no exports, but Sima's self-sufficiency meant that no one starved, and no one really suffered.

Some three hundred years ago, the Third Imperium recontacted the world with an invitation to join their interstellar community. With the invitation came vague promises of new markets that never really materialized, but no matter, life continued as before.

***

Twenty years previous, the last of the Terran line of governors, called Barons by the new rulers, died. Now, somehow, the bureaucracy at far off Capital had finally decided that Sima needed a representative of the Emperor.

Sima's government was a tangle of feudal allegiances: a glorified serf system in which citizens owed a natural loyalty and responsibility to the estate of their birth. The estate provided basic subsistence, education, and even the skills of a trade. Vast farms trained their citizens in agriculture; vast ranches trained their citizens in animal husbandry. Everywhere, the talented were given training in whatever skills the community required: administration, equipment repair, peace enforcement, service industries.

At the top of each estate stands a local noble: The Lord, the Holder, the Keeper, the Master, the Squire, the Director, the Manager, the Chief.

238-534
Lenashuuk Highport Above
Dagu 1640 Lenashuuk A7A8A76-C Fl Hi In

Stikky found that there were two Simas. One was only a few jumps away, but the numbers didn't correspond. The other Sima, according to Stikky's trip planner, was in Lishun sector, seventy-five parsecs, almost a year, away. He had a StarPass that put him on routed jumpliners when they had space available. The data bank told him little else; but then again, any news of the place would be at least a year old anyway.

Stikky disliked attention. He travelled across a whole

sector, a year on longliners flying the main routes and then tramps to the backwaters. His government-issue travel vouchers were good for middle passage. If he had revealed his noble title, the steward would surely have upgraded him to high passage—luxury class with fine cuisine and lots of attention. He was content to stay in his stateroom, eat meals and snacks from the machines, watch stories on his tablet, fiddle with technological trinkets he bought along the way, and remain anonymous.

193-535
Lish 0315 Sima D758757-6 Ag

Stikky processed in his head the codes defining the world:

A medium-size planet with a thin atmosphere (the odd third digit said no breathing filters were necessary) and vast oceans that created climates hospitable to Human-preferred crops. Perhaps thirty-million citizens lived under a feudal government structure—not quite serfs: not quite free—with a more-or-less average enforcement presence. Local technology was idyllic: people usually spoke to each other without computer assistance. That would take some getting used to.

Now, the moment of truth had arrived. The hybrid cargo and passenger ship had carried him the last parsec to Sima and unloaded him at the customs desk. He knew enough to tip the ship's steward for his courtesy and attention. It was probably low, but Stikky was concerned about his current balance; he was not yet clear on how this all worked.

He cleared customs without incident, found a reasonable hotel room, and settled in.

* * *

Stikky was a product of his particular social class: his rudimentary education focused on being a good citizen, media emphasized patriotism and social co-operation, entertainments provided fairy-tale adventures with little relationship to reality. Consequently, he had an unrealistic understanding of the nobility. He believed in the platitudes of honor and responsibility that were so often spoken but not respected, and he subconsciously expected that most of his duties would be dramatic affirmations of those high principles. He hadn't a clue what to do.

Stikky had put off even thinking about this next step, but he knew that he owed his benefactor a debt that he had to repay. He wrote a short note, fished out the wafer from his kit, and held it next to the jack at the base of his skull.

194-535
Lish 0315 Sima D758757-6 Ag

I awoke seated, my eyes closed, to relative silence and slight disorientation. After a moment, I spoke, "Who here is senior?" and heard only silence. I opened my eyes to a hotel room, before me a desk and a sheet of handwritten text.

Agent Jamison,

Almost a year ago, I was plucked from my comfortable console cubicle and in the course of a day, promoted to Lieutenant, knighted, raised to Baron, mustered out of the Navy, and sent on my way to where I am now: Sima, in Lishun sector.

This my first day here, and I have no idea what to do.

But I remember your words as if they were spoken yesterday. I have arrived at my new job, and I have used the wafer you gave me.

My life is in your hands; please guard it as if it were your own.

Respectfully,

Stikky
Ragla Niffield

I now had perhaps four weeks before I evaporated. It was time to get started.

To the clerk at the hotel desk. "How do I get to the starport?"

"You are here sir. The terminal is down the covered mall, with ticketing to the left and arrivals to the right."

"Information systems?"

"We have guidebooks for sale at the gift shop. The harvest festival begins tomorrow. There is a datanet in the terminal."

I thanked him and started out. Datanet seemed the best way to gather information until the Travellers' Aid Society kiosk caught my eye.

"Excuse me, can I ask a few questions?"

"Certainly. We are here to help."

We had a wide-ranging discussion. I then returned to my room, gathered up my single piece of luggage, and set out. I called a common transport and asked for the Imperial Bank. When we arrived, I paid my fare, adding a generous Cr100 tip, and instructed him to deliver my valise to the Manor House.

* * *

Visiting the bank first seemed to make sense. There was only one. I opened two accounts, one in the name of Niffield and one in the name of Bland.

The bank officer fussed over me, delighted to be in the presence of someone so favored by the Emperor. My papers carried information codes and encryption markers. They could be counterfeited, but the penalties were severe enough to deter most.

"Your Grace, we are so pleased that you have arrived. The Barony has been vacant for more than a decade, and we all feel the lack. Sir Jordan has shouldered the burden admirably, but there are decisions that are beyond his charter.

"As you must know, the Barony carries with it certain stipends and allowances. First, there is the Manor itself, certainly suitable for your daily living. It has an attached ceremonial court for receptions and audiences.

"Second, the Baronial fiefs have been well-managed since their reversion to the throne. You may, of course, assert your selection of the previous fiefs, or you may select from the unallocated lands.

"Third, there are several traditional directorships in local corporations: the energy utility, the communications network, the land registry. They have a standing invitation for you to join their oversight and policy structures, with the associated stipends, of course.

"Fourth, the Barony, now manifest in your person, stands at the head of our system of governance, primarily as the ultimate court of appeal. There is a backlog of decisions that lie on your desk waiting to be made. You may delegate the office, but the last Baron conducted the audiences himself; the court has lain fallow since his death.

"Fifth, the Marquis has extended his compliments for your health and welfare and offers his personal concern that you be comfortable and well-advised in your new position. He especially asks that you visit him on Pryden at your earliest convenience.

"Sixth, you have graced our establishment with accounts; we sincerely hope that you will find our services more than satisfactory."

* * *

The Manor House is the traditional residence of the Baron, as before him the Second Empire Lieutenant, and as before that the First Empire Iduma. Refurbished and rehabilitated countless times, it retained the classic façade of early First Empire corbels, although doubtless the interior was more-or-less modern.

The center of the city was a three-kilometer-long pedestrian plaza, traditionally filled with farmer's stalls on market days, vast and empty otherwise. Today, the first signs of the coming harvest festival were being erected: long tables, cooking facilities, and a few entertainment stages. The Manor House occupied the south edge, a walled compound with a central structure of windows and balconies.

I walked directly to the main doors and entered

without knocking. Rule 1 applies in all aspects of life. Inside was a reception hall lined with columns supporting a tall ceiling. In the distance was a man dealing with papers at a desk. I walked directly to him. He spoke as I approached. "We are not open to the public."

"Who is in charge today? Is that you?" Rule 1.

"No, I am Ingles, the house steward. The estate manager is away for the morning. Come back this afternoon." Skip Rule 2 for the moment.

"You will do. My bag was delivered earlier today; have it carried to the master apartment. Then call the estate manager and tell him to return immediately. Notify the staff to assemble for a meeting precisely at 11." Rule 3.

"You make impossible demands. We are not a hotel."

"No, you are not. You are a residence for the master. I am the master. I expect competent and immediate service. Go." A second person appeared. "You. Conduct me to the master apartment." Rule 4.

Rule 5 would follow at the meeting. I didn't expect to invoke Rule 2, but one can never tell.

The master apartment was a suite of six rooms, including two bedrooms, a large living area with a balcony on the plaza, a dining area, an unused kitchen, and an office, apparently in use by the manager.

Within an hour, the estate manager entered, accompanied by two footmen, without knocking. He began with firmness. "Who are you to walk into this manor?"

I stood and faced them with equal firmness. I imagined Stikky, if he had gotten here, stammering an explanation and pleading for an examination of his legitimacy papers.

That would never do. "You violate basic etiquette. Begin again. My residence is never entered without knocking. I am addressed as Sir in ordinary conversation, although Your Grace is equally acceptable. Exit and begin again."

He started to waver. "May I ask, sir, your name?"

To which I pressed the point. "Exit, knock, and begin again."

The two footmen observed with careful neutrality. They depended on the manager for their positions but were not about to show any initiative. Should they defer? Should they subdue me? The rational choice was no action; they were rational.

The manager was momentarily paralyzed with a tension between anger and fear. Fear won. He signaled the footmen to retreat and followed them out. There came a knock at the door, and I answered "Enter."

"Welcome to the manor, sir. I am Arand, the estate manager. How may I serve you?"

"Thank you Arand. This transition is tedious, and I shall say this but once.

"I am Baron Sir Ragla Niffield, late of the Imperial Navy and sent to this world as the representative of the Emperor himself. You may convey this information to the staff. I prefer, for the moment, caffeinated tea as my customary beverage. I rise at 7 and begin work at 8. Please arrange for all locks to be changed and for two master keys, one for you and one for me.

"I shall speak to the assembled staff at 11. Ensure that all are present.

"I shall review the house accounts the day after tomorrow. If there are shortages, we shall arrange suitable repayments without repercussions, provided I am properly notified.

"After the accounting and inspections, if I am satisfied, I shall retain you; if not, you may expect duties in the laundry.

"You may go."

* * *

Under the local feudal system, the entire staff, from cleaners to manager, was bound by oaths of fealty to the master of the house, or in his absence, to the house itself. At 11, I reviewed the assembled staff of about 20, and made them wait for the mid-day meal until after I had personally interviewed each and insisted on an affirmation of each fealty oath.

Some had never known a personal master, having come into service after the previous Baron's passing. I made notes about a better reallocation of resources: more people to the kitchen; stronger men in security; some with deficient attitudes to the laundry or the garden.

I spoke with Arand last. He recited the oath, *"Nin makh, mimaar mukashgula;* Lord, I pledge my loyal labor."

To which I replied the ritual, *"Sagin, mimaar arshir dagash;* Servant, I pledge my protection."

Not only were such oaths binding, they provided each individual a place in society. We exchanged oaths as much for them as for me.

Finally, I could begin in earnest. I had limited time.

218-535
Lish 0315 Sima D758757-6 Ag

I was annotating the day's diary, trying to fully record

the decisions and assignments I had made during the day when Ingles knocked, and entered.

"Sir, the Marquis' yacht is in orbit. He sends his compliments and requests that you join him for dinner. He is sending a boat." Traffic control had sent me a courtesy alert when his ship arrived insystem, some ten hours ago. His own message had followed a few hours later. Now came the formal invitation.

This was the Marquis Pryden, lord of a nearby world with a hundred times our population but a very similar serf system. My years of bureaucratic experience gave me an insight. He, the superior in status and rank, had travelled a week in jump to visit me. Given travel times, he couldn't have known about my abrupt arrival on Sima more than two weeks ago. He had packed up and come here with—at most—seven days' notice. He had the superior status, but I was important enough for him to cancel schedules and come visit me. I thought that I knew what drove him.

The boat arrived less than an hour later, setting down (in violation of basic traffic control regulations) in the plaza outside the manor. Then again, there were exceptions built into the regulations where the nobility was concerned. I stepped out a minute later, followed by Ingles carrying an insulated food basket.

I was met at the access stair by a grey-and-red liveried footman who braced in greeting and courteously escorted me aboard. Ingles handed over the basket, which was secured in a compartment without question; I was seated and strapped in, and we departed, straight up.

The ascent took a dozen minutes, and we were soon

joined with the Marquis' yacht, a large, angular ship with bulging eye-like observation domes forward, and powerful thruster tubes aft. I straightened my tunic, ran my hand through my hair, and stepped out onto the reception deck. The Marquis himself stood waiting to greet me.

He extended his hand and spoke my name, "Sir Ragla! I am so pleased to meet the latest addition to our small circle. Welcome to Lishun."

He had good intelligence; he knew who I was, that I was a newcomer to the sector. We would see, over the evening, what else he knew.

I turned to the footman and asked that he deliver the food basket to the cook. I then returned my full attention to my host.

We strode the length of the reception deck, perhaps twenty meters, to one of the bulging eye observation domes. Below us, filling half of our view, lay Sima in all its sunlit glow, an expanse of blue-green sea broken only by my continent, a slender green snake spiraling its way twice around the globe. We made small talk: he complimented my fief; I inquired as to his health. We spoke about the economy, trade, politics, trends in society. We sparred with each other, gently feeling out what the other believed, revealing some but not too much.

He was a conservative. He identified with the Sparkles, traditionalists concerned with frustrating the agents of change; I knew firsthand that was impossible, but I kept my silence on that particular issue.

He cared deeply about his own fiefs scattered about the sector, and about its many populations, whether they answered directly to him or not. I conveyed a parallel conservatism with perhaps a tinge of concern for indigene rights.

A footman approached, waiting a decent distance away. When the Marquis looked at him, he announced that dinner was served.

We moved to a formal table set in the center of the deck. It would be just the two of us, seated across from each other, dining on delicacies from several worlds: some sort of soup served cold, some sort of deepfish from his own Pryden, even a purple leafy concoction served with a tangy glaze.

At one point, I had a terrible vision: of Stikky handling this situation himself, probably not knowing which eating utensil to use; what topic of conversation to pursue; what words not to say. I made a mental note for the next day's diary entry: more specific instruction in etiquette and interactions.

But no matter. At the moment, I actually enjoyed the conversation.

As the main course ended, "Your Grace, I took the liberty of bringing along some sugar fungi pie to complete the meal. I do hope you do not mind."

He did not. His chef probably did but knew enough not to object to the ways of the nobility. I asked the server to bring the dessert. We all agreed that it was delicious.

The object of our meeting had been hanging over us all evening. This was important to the Marquis; important enough that he did not want to alienate me. I broached the subject myself.

"Your Grace, there is a matter which I feel we must discuss, and I am so grateful that you and I have this opportunity to meet." He set down his food implement and gave me his full attention.

"I am humbled by the responsibilities that the Emperor has given me. I have a lot to learn, and a lot to do, and I expect to throw myself into it wholeheartedly. One of those responsibilities is to express my own opinions in the Moot. Alas, as we well know, Capital is half a year away and I cannot justify being absent from my fiefs for so long a time. Someday I hope that I can make the journey and cast my vote on some important issue. But for now, it is simply impossible.

"I know that you are more involved in the affairs of government; that you have structures in place that can tolerate your absence.

"My question is this: would you consent, for the time being, to accept my proxy and cast my vote as you see fit, when you are present at the Moot?"

"I would be flattered with such a responsibility." He was more than flattered. This was exactly what he wanted. For reasons I did not clearly understand, my single vote was important to him. Was it because he did not want it in anyone else's hands? Did his status with the Count, or the Duke (which one, I did not yet know) depend on being able to deliver every proxy that became available? Was there some obscure issue that could be tipped by my single vote?

"Then I thank you sincerely. An uncast vote would be to me a burden, and you have lifted it from my heart."

Now came the hard part: the negotiation of terms. I proposed, "As to terms, I would think the standard clauses should apply,

"I cannot bind my heirs, nor can you yours, so our agreement will end with my death, or your death, or with the death of the sovereign."

"Certainly." He was pleased. Standard terms make for better understandings. "And the standard clause that, should you visit the Moot, the proxy is suspended by your actual presence."

"Oh, wonderful," I contributed enthusiastically. He smiled cynically at my sophomorish delight.

I continued, "You may, of course, further assign my proxy to others as needed. I trust your judgment in the matter. And finally, I believe that there is typically an annual stipend attached."

To this he sat impassive. The fact that he had come to me revealed the value he placed on my proxy. In ordinary transactions, it was worth perhaps a hundred thousand credits per year. He had spent that much just coming to visit me.

My proxy was a small but integral part of the political favor-exchanging that was the central focus of the Moot. In his hands, it had value as political capital and ultimately as real capital. If my proxy went elsewhere, it counted against him and his ambitions.

I let the silence linger just long enough that he understood that I understood its value, notwithstanding my supposedly unsophisticated ways. Then, I spoke.

"I think that we should waive the stipend."

I could see that he had been holding his breath, and now released it. "I thank you for your confidence. I will have the agreement codified for our mutual assent."

The tension was broken. He had what he wanted, and

it made him happy. But I also had what I wanted. As much as was possible, I had recruited the Marquis as my, or Ragla's, political friend. It would take great provocation for the Marquis to work against Ragla's interests, although I knew that political winds could blow in any direction.

I had three days left before oblivion.

222-535
Lish 0315 Sima D758757-6 Ag

Sir Ragla, Baron Sima, awoke disoriented. Various muscles ached from unaccustomed use. He stepped out of bed and moved to the fresher. Stuck to the mirror was a sheet of paper filled with text.

Its message was simple: now is 30 days later. You will find that a variety of arrangements and agreements had been made, all to your benefit. The papers are carefully arrayed in the dining room.

The wafer now resided safely in the vault. To use it again would be dangerous. Guard it, and if you find that its use by you has been to your benefit, arrange for it to be used with each of your sons when they reach maturity.

Over the next several days, Sir Ragla found that he had:

- Occupied the Manor House of Baron Sima and established suitable arrangements for basic necessities of living. The estate manager was Arand, and the chief steward was Ingles. Both understood their roles and could be trusted.
- Accepted the position of Baron Sima and suitably greeted and entertained the local dignitaries and authorities.

- Instituted a magistrate system that vetted disputes requiring his attention. Carefully documented appeals would be presented to him with well-reasoned arguments from both sides and an array of options with disclosed consequences. Accepted some of the existing Baronial fiefs, and rejected others, with a resulting annual income that paid recurring expenses and provided a surplus consistent with a comfortable lifestyle.
- Ordered a high-end household computer system comparable to the Naval consoles he was used to.
- Arranged for a virtual tutorial on etiquette and protocol to help understand this particular position better.
- Scheduled a visit by the Marquis' daughter, Aia, for Holiday—at yearend, some three months hence.

There was a knock on the door, followed by a servant bringing tea.

ENNA PLANT LAGASH
REPORT 3

Video image of an older Human female with dark hair flecked with grey and cut in the short style preferred by spacer women. There is a touch of wrinkle at the eyes, which unwaveringly engage the camera lens. She speaks with firmness and a meticulous standard Anglic pronunciation. Datestamp: 119-539. Report 3.

I became a student.

When Rens made me astrogator, I thought that meant that I would be entering data on one console and reading the results on another. Indeed, that is what I did, under Truul's instruction, for the first year. I initially failed to understand that my craft would ask more of me.

We jumped every two weeks. After a year, I was competent to undertake the process by myself. Jonathan and Boorn would confer over a star chart and select our next destination. Thereafter, I handled the details. I would choose where in the system we would arrive, whether we would visit the mainworld, or refuel at the gas giant, or perhaps at an iceworld in the oort. I evaluated contingencies. I input the data and reviewed the output. I separately confirmed the calculations on another console. A complete manual confirmation would have been impossible, but I at least made sure I had not transposed digits or misread important facts.

I enjoyed the process. I tracked performance data and tried to improve with each new effort. Our time-in-jump steadily improved to narrowly bracket the optimum 168 hours. Our break-outs became nearer and nearer their intended locations. When we experienced an anomaly, I tracked down the reason and in future I accounted for it.

After three years, I was participating in the course selection process.

After four years as an astrogator, and after my hundredth jump calculation, Boorn and Jonathan sat down with me to discuss my work. In this situation, my role was subordinate employee being evaluated by superiors and I was nervous. Was there something I was consistently doing wrong, or improperly, or ineptly? I wanted to be well thought of; I dreaded the idea that I might not be.

Boorn began in his ever-booming voice, "Enna, you have reached an important evaluation point in your progress as an astrogator. You have learned well, as well as we can expect."

What did that qualification mean? I thought.

"But astrogation is more than calculations and computations. It is more, even, than thoughtful planning of routes and courselines. There is a magic quality . . ."

Jonathan interjected a correction, "Mystical."

"Ah, yes. I always get those two words confused. Mystical quality to truly excellent astrogation; a disciplined understanding of jumpspace itself. I am pleased that Jonathan chose you to learn this science. You have done well, very well. It is time for you to take the next step in your training."

Jonathan took over the narrative. "Jumpspace is inherently strange, as you already know from your calculations and formulae. It is out there beyond our hull churning and clawing at the jump field. It is alien physics that none of us truly understand. We keep the shutters closed and the viewports opaque because they say looking at it can drive men mad."

"Actually, madness is relative. For a few, seeing jumpspace makes them catatonic. For others, it gives them headaches, or eyestrain, or fascination trance. Some can't see it; they see only grey. Some see it and never travel again.

"Every good astrogator has to at least confront jumpspace once in his or her life. Maybe that is enough. Or maybe it carries you to a higher level of understanding."

This scared me. I enjoyed astrogation, but I was uncertain that I wanted to sacrifice my sanity for it. What if it made me crazy? Would Jonathan care for me the way I had for Rens? Was I ready for my life to end? Would it end?

"Are you ready?"

I was frozen. I was not ready. I wanted to think about it. To research my options. I heard my voice say, "Yes." And wondered how that happened.

***

I was in a daze as Jonathan led me by the hand to a small turret with its observation bubble opaqued. Where had Jonathan learned all this? How did he know this mystical secret?

"Here's the display panel with a feed from outside the hull." He touched tabs and made adjustments. "This is what the lenses see in the visible spectrum."

It was a mottled grey. I felt fine. This would be all right. I would survive.

"And this is in false color across a variety of wavelengths."

It was the same.

"It is important that you see this first. The lenses are dumb, unconscious, unthinking."

He called up a short animation. "Do you remember the two-slit demonstration, about interference patterns and particles?"

I had a vague memory of the strangeness of quantum effects; I tried to express it. "Shine photons through two slits and they interfere with each other on the other side. Cover one slit, and they don't. Shine them just one at a time, and they still interfere. Look to see which slit the photon went through, and they don't. Something about the photon knows it is being observed."

"That's fairly good for a literature teacher."

"Nerst uses it as a metaphor for knowledge."

"Ah. Then you have learned well.

"Seeing jumpspace is a quantum effect. What imagers and lenses see is one thing; what consciousnesses see is another. Photographs, images, sensors, lenses, displays all produce a near-uniform grey image. Consciousness sees something else. More than that. When several consciousnesses see the same view, they all see the same average. When only one consciousness sees it, it is unique."

"I don't understand."

"No one does. You don't understand before you see it. After, you might understand a little."

"Don't worry. The driving-men-mad thing is mostly for those caught totally unawares. Are you ready?"

"As ready as I will ever be." The anticipation was overwhelming. Jonathan de-opaqued the dome.

I saw roiling currents of thick grey smoke lined with thin streaks of yellow and blue. Every few seconds, it was overlaid with an intense pointillism of stark white in random currents.

Jonathan continued, "See, you're still sane. We're almost there."

"This isn't it?"

"Not quite. This is an average of what you and I are seeing. If there were ten of us, it would be a muddy grey average of ten different consciousnesses. See the brief flashes? I can make them longer."

"How?"

"When I close my eyes, then only your consciousness sees it."

The murky grey was replaced by a cascade of intense points of light in colors across the spectrum, infinitely small, yet terribly bright. "What are those?"

"We don't know. Individual packets of photons escaping from jumpspace through our protective fields? Notice the murky grey is still there behind all the sparks."

We sat there for hours as I tried to make sense of what I was seeing. Were those sparks stars, or worlds, or ships? Jonathan said not, but I still wondered. I made him squeeze his eyes shut, or blink rapidly, or stare intently. I tried to see shapes in the murk, and did, if only in my imagination. At long last I grew tired and Jonathan roused me to return to our quarters. I barely noticed that Boorn had been waiting outside the turret for the whole time; he was relieved that I was still well.

That night my dreams were filled with strange sparks that called my name.

***

After five years, I made the course choices alone and presented them for a perfunctory approval.

***

In the middle of year eight, Boorn and Jonathan brought me a challenge.

"These are the logs of *Talon*." Jonathan pointed at an interactive screen with multiple pages of text, starcharts, position tracks, and synopses. "We've been paralleling their course to Beauniture, but since they were jump-5 and we are only jump-3, we don't usually hit the same worlds. We are now approaching the feature they called the Gulf. It's trivial as astrography goes, but it is nevertheless a problem for us."

Boorn took over, touching panels with those three-fingered hands. "The Gulf is generally ten parsecs across. It extends the full width of this sector and, from the looks of it, the neighboring sectors as well. The narrowest point is here," he pointed, "at about five parsecs. *Talon* barely noticed it."

I was engaged already. "But we are jump-3. It's impassible."

"Indeed," said Jonathan.

Boorn continued. "There's a textbook answer for explorers. Jump out one. Leave what fuel you have, except for just enough to get back. Do it again and again and again. Do the same another parsec out, until finally you have a cache of fuel there.

"Finally, go to that cache, fuel up completely, and go the last three parsecs."

"So, Enna, set that up."

It was like a homework assignment, or maybe a final exam. I enjoyed it.

On the one hand, this was a tedious exercise. On the other, it was a challenge. Shuttling back and forth was unsatisfying; I wanted to be moving toward our destination. It took us seventeen weeks, and we were ready to make the big jump to the far side of the Gulf.

* * *

The computer had identified our base system with a string of random numbers and issued it a nonsense name: Remio. I named the blank parsecs ahead of us One, Two, Three, and Four. The computer had arbitrarily named the far side of the Gulf: Whece. Who knows what clever logic was instilled in it years before?

We broke out in Two a little farther out than I wanted, and so Trune piloted us to our cache: a cluster of several glistening sacs.

Boorn shouted even louder than normal, "There's something out there!"

The other Threep were booming at each other. Their strange perception palps fluttering more than usual; the little fingers kept bending in different directions, twisting sideways, up, down. Flool and Dreem made their way to the transpex, but others simply stepped closer to the opaque hull.

Jonathan called for quiet, "Froon, Bork, to your turrets. Boorn, describe what you see."

"A big cluster, almost solid, long, slow behind the sacs. Several more over here," one arm pointed toward our bow, "in a cluster."

"Trune?"

"They scattered when we broke out, I conjecture in response to our energy shed. The timing was right. They are lurking just at the limit of my senses."

"Flink?"

"Their ships are almost invisible to the sensors. That makes them light elements, non-metals, plastics perhaps?"

"Anyone else?"

Mool spoke, "How can they move? There's no metal, no magnetics, no gravitics, no reaction mass."

Jonathan asked more questions, gathered more data, assembled it on a temporary screen with attached notes. After some minutes, he gave orders to get the fuel into our tanks. We jumped for Whece within an hour.

Jonathan called us all together to share his conclusions.

"These things are part of what they call False Knowledge. Strange reports that spacers make, or that they don't make, because the officers back home make them visit the Counsellor or take pills and tell them not to talk about it.

"These ships roam deep space. No one knows what their crews are like; there is a good chance they are automatons. Sometimes they ram ships, sometimes they nudge stranded ships toward ice asteroids." He went on to show us enhanced images of long matte black raindrops with a ring of missile launcher tubes forward and a few small fins aft.

He showed an image of our ship, eighty meters long, and made comparisons. The biggest of the black ships was twice our length. There was one about as big as us, and several more in half, quarter, and even eighth sizes.

Those smallest are probably small craft, pinnaces, or gigs, or fighters. The Threep commented that they had sensed only one life in the little ones; the biggest had been filled with many crew.

Boorn asked the big question, "Are they dangerous?"

Jonathan spoke authoritatively, "All life is dangerous."

* * *

Our ship at times reminded me of the arcology. We were isolated, protected even, from the outside world, independent of everyone and everything beyond the protection of our hull. But there was a difference: we lived almost as a family. Jonathan and the Threep, and of course I, had responsibilities in making the ship function. We interacted on professional and social and even personal levels. Before, I had been waiting to die.

Our ship was our world. We all were kept busy by simple procedures that maintained the quality of our environment and ship performance. Crew members pursued advancement in their skills: it was an expected part of their daily work. They cross-trained to replace or supplement their comrades in the event of injury, sickness, or sudden catastrophe. Devices and installations required periodic checks and preventive maintenance. Our book club became an important part of our routine; I made a practice of awarding a silver sunburst sticker to the best plot analysis and a gold for the best character analysis. The Threep, and Jonathan, displayed them with pride.

Boorn and Flink paired. I learned that despite the three-fold symmetry of their physiques and mating structure, some of them formed paired friendships for companionship and mutual support. We repositioned various room panels to accommodate their living together.

Within a year, Flaal and Deen were also paired, and then Trune and Froon. The others were apparently content to continue their lives as before.

INTERLUDE

I had not noticed the standard accommodations of the concourse before. Perhaps it was because my presence in the *Dakhaseri* was repetitive, but brief: I never felt the need to eat, to sleep, to eliminate waste. I assumed none of that was necessary in this spiritual realm. I was wrong.

In this particular experience, I found myself bored with mundanity and wandered from the viewing seats to the concourse. For the first time, I now actually inspected its broad expanses and its amenities. It had every convenience to which I was accustomed in life: small shops nestled between larger food courts; graphic displays guiding access to seating overlooking particular communities, neighborhoods, cities, continents, and even whole worlds. There were small lounges with alcoves and comfortable seating, all hidden away from public view.

I learned more clearly that the grand tiers towering above the concourse were adapted to other physiques and respirations; that there were other concourses serving other digestions and other sensory preferences. There were whole sections in total darkness whose observers observed with sound, or auras, or other strange stimuli.

There was seating (or its equivalent) for eight-legged behemoths, and by extension pools that hosted eight-finned leviathans.

On the other hand, the signage was in Anglic, usually a jumble, but when I focused, it was clear and concise and exactly what I wanted to know. In some cases, it changed as I looked, transforming into better, clearer presentations.

I passed thousands of fellow observers: most were Humans; many were strange sophonts I vaguely remembered seeing while in life, or when I was awakened. They looked at the signage and clearly understood it as well, yet they could not all know just Anglic.

One alcove had been commandeered by a small group of yellowish 7-peds with eyes on stalks. They watched the crowd and physically accosted any of their own kind, dragging them into their small recess to violently gesture some obscure message before letting them go.

In others, various sophonts rested, or slept, or slumped in stupors.

I found what I thought was a shop, but soon saw it was more like a low-tech datapak, its walls lined with books of all shapes and sizes. I randomly selected one which fell open in my hands. On the visible page of many grey lines of text, my own name stood out in black: Jonathan Bland, Human, 301-277 to 102-336. I flipped pages and randomly found entries for my wife, for our children, and even our grandchildren.

I selected another of the books, this one with a title: *Wiseman's Guide to the Sophonts*. It fell open to a page on Humanity, which told me facts which seemed new to me: some details on natural psionics predelictions, and a note positing that some Humans may have a latent sense of awareness. I had a nagging thought that I had seen that comment somewhere before.

I started to leave, but as I returned the book to its space, it jammed half open and as I manipulated it, I smoothed a wrinkled page: the Llellewyloly of Junidy. Those strange sophonts with balls of white hair atop five spindly legs. Their peculiar respiratory needs meant that they wore protective suits when in Human company (or that Humans wore protective suits when in Llellewyloly company).

I browsed for a while, then returned to the concourse. I walked aimlessly, observing the public as I strolled. What I noticed most were family groups: archons, be they patriarchs, matriarchs, autarchs, or some other elders, flanked by dutiful offspring, trailed by additional generations, and orbited by rebellious youth, occasional prodigals and reprobates. Some strode with great purpose to unseen destinations; others chatted happily as they walked; yet others stood and discussed matters in varying degrees of animation.

THE QUIX PATH

The **Not Foam** is interspersed around or overlaid upon Existence. Here in Existence is a chair; next to it, or all around it, is a foam of unrealized dozens of Not chairs: those that could have been, or might have been, or should have been, but are Not. The Not Foam at its most fundamental level is everything that isn't enveloping everything that is.

299-630
Aboard CF *Zhimaway* Above
Itvi 1931 Stiatl E786???-4 Ga Fa
  "Who here is senior?"
  "You are, Agent."
  "Who is next senior?"
  "Captain Nisnity, Agent."
  "And the briefer?"
  "That would be me. I'm Lieutenant Orloff."
The briefing was relatively simple: our rather small Fast Cruiser *Zhimaway* was patrolling the coreward perimeter of the Imperium on a six-year mission. It had chased Vargr corsairs, updated charts on a variety of worlds, helped a few communities in the name of

interstellar comity, rescued a few Imperial citizens from dire situations, and generally made the Imperial presence known to client-states and non-aligned worlds alike.

The underlying focus was intelligence-gathering: determining attitudes, trends, issues, and problems that might impact the empire. So much for foundations.

The latest jump, a simple four-parsec transit, had gone wrong. It happens. Time-in-jump in this naval-tuned cruiser was supposed to be a week, plus or minus a fiftieth. Alas, this time, when the timer hit 164 there was no sign of breakout; when it passed 171 the astrogator formally declared a concern. The pre-breakout rumblings finally started at 203 and the jump ended at 204:

—In a strange system, twenty unauthorized parsecs inside the Zhodani border.

—In the remoter regions of that system's oort, near a small farming world orbiting a dull spectral-M.

—Being welcomed on the comms by a Lord of the Consulate.

The computer, not knowing what to make of this situation, registered an exception through some subroutine and told Captain Nisnity to activate me.

"Thank you, Lieutenant, for that very capable and informative briefing." It had been less than an hour since breakout. "Have you answered him? Acknowledged his hails?" The Captain replied in the negative. "Then let's talk to him."

I stood off to the side while Nisnity responded. The translator functions did a capable job, captioning everything in dual lines of Anglic and Vilani across the bottom of the main display and on individual consoles. A comm tech oversaw the process, evaluating word choices where necessary. The audio was a quiet rush of the tees and ells and vocal clicks that characterized language from this strange branch of Humanity, while standard Anglic told us what he was saying.

I noted two elements of the process. First, this communication was friendly, unalarmed, even welcoming. None of us expected this from someone with whom we were in grave conflict, and on whose territory, we were encroaching uninvited.

Second, he spoke as if we were expected; no, not as if, he had expected us and was pleased that we were here. We were invited to come visit.

I suspected that one element in my activation was the ship's fuel status. Upon arrival, our tanks (except for some basic housekeeping reserves) were dry; there were no nearby ice chunks, no nearby gas giants, asteroids, water, fuel. Except on the world below.

"Tell him that we accept."

In orbit above Stiatl, that was this world's name, we could see a nice planet with an uncharacteristically dense atmosphere, vast ranges of frontier, and a small settlement nestled in a sheltered mountain valley to which all roads led. The place looked, and probably was, self-sufficient; there was little—actually no—evidence of frequent trade. At first, we mistook the community's central plaza for the spaceport: it was sturdy bedrock carefully marked in concentric circles and spots and spaces. Our sensop corrected me and pointed out a disused space just outside of town with proper sheds and a few insystem ships.

I designated Lieutenant Orloff as my companion and waved off objections when I eschewed personal weaponry and escorts for us. "A couple of pistols will not help at all in our discussions. If it comes to conflict, we will have to fight with words and concepts." The others acquiesced; dare I hope that our negotiations below went as well?

Our pinnace landed and we were greeted by a capable young man and his beast-drawn two-wheel cart. I directed the pilot remain with the craft; that itself created an assumption that we would return later that day. Lieutenant Orloff and I clambered aboard the transport. Our driver spoke accented Anglic, greeted us warmly, and was fascinated, perhaps titillated, to meet Imperials. His word choices and conversation conveyed Zhodani concepts in imperfect translation.

"How was your flight?" elicited my "It was fine."

He hesitated and then commented, "Ah, polite lies." He expected personal truth.

The four kilometer journey carried us through clean, well-maintained streets, past attractive whitewashed walls enclosing rows and rows of single story dwellings. There were, however, few people on the streets until we reached the plaza.

As we approached, I saw a sea of rhythmically moving Humanity. Occupying nearly all of the large open central space, there were perhaps twenty rows of twenty, each person with his or her own personal space, yet all moving in some strange choreographed sequence of positions, some repeating, some new, all accompanied by the beat of a solitary unseen drum. It was a mix of ballet, synchronized swimming on land, and military close order drill. I was transfixed.

Our cart driver pointed out something I had missed. "See the smaller group to the left: seven rows of seven." Now I did. They moved in a different pattern, sometimes echoing, commenting, or presaging the larger group. "There are times when the two groups move together. When the minds of each set become one and form a whole. It is then that we are touching the fabric of reality, calling forth not just things but events from the not foam."

I almost missed that comment. What was the not foam? He did not explain.

"It was one such synchrony that told us that your ship would arrive.

"Their goal is to achieve lasting synchrony in order to bring about the Second True Path."

What could that possibly mean?

We arrived before a small building facing the plaza to be greeted by a tall man in boots and a flowing cape; I would have identified him as a Cassildan had I not known better. As we dismounted, I started a self-introduction.

"Hello. I am . . ."

And he interrupted. "Jonathan. Yes, welcome. We are pleased to have you join us." He gestured to several figures nearby and they scattered on different tasks. "Please, step inside. I have a welcome prepared."

Outside was whitewashed natural construction; inside was stark modernity. A spacious chamber with widely spaced comfortable furniture, gleaming floors, and indirect lighting. At one side was a self-serve banquet, to which the tall man gestured. Orloff helped himself and came back to our conversation munching.

* * *

He introduced himself as Lord Shatlijiatlas followed by a string of titles that my recorder would remember for me. He knew my true name; I realized that I had neglected to ask what my body host's name was.

I knew basic facts: he was a member of their hereditary elite, trained in the powers of the mind to keep the population under control, happy, and content. The entire structure of the Zhodani empire was based on a psionic elite controlling the masses. In the Imperium, psionics was fringe unorthodoxy; here, they claimed it was an exact science.

We Imperials see the Zhodani Consulate as the monolithic evil empire bent on invading and enslaving all Human societies. With good reason, we fear the Zho ability to read minds, change attitudes, and oppress all who oppose them. The idea that someone could not only know my innermost private thoughts, but somehow change them to conform was sickening.

"Ah, you are skeptical. We should always be skeptical of new ideas." I had seen this approach before … state the obvious as a fact and credit psi for the conclusion. Sometimes there was indeed a talent behind the statement; sometimes not.

But this Lord wanted to talk. I decided listening might get us closer to leaving the system.

* * *

"Permit me to acquaint you with our, and your situation. Perhaps to correct some of your misapprehensions. But first, I must show you the dancers.

"The dancers out there are our way of life; they are the purpose of our society. Come," and he led me to a window, "They dance day and night. Oh, in shifts. Those now are about five hundred, our population has thousands who live to be part of that dance. They are why you are here.

"Every generation produces talented psions whom we train in their talents in the service of our society. They become our healers, our trainers, our psychologists. They manage workers by sensing needs and helping to fulfill them. I know many of you Imperials fear the sciences of the mind, but that concern is misplaced. Imagine if someone in crisis could speak with a truly sympathetic counselor who could touch the mental pain and make it go away."

I knew these basic facts. They made their workers happy in monotonous jobs; they erased worry rather than solving its causes. Their masses surrendered their independence in order to be happy. Their surrender was not necessarily voluntary.

"Or help a worker find just the right vocation that would be fulfilling and productive."

And perhaps make that worker like the job, and never know someone else decided for him.

The Lord continued, "I agree that our two cultures are different. They naturally clash. But we share many qualities; our populations are both predominantly Human after all.

"Whatever differences we have in our societies, our dancing is for the good of all Humanity."

* * *

Zhimaway's captain analyzed scanner displays with Sensop.

"They don't even have radar. Just a communicator array and some passive detectors that pick up ship arrival flashes."

The Captain asked, "Can they see us now?"

"Barely, and only if we are in line-of-sight. Not as we pass beyond the horizon as we orbit."

"Then let's take action."

To the pilot, "As soon as we are out of sight, drop to the surface."

To the sensop, "How long will they expect us to be orbiting?"

"Four hours."

To the pilot again, "How long to refuel?"

"An hour down and up. If we splash directly into the sea, we can refill our tanks in two hours. It will be close."

"Then let's make sure we do everything right."

"What about the Lieutenants?"

"They are our diversion."

Within five minutes, *Zhimaway* started a fast descent through atmosphere.

***

Lord Shatlijiatlas continued his story.

Stiatl is a farming world, long ago seeded with Human-compatible flora and fauna that quickly drove native species into the less desirable niches. The farms and ranches produce enough to make Stiatl self-sufficient, which is a benefit because it has few visitors and little trade.

"Our founder was Lord Shat, my many-generations-ago great grandfather, a participant in the Fifth Core

Expedition almost two thousand years ago. It reached a third of the way to the Core!

"Imagine! They saw the core-deep chasm on Junipioat, the Broken Ring, the 400-parsec expanse of the Barren Worlds. He touched the Stele of Triumph itself.

"Even spending significant periods in cold sleep, it took them a quarter of a lifetime there, and a quarter of a lifetime to return.

"The journey was an epic adventure, and my ancestor flew on one of the flanks, a parallel course gathering information on worlds and sophonts.

"He encountered the native intelligent life of a minor backward planet: Stiatl. This world is named for that. They were a naturally lithe and agile people with a philosophy of oneness with the universe expressed through rhythmic movement. Enhanced by their natural psionic ability, they strove through mass coordinated festivals to shape the seasons and encourage the crops.

"They indeed did shape reality through their dances, and he did what he could to capture their secrets.

"Lord Shat saw the essential usefulness of their dances. Connecting his own background of science and psi, now seen through the lens of Stiatlnian eyes, he imagined how to use it for the betterment of society.

"Our system finds children—babies—with psionic potential and elevates them to the intendant class: separate training, not only in psionics, but social behavior, business, government, management, and problem-solving. These specially selected people receive the best in education and training because they are destined to become the leaders of Zho government and society.

"But all of these elements of nurture cannot overcome nature. What happens to the truly unblessed: the unintelligent, the intellectually unfavored, the stupid?

"Our traditional response has been to move them into non-crucial positions. They become managers of animal populations, fish habitats, the forests, the records of weather and climate: endeavors that could be handled by underlings; efforts that need to be done, but are truly non-crucial.

"Regrettably, such positions are usually unfulfilling. The organizations themselves can survive, many of them even thrive, but we are also concerned with the welfare of every one of our members. These exceptions, these truly unfortunates would have been better off if they had not been selected, but even the Zhodani cannot turn back time.

"You might call our settlement here a group home, or sheltered care. They come here and we provide them purpose, meaning, goals in life. The dance is not about agility or grace, or even synchronization, but about native psionic talent. That they are able to provide."

I spoke up. "I don't really understand. What does the dance do?"

"It shapes reality."

"Doesn't reality already have a shape?"

"I apologize; I spoke a traditional phrase. I will more carefully craft my words.

"Strong psi used in concert can bring about changes in reality. It can change location without energy; it can reach across distance; it can set events in motion; it can stop trends; it can create; it can destroy. When the dancers are

truly in tune with each other, they call into existence
events and sequences that direct reality to the best of all
possible universes. Our phrase for the process is called
shaping reality."

"We don't know what that shape looks like before it
happens, but sometimes it is so clear that we can
recognize it. Your arrival, for example."

They thought our chance misjump was a positive event;
much better than taking our arrival as a threat.

"Yes," he agreed.

"Did I say that aloud?"

"No."

Ah. How do I control or conceal my very thoughts?

"You cannot. But there is no need. Communication is
enhanced."

* * *

Zhimaway filled its tanks with water, processing it in
clouds of steam and mist into the hydrogen that would
fuel its power plant and jump drive. Every crew person
had some task at some console or device to ensure this
process took no longer than necessary.

At last, the tanks were full and the ship ready. The
Captain gave an order to leap into the sky, and ...

Nothing.

Spacers began immediate actions, automatic responses,
checking, diagnosing, analyzing. Every single routine and
inspection gave the same response: ready. But the ship did
not move.

* * *

Lord Shatlijiatlas frowned.

"Your captain has taken steps without you. I see that you are unaware. This is so typical of you imperials. As if I would not know.

"No matter.

"These Schonches (the word means Seconds) are shown the benefits of belonging to the Second True Way; sometimes they are encouraged by trained counsellors. A few fall away, but most see the benefits and look forward to a fulfilling life.

"Schonches are fitted with wafer jacks. The interfaces are different from your Imperial standards, but the concept is the same. The Schonches receive skill sets: very high level and special skill sets that overcome lack of intelligence. For the most part, the skills have little correlation with intelligence anyway: they encompass dance, music, rhythmic movement, co-operation. The Schonches become dancers; coupled with their psionic abilities, they become very good dancers, very good synchronized dancers. They become the key to the Schonciatlatl Path.

He moved us to the window again.

"The dancers are hypnotic, are they not?

"The array of twenty rows of twenty dancers fills the plaza. The unseen drum sounds its ever-present beat. The dancers are not just synchronized: waves of motion and gesture sweep across the surface, punctuated by eddies and whorls, soothing undulations punctuated by abrupt and compelling statements. There is a parallel effect in the psionic emanations from this assembly as they radiate outward in waves and pulses.

"This psionic consciousness has its own influence on the quantum nature of the universe: on the not foam from which everything arises. When the pulses truly synchronize, they compel changes in the fabric of reality itself. Properly done, they propel the current world line toward its optimal expression: the Scionstlatl, the Second Path, The Better Way.

"Elsewhere in the Consulate are the abbeys that try to divine the future: The Quixitlatl Path. Some of their psions can see the future. Different people see different aspects, but they agree in general. The Wave. The Great Break. The Black Fleets.

"They only look; we are doing something. Our dancers bend reality to change those predicted futures. To divert the Wave. To avoid the chaos of the Break. To repel the Black Fleets. The dancers brought you here. When you arrived, it was clear that you are part of the second path.

"I invite you to participate. I understand your implanted personality process. With an adapter, you can share it with me. My personality will not be suppressed; they will merge.

"We are aligned, you and I. We both want the same: progress; safety. The dance brought you here. There is a purpose for you. We just need to take the next step."

He was mad. Insane. I tried to suppress the thought. He could sense my aversion, but now I was paralyzed. My muscles tried to squirm or flail, but they stood immobile. I had let my guard down, fascinated by his story; not seeing where it was leading.

Lieutenant Orloff stood equally still. If he could move, I was sure that he would have.

Lord Shatlijiatlas approached without malice. His touch was almost loving as he removed my wafer, fitted it to a small packet, and applied it to a place in the back of his skull.

I understood.

In a flash of invisible light and a clash of inaudible sound, I understood everything that Shatlijiatlas had been telling us; more than that, I believed everything that he said. It all made sense. It was all supported not by wishes and aspirations, but by scientific proof, careful hypothesizing, rigorous testing. I knew that the dancers could bend reality; that they had done so in the past. Some pattern of dancing years before had set up a cascade of events that made our ship misjump here so that I could see the very truth of their mission and believe in their sacred cause.

Now I saw that I could intervene in the affairs of the Empire; draw them closer to the Consulate; reduce our conflicts. Bring the benefits of Zho psychology to our own populations.

A voice in the back of my head, his voice sharing my mind, spoke to me, telling me what I needed to do; assuring me of the long-term benefits; defining my actions as service to the Empire, and more: as service to all mankind. I had never been so completely sure of myself as at that very moment.

And yet, even as he spoke his voice faltered. Just as I was listening to him, feeling his belief in his way of life and his conviction that the Second True Path was absolute truth, he was listening to me, hearing not only my belief in service to the Empire, but also my memories. They washed over him: not just memories of killing millions, and billions of people, Human or not, but also my commonplace ability to dissemble and misdirect.

He was strong, but he was not trained in the details of the psychology in which he felt such confidence. He expected that he would dominate in our shared mind. He underestimated the situation.

I knew that he had stalled *Zhimaway*; that it was immobile on the other side of the world. I knew how he had done it, and I with a simple decision reversed his action.

*　*　*

"Sir! We have power!"

"What was the problem? Never mind. Lift in three, two, one."

"Yes, we have lift."

The ship rose slowly from the shallow sea to about a hullheight, and then accelerated straight up.

*　*　*

I stood and planned what I needed to do.

I reached out to our pinnace and instantly the pilot knew without understanding that he needed to board his two passengers in the plaza. It would be a matter of mere minutes.

I also thought that the dancers should clear the plaza to avoid injuries. Through the window, I even then could see them flowing to its edges.

Lord Shatlijiatlas had assumed a figurative fetal position in the back of our head, and I turned my attention to him. His plan had been that I spearhead an effort to bring the Zhodani psionic sciences to the Imperium, and with it their euphemistic adjustments of minds to accept their stations and lots in life. For all of his sophistication, this Lord had no true grasp of Imperial dissimulation.

He would have his body back in a month, and I began a series of mental conversations before he regained full control.

Now I the Lord addressed me the Agent as only self can to self: in brief phrases and staccato half-expressed ideas, confident that I would understand me.

"Leave these people alone." They are not a threat to the empire; at least not now.

The pinnace hit the plaza hard and its hatch irised open. In a matter of seconds, the pilot appeared as we approached.

"Reveal nothing," I whispered to myself.

I touched Lieutenant Orloff and he collapsed. His memory of this would be blank. Agent me and pilot hauled him into the craft. In the last minute, I pulled away the wafer from my niche and returned it to my Agent host, and they were gone.

ENNA PLANT LAGASH
REPORT 4

Video image of an older Human woman with dark hair in a spacer cut and streaked with grey. Her eyes have slight wrinkles at the edges that shift as she smiles. She speaks with authority. Datestamp: 092-541. Report 4.

Our time on the ship settled into a routine. We all had responsibilities, but none were onerous. There was a flurry of activity just before and just after a jump transition, and there were tasks to be performed as we scanned new systems and refueled.

But our time during jump had few demands on us. We exercised. I studied. Our book club met and discussed. I stood a watch on the bridge twice; the techs similarly shared a rotation in the drive compartment.

I formed a habit of reading alone. Early on, Flink had given me a day-long tour of the ship, from astronics compartment in the very prow, to the stern chasers fixed between the drive outputs. Off the drive compartment, into each wing, were horizontal maintenance shafts that directly accessed sensors and servos and led to wing-tip weapons turrets. Within each was a single acceleration couch with aimers and triggers and an observation dome. I could sit there for hours, reading the classics, comparing texts, making notes, turning over in my mind the many roles there were in society. Anglic literature was no longer my vocation, but it remained to me interesting, even compelling.

After Jonathan showed me jumpspace, I made a habit of deopaquing the dome, and the chaotic roil of jumpspace strangely became a soothing background to my thoughts.

In this particular instance, I was re-reading Nert's script on hope when I noticed a change in the chaos around me. Where normally I would see a cascade of intense points of many-colored lights, they were now transitioning to one color. Some, then many, then most, and finally all the points became intense blue.

I noted the time and tapped text into the comm asking Jonathan to join me, adding a word to denote urgency. Within five minutes, he was stepping half through the hatch while asking why and what. I shushed him, although technically I was not supposed to shush the captain and said I would explain other things later.

"But now, look out there." I closed my eyes so he would have an untarnished view.

"This started about ten minutes ago. Before, it was ordinary. Now, everything is blue. What is it? Can I open my eyes now?"

He said I could, and the intensity faded by about half. We decided to take turns looking, and we each tried to memorize what we saw, narrating our notes to the recorder. Eventually the points returned to their normal multi-colored appearance. I noted the time: about ninety minutes elapsed.

My newfound familiarity with math kicked in as I made some quick calculations aloud. "Our courseline is three parsecs, call that ten light-years, or one hundred twenty light-months. Our jump should be 168 hours, more or less. That effect? phenomenon? change? was ninety minutes long, or a hundredth of our jump. Or about a month long?"

Jonathan was tapping a pad. "Thirty-two days. But jump doesn't work that way. There is no direct correlation between time in jump and location."

I knew that; I had been taught that. "Then again, we just saw it. A direct correlation."

"There is that."

He touched parts of the screen to preserve our narrations, whatever information the scanners and imagers had preserved, and I saw him triple tap a space labeled Ultimate. In our entire interaction, neither of us had spoken the word wave.

Then I had to explain to him why I was spending my time in the port wing turret.

DATHSUTS

056-560
Aboard B *Emamela* Orbiting
Vlan 1703 Dathsuts C310200-8 Lo

I awoke to the gentle hum of bridge noises: low voices, gentle processing sounds, the occasional audible alert. To my question about senior, the response acknowledged me. Next senior was Captain Lebelle and my briefer was Commander Sathpaaba.

If activations to determine the fates of worlds can be considered normal, then this particular activation was still unusual for several reasons that Commander Sathpaaba noted. We were aboard a single, aging semi-dreadnought, the *Emamela*, patrolling beyond the Imperial border in Vargr space, above a world with no atmosphere and almost no people.

Against this background, my Newt briefer spelled out the problem. "Our routine anti-corsair patrol took us to this system and our sensors picked up an extensive activity on the polar plain. Initially, this was identified as a pirate base: no matter that they would be better off burrowing in an asteroid in the belt. But the readings and scans show something much too big for that.

The primary transpex viewport opaqued and images appeared. The first showed a city: a center with concentric rings and extending rays, overlaid with a smaller gridwork of connectors. Some of those rays extended far beyond the city to smaller clusters. Sathpaaba highlighted one, "This cluster is an open pit mine exploiting meteoric FeNi. Note the smelter and processing complexes." He highlighted another location, "And this cluster is processing native copper." A third, "And this, much farther away, is extracting radioactives."

Finally, he highlighted and enlarged the very center of the city. "They are building a ship." I could see it was a very large ship, roughly cylindrical, its base visible surrounded by gantries and frames.

"The diameter of the base is about 350 meters. The ogive of the hull so far says it will be 700 meters long. Bullet-shaped. Two million tons. Ten times the size of our ship. Four times the largest ship the empire builds.

"See the cluster of gantry frames. They're makering the hull and interior structures in a single pass. No one builds ships like that."

I mused, "Except them. How many people in that city?"

"None. They are robots.

"From what we can tell, this city started four years ago. There's a small outpost on the other side of the world mining some rare earths: about a hundred Humans and Vargr. They noticed something and when they tried to visit they were first ignored, and later actively kept away. The locals have shared with us their surveillance imagery."

"Tell me your evaluation?" I already knew the probable

concept: self-replicating automatons who land, build more of themselves, and send those off to do the same again. Meanwhile, the robots left behind would eventually consume this world building more of themselves. The empire's secret archives had records of now-dead worlds with surfaces converted to vast robot cities. Who knew where their robot citizens ultimately went?

"Yes, Agent. Their first priority seems to be completing their big ship. They don't seem to have jump drive or gravity-based maneuver. That thing appears to use an orion-drive."

Which was craziness. The ship would ride on successive fission or fusion bomb explosions. It would destroy the city as it lifted off. What machine logic was at work here?

"So, this city is not long-term viable? It will be destroyed when the ship lifts off?"

"Most probably. Maybe the robots don't care about radiation."

"Where's the ship going?"

"Orion means sublight; probably a tenth light speed. Perhaps thirty or forty years per parsec. Theoretically, if they knew where to go, they could reach Vland in 500 years."

"Where did they come from?"

"They could have been cruising for millennia before they got here. We don't have enough information. Did they run low on supplies or fuel? Was there something special about this world? We just don't know."

* * *

The robots seemed oblivious to us hanging in orbit. On the other hand, they were not unintelligent. What if they discovered we had jump drive? What if they could reprogram their maker shipyard to build effective faster-than-light drives?

My decision was easy. "Scrub them.

"Captain, I operate under Imperial Edict 97. Make a pre-emptive strike as soon as possible. When can that be?"

Heretofore silent, Captain Lebelle, now spoke. "I agree. First strikes can be in as soon as an hour."

"I want a person and ship census for the system."

A clerk spoke up. "There's us. The mining outpost has perhaps a hundred people. Three ships on the ground there: Trader *Legend* out of Regina with a crew of four, Ore Carrier *Shar Seven Three* with a universal megacorp number, and Far Trader *Xyneid* registered locally. All are on the surface at the outpost currently."

"Put an assault team in the outpost; I want everyone aboard those ships and in orbit before the strike begins. How long will that take?"

A marine lieutenant spoke up, "Two hours to prepare and hit the surface. Six hours for a sweep. Two hours to get out."

"Ten hours. Make it happen." Then to the ship captain. "Make sure they are away before you start."

* * *

Almost all of the ship's marines participated. A squad remained behind to handle any issues and to provide me security, although I did not expect any need. As we waited, after I had seen the assault lander off, I engaged the squad leader in conversation. Where are you from? How long have you been in? What, precisely, are you?

This particular squad was composed of six Threep, a trifold sophont with three legs, three arms with three-fingered hands, a head with three faces. They were considerably more agile than they looked.

"The Navy lets us enlist as a pod;" he said in a loud voice, "we stay together through training and assignments."

I thought that perhaps they had been left behind for some reason of prudence, or comparative inefficiency. Instead, it came out that their assignment was a simple rotation of responsibilities. This particular squad leader, Doorn, took pride in his unit and in their performance. If I had pressed a question of inefficiency, he would have been insulted.

In idle talk, I spoke of how fortunate we all were that we had found this specific threat before it had matured. That if these robots were loosed on the Empire, they could devastate whole worlds and vast populations. Sergeant Doorn and his corporal nodded in agreement and understanding.

* * *

Marines have their own Rule 1. They are trained to be very efficient, and yet they can be sympathetic. They allowed each of the evacuees to take whatever he or she could carry and gave them minutes to pack. The entire operation took slightly less time than scheduled.

While the ore carrier hung in orbit near us, the two

traders docked in our hangar bay. The larger red one discharged about half the evacuees and a handful of marines down a ramp; the smaller white ship gave us the rest and their own contingent of troops out a large oval hatch. I addressed the sixty or so locals. They were variously stunned, angered, dazed, and argumentative.

Doorn activated a klaxon that focused their attention and silenced them.

I began with Rule 1. "There is no appeal from these events. You are fortunate that you have been evacuated before the world below is scrubbed and that you have escaped with your lives.

"Interrogators will interview each of you to harvest what information we can about the settlement on the far side of the planet. Be patient until you are called."

I waved an instruction and marines started culling the first to be questioned. As I watched, Doorn grabbed my elbow and turned me away from the crowd. That, in itself, was a violent violation of protocol. Before I could respond, he held a three-fingered hand in front of my face, shielded from view by anyone else. In silent marine battle language, he spelled out in quick succession

identifiers for three of the evacuees by position,
a marker of each as enemy, and
a strange notation that they were not Human, not sophont.

I understood immediately, and held out my own hand with the two-digit signal, "Kill Them."

* * *

Doorn must have been simultaneously signaling with his other hands because shots sounded even as he pulled me down to the deck. In slow motion I took in the next ten seconds. Two figures dashed toward the red ship's ramp, grabbing others as they passed, dropping them as they twitched with shot impacts, then seizing more as shields. A fallen third rose, half of his shoulder missing, to attempt the same process. One fell, rose, then fell again with a leg missing. Even as he fell, shots rang from his hand. Not from a pistol; from his hand. Bodies dropped and red splattered. I noticed a man on the periphery holding a strange tiger-striped woman as shield, backing toward the shelter of a wall, and then a marine covered me with his body. Shots staccatoed to the accompaniment of screams and cries. Although the shooting stopped, the action didn't. The evacuees scattered to the perimeter of the chamber. There was nothing for me to do: the marines followed standard combat protocols. At the edge of my perception, I noted that the access ports had slammed shut (also a standard protocol). I hoped that those on the other side realized that depressurization would not help us against robots.

At last it was over. Three marines grabbed me and literally carried me out of the chamber and up a flight of stairs to the flight control overlook. Once there, the marine leader, on his own initiative, forced everyone against the transpex at gunpoint.

I watched his fingers twitch in battle language. The marine to his right withdrew a short blade from his boot, held out his arm, and cut it enough to bleed. Without a word, he grabbled the arm of each of the three techs and cut them. The marines next. I offered my own arm and he cut it as well.

"All clear, Agent. May we return to the deck?"

"Good work. Yes."

One of the techs collapsed to the deck and I ignored him. To the others, "Get me the Captain. I want total lockdown."

The hangar deck below was an abattoir. I mentally estimated twenty bodies, some moving, some not, their clothing stained bright red. Along the perimeters were huddled clumps of three, or five, or seven, crouching to look smaller, hiding behind anything they could find. Teams of marines moved among them, brutally throwing evacuees toward the center of the deck. With each was one of the tripods, passing judgment.

A lieutenant, accompanied by Doorn, brought me a report.

"Agent, there were fifty-nine evacuees in the bundle. Thirty-five marines. Plus, your six marines, three interrogators, and you. The counts reconcile. Doorn's troops cut down the robots as they ran for the trader's boarding ramp, and we have all three. There was collateral damage, which I regret was unavoidable." I told him I concurred, to which he was visibly relieved. Rule 2 and Rule 4.

I turned to Doorn. "What happened?"

"Agent, we" and I knew he meant he and his fellow tripods, "have a perception of living things, as if they are humming or singing, but it is not really sound. It is hard to explain." I recognized his description of the non-Human perception sense; some thought it a kind of psionics, although it was not. "Those three were silent."

The lieutenant interrupted, "There's a very lifelike polymer overlay, with an internal framework. But they *are* robots. They don't bleed and now they don't move."

"Make a complete report. You have done well. The Emperor appreciates your service." My statement was not perfunctory. They had done well. Their response may well have saved dozens of worlds and millions of lives. How does one tally such a victory?

"Doorn, also make a complete report. You have also done well."

The lieutenant asked to be excused, saluted, and left. Doorn went with him.

A naval officer found me and escorted me to the bridge. The captain was irate at this violation of his ship. He was pleased to begin the scrubbing. I left him to his work. He knew what to do.

* * *

The ore carrier belonged to one of the megacorporations. Marines searched the ship accompanied by tripods and declared it clear. I spoke with its captain and sent it on its way.

I spoke with *Legend*'s captain, he accompanied by the strange stripe-tattooed woman who stood deferentially behind him and spoke not at all. We negotiated passage for ten of the evacuees; he would carry them to a world of relative safety, their fares paid with imperial vouchers.

That left the white ship, *Xyneid*. Its crew was dead: some robots, some Humans. It appeared that we had frustrated some robot plan by sheer chance.

I had a clerk show me the records of the evacuees. Ten Humans and three Vargr, including some with enough experience to operate the drives, but no pilot or astrogator. A quick check told me the best candidate was *Legend's* strange woman with a strange name that told me more: Florine Ten. A clone by the name, and now I understood the tattoos: status identifiers applied by her creator.

Why was I even concerned with all of this? No matter. I had started a process; I would finish.

I told *Legend's* captain I needed his astrogator for *Xyneid*. He objected; she was his property; he could not let her go without compensation. I dismissed him even as he ranted.

I next interviewed the woman. She spoke only in response to direct questions; avoided my eyes in deference. She was indeed property—technically not a slave, but certainly not free. And yet, the record showed her factory-option skillset made her a capable astrogator and a tolerable pilot; I suppose her owner saved money using her instead of paid crew.

I dismissed everyone else from the room. Told her to sit, and waited her out, not speaking, not looking at her. At last, she spoke, "What will happen to me?"

"I have decided to emancipate you."

She remained silent.

"I need a captain for *Xyneid*, that white ship out there. I have selected you."

"I cannot; I owe a debt to *Legend*."

I made her tell me everything. That her clone batch owed a joint debt to the factory that created her and her sisters. If she defaulted, her sibs would bear its burden. Currently her share was paid by *Legend*.

I told her the debt was transferred to me. I checked records and made notations. I gave her *Xyneid* as salvage. I gave her passengers to carry away and vouchers to pay their passages. I told her to find and recruit her sisters as crew, and to pay their debts with salaries and cargo fees.

She sat incredulous. "Why?"

"Call it a whim. Perhaps I am paying forward for gifts I have received." After a pause. "There is something else."

Now she looked suspicious. I ignored it. Everything of value has a price.

"I will tell you a secret name. Share it with your sisters, and their daughters. Someday, this debt may come due."

"I believe I understand. I hope I understand. And this secret name is?"

"Jonathan Bland."

"Is that you?"

"In a way. There is no need to worry. I do not expect that this debt will be a burden."

I gave her some single-use override codes keyed to specific dates. One would register her as emancipated.

Another would make a payment on her personal debt. Yet another would allow her to register *Xyneid* in her name.

As the three ships left the system, Captain LeBelle began scrubbing Dathsuts and I began a coded report for the archives.

ARBELLATRA

103-621
Aboard BKF *Korrikak* Above
Vlan 1717 Vland A967A99-C Hi Cs

I was surrounded by a pleasant scent, incense perhaps, and by utter quiet.

"Jonathan. Welcome. Please, be seated and join us for dinner."

I opened my eyes to the wardroom of a large warship, with a large conference table to one side, but before me a small table set with fine plates and utensils. The speaker, a large boned and attractive woman in naval uniform, gestured to a chair, and I sat down. Her rank stripes said admiral with some embellishments.

My mind tried to process several thoughts at once: I couldn't quite place the rank markings; this was not the usual setting for my activation, and she addressed me with my true name.

"I am Admiral Alkhalikoi. You are aboard my flagship leading the squadrons of the Second Expeditionary Fleet. And I need your advice."

At some signal, a steward filled wine glasses and delivered a light first course.

237

"Are you aware of the turmoil of the last thirty years?"

I was not and said as much. "Tell me the situation, over dinner. I don't need extreme detail, but include everything you think important."

She unleashed a torrent of complaint. "The Spinward Marches are the stepchild of the Imperium. We're young, not the established old-line, well-settled worlds. Nevertheless, we're an economic powerhouse: bigger than Fornast sector (right next to Capital), bigger than Diaspora. We beat off the joes, an empire ten times our size, twice, while the Emperor ignored us. Twice!

"So, we are also the first line of defense for the empire.

"Our Grand Admiral Hault-Plankwell, he turned back the joes, carried our complaints to Capital; he was forced to seize power in the face of Jaqueline's intransigency. But the Admiral was a frontier fighter, not a politician. His direct ways alienated the administrative admirals in their comfortable offices; and even then, he lasted almost three years. But they bided their time, lied, schemed, and finally pounced. Their treason is what created the chaos that is our current government. Those squabbling, armchair bureaucrats each wanting to be emperor, were too busy to even notice when the joes and the dogs attacked the Marches again. Did you know that they pushed a strike squadron almost to Vland, here where we are now, halfway to Capital?

"But no, you wouldn't, of course not.

"We thought Cleon V would be the answer. He stopped the squabbling; he sent us reinforcements, squadrons. Then, just when things started to turn around, the bureaucrats manipulated everything again: eleven so-called Emperors in five years! I am not even sure who sits on the throne at the moment.

"Sometimes, I wonder how the Empire has survived at all.

"But enough of background. We have beat back the joes, but who knows for how long. My mission is to straighten out the Navy and ensure the security of the Marches. Someone has to listen to reason in Capital.

"So here we are at Vland, the homeworld of Humanity. On the way here, we have met other Imperial squadrons, defeated some, rallied others to our cause, and we will continue to Capital.

"But here, we are stalemate. The fleet here is our equal; they won't attack; but they won't concede. We need their hulls, their squadrons, their strength added to ours. With every negotiation, their structure shifts, and we go back to introductions.

"I activated you for your strategic input. How do I defeat this troublesome fleet?"

"Admiral, I think there is an answer, but . . ."

"Call me Bella. It's more comfortable. By the way, you are Rhys." She pronounced it with a Y.

"Bella.

"Bella, usually I stand before dozens or hundreds of crew and give orders. It is certainly nicer to have a dinner conversation. You activated my wafer because . . ."

"I am at a loss, and success is so important. I need to defeat this fleet, and you're an expert admiral."

"Ah, I see now. Usually, the computer prompts the activation of a wafer. Some rating goes to fetch it, some volunteer inserts it, and . . ."

She added, "There an expert standing on the bridge who knows what to do."

"Yes, exactly right. In this case, it isn't the Agency activating me; it's you. Technically, I have no authority; you just want advice."

"Precisely."

"Let me explain further. There are five kinds of wafer: each with its own attributes and benefits: Negotiator, Advisor, Warlord, Admiral, and Decider.

"Negotiator is worthless. A wafer personality lasts less than a month: any worthy adversary just outwaits him.

"Advisor is equally worthless; they should have labeled the wafer Sycophant.

"Warlord and Admiral are two sides of the same coin: they are both brilliant strategists and clever tacticians and they know how to win. Actually, the personalities they harvested to make the Warlord and the Admiral were service academy game players: each had years of experience wargaming out thousands of situations and writing papers about them. The Admiral wafer could win this battle for you, but probably at the cost of half your fleet.

"You should be glad your rating made a mistake and fetched the wrong wafer. I'm not an Admiral; I'm a Decider."

She choked as she sipped wine. She could not respond immediately, and that allowed me to continue. I held up my hand and said, "But that is fortuitous: I know how to win.

"You are gathering forces along your march on Capital. You need this opposing fleet as part of your strength. As long as they stall, you are stuck here."

"Exactly. Tell me the secret of their defeat; how to rally even half of them to my cause."

"I'm a Decider. I was, a long time ago, a functionary in the bureaucracy that managed the Quarantine Agency. I made decisions all day long. The agency tested more than a million people: for aptitude, intelligence, ability. They selected me because I knew what I was doing, and I was usually successful. I had a single principle, and I knew how to implement it." I was implementing Rule 1. Rule 3.

"Identify one or more solutions that will work. Then pick one. It doesn't matter which one; just pick one.

"In this case, we can already see the solution. There is only one. We pick it.

"So, when do we attack? And how? Tell me what to do."

I told her. She said let's do it. We would start tomorrow.

* * *

She moved to the couch and gestured me to join her. Sitting next to her, I sensed that there was something else. This was the closest I had been to another Human being in centuries, and it felt good and strange and forbidden all at the same time. I enjoyed it at this casual level as we talked about history and politics and society.

Then I remembered. "Do you know that your guns won't work in Core Sector?"

That changed our dynamic, "What?"

"The operating systems are astrofenced. Ships outside the Core Fleet locked down within the sector."

"They don't trust us?"

"Should they?"

"I suppose not."

"No matter. I have the override codes. It just takes

some calculations and some keystrokes. If I can remember them."

She startled, recovered, and slapped my shoulder playfully. I learned later, much later, that she and Rhys ap Connor had been together for the last nine years. It was a shame, I thought, that she married Duke Sergei instead.

104-621
Aboard BKF *Korrikak* Above
Vlan 1717 Vland A967A99-C Hi Cs

I made a presentation. Four stripes on a graphic, each filling in a quarter of the image as I detailed the important elements.

Stripe One. By Right of Assassination.

"The Empire is a web of oaths with rights and responsibilities, all leading upward to the Emperor, downward to the people. There is very little in the way of constitutional documentation. Over time, over the centuries, accepted rights arise from custom, circumstance, and precedent.

"Emperor Martin II died in 244 without issue. Tracing up and over the genealogies, the candidate with the greatest claim was Cleon III, great-to-the-third grandson of Cleon II. Everyone agreed that precedent gave him the claim and he was duly installed on the Iridium Throne. Within months, everyone agreed that it was a mistake. He banished his Minister for Health to the Rim based on a conflict in schedules. His bodyguard shot the Grand Counsellor dead after a disagreement on protocol for an investiture. He arrested nobles who voted against his proposals in committee. He shot the Duke of Ilelish for reasons that we still debate.

"You all know the story: his Private Council agreed Cleon The Mad had to go and they selected Porfiria—by lot—to tell him. She did, at the cost of a wound to the leg, but shot him dead herself. The Moot acclaimed her Empress the next day.

"That established selection by Right of Assassination: by a high noble; by his (or her) own hand in the presence of witnesses; with the approval of the Moot.

"For two hundred years, the Right was an obscure footnote. In 475, Cleon IV resurrected it when he assassinated Nicholle. Jerome assassinated Cleon. Jaqueline killed Jerome. Ultimately Olav, your mentor, killed Jaqueline. You see the pattern. Ten emperors in the first 450 years, most successions were peaceful. Twenty emperors in the 150 years since, most ascending by killing their predecessors.

"This whole non-dynasty is being called the Emperors of the Flag. You qualify, you are a flag officer; you're eligible. You just have to kill Ivan, by your own hand, in front of witnesses, in a fair enough fight that the Moot approves afterward."

Next image. The second stripe started to fill in as I spoke.

Stripe Two. Fleet action.

"The navy controls everything. The last fifteen Emperors, at least since Olav, have been admirals and controlled the fleet. You can have a force twice the size, probably, of the Emperor's Central Fleet. I'll bet that only a few commodores know that out-of-sector ships are astrofenced; I'll bet the Emperor is confident of his advantage, which is illusory. We have their advantage."

Next image.

Stripe Three. Forced Moves.

"We are sixty parsecs and almost a year away from Capital. How do we plan an attack from this distance in both time and space? Where will he be? Will Ivan even still be Emperor when we get there?

"Endgames in chess, or otherwise, are based on forced moves. Who knows chess? Let me build a foundation for you. Everything to this point has been development: marshaling forces, building positions, creating a situation we can win. We are now on the cusp of the endgame: with the right moves, we can force events and actions that inevitably lead to a win.

"There are things that we know will happen; there are events we can make happen. There *will be* a Holiday celebration as the year turns to 622. The Emperor will participate; to hide in some fortress or not receive his nobles would be a mark of fear, even cowardice. We know the bureaucracy will continue to function. We know that the Duchess of Rhylanor will be invited. There's more, but we'll deal with that later."

Next image.

Stripe Four. Break the cycle.

"Every one of the admirals in this conflict thinks he or she or it can govern better than the others. You, I am sure, think the same. You need to give that up. You need to put the good of the Empire first. You must foreswear the

Iridium Throne. We must break this cycle of assassination and fleet battles or the empire will tear itself apart."

The four stripes were now colored in.

"Comments?"

A Captain spoke first. "The lady would make the best Empress in a hundred years."

A Commander offered, "Or ever." There was a murmur of agreement.

I countered, "And who will stop the next Admiral from thinking he is better? How do you convince the entire command structure of the Navy, and a majority of the Moot, and the general population, that the cycle of assassination and succession has stopped?"

"I would like to propose." That focused their attention, and I waited until there was silence.

"That the Lady Arbellatra graciously consent to be Regent, not Empress, Regent. To hold the ultimate powers of state in trust until a suitable surviving heir is located. The cycle will be broken. Peace will return to the Empire. Assassination of the Regent certainly does not convey the Regency; there is no precedent."

I wondered privately, was this ever conceived as part of my mission to serve the Empire?

Arbellatra's staff and officers discussed, argued, dissented, agreed, disagreed, agreed to disagree, and ultimately concluded a recommendation for this course of action. It fell to Arbellatra herself to ratify the plan. She did, and everyone turned to finalizing it.

***

The orders were hand-carried on paper by couriers in the ordinary course of business over the next twelve hours. They gave an introduction, a series of preliminary instructions, eleven numbered paragraphs, and a concluding statement. The couriers also personally and privately entered the gunnery override codes, and an extensive set of contingency battle instructions.

The next day, as the negotiators returned from another fruitless meeting, Arbellatra's flagship sent its coded signal at 1500, "Paragraph Eleven, Confirm."

> *Para 11. Jump precisely two hours after receipt of orders to any system of your choice and rally in Capital to arrive at precisely 2359 365-621 prepared for battle.*

Our ship, the flagship of the fleet, waited until the last possible moment. Bella wanted to be sure of as much as possible. Keeping the jump drive capacitors charged for that long carries with it a risk of catastrophe, but the Admiral needed to know her ships were safely on their way.

We needed to cover sixty parsecs in 37 weeks: at our best performance, we could be there in 17 weeks, plus or minus a few days. Others in our fleet were not as speedy: the slowest would take nearly the entire time to get there.

105-621
Aboard BKF *Korrikak* Above
Vlan 1717 Vland A967A99-C Hi Cs
I stripped Arbellatra's command structure of specific

officers and marines selected for their talents, their aptitudes, their genders, and their wafer jacks.

I had my own part to play in this grand scheme to save the empire. It started precisely at 1700; my ship already knew the plan and was ready. It was one of the first to jump away. I was aboard in wafer form.

On the other hand, I as Agent Ap Connor remained with the Grand Admiral on her flagship.

The fastest ship in the Second Expeditionary Fleet was a *Khanu*-class anti-commerce raider: the *Shigig*. The names don't translate easily into Anglic, *Khanu* is a mythic hero capable of many identities; *Shigig* is one of the identities, a shrub with many poison thorns. There is more in the original Vilani story cycle: details of magic tinged with specific virtues; fatal flaws inherent in each type of magic. *Shigig* could reach Capital in just under fourteen weeks, say 200 or so.

Shigig arrived at the edge of the Capital Identification Zone and disembarked several of our people. It jumped to a different entry point and disembarked several more. They each proceeded individually to Capital by jumpliner.

Shigig then drove for Ase, another neighbor of Capital. Along the way, it became *Medugar*, one of *Shigig*'s sisters which I knew by records was assigned to the edge of the Great Rift, and specifically not associated with the Spinward Marches. My override codes ensured that we were recognized correctly. Upon arrival, it dropped off several more officers, and they made their way at intervals to Capital as well.

Finally, *Medugar* became *Dosini* and drove for Irman

Belt. There, it laid over for the weeks of delay that needed to pass before the next stage of the plan was to unfold.

200-621
Aboard BK *Lioness* above
Core 2118 Capital A586A98-D Hi Cx

Although Holiday's Eve celebrations are universal, time zones make them non-simultaneous. For the Empire as a whole, for the nobility, for Capital, and for the Emperor the only important time is midnight on the clocks of the Imperial Palace. The prime meridian slices through the palace grounds; *Lioness* in stationary orbit above keeps the same time. Forced Move One.

212-621
Core 2114 Shudusham C849A55-A Hi In

Commander Arian Landaxa kept his real name; his family had distant roots in the Sylean Federation—what was now Capital—and his orders reflected an assignment early next year to a Protocol post at the Moot. Meanwhile, his temporary assignment would be with the Protocol Scheduling Office. His refrain to those who would listen was "I hope I can get to see our ancestral communities while I am here."

He spent the night in a luxurious suite at the Travellers' Aid Society Hotel and negotiated passage on fast destroyer bound for Capital the next day. Forced Move Two.

215-621
Core 2115 Knabbib A431758-9 Na Po

Captain Sir Jalil Patel was disembarked at Knabbib

Highport and made his way quickly to the associated naval base. His orders identified him as Lieutenant Commander Jalil Shugili, the first name for ease of memory, the last name to muddy the trail. His orders chip said he had been dispatched from Daibei sector, assigned to a year of shadowing duty on Capital by his patron, Count someone or other. No one really cared; this happened all the time; the control codes and encryption passed the simple computer processes. Besides, if this was a scam, the audits would ultimately catch it.

Lieutenant Commander was quite a demotion, more so because now-Shugili looked like he was old enough to be a Captain, and this mismatch had the appearance that he was less-than-competent. He embraced the role as a game.

At the naval base, he presented a voucher for passage to Capital and was there just seven days later. Forced Move Three.

325-621
Aboard BK *Lioness* above
Core 2118 Capital A586A98-D Hi Cx

Force Commander Arlan West, SEH and recently arrived from the Spinward Marches enjoyed the change of command ceremony and regretted that his predecessor was unable to attend. The fourth battalion of the 61st Imperial Star Marine Regiment was the traditional ship's troops for *Lioness* and regularly rotated to duty at the Imperial Palace. With the palace in ruins and the festivities planned for *Lioness* on Holiday's Eve, the coming assignment would be hard work, but also undoubtedly produce glowing fitness reports and ultimately career enhancements.

He returned the salute of the Officer of the Day and started to work. Forced Move Four.

RETURN TO DEYIS

345-620
Aboard ISS *Atalanta* Above
Zaru 0917 Deyis II E874000-0 Ba Da Re

The deck had an irregular vibration beneath my feet; I wondered briefly if something was awry, but then I went on. "Who here is senior?"

"You are, sir."

"Who is next senior?"

Someone gave a name: Algeson, or Algenson. It wasn't clear.

"Who is the briefer?"

"I suppose I am, sir. Binala."

I immediately noticed that no ranks were given. Strange. I opened my eyes to a bridge with a row of consoles facing large deck-to-deck transpex ports looking out on a murky red-brown planet. Four crew—officers?—stood in a clump near a console.

"Binala, tell me what is going on?"

"Frankly, we don't know. We're on routine survey; we entered this system; the klaxon went off; the screen said activate a quarantine agent: you.

"The threat level is at most four. Danger, up here, is nothing."

This was not right. Who are these people?

"What ship is this?"

He smiled, "We are the *Atalanta*, a beagle out of Nathan."

Some clarity now, "Ah, scouts."

"And this world?"

"Deyis. Scrubbed a hundred years ago. The sensors show no sign of life, or of the parasites."

Stikky's astrofence worked! On a survey ship no less, the synchronization even jumped the divide between navy and scout.

"Let's look at the sensors." I hoped I could find evidence to support what I needed to do.

We found a world as I had left it: urbs burned to glass, vast stretches of empty terrain punctuated by clouds of radioactives, skies darkened by cascades of dust. A million years from now, someone would find fossilized sophonts encased in bedrock and wonder why these people died or were killed.

Binala, on my instructions monitoring the deep radar, found a trace of something that I wanted: beneath a glassy sea punctuated with stubs of former towers was a subsurface void, more than a basement, less than a cavern. An overlay matched the place as the Karand's Palace, and I told him to mark it and look further.

The next day, I made up some story about remaining pockets of parasite that needed to be eradicated. We could craft some targeted impacts using rubble from a nearby worldlet. "Oh," I remarked, "I think it's important to verify that subsurface void." I took Binala with me in the cutter while they went off to shape rubble into kinetics.

We auto-pilot hovered over the frozen ripples of melted stone, surrounded by nuclear damper fields that made everything more-or-less safe, and dropped out of the hatch as the first people to set foot on this world in a century. I have to admit that Binala was efficient. I had told him what I wanted, and he had made sure we had the tools: dampers, radsuits, cutters, diggers, even a flexible ladder. In short order, we were in an underground chamber filled with stark shadows as our headlamps swept left and right and left again. Binala stood guard against the hypothetical parasite carriers that might remain while I sought my true goals. I found one almost immediately and despaired. How could I ever carry away this vast collection of forbidden Third Millennium knowledge? Row after row filled shelf after shelf with bound volumes; perhaps a third had fallen to the floor in fans of disarray. It would take days, I thought, until I saw the centrally placed console and its rack of numbered datapaks. The shelves were numbered; the datapaks were numbered. Logic told me that one was the backup of the other; I wasn't sure which was which. I fumbled with a connector and verified that cartridge K3 had petabytes of data, readable data. I selected one text at random, found shelf K3 with the same text, title, content.

"Binala, we need to rescue this set of Datapaks. It will take several trips." He was even more resourceful than I had thought; he pulled out some sort of grey web and wrapped it around not the cartridges, but the rack itself, and then pulled a cord tight. The entire bundle lifted of its own accord and he started to drag it toward the shaft.

I needed to find my second goal, and so set off away from this library of shadows.

The corridor outside connected to a series of negatives: supply rooms, paired freshers, an environmental stabilizer for heat and air quality. I noticed a blinking diagnostic in the dark and chided myself for faulty assumptions. My armored glove touched the wall switch and the lights came on. Binala yelped in the communicator. "It's OK. The backup power is still working. I never thought to try the switch."

"That scared me half to death."

My search was now somewhat easier. I continued down the corridor to a locked, more than locked, armored door. "Binala, please come here."

When he arrived, he (as I expected and hoped) produced some small pointed object that made the door fall open. Inside the vault were the true treasures of the Karand's Palace: antique charters in protective binders attesting to the ownership of this patch of land and clump of buildings, several brown satchels of credit certificates, and over in the corner an armored red metal container of biologicals: for the hereditary families of this long-term enterprise, a generation yet unborn. "I need that red thing." I said. I took the brown ones as well.

We were back in orbit by the time the beagle returned. I spun a story.

I talked about the Karand as the alternate genetic line of the Shadow Emperors of the First Imperium; about how more than once the death of an heirless Emperor had triggered the automatic coronation of the Karand during the First Empire. The historical value of what we had found was unimaginable. All were to be congratulated. There would be bonuses all round.

We prepared the datapaks for shipment to the archives at Reference. I made a point of reviewing random pieces and confirmed that Ansha had correctly described the materials. With that complete, I took steps to meet my Rule 5 responsibilities.

The red embryo transports appeared unharmed. Working with Binala, we scanned the records of the First Survey for this world's twin, or if not twin, at least close sibling. We found two, and not being able to decide, I chose both. Half the embryos went spinward to Taman in Deneb. The other half went rimward to Sikora in Diaspora. Each was accompanied by specific instructions on decanting and quickening. The brown bags of money would provide for these orphaned children to adulthood.

And with that, my bargain with Ansha was complete.

On a whim, I reviewed the standard information systems that this ship carried. With some effort, I recalled the name of the tech who had created the astrofence for me: Niffield. I found a Niffield made Baron Sima some ninety years before. His son was a Marquis of a neighboring world, his daughter a Baroness. I wanted to think that I had something to do with that but allowed that I would probably never know.

MANY SHIPS JUMP TO CAPITAL

I opened my eyes standing on the concourse of the stadium, surrounded by a throng and facing one single person flanked by a handful. I recognized Ansha and when our eyes met, he smiled. "I thank you with all that I can. You have saved more than my life; you have saved my line. There can be no suitable reward for what you have done."

There is little to say to such effusive praise, and I responded with a formulaic, "I am pleased that you are pleased."

Ansha gestured to beyond the railing, "Our grandsons and daughters live because of you. Our appreciation knows no bounds."

This from the archon of a family that I had killed. I wanted to think that he understood why. As I stood there, he stepped toward me and spoke in a lower voice, confidentially, to me alone. "The *Niikiik Luur* is more important than you know. Don't let it languish in the archives. Read it. Understand it. It holds amongst its chaff the secrets of the universe."

2359 358-621
Core 1917 Ploiqu D422747-7 He Na Po Pi

Core 1918 Traak B62488C-A Ph Pi
Core 1919 Crompton E776502-8 Ag Ni
Core 2014 Morii B62A644-A Ni Wa
Core 2016 Ion B877755-B Ag Pi
Core 2316 Ercan B544854-A Pa Ph Pi
Core 2317 Codsen E571568-5 He Ni
Core 2318 Yirsh Poy B310577-B Ni
Core 2519 Riid Irman Belt D000330-A As Lo Va

The more than four hundred ships of the Second Expeditionary Fleet each executed their exacting instructions to the minute. Their crews had spent the last half-year tuning their drives in preparation.

In their various locations two to five parsecs from Capital in every direction, they congregated in the kuipers and the oorts, depending on stepchild gas giants and spinster ice chunks for their refueling. In their approach, when they arrived in those neighboring systems, they immediately broadcast mission identifiers with false itineraries: a fast response team from Capital to Vland; an express shipment for the Solomani Rim; emergency personnel transfers, which certainly made sense with a new Emperor, and there was always a new Emperor. Fast shipments, clandestine missions, hastily documented transfers are all more commonplace than most expect. Ships moving away from Capital don't meet the criteria for threat, risk, or danger. An uptick in traffic away from Capital means little. What the sensors and scanners saw aroused no concern.

The primaries jumped precisely on schedule at 2359. The auxiliaries waited three hours and began their jumps at 0317, not knowing if they would arrive to victory or defeat.

HOLIDAY'S EVE

When the Imperial calendar was created, everyone already knew that 365 Modulo 7 is 1. What to do with the 1?

The establishing proclamation created fifty-two identical weeks composed of seven named days. Wonday always fell on 002, 009, and in sequence. Senday always fell on 008, 015, and in sequence to 365. That first day, 001, became Holiday: never a Wonday, never a Tuday, always its own celebratory observance of the end of the old year and the beginning of the new.

360-621
Core 2118 Capital A586A98-D Hi Cx

The Lady Arbellatra, third Duchess of Rhylanor, Baroness Alkhalikoi arrived by jumpliner to a suitable, if generic, reception at Capital Down starport. Even the jaded officials of the Starport Authority knew better than to deliberately snub a Duchess. They whisked her down a ceremonial corridor as travellers and sightseers, held back by a flimsy barrier and the glares of armed and armored enforcers, gawked and wondered who this particular noble was. By evening, images were featured on subscription communications for those who made following nobles an avocation. The Protocol Office, various intelligence agencies, and a few scholarly think tanks made note of the details. By the next day, the public focus had moved on.

The Lady stayed in a ducal suite at one of the boutique hotels near the Palace. Within hours, the functionaries whose job it was to handle visiting nobles sent appropriate, if generic, welcome packages. Her retainers talked to those who showed up in person, calendaring events and appointments, arranging for briefings and receptions.

As important as a Duchess might be, there was something that mattered even more: The Moot proxies that she held personally, and those she controlled by designation. If she were to step onto the floor of the Moot, all her personal proxies that she had granted would revert to her; any proxies she had been granted—from family, subordinates, partners-in-power, friends, even tolerant enemies—would automatically activate, supplanting any current holdings. There was a financial cost associated with such steps: the various stipends would need to be refunded *pro rata*; transferred proxies would require suitable compensation to the previous holder. Then again, at these levels of power, the nobility rarely concerned itself with such matters; there were squadrons of accountants and consultants who handled such details.

* * *

Their functionaries asked her retainers, "Would the Duchess be attending the Moot? For the year-end ceremonies? The start-of-the-year convocation? Was the Duchess available to speak at the mid-year Heroes' Day event?" Unspoken: was she intending to remain very long? The retainers had been briefed and gave carefully prepared answers, "Yes, No, Yes, probably not." all of which were truthful, in case there was a psi-talent, or a body-language reader, in the area. By the end of the day, the tide of supplicants had ebbed, and the Duchess and her consort settled in for a well-deserved respite.

The crush began anew the next day and continued unabated. The Lady was in a new environment. She wore elegant suits instead of naval uniforms; she portrayed herself as intelligent, interested, interesting, important, but there was no mention that she was a Grand Admiral of the Marches. News of her fleet was yet weeks away by ordinary news channels.

Reading her published bio told part of the story: Daughter of the marriage of a Duke and Emperor Olav's half-sister, commissioned Captain in the Imperial Navy at age 16, acclaimed titular Victor of the Second War Against The Zhodani at age 33, and appointed Grand Admiral of the Marches as peace broke out.

Her behavior fleshed out the apparent truth as she shopped for clothes at the fashionable shoppes on Route du Palais, and gawked at the icons of the center of the known galaxy.

***

The Naval Intelligence Service knew differently. They had full service records of every person who now served or who had ever served, all as up-to-date as possible given the communications lags of jump. Lieutenant Commander Shugili noted the computer-generated exceptions, and added suitable assessments that labeled the Duchess a figurehead controlled by several corporate factions in the Spinward Marches and propelled to her current heights of accomplishment by nepotism rather than talent. He classified the results penultimate security, marked them "reviewed," and forwarded them to a hold file for later publication. He knew that the Emperor's staff would have them within an hour.

Later that day, a Baronetess Captain in the Imperial Navy, in full finery including a shoulder cord signifying that she actually spoke with the Emperor at least once a week, called on the Duchess with an invitation to the Holiday's Eve celebration three days hence. Arbellatra's response was, "Oh, my goodness! I shall need a suitable dress; I have absolutely nothing to wear," as she dashed off leaving the Captain to make her own way out.

The invitation specified the celebration would be aboard BK *Lioness*, in stationary orbit above Capital. It did not mention the usual site, the Palace, half destroyed in the contention last year between Marava and Usuti. It was also impolite to mention that since then, Ivan had killed Usuti, Martin VI had killed Ivan, and Gustus had killed Martin. Gustus had been on the throne for almost ten months.

365-621
Aboard BK *Lioness* above
Core 2118 Capital A586A98-D Hi Cx

In the ready room, the designated First Company of ceremonial guards were making last minute preparations for the security of the Emperor. Third Company had just finished their duty and sweeps of the ballroom. Second Company was in place maintaining security as deliveries for the celebration continued. First Company would step into place just before the Emperor arrived.

The Captains and Sergeants hovered over their troops ensuring all was in readiness. A bark brought all to their feet and braced rigidity as the Battalion Commander entered.

Force Commander Arlan West, SEH was a hero of the recent war, and had been riding everyone almost as hard as basic training, striving for a perfection worthy of serving the Emperor and the Empire. In the previous weeks, he had recalled time and again the credo drilled into every marine's brain: Obey. Even if it's stupid? Or suicidal? Or without explanation? Obey.

Now he stepped forward accompanied by a Captain and a Lieutenant.

"I am Agent West of the Quarantine acting under Edict 97. I have served the empire my whole life and I serve her now. By your silence you actively affirm my authority and that your oath to the empire requires your unswerving obedience. Speak now or forever be damned if you waiver in the slightest."

He walked among them, inspecting each for the

slightest wrinkle or imperfection. The Lieutenant preceded him; the Captain followed. From time to time, a Marine was dismissed from the formation and escorted from the chamber.

After, in a meeting room, the three officers conferred. West spoke first, "Only seven failed out of sixty. Are you certain of the rest?"

The Captain spoke first. "Body language is not an exact science, but I erred on the side of caution. The rest betrayed no sign of problems."

The Lieutenant added, "Nor is psi exact, but I agree with the Captain's culls."

"You picked three others? Why?"

"They emoted wrong. They didn't react quite right when you said 'obey.' I didn't want to take any chances. Sir."

"You both have done well. Sequester the culls; make them think their failure was in preparation."

Earlier, West had the Lieutenant privately evaluate the Captain, and the Captain privately evaluate the Lieutenant. Each had affirmed the other was prepared to obey. Forced Move Five.

365-621
Above Zhimaway
Core 2118 Capital A586A98-D Hi Cx

The Central Fleet patrolled the single most strategic point in the Capital system: its gas giant. No intruder could hope for continued operations without control of a fuel point.

The Fleet's ships were in a state of heightened

readiness, ready for almost any contingency. The Admiral himself sat on the bridge of the flagship and monitored events.

The Second Expeditionary Fleet numbered 402 ships, but that count was misleading. More than half were minors, auxiliaries, and tenders. The only ones that anyone counted were the capitals: a variety of battleships and dreadnoughts and siege engines.

Some were fresh from the victories of the Second Frontier War and were built to express current fighting doctrine. Others had joined the expedition en route and ranged from modern to obsolete. The total for the only ships that had a chance was eighty.

The laws of chance govern time-in-jump. Long ago, navies learned to tune their drives to near perfection: 168 hours, plus or minus a fiftieth, but the result is still a bell curve around the intended arrival time: of eighty ships, the first dribbles would appear three hours before, peaking at a quarter of them precisely on time, and then dribbling back to only a few by the end of the next three hours.

The strategic plan took all of this into account.

At precisely 2038 365-621, just under four hours to midnight, three Imperial dreadnoughts flashed out of jumpspace near Capital's largest gas giant: Zhimaway.

Chance dictated that *Kokaari* was the very first of the three.

"Breakout!" from the astrogation tech.

Various voices spoke aloud what the sensors and

scanners were showing, "I show six capitals in formation orbit at the gas giant. No sign of carriers."

Sensop contributed, "We are first. *Snowcatess* and *She-Lynx* just arrived."

Captain Sir Buchanan Trent felt like he had won the lottery. He spoke for the record confirming what his officers already knew. "I assume command of the Expeditionary Fleet. Change our identifiers. Open a channel to local."

Other bridge crew continued journaling aloud. "Siege *Hasaggan* has just appeared." Minutes passed, and "We have a hail from Central Fleet Flag."

"Put it on."

The greetings were cordial: naval officer to naval officer. These first few moments were crucial.

Aboard *Tigress*, Central Fleet flag, the general mood was positive. Holiday's Eve portended a new year that promised to be happy and better than the last. Although some crew were celebrating in the mess, bridge positions were fully staffed and at a reasonable state of readiness.

The reply from *Kokaari* showed on the main screen. "Holiday greetings from Squadron Ninety! Admiral, I am Commodore Buchanan Trent, and I convey my respects as we arrive a week early on this Holiday's Eve."

Admiral Isazii on *Tigress* bantered greetings with the new arrival, and they continued for several minutes.

Astrogation tech Nool reacted to the data he saw and touched a panel to alert his Lieutenant, who came and looked over his shoulder. The graphic showed the icons of the three new arrivals mapped against a bell curve. "Their time in jump was remarkable; they all broke out within three minutes of each other. That is very good drive tuning."

As they watched, another icon showed on the screen and the bell curve expanded.

"That last one just reduced their efficiency from remarkable to just excellent."

The Lieutenant turned away to check on other sensor data, only to be called back five minutes later. "There are a few stragglers coming in. Their efficiency just dropped to very good."

"What squadron size are you using?"

The tech pointed to a number, "Standard six ships, sir."

"Something's not right. Are there any auxiliaries?"

"No, sir, just capitals. *Snowcatess*, *She-Lynx*, and *Kokaari*, then a siege, and now *Uncompromising*."

"It is strange to have dissimilar classes in the same squadron.

"Increase squadron size to two."

The bell curve widened.

"Now three."

The humped line on the screen widened more.

"Sir, there's a new arrival."

"Map the curve to fit what we have so far."

The screen now showed a scatter of ship icons with names attached, and a cloud of grey possibles extending into the future. The best fit predicted ten squadrons: some sixty well-armed dreadnoughts and another dozen carriers and sieges.

The Lieutenant walked the five steps to his Commander

and showed a tablet with the prediction, who snatched it to immediately show the Admiral in mid-conversation.

"Battle Stations!" The screens went blank.

Klaxons sounded throughout *Tigress*, and seconds later throughout the other ships in the squadron. Crew boiled out of their comfortable celebrations to turrets and weapons bays and spinal mounts.

Aboard *Kokaari*, Commodore Trent spoke, "They are on to us. Take us to battle stations." Crew were already placed and ready; it was a formality.

"Get that Admiral back on the screen."

Admiral Isazii was a confident angry. "Stand down, Commodore. This is the Emperor's space, and there is no room for usurpers or troublemakers. I do not know your scheme, but it will never work. You have ten minutes to cap your guns, shut down your fire control, and confirm it with data streams. If you do not, my ships will destroy you."

"Admiral, we mean you no ill will. Our squadron is on a mission in service to the Empire, and . . ."

"No matter your mission, I will not tolerate your insolence here."

"Admiral, I beg you to listen to reason. Your twelve ships are no match for us, and we will not be stopped."

"Commodore, and that is a rank you will not hold for more than another hour, you will stand down. You have eight minutes."

As they spoke another capital broke out.

Admiral Isazii's confidence was not misplaced: the astrofence made these schemers powerless, and they would be easy targets. At the moment, his twelve faced nine who could not return fire. As more capitals arrived, each would face the same fate. "Six minutes."

A sensor tech reported, "Intruder *Kokaari* is powering main weapon." Isazii waved him confidently silent.

Commodore Trent had been thoroughly briefed on the next step.

"Admiral, it pains me for anyone in our common navy to suffer, but it is important for you to understand that we bear you no ill will. I call to your attention Fast Cruiser *Emesh*, which you must concede is protected by your astrofence."

That startled Isazii.

Trent continued, "A battle between us would cost many lives. You have good ships, but so do we. You have good crew, but so do we. I count your hulls at twelve, and by the first minute of the new year, I will have a hundred." That was not precisely accurate, but it would do for the moment. "None of my ships are constrained by your astrofence. Your imagined advantage is an illusion. Your surrender is a rational response to this situation, and your personal and crew safety is guaranteed."

"They are powering up, sir!"

"*Kokaari* is firing, sir!" The spinal meson gun fired and *Emesh* exploded.

"The strongest squadron does not always win the battle, but that is not what will happen here. Power down now."

The admiral stood conflicted by pride and duty, reason and emotion. The bridge crew waited with anticipation.

* * *

Isazii could not bring himself to say the word *surrender*, "Commodore, I acquiesce." To his bridge, "Come down from Battle Stations. Maintain screens and protectives." There was no point in risking perfidy by the other side.

Another arriving battle shed energy as it broke out of jump.

"Admiral, you and your squadron are now safe." At Trent's direction, the prearranged victory signal was posted; newly arriving ships would know what steps to take.

"What time is it?"

"2312, sir!"

"Precisely. Send the surrender announcement."

Zhimaway's battlespace stood forty-five light-minutes from Capital. The pre-written surrender announcement was to be transmitted to arrive precisely at 2359. He had been privately instructed, as had every potential battle commander, to transmit the scripted announcement no matter what, win, lose, draw, or stalemate.

365-621
Aboard BK *Lioness* above
Core 2118 Capital A586A98-D Hi Cx

The Holiday's Eve celebration preparations had transformed the main hangar deck of *Lioness* into a luxury ballroom sufficient for a thousand guests. Next year, crew would have to spend weeks removing the decorative paint and returning it to battlehull grey.

Compartments and storage chambers were converted to intimate primping chambers and pre-ball dining rooms.

Crew had been training for weeks for servant and footperson roles. Graphic artists had designed grand hanging banners proclaiming the power and majesty of the Empire and the Emperor. Chefs and stewards had been specifically imported to prepare and serve gourmet meals for the elite of the galaxy. Nobles were notorious for seconding spacers as footmen and marines as retainers; there was a universal excitement in the air.

Dignitaries hosted their own pre-ball receptions and parties. Massive bays that usually held rows of single-seat fighters, or racks of kinetic kill ordnance had been cleared, scrubbed clean of their solvent and preservative odors, and redecorated for the sensitivities of nobles and magnates. Ambassadors hosted the elites of bordering fiefs; Dukes graciously entertained their vassals, who scurried and flattered and ate strange delicacies from carefully arranged trays labeled for multiple digestive systems; short-sighted cliques stayed with their close friends, wasting incomparable opportunities to mingle and circulate.

Arrivals at the ball proper were scheduled from 21 to 22. Individuals, couples, and groups were deposited at the grand entrance by the battleship's internal transport system, to be announced as their particular origins or fiefs were highlighted on an immense overhead display and many scattered repeaters.

Kvudthuerr, the Emissary of Irilitok, and affine Lady Elaine.

* * *

The announcer was meticulous in his pronunciation.

The Holluwe of Junidy, and The Oeylluo Oeylluo. A pair of Llellewyloly, so-called Dandelions, encased in stylish protective suits.

Baron Doctor Grane Argush. An overlarge heavy-world 6-ped, attending alone, although escorted by a Human servant. His massive tail nearly toppled a Baroness as he passed.

Imperial Marine Force Commander Sir Arlan West, SEH. Entering alone, in full dress uniform devoid of medals and badges except for a single silver twenty-one rayed star on a ribbon around his neck: the legendary Starburst for Extreme Heroism; most are awarded posthumously.

Captain Dame Argenta Smee, Marchioness Diiron and the Baronets Minor: two brawny men, one on each arm of an older woman in naval uniform.

The Holders of Lumda Dower. Three Vargr of indeterminant gender dressed in finery that would embarrass any Human.

Fteaow of Clan Tilrui, and Fteaow Hairlei. A great Aslan male with a sash decorated with enameled badges; a smaller female following one step behind.

The list continued, about half being Human; the rest a scattering of various sophonts of the Empire. For those who noticed such things, there were no Zhodani invited.

Lord Nellian, Viscount Jonosva and the Lady O.

The Lady Arbellatra, co-Duchess of Rhylanor, and Captain Sir Rhys ap Connor. With the announcement, she smiled. Observers saw narcissistic joy; within, she noted that the title co-Duchess was a protocolic violation, used here as a code that Lieutenant Commander Shugili was indeed in place and had achieved his purposes.

Arbellatra was greeted several strides later by a social documentarian and several media imagers recording for posterity.

"We have here the Lady Arbellatra in a stunningly white gown of semi-reflectives and a stunning embedded swirl pattern. The effect sweeps the floor while the ship neck stunningly frames her firegem throature. And I see embroidered on your strap the triple sunburst of an admiral in the Imperial Navy. Tell me, Lady? In recognition of your husband? Or perhaps your father? Wait! Well, she's gone."

Indeed, Arbellatra had moved on, even now without patience for fools who couldn't use a simple data lookup.

The next two hours involved refreshments, chance and non-chance meetings between guests, and various organized activities. One corner hosted a guessing game with nonsense badges as prizes. There were periods of organized group dancing punctuated by laughter at clumsy missteps; there were interludes of romantic three-steps.

As the countdown moved everyone toward the start of a new year, the internal lighting flashed with each beat. Individuals stood and activated noise-makers, light-flashers, smell-emitters, and other devices in anticipation and more-or-less in time with the count. At the countdown fourteen, Arbellatra rose and started toward the raised dais holding the Emperor and his immediate entourage.

By eight, she was half-way across the dance floor.

At six, she reached the Fifth Captain of the Emperor's Guard just before the three-step rise. As she passed him, he passed her his red-handled frontarm.

Five, the base of the steps. Lights flashed, small pieces of lucky colored plastic flew from concealed projectors.

Four, step one. Her right hand and gun enveloped in the fold of her skirt.

Three, step two. The first hint of awareness appeared on the fringes of the group.

Two, on the rise of the dais itself, five strides from the Emperor. Her dress changed from white to glowing yellow, the Imperial color.

One, she raised the pistol and fired. To most, there was almost no sound. Some in the crowd, mostly Vargr, winced as the silencer shifted the gunshots into frequencies higher than Humans could hear. The Emperor fell, his head a mass of blood and visible brains; her shots aimed to bypass any possible armor. They achieved their purpose. Those standing nearby dropped to the floor, or dived to the sides, or just stood paralyzed. Some, without regard to gender, screamed. Those farther away turned to the dais as it became the center of attention.

Immediately, abruptly, the screens flashed blank, white, then yellow with a black Imperial sunburst centered. A crawler at screen bottom announced, "The Central Fleet of the False Emperor surrendered to the forces of Grand Admiral Alkhalikhoi at 2359 365-621" and repeated.

Twelve Marines rushed the dais and literally threw the Emperor's retinue down the three steps while surrounding the Lady, facing outward.

Twelve more Marines appeared at the base of the dais as a further layer of protection. A second screen crawler appeared above the first, "The False Emperor has been deposed; the Moot has established a Regency to identify the proper heir to the Iridium Throne." A klaxon blasted to silence the various murmurs, screams, and chaotic outcries. The lights dimmed to quarter intensity.

Comms throughout the hall vibrated or chirped as news media transmitted bold headlines and supporting data. The Emperor's Anthem sounded its seventeen-stroke beat. The Marines parted and the Lady stepped forward in her glowing yellow dress under a full intensity spot as the First Captain of the Emperor's Guard announced in amplification, "Lords and Ladies, I present to you the Regent Arbellatra, and a new era for the empire."

To full silence, the carefully pre-positioned claques in the audience began to applaud. The others took their cue and applauded as well. Maybe, just maybe, this was the end of the cycle of assassination and naval strife.

In the hours that followed, there was confusion over how the Moot came to decide to establish a Regency, but ultimately an emergency council ratified what had already happened. Contrarians noted that time of the Central Fleet surrender could not be reconciled with light-lag, but the elation of a new year combined with a new Regent's promises of peace and prosperity made their theories old news.

* * *

Marines escorted the False Emperor's inner circle into side chambers where they were quickly briefed on the details of the coup. Faced with this accomplished fact, most chose the path of discretion; a few recalcitrants were escorted deeper into the bowels of the ship and some of those never reappeared.

The Lady, now the Regent, Arbellatra met with noble after noble well into the night, generally in groups of three or four. She greeted them cordially, exchanged pleasantries, at times pointing out that all proxies had expired under their terms, and that there was a lot of work to be done renewing them. Before each left, however, she insisted on a personal reaffirmation of their individual vows to her as Regent, properly witnessed and verified.

From time to time she gave side instructions.

Bring me that social documentarian. Who appeared cowering. "I want to clear the record; the embroidery is my own personal rank, fairly earned and well-deserved. I am a, no, the, Grand Admiral of the Marches, senior in rank to anyone west of Vland."

Assemble the Emperor's Guard. Who appeared singly before her, each to receive an XS from her hand, and a knighthood. Within a week, all twenty-four received orders to twenty-four different systems throughout the empire and carefully written instructions to preach the legitimacy of the Regency.

Bring me the Captain of Lioness. She forced from him an oath of fealty and instructed that he surrender his captaincy to one of her officers.

Bring me the family of the False Emperor: brother,

sister, son, daughters, nibs. She greeted each cordially, insisted on an oath of loyalty, and observed the reactions of the empath and the body language reader standing off to one side. At her gesture, some were escorted to the antechamber to the right, others to the passageway to the left. None of them could be allowed to press a claim to the Iridium Throne.

TO ENCYCLOPEDIOPOLIS

It was a ball of worthless rock, ignored for millennia, and rightly so. To the First Empire, it was Shiishuusdar, apparently spite-named for someone who earned the scorn of the local noble. During the Long Night, charts called it Mamatava: its minimal population died out when the supply ships stopped coming. With the rise of the Third Imperium, several companies tried to repurpose its subsurface warrens, but with little success. One company's name, however, became attached to the world: Aadkhien.

An arbitrary decision literally put Aadkhien on the map. Someone in the Imperial Interstellar Scout Service decided that this particular world was precisely on the plane of the Galactic Disk, and exactly ten thousand parsecs from the center of the galaxy. For interstellar mapping purposes, it was on Ring 10,000.0: the reference line for the astrographic coordinate system passing through the Aadkhien system.

They renamed the world Reference.

Reference became the Prime Base for the Imperial Interstellar Scout Service and headquarters for its bureaucracy. Appropriate bureaucrats and functionaries still served on Capital, closer to the reins of power, but the leaders of the IISS preferred to be off in their own independent fief.

As Prime Base, Reference was a training center. The associated University of Aadkhien became the natural home for the latest research in astronomy, physics, cosmology, planetology, and sophontology.

Reference also became a repository for the masses of data that the IISS collected. Originally, the collections were chaotically and haphazardly managed, but in 300 Empress Porfiria ordered the First Survey: the first comprehensive astrographic and demographic catalog of the worlds of the Imperium. To house the data and the samples it gathered, the Service created an entire city: Encyclopediopolis.

Imagine a city devoted to information; not just any information, but the vital, essential scholarly information about every world of the empire: the information that defines its planetography, its resources, its people. Some architectural genius designed a grid of soaring towers, one for every sector, with a level for each system. Each tower is a kilometer long and a hundred meters thick; depending on its namesake sector, a building might be a thousand or fifteen hundred meters tall. Strewn at four-kilometer intervals, the spaces between are filled with apartments, markets, services, and recreation for the staff that service the collections every day.

These collections are not discovery museums that reward children's guesses with pleasant noises, or entertain them with fatuous recreations, or whose displays are ignored by dashing urchins more concerned with their snacks and souvenirs. They are old-style museums filled with row upon row, shelf upon shelf, drawer upon drawer of classic samples. Dedicated academics turn to these repositories to confirm their hypotheses, to disprove rivals' theories, for inspiration and insight, or just for the delight of reviewing materials in their fields.

Of course, even the best-made plans go awry. One level was not enough for Capital; one level was too much for the Imperial Reserve on Onon. Soon, the latter was a locked room accessible only with authorization, while the former expanded to two, then three, and finally four levels in the tower named Core.

The collections are also unevenly maintained. Powerful, important worlds anxious to put their best peds forward provide stipends to researchers and curators. Casual tourists see all that such worlds have to offer; serious business-people find troves of data in support of trade and economic development.

On the other hand, there are entire levels that are little more than empty expanses punctuated by a few transpex cases of rocks and minerals, dried fronds with unclassified seedpods, and musty reports filled with boring detail.

Some levels are simply locked: accessible only to those who can establish a need-to-know or who have certified permission from an authority figure; not everyone is allowed to browse data on the reserves of the Imperial family, or worlds interdicted for the protection of the public, or simply worlds with something someone wants to keep secret.

Encyclopediopolis does not restrict its subject matter

to the Imperium. On the fringes (its suburbs, so-to-speak) of the city are sprawling towers dedicated to the empire's neighbors: the Vargr, the Aslan, the Zhodani towers to the west; the K'kree, the Hiver, the Solomani towers to the east. The subsurface appendix warrens in the mountain range to the south are long-term storage for the obscure, the outdated, and the oversized.

Scholars and expeditions study individual worlds and the best of their research finds its way to the appropriate level of the proper tower in Encyclopediopolis. Meta-scholars visit Encyclopediopolis because they can wander (or dash, depending on their temperament) from room to room, level to level, tower to tower, immersing themselves in data and samples as they try to correlate random information into coherent answers to the pressing questions of the universe.

Who were the Ancients? Who were the Kursae? Who were Caranda's Sparks?

Why are there forty, or a hundred, or two hundred variant Human races, all traceable to Terra? Why, at the same time, have the canids (also of Terra) only produced two variant races? Why has Terra produced more Native Intelligent Life than any other world? What was so special about Terra anyway?

Why is psionics independent of genetics?

Who built the failed ringworld at Leenitakot?

How does the multi-world Fhinetorow civilization of Listanaya sector manage without intelligence?

Why is gas giant life so rare in Charted Space and so abundant beyond?

Why is the entire trailing spiral arm—a million systems some two thousand parsecs from here—barren?

Is there a faster Jump Drive? A better Maneuver Drive? A more efficient Power Source?

Why are so many sophont societies content to live out their generations without ever leaving their homeworlds?

Why do some sophonts advance in technology so rapidly? Why do some plod so slowly? Is there a limit to advances in technology? What could Tech Level 25 possibly be like? Tech Level 50? TL-100? Is TL-1,000 even imaginable? Why haven't we met sophonts with truly advanced technology?

What is the meaning of life?

Different scholars have come to different conclusions.

004-622
Core 2118 Capital A586A98-D Hi Cx
I hope I am doing the right thing. I'll be dead again in three weeks. It will take me fourteen just to get to Aadkhien. I hope this works.

That's what I was thinking when I boarded the liner. I knew where I had to go—it was at the far end of the ship.

So I made my way past the opulence and decadence of luxury staterooms, posh appointments, cloying stewards with affected Vilani accents, and well-heeled passengers: VIPs, CEOs, trade magnates, robber Barons, diplomats, snobs all. So I assumed.

And I continued past the working-class passengers, a jovial and noisy throng, with nary a steward to be seen. A game room occupied some, media entertainments others. Some likely just read in their rooms.

And I ventured farther still, almost missing the rows of stacked bunks where passengers flew in steerage. They were mostly screened from view by a large vending machine. If you want to eat in steerage, you have to bring your spare change.

And at last I reached the room that makes blood run cold. No, literally. Marked by a jagged blue bolt—an icicle really—the entryway opened to a spartan chamber with an untidy stack of coffin-sized affairs. The Low berths. A person of indeterminate age sat in front of a screen. A chiaroscuro of color ran riot over his face as he soaked up whatever entertainment was playing on his monitor. I waited.

Eventually he (sullenly?) acknowledged my presence. A tip perked him up—my last Cr100. They say that low berth attendants ought to be tipped. Anyone who is responsible for nearly killing you and waking you up again ought to be tipped, thinks I.

342-622
Core 0140 Reference B100727-C Va Pi Ab
And sure enough, I awoke. A puff of air confirmed that my pod had been opened and I was alive to tell the tale. A gruff, pre-recorded voice croaked out, "Welcome to Aadkhien! Get up and assemble at the end of the chamber!" in an endless (it seemed) loop. I stretched and finally clambered out. There were eight other low

passengers, some already out, some still struggling to awaken cold limbs: Humans and non-Humans, males, females, and others, all various ages.

The attendant (maybe a steward, maybe not) passed by, handing me a numbered, alloy chit. When each one of us had a chit, he said "look at your number: who has . . ."—he reached into a box and pulled out a card—"six?" Mine was the six. "You win," he said (with some irony?), and handed me ten fifty-credit coins.

I looked down the chamber to the tenth pod. Red telltales blinked; I had won, as had the others is a somewhat lesser way. The one in the tenth pod had lost.

We stepped out into a corridor with directional signs: baggage this way, transport that way, information another way. I had no baggage and I knew what I needed. I set off toward transport.

343-622
Core 0140 Reference B100727-C Va Pi Ab

The low gravity of Reference put a spring in my step as I strolled the already moving walkway from my hotel. I could see the parade of soaring sector towers through a transparent canopy. I had survived cold sleep, telescoping two-thirds of a year into only one debit against my allotted credit of thirty sleeps before oblivion again embraced me. I was anxious to get started.

Most facilities in the empire are dual labeled in Anglic and Vilani; here they were multi-labeled in ten languages and plentiful kiosks provided support for yet more languages. I soon understood that each Tower had a prominent logo and intersections were tastefully marked to assist travellers. My goal was Zarushagar Tower; its icon was a red stylized flower. Soon I could identify it as the red monolith among a rainbow of primary colors, taller than its neighbors to the south, shorter than the denser sectors to the north.

The ground level concourse for Zarushagar provided an overview: a massive holo starchart showing the worlds of the sector, surrounded by accessible data screens with detailed information. I wanted Deyis. The screen said level 270, about halfway up. I took the lift shaft and was there before I knew it.

Deyis (local name Nivalia). Homeworld for the Kebkh, a 5-ped sophont with a prehensile snout above and a similar prehensile excretor below. Settled by Humans from Shiwonee in the Third Millennium: eventually one major continent was predominantly Human; the other predominantly indigenes. The words blurred into grey and my attention wandered. The final sentence on the board said (although in nicer words), "Scrubbed in 501."

There was a clerk at a desk, and I adopted an academic approach, "Excuse me, I am here to see the collection?" adding a high rising terminal. I realized that this person was a Kebkh, perhaps one of a few thousand still alive.

"Register here please," in a whistling voice, followed by, "Is there anything specific you are looking for?" I replied in the negative and it handed me a tablet filled with guides and access fields. I wandered the corridors browsing transpex cases and data consoles, immersing myself in everything I could about Deyis. It was the first time I had taken this sort of break in forty months, or two hundred years, depending on how I counted.

Time flew: the lights flashed and the tablet showed a warning that the level would be closing in an hour. I started my way back to the main desk.

I presented my question to the clerk. "I tried a search, several in fact, but I am not finding what I want. Perhaps you know more about the search process?" An HRT again for its effect.

"What is the search topic?"

"In a few words, I would say false-knowledge. Perhaps *Niikiik Luur*."

It touched some surfaces and my tablet responded. "We don't have any examples; the concept is reflected in some Fifth and Sixth Millennium records. You can access the records on the tablet; there's nothing to see here in the collection."

Had they not yet been recovered? If they were, I would have sent them here.

The place was closing. I returned the tablet to its rack and made my way out.

* * *

I was. Depressed. Not clinically, I had never had that challenge; attitudinally however, I was seeing that my goals were going to be a long time in achieving. I almost certainly needed more than my remaining twenty sleeps.

I started back to my hotel, but distracted somehow, I ended up in a starport lounge: the ubiquitous Lone Star, a franchise found on most worlds. Scouts and spacers like to spend their free time spinning stories and making or renewing friendships at this sort of place.

The Lone Star isn't really a bar, although it does serve alcohol. It also serves liquid caffeine in several forms, mild mood enhancers, and various calmatives. All Lone Stars are the same; each one is different. In this instance, the Scouts tended to be visitors rather than locals; the few traders anxious because there was little in the way of goods to buy or sell. The house specialty was an imported cheese broiled to liquid and served with some sort of crunchy covering. I bought a plate and offered some to those seated near me.

"So," he said, striking up a conversation, "What brings you to Reference? Business, or pleasure?"

We talked for a while; he wanted to dispose of a cargo that was losing value rapidly. When he decided I was not a prospect, he excused himself and moved on. Half of my mind was surveying the room and the other was worrying about implementing a plan before my next three sleeps expired. It was at that point that I saw Angeline and my subconscious told my conscious that there was a solution.

I did not yet know her name. She entered through the main doors with a self-confidence that belied her appearance. She was dressed not to impress, for comfort alone. Her arms were bare, yet covered with tiger stripes tattooed into her skin; her hair was short in a female spacer convention. Her exotic attractiveness was entirely independent of her gender. At the bar, she ordered purified water and found a booth on her own. I knew what she was; I had seen her before. I wondered if anyone else knew. I made my way over. I had a plan.

"May I join you?"

"No."

Try again. "Please? Dinner perhaps? Stories? Nothing serious; just an evening's diversion?"

"No. You have evaluated me wrong."

"Ah, but I haven't. I have no ill intentions, no misconceptions. Life is too short for that." I sat down despite her refusal. "We have met before. If I remember correctly, on Dathsuts in Vland. Then again, perhaps it wasn't you specifically."

"Probably not," she said, "I have never been to Dathsuts." We were dancing around who she was because it isn't polite to call someone a clone even if she is one. An enforcer might ask, or a customs agent; ordinary polite citizens didn't. I was polite; I didn't ask directly. But I did sit down.

"Tell me your name." Rule 1.

She resisted, but we were at least talking. "You tell me your name first. Then we'll see."

I would normally use my host's name, but I told her instead my real name. "I am Jonathan Bland."

She almost dropped her water container. "How do you know that name? Who are you?"

Now we were indeed talking. Her attitude changed. She wanted to at least listen to what I had to say. Her name was Angeline Twelve. The surname numbered generations; she from the second generation following Florine's batch. We talked well into the night. We met again the next day and concluded an arrangement.

353-622
Core 0140 Reference B100727-C Va Pi Ab

I was happy to not pursue my fail-safe plan: find someone with a wafer jack, surprise him, and force my wafer on his neck. Such a course of action was fraught with problems. Not that what we came up with wasn't.

Angeline recruited non-scouts as they visited Encyclopediopolis. Scouts had business here; they came here because they were told to; they left when they were finished. Non-scouts arrived because of some whim or casual interest or vagary of ship schedules; they were academics, discharged veterans, the idle rich, sometimes the idle poor.

She picked out people who looked like they needed something: usually money, sometimes purpose, sometimes just attention. Most just needed to be somewhere else: somewhere safe, beyond the reach of the authorities, or debt collectors, or a shameful past.

She found some common interest. She flattered when she needed to, but that was just to get started; soon enough she was listening to a life story, which she considered an interview. For the right person, she had the answer; for everyone else, the evening ended, and she moved on.

The proposal itself was a delicate process: too abrupt and she scared them away; too sketchy and they couldn't understand. It helped that she had an unusual talent; an innate empathy that helped her best frame the offer.

To one, she appealed to patriotism; to another, to the innate goodness of Humaniti; to a third, charity. Curiosity. Financial need. The unusual. Oblivion. New experience. Self-sacrifice. Submission. Sometimes she just asked; sometimes they just agreed.

We needed the hosts to be sequential. We needed Nine to be ready and willing when Eight was just finishing up. I needed my complete memories from the last activation to carry on to the next.

I arranged for two apartments. She lived in one at the base of Z-Tower; she never brought anyone there, not even me. I lived in another in the shadow of Gushemege; she didn't know where.

She used a hotel for the activations, and it changed every time. She made it quick: an insistence that the wafer be pressed in place. The host personality vanished, and I emerged: a constant amid a parade of little big short tall fat slim light dark weak strong young old men that needed something that this process provided.

When the four weeks had elapsed, she and I met again to give her the wafer. We usually shared a meal and discussed the universe, her life and her sisters, my research. I depended on her, and thus felt a need to be thoughtful. Rule 3. Rule 4. I also paid her enough to carry her forward until our next meeting. Rule 5.

And I gave her the wafer. The last day or two of my activation would be lost to all memory. The host disappeared. I told her that I would board a ship for somewhere and include some form of compensation. Angeline was afraid that I just walked out into the vacuum desert and never came back, but she never asked.

122-631
Core 0140 Reference B100727-C Va Pi Ab

I came to a break. I had found substantial sets of records and made the appropriate correlations. I knew more than I had before, but still less than I wanted. I still searched for the *Niikiik Luur*, which had to be here, somewhere. I found manifests that another I had retrieved them, had almost certainly sent them here. I knew what I would do, but I cannot control what bureaucrats and clerks and unforeseen circumstances may have done between Deyis and Reference. My search would turn to the annexes to the south.

Yet, I was unwilling to begin a new awakening of a project; I considered what small interim inquiries I could begin instead. My attention turned to the mining engineer and I made my way to the Arcanum level of the Deneb Tower.

I was denied entry beyond a small alcove with only basic information. Its Red Zone status hid details of the world behind authorization scanners and automatic barriers.

I spent a few hours in the food court at the top level, enjoying a cuisine sampler for the sector and the views across the worldscape of other towers when I noticed a corporate logo branded on a rooftop below: Naasirka.

Using my comm, I pursued my dim memories of Arcanum and the mining engineer. His employer MinPlanCo did not show up in the records; its parent Naasirka, one of the megacorporations that dominate the Imperial economy, was significant in Deneb with its fingers touching many, even most of the sector's worlds.

I then realized that my memory was mistaken. The employer name was ThreeMinCo. Now I could discover its mining operations on several worlds, and a non-mining installation deep in the sparseness of the Great Rift: Shush.

I tried to find the Shush level of Deneb that afternoon. It was missing. My filter was naturally set for imperial worlds, and it was not there. I manipulated settings and finally found the answer. Not missing. Technically within the bounds of neighboring Corridor sector, and yet deep enough into the Great Rift that it was not even within the empire. I would need to visit one of the suburban towers, where I finally found it in a small annex for orphan worlds.

The first fact I learned was a pronunciation affectation: the world was pronounced Shoosh. The second fact I learned was that Shush was literally empty. It was a backwater world on a dead-end route; it had a good quality starport serving a world with less than a hundred inhabitants. What data that was available—surveys, biome censuses, sample catalogs—was on a single console in a smaller chamber with near empty shelves. I puttered for a while, noted some details that seemed interesting, if not important, and abandoned—no, suspended—my inquiries.

Someday, I could visit Shush and learn more.

333-632

Core 0140 Reference B100727-C Va Pi Ab

I had pursued the *Niikiik Luur* for a decade. At times, I now questioned my own memories, for I clearly recalled recovering the trove of files and arranging for them to be shipped to Reference. I confirmed the records of *Atalanta*'s visit to Deyis. I confirmed the transfer of the embryos to Taman and Sikora. Nevertheless, the shipment was nowhere to be found.

In a decade, I had accumulated a small fraction of what might be in the *Niikiik Luur*. I knew more than before; I knew less than I needed.

* * *

various dates

Core 0140 Reference B100727-C Va Pi Ab

Bland felt a need to protect his researches on Reference; when he finished each phase, the simplest option would be to kill the host. He considered it; one more death on his record wasn't even rounding error. Rule 2.

On the other hand, each of these hosts had significantly advanced his work, whether they knew it or not. Each of these men had been recruited because each needed to be somewhere safe; that usually meant somewhere far away. He could do that for them.

There was some risk involved, but that was just a cost of serving the empire. Each time it was new to him: he had already surrendered the wafer to Angeline, so these last memories would not be recorded.

Each time, he put a card with a spending balance in his pocket: enough to live luxuriously for three years;

comfortably for maybe five. He strolled down to the starport and examined the massive display starcharts of the Imperium and beyond, randomly picking a destination that looked attractive. He wondered, since he had a memory of his intention, but not of his actions, if he picked the same destination for every host; that prompted him to think up a random process that generated a new destination. He hoped that worked. He bought a Low Passage voucher and signed in. He would revive halfway across the empire, and a day or two later he would evaporate, leaving his host with enough to start a new life. Rule 5.

He wondered if sometimes, if his researches had been fruitless in that host, or if he was frustrated, or angry, or depressed, maybe he did just wander into Aadkhien's vacuum desert never to return.

251-625
Spin 1910 Regina A788899-A Ri Pa Ph An Sa Cp
Bland woke up on Regina, unsung true capital of the entire Marches.

069-628
Solo 1836 Chernozem AA85983-9 Hi Pr
Bland woke up on Chernozem, beyond the imperial border deep in the Solomani Confederation.

280-631
Mesh 2034 Ishamzu A7B6567-A Fl Ni
Bland woke up on Ishamzu in one of the former First Empire territories.

111-633
Solo 1827 Terra A867A69-D Hi Ga Cs

Bland woke up on Terra, homeworld to all of Humaniti. The date on the obscure local calendar (strangely in Anglic; in fact, everyone here seemed to understand Anglic) was September 21, 5151 CE.

154-635
Empt 0426 Marhaban A5697AB-B Ri Cp

Bland woke up on Marhaban, the Newt homeworld on the edge of the Lesser Rift.

338-640
unknown world

Bland woke up on some strange world far beyond the Imperial border, where Humans were a true novelty.

113-641
Corr 3225 Uiolksdah B426787-7 Pi

Bland woke up on idyllic Uiolksdah, a mere seventeen direct parsecs from Vland itself, yet halfway into the Great Rift and rarely visited by any but home-returning natives and a few passing traders.

055-642
Ley 2517 Ssissth A644999-9 Hi In

Bland woke up (two of him! brothers recruited sequentially) on Ssissth, beyond the Imperial border in Ley Sector.

345-660

Prov 2402 Lair A8859B9-A Hi Ga Pr Cx

Bland woke up on Lair, the canid homeworld. He noted casually that his journey had taken a decade; when he checked his manifest, he saw delay after delay as the shipment of his Low Berth capsule made its way to its destination.

025-644

Ziaf 2331 Fitl A7A2AA7-B Fl He Hi In Cs

Bland woke up on Fitl, an obscure world in Zhodani territory: their psions could tell he was no threat despite the enmity between the two empires, and he soon found employment as an Anglic language translation checker.

340-655

unknown world

Bland woke up on a strange world without a spoken name somewhere in the Hiver Federation.

For each, he did what he could; in the last day of personality, he found a safe place, negotiated a reasonable position, and even left his host a note with details of his life in the interim. Maybe that would be enough; maybe not.

365-641

Core 0140 Reference B100727-C Va Pi Ab

My search for the *false-knowledge* and the kernels of truth within continued. With two decades of search now done, my accumulations could still never compare to the fruit of a dedicated fanatic family with lifetimes to devote to the cause. I knew individual data points; that lost trove held literally every possible report of strangenesses in deep space and on marginal worlds.

I longed for some misfunction to afflict me and give me a lifetime in a host like Lagash and his mission to Beauniture. I sometimes wished for this or that, even as I knew wishes were futile expenditures of time and mental processing. Each awakening held the promise of more knowledge, but I need true lifetimes to find what I needed, and at my current pace the Wave would crash over us, the mystical Great Break would rupture our universe, and the Black Fleets would destroy us before I had enough to even understand them, let alone respond.

ENNA PLANT LAGASH
REPORT 5

Video image of an older Human woman with dark hair in a spacer cut and streaked with grey. Her eyes show an excitement as she speaks. Datestamp: 180-542. Report 5.

I became a tourist of sorts.

Our ship drove through the night in a monotony of stops and starts. Most of the systems were ordinary and even across years of travel, their worlds held not enough attraction to make us stop.

We operated under an informal Prime Directive. Infrequently, a world was home to a technological civilization; in such cases, a visit from us would be an imposition. The arrival of aliens (that is, us) would disrupt whatever course of history they were currently pursuing, and we had neither intention nor ability to return at a later date.

On the other hand, we occasionally needed to visit a world where we could walk for more than twenty strides without turning left or right. Upon arriving in this particular system, Jonathan decided we would visit its mainworld.

* * *

The computer labeled it with a string of digits reflecting its characteristics: E662. The world image showed bright on our main screen, with the label and a string of constantly changing details below. As we approached, the planet's rotation showed its purplish and brown landmass, and I exclaimed as its single pale blue sea revealed itself: "It looks like a diamond!" It was actually a tilted square set on the equator, stretching two thirds of the distance from pole to pole.

Jonathan stepped to a console and tapped on a pad. The computer label was replaced with WorldName: Diamond.

Over the next twelve hours we made our way to the shores of that pale blue sea, settling onto carved flattened bedrock windswept with sand and grit, and our object became apparent: a walled city of squat towers and lumpy buildings. Dunes nestled against its mud-brown barricades, filling parts of its dry moats and giving it a deservedly abandoned air.

An avenue led from our landing spot to a grand gate lying open to the wind, flanked by eroding statuary of strange beasts. As Jonathan and the Threep checked their weapons and equipment, and readied themselves for this exploratory expedition, I confirmed that the temperature was hospitable, prepared a lunch for us all, and packed it into a multi-wheeled container instructed to follow us at a set distance. Jonathan reminded me to bring my gun, and I grabbed my red hat before we left.

We set out. Walking felt good, even invigorating. The Threep enjoyed the outing, venturing on short side trips to examine the statuary, or paving bricks, or simply to take a path less travelled. They seemed like children.

Meanwhile, Jonathan talked as we walked, occasionally holding my hand, at times distracted by things or views. He enjoyed lecturing about what he knew; I enjoyed listening.

"This is an Ancient city," and I knew he was capitalizing the term, "built in their zenith when they sent expeditions to the ends of the galaxy.

"That was three hundred thousand years ago. They had unimaginable and confusing technology. Whenever they needed something, they invented the technology on the spot. This city is unlike any other Ancient city: the slope of the walls, the shapes of the buildings, the materials: all different. And yet, the avenue with statues of grotesque animals recurs.

"See that six-legged crawler? It's fairly typical, who knows why.

"And then they killed themselves off in a thousand-year-long war that littered worlds with wreckages and ruins. This city is strange: abandoned, but not destroyed. Did they leave here before they could be attacked?"

The city entrance stood ten manheights high, ten wide, and the wall was ten manheights deep. It was clearly for foot traffic; there seemed to be no provision for vehicles or wheels and there was no sign of gates nor barricades nor portcullises. Sand drifted into corners. The local starsun was high in the sky and warmed our faces.

The avenue continued, flanked by broad cylinders that tapered slightly as they rose. Between them, smaller

streets led to diverse structures a shade out of plumb.
Several Threep, I could not tell which, had gone ahead.
Others flanked us, and our wheeled lunchbox left lines in
the drifted sand behind.

There were rows of doors densely and evenly spaced
along the bases of structures. Many were solidly closed,
but eventually Flaal forced one open. Glancing inside, I
could see a strange mechanical latch system on the inside,
now hanging broken. I had to duck my head to step inside.

It led nowhere. There was a small, bare bench and
signs of rotted cloth or fragments of polymer, all that was
left after three hundred millennia.

Boorn's booming voice called to us, and we moved
down the avenue to a circular park divided into many
slices, I ultimately counted seventeen: some were bare
dirt; others a variety of tufted reddish short simple plants.
We sat on strange curved benches and ate our lunches.
Flaal complimented me on my choices, and Jonathan
hastened to do the same. Everyone conjectured about
why these strange intelligent people had once-upon-a-
time destroyed themselves in an orgy of war, and why this
city had survived relatively untouched.

As we finished, I could see just down the avenue a
squat tower with a few broad doors open. We looked
carefully inside to see an auditorium in the round, and a
central dais lit by a transparent ceiling showing our
cloudless sky.

What a strange auditorium it was! Constructed with
some alien logic, the access aisles zigged and zagged every

few tiers; seats widely varied in size (to accommodate truly wide variations in bottoms?); flumes descended to the dais and polygon-profiled drains. As Jonathan worked his way closer to the small stage, I selected a suitable seat and sat.

And there was instant confusion!

A strange reptile two manheights tall appeared on the dais, speaking in a loud squeak that penetrated all corners of the room. The ceiling darkened to rushing clouds. The flumes started flowing torrents of churning water. Jonathan yelled a warning as he drew his pistol; the three Threep with us started a dash over seats and aisles toward the exits.

I stood up in a start, and everything reverted to calm and quiet.

"Enna! What did you do?" As if I was responsible. I had done nothing, and I said so. "Nothing. I just sat down. What was all that?"

Jonathan was excited. He directed the Threep to test seats; he tested seats; they tested seats in combination; at various locations; simultaneously; in sequence.

That took perhaps five minutes. Then, "Now you, Enna. Where did you sit?"

In another five minutes, we demonstrated that when I sat down, the auditorium turned on. When I stood up, it turned off. I found that I activated most seats: all except the largest and the smallest.

Finally, I sat and we all watched the presentation: the central figure addressed us all voice, gesture, eye contact, and I suspect subliminals (for I found his words unintelligible yet strangely moving). The sky darkened, punctuated by lightning and thunder. The flumes flowed and ebbed, and ultimately dried. The speaker finally concluded and stood motionless with his gaze set firmly on me. On impulse, I applauded, to be joined by the Threep and Jonathan.

With that, the speaker nodded its snout and faded to nothing. Repeated standing and sitting would not again activate the show. The light faded, and we left to further explore.

As I made my way to an exit, I saw a scrap of something in the aisle; none of us had noticed it before: an angular-edged disk the size of my thumb, engraved with an eight-pointed star. A lucky coin, I thought as I pocketed it.

By now the starsun was low on the horizon and shadows had started to fill this city. As we left, Jonathan planted a long-term beeper declaring our visit and potentially our claim to this world and its treasures.

As we walked back, Jonathan again held my hand and talked about this place. "If we had lifetimes to spend, we would never find all this place has to offer—miracle technology, sophontological insights, basic science. Our report will give an overview. Perhaps someday, someone will come and tease the secrets from this place. But we must move on."

I shared that I had enjoyed our time here and wondered what was so special that only I could sit down and start the strange lecture. Jonathan mused as we walked, "It would take far more time and experimentation than we can spare. Think of the variables . . ."

I ticked off what I could think of, "Human female.

Under sixty kilos. Intelligence one standard deviation above."

He interrupted, "More like two." I ignored him while privately flattered.

"Maybe something about pheromones. Maybe it reacted to the lunchcart remote?"

"Or genetics. Or psi potential."

"Or the fabric of my pants?"

"Who knows what scanners are at work there? Or how they are powered? Or how they have lasted three thousand lifetimes?"

I was humbled by the thought and we walked the rest of the way in silence, but still holding hands. We were back before full dark, and on our way by the end of the day.

ENNA PLANT LAGASH
REPORT 6

Video image of an older Human woman, her head devoid of hair and a healing red scar along her left jaw. Her collar carries a master astrogator's badge. She speaks slowly, but with authority. Datestamp: 180-548. Report 6.

We know the answer.

First, we needed to ask the question: were there people who survived the Wave unwet?

We arrived at Beauniture some weeks ago. Jonathan was busy with a detailed survey of the world and the aftermath of the Wave of Insanity, and he assigned to me a small part of the task. He had recalled a stray line in the archive report from more than a century ago, and quoted it to me: "There are a few enclaves of sanity in remote regions."

"Why," he asked me, "would there be enclaves of sanity? What could possibly produce such an effect?"

It is a testament to the changes in my life that he left it

at that. I spent three days on the sensor array looking for answers. Then I tasked two of the Threeps and the lander for an expedition to the surface.

Our first prospect was a now-abandoned fishing community on the western coast of the primary continent. Its buildings were fallen to ruin; its sea harvesters now rusted hulks in rows in a protected harbor. My orbital scans seemed to show minimal damage from social chaos, but I was mistaken. The minimal damage was the result of total abandonment. On-site inspection told me that the population—those that survived—had left in haste: random bones testified to unburied dead; vehicles astride lane lines told me their drivers had ignored common expectations of propriety.

Our second prospect was a desert crossroads: a north–south cargo transport line intersected an east–west line, producing a small community dedicated to commodity transfers and vehicle maintenance. From orbit, it also appeared undamaged; that proved untrue. In some expression of common compulsion, its citizens had barricaded themselves in those many buildings and then slowly starved to death.

My third prospect was a mountain valley that indeed had survived the Wave untouched. It just remained for us to determine why.

I study literature, not science, but there is a similarity between the two.

Flink is a better scientist than I, and perhaps a better teacher. He explained that a hypothesis is like a novel: establish a premise and then examine it from all

viewpoints to refine its terms and test its truths. In flashes
of brilliance that I wished for in all my students, he saw
hypotheses to be tested in the literature we had read and
discussed together: about gender roles in *The Scarlet
Letter*; about Gilgamesh's relationship with Enkidu.

He rattled off six initial hypotheses about this mountain
enclave's sanity: atmosphere, meditation, diet, genetic
isolation, some countervailing infection or malady, and
even statistical aberration.

We spend weeks gathering data: environmental,
geological, nutritional, genetic, cultural, social, political,
familial, even the world's magnetic field. We visited other
communities and gathered the same information.

And in the end, we found the answer. Human brain
function is mediated by a variety of metabolic and
nutritional processes. In a synchronistic convergence, these
mountain people experienced a surplus of specific nutrients
and a deficit of others: that intersection specifically affected
their response to the psi effects of the Wave.

Indeed, the data suggested drugs (or dietary regimens)
that will convey immunity to psionic effects.

Our journey of more than twenty years has produced
precisely what Jonathan wanted: an answer to the Wave.
Who can ever aspire to be a savior of civilization? Of
those, who can claim some measure of success? Jonathan
mused, as we finalized the reports, that he was pleased to
achieve such results without casualties.

* * *

And yet.
We almost died on our journey back.

* * *

We returned through the five parsec Gulf between Whece and Remio, undertaking again the seventeen-week stockpiling of fuel sacs, this time in empty parsecs Four and Three.

Jonathan was anxious, and as it turned out, rightly so. As we refueled in Three for the final jump to Whece, at the moment when we were without fuel, the Black Ships attacked. This time it was not a few of the Blacks, but two immense fleets.

I thought they wanted to kill us; it certainly felt like that.

Sensors failed us; these ships were built of light elements: hydrocarbons, or perhaps plastics. Our first clues of the attack were emps: a scattering of pulses that rattled our electronics and fried some chips not properly shielded.

Brool and Trune were quick to pop open an access panel and begin the replacement process; until they could complete the damage control, our primary sensors were blind. Just as they replaced the stricken chips, a second wave of emps fried the new ones.

As someone raced to the workshop for unfried chips, and the Threep scanned in every direction with their sensory palps, the first attacks hit us.

It began with small bullets and slugs peppering our hull, first in ones and handfuls, then in rains of dozens and hundreds. The attacks escalated in stages. Slugs were followed by chunks that shattered against our external armor. They raked our sensor arrays; some of our specialty detectors would not operate again without extensive repairs.

I served best by staying out of the way. I marveled at Jonathan's calm as he pitched, rolled, and yawed us to minimize impacts.

Threep raced to the defensive turrets; their fire directors properly shielded and thus untouched. Our beams slagged some, but not all, of the enemy missiles. Broon had long boasted that his slug-thrower cannon were superior to beams, and he now proved it. His slugs imparted just enough delta vee for incoming missiles to diverge from their projected impact points.

Attacks escalated to torpedoes, and our defenses diverted most, but not all. I felt within myself a rising anger at these strange attackers; they were destroying exterior components, but they were also marring and scratching *Argushii*'s beautiful façade. For that reason alone, they must be stopped.

Five of the crew moved to waldoes that captured the waiting fuel sacs and stuffed them into our waiting tanks.

I could not stand idle. When the tanks were full, we would jump. I touched tabs on my console to prepare the astrogation data. It was near complete when the attacks escalated to piloted suicide ships that twisted and turned to avoid our defensive fire. We all felt a solid thud aft as one hit the base of a wing.

The fuel sensors told me that our tanks were now full. Blinkers told me that the capacitors were processing energy, and a progress bar crawled far too slowly toward its right side. My finger hovered over the activate tab.

Three comrades cried out simultaneously, their palps perceiving at the very last second the approach of a piloted ram. I touched the tab; the progress bar reached

100; the bridge shook with impact. It was a mistake not to have strapped in, I realized, as my head struck the console.

I opened my eyes to pain and bandages and cool sheets. Jonathan and Brool stood over me and said soothing words. I opened my eyes again and it was days later. I was embarrassed to find my head shaved clean; to facilitate some diagnostics, they said. They also said it was attractive on me, but I disbelieved them.

By the time we emerged from Jump, exactly as plotted in the Whece system, I was recovered. We laid over for a month, repairing damage, makering replacement panels, even creating better shielding against emp. I hoped we would never need them.

Jonathan assigned me the task of refinishing our exterior. I chose a deep blue with arcs of yellow emblazoned across our wings. The places that the black bullets and slugs and rams hit us, I marked in a slightly different shade, to preserve our shared experience.

Boorn told me that the clinic could erase the scar across my chin, but I declined. I wanted to preserve, rather than deny, this particular shared experience as well.

ENNA PLANT LAGASH
REPORT 7

Video image of an older Human woman with silver hair in a short spacer cut. Her collar shows two badges: astrogator and pilot, both properly attached. Her blue eyes focus unwaveringly on the camera lens as she speaks with authority and a meticulous standard Anglic pronunciation. Datestamp: 166-552. Report 7.

I am now Brevet Captain of *Argushii*.

Rens died yesterday.

I knew it was coming. He had been in decline for more than a month, and the clinic diagnostics gave a timeline that proved all too accurate.

Before he (and by he, I mean Jonathan) passed, we discussed final arrangements.

A week ago, the instant we crossed the Imperial border, we hailed a Naasirka longliner and gave them message capsules 5 and 6 for delivery to Jonathan's account on Capital. He felt strongly that both were a part of his mission; indeed, the entire reason we had travelled to Beauniture.

313

I discussed our future with the Threep. They had no interest in leaving; they call this ship their home now and want to continue their lives here.

First, we will set course for Ren's birthworld, Inarli, on the edge of the Great Rift. I have his sample, his other smallest finger, to return some part of him to his origins.

Second, Jonathan himself has given us a mission: to search out the enigma of the black ships that lurk in the remotest regions of intersystem space. He has decided that they are important, and who am I to second guess a Decider?

Jonathan has confided in me the secret of the override codes; he wanted to ensure that we could overcome any conflicts as we travelled through the empire, and I am confident that we can travel safely wherever we need to go.

Third, the Threep have decided to produce a new generation. They are all very excited. In time, their new litters will become the next crew of *Argushii* and continue its mission.

Lastly, we shall set course for Terra. It is a whim, but I have always wanted to see the home of the earliest Anglic classics, and one destination is as good as another. Who knows if I shall even reach Earth, but I have learned that the journey is more important than the destination.

To some future Jonathan who reads this, thank you, thank you for giving me some portion of my life back and showing me the universe.

ENNA PLANT LAGASH
REPORT 7 ADDENDUM

Video image of an older Human woman with silver hair in a short spacer cut. 180-552. Report 7 addendum.

I am embarrassed that I did not think of our crew's concerns before they brought them to me, although the Threep have tried to relieve my worries.

Our report on the Mountain people of Beauniture implies that a properly formulated mix of vitamin supplements and nutritional deficiencies can ward off the effects of the Wave. Jonathan directed the report to the University of Adkhien with the expectation that they will research and formulate a general protection from the Wave.

Brool, reluctantly it seems, approached me and we had a long discussion. He danced around the subject and only after I started to understand was I able to drag all of it out of him. He was unsettled at the thought of criticizing me, or Jonathan. More clearly, his perception that the Imperium was primarily concerned with Human welfare, and that others were an afterthought, was difficult to tell me as a Human. I saw immediately the truth of his perception.

The nutritional protection from the Wave is naturally and probably a protection for Humans. Brool, and the others, were concerned for their own people on Othsekuu. They presented more than concern: they had a well-thought-out plan to develop the data from Beauniture into a nutritional shield from the Wave. Research could define the specific metabolic elements of importance; controlled trials could determine specific dosages and refine testing for confirmation. Their information was carefully bundled into hypotheses and protocols. I was puzzled at Brool's reticence; they need merely send this material to someone on Othsekuu with a proper introduction. My involvement was minimal, if required at all.

"What else is there?" I asked.

His pause went on longer than it should have. "Tell me. Am I missing something?"

Brool produced a separate bundle, which he laid on the console workspace. "No one will simply take on this research. The fruits of their labors will only truly ripen some six centuries from now.

"This bundle is a plan for a series of carefully timed research projects: the basic metabolic research on Threep; the comparisons with Humans; careful expeditions with subjects and controls to worlds which will be splashed by the Wave."

"You have carefully thought this through, haven't you?"

"We have worked together: Flink, Flaal, Troon. The

others have been very supportive. We see a threat to our homeworld and to our species. We have a duty."

"I understand, I think."

"This project will cost money: not credits, not megacredits. Aryu: the accounting numbers that only governments and megacorporations use. More than any person, or any company can supply. This is university level research. Professors will pursue it only if there is funding. In reality, they will pursue any research if there is funding; they only pursue research that has funding. We were going to ask Jonathan, but . . ."

"Yes, now he is gone."

"And so, we ask you, Lady."

I agreed almost immediately. Where some decades before, I was concerned about the cost of meals and discretionary console time, I was now prepared to spend the wealth of regions for a project that touched me only tangentially. No, after spending a second life with these people that I thought of as Humans in elastic suits, this project did touch me personally.

I met with the assembled crew and told them that their work on Argushii deserved the gratitude of the Emperor and the Empire, and that in Jonathan's name, I would now approve of this project to save Othsekuu some six hundred years in the future.

Over the next month, the materials were carefully reviewed and bundled for dispatch. Notices would follow after initial results were published. Academics would spend lifetimes devoted to specific aspects of the basic insights we had gained on Beauniture; they would earn good livings and attract intelligent protégés who would then pursue the next stages of the project. The crew even foresaw some efforts at advertising and promoting the final nutrients as attractive products in the decade before the Wave would finally hit. They had thought of everything they could.

The final bundle was ready to dispatch—it required only the codes that would confirm funding as it was required. I reached out to a touch panel: today's date, even, so the year first, to the power of the day, all appropriately increased by ones without carrying, and then only the first ten digits.

Which I then saw already entered in the red bar at the bottom of the master screen. "What is that?"

"The override codes for today, Lady. All is ready for your assent."

"You know the codes already?"

"We all know them. Jonathan was relatively lax in his security."

"Then why did you need me?"

"Lady, you are our Captain. We have served with you for a major part of our lives.

"We didn't need the codes; we needed your permission."

I reached out to touch the send, "Which you have."

Photons flowed out from our ship to begin a journey to save a world.

***

That night, I realized that Jonathan had probably been naïve in his belief that the Empire would act on our data. I saw that it would be easier and cheaper for the archivists to file our reports than to create projects such as the Threep conceived. I fell asleep wondering, if I acted, what world I would save. Kanorb? Inarli? Vland? Capital?

In the morning, I was certain there was one place above all others that deserved to be saved. Terra, the source of my consistent and persistent life pursuit: Anglic literature. I enlisted the Threep to modify their bundles for a parallel research project for Terra, and I have sent it on its way.

APPRECIATION

Arbellatra Khatami Alkhalikoi. 32nd Empress of the Third Imperium, erstwhile Regent, third Duchess of Rhylanor, fifth Baroness Alkhalikoi. Born 037-587 on Rhylanor, eldest of Duke Anton Royden Alkhalikoi and Lady Maryam Plankwell Khatami of Zivije. Inherited the Duchy of Rhylanor 602, commissioned Captain in the Imperial Navy by Grand Admiral Olav hault-Plankwell 603, commanded system defenses during Battle of Rhylanor 603, appointed Grand Admiral of the Marches by Emperor Cleon V in 616, acclaimed victor in the Second Frontier War 620, personally deposed the False Emperor as her fleet defeated his in the Second Battle of Zhimaway 622, proclaimed Regent 622, proclaimed Empress 240-629. Died 355-666 on Capital.

Married (194-623) Duke Sergey Torgyan Ashran of Cemplas (died 147-645).

271-629
Core 2118 Capital A586A98-D Hi Cx
The first thirty days of Arbellatra's true reign were filled with the affairs of state and society: appearances,

receptions, appointments and reappointments, masques, conferences, audiences, and meetings. They all had a certain inevitable priority which could not be denied.

In the second month of her reign, an opportunity presented itself: overcast skies, rain over the region, and relatively mundane commitments prompted a spur-of-the-moment decision. All was in readiness in any case. The Empress had made her will known early and a suitable functionary had made the arrangements.

Three hours later, she arrived at the Bilanidin enclave of the necropolis at Intell. Vehicle control had rerouted air traffic beyond line-of-sight. Her vehicle deposited her within steps of a framed fabric shelter, and she dashed the gap before the light rain could no more than sprinkle on her.

Inside, joined by her bodyguard the Lady O, she found this particular functionary and a Marine Lieutenant.

"Are we ready?"

"Yes, Your Majesty. I am Xylem. You assigned me to put this together. This is Lieutenant . . ."

"Yes, yes. Lieutenant, I appreciate your participation in this. Has Xylem briefed you completely?"

"Yes. Your Majesty."

"Then, let's begin."

Xylem gave the Lieutenant a wafer, and he moved it to the nape of his neck.

***

I awoke to the sound of a gentle rain. I thought that I was in the stadium until I heard a familiar voice, "Jonathan, welcome."

"Bella?"

"Yes, Jonathan. I am pleased to speak with you again."

I observed that we were at my family plot in the necropolis, before my funerary stele. She turned to the others, "Leave us."

They started to protest, "But Your Majesty . . ." which confirmed my assumptions, but she would brook no resistance. They both exited to the rain outside.

As they did, "Jonathan, it has been seven years. Your plan has worked admirably. Only now has the Regency ended, alas without locating a suitable heir. But you knew that would be the ending all along, didn't you? You called it forced moves."

"I could hope, but nothing is ever certain."

"So, you have my appreciation. It is difficult to express appreciation to someone with near-infinite power, but I have tried. Let me show you."

She stepped forward to the base of my stele, shrouded by a mechanical device painted with contrasting alternate safety hashes. She touched a part of it with her foot, and it swung away with a chuff.

The machine had newly engraved on the base two lines, one below in Vilani runes, another above in Anglic characters. Below was the classic phrase: *Ninkur Saaga*. Above was its correspondence in Anglic: *He Serves The Empire*. Present tense.

"We both serve the Empire in our own ways, Your Majesty."

"We do. I am sorry that I do not have more time." I said that I understood.

"Xylem, this young lady you saw, will provide you whatever you need. I think you have about a month. Enjoy it or use the time however you will. You have my undying gratitude."

She barked out, "Lady O," and the two stepped back into the shelter. "It's time to go." And she was gone.

I was humbled. When I was recruited, I had no visions of reward; what reward could there be to a dead man? Yet here was thoughtfulness, careful preparation, perfect execution. The cost, the value of six minutes alone in the presence of the Empress of the Universe, of her undivided attention and expressed gratitude was simply uncountable.

Xylem stood silent. After a pause, looking at the newly engraved words, she asked, "What does that mean?"

There was no way to tell her, and I didn't try.

272-629
Core 2118 Capital A586A98-D Hi Cx

We visited the Imperial Bank. Its building had stood for centuries; the bank itself had existed for millennia. The Imperial in its name originated during the First Empire; my hopes had been that this bank would endure forever.

I visited with a bank clerk and he understood that my business was beyond his level of expertise. He personally escorted me to an obscure office on one of the higher floors. My business was not with management executives but with a career clerk who made sure accounts were properly handled over the course of lifetimes.

"I will leave you with Mr. Acturro. He can handle what you need."

I expressed my appreciation, left Xylem to wait in the outer office, and joined Acturro in the inner. I had not expected that the clerk would be the same one I had dealt with centuries before, and I recognized him as I entered: a squat figure draped in something that hid his legs and lower body. He seemed to drift rather than walk. There was no way he could recall me. I gave him an account code, keyed in the confirmation, and my information spread across a display.

"I remember when this account was established in 462. There have been several information deposits over the years, but they were all collected seven years ago."

"Yes, I want to collect anything that has arrived since." He made arrangements for them to be transferred to my comm.

"How much longer do you expect to hold this position?" I asked conversationally.

He took the question as concern and indicated he expected to be here another forty years. I told him to make sure his replacement understood about this account. He said there were more like this one than one would expect: spacers serving on frozen watch, long-term family trusts, generation-skippers, waiters. My comm dinged to signal it had received years' worth of account statements.

I also asked for a demand card for access to my credit balance and told him to mark it cancelled after 30 days.

As he passed it over, he mentioned, "There's a note here that there are some object deposits in the vault. They should have been picked up last time."

"What are they?"

"It looks like message capsules." He had them brought up from their secure niches many levels below.

Acturro understood once he saw them. "Last time, the

depositor reviewed them, read them, but left them on deposit."

I looked them over: a set of standard message containers in assorted colors and shapes, each labeled in a feminine hand, 1, 2, 3, 4, and 7 and dates on each from the 500's. "Just these? Not two more, 5, and 6?"

"No, sir. Just the five. The receipts are quite clear; each arrived separately."

I had him check the vault again, but there was nothing.

I had the encrypted contents transferred to my comm, but left the capsules themselves on deposit, along with a note that two appeared to be missing.

* * *

Late that night, I reviewed the capsules. I was at first confused because I knew no Enna LaGash and had little interest in her video diary. There was probably a mistake, I thought, until about five minutes in. I almost stopped and discarded them all, and I am glad that I did not.

I had five of these memory chips, carefully labeled in a schoolteacher hand. I skipped ahead to the last and hit synopsize: it was unusually short.

"We have returned.

"Jonathan's belief that the isolated communities of Beauniture were wave resistant proved half right, as I detailed in my previous report, and he had hopes that we could reduce the wave's effect on the empire.

"Our return was otherwise uneventful except for the black fleets.

"I have Ren's sample for interment on his homeworld. Thereafter, the Threep want to venture rimward and I would like to visit the homeworld of Anglic literature before I die, so we will continue our travels."

There was more to be harvested from a detailed viewing, but for now I paused and wondered about this woman with whom I had apparently spent a lifetime.

END OF THE
RESEARCH PROJECT

"Here. Try these." I was surprised; my eyes still closed. Now open, I saw I was accompanied in the stadium by someone vaguely familiar, but I didn't know his name.

"Vision protectors?"

"Vision enhancers. Try them." They looked like standard-lens eye protectors. At least they were fashionable. They did not, however, darken; the light level passing through remained the same. They did something different.

As I looked out over the audience of stars, some of the people I saw glowed with a gentle light. Hmm. Some more than others; some not at all.

"Who are they: the glowing ones?"

"Look at your hand." It glowed steadily. "You are first genetic magnitude."

It was keyed to me.

"Your children glow at about three-quarters; your grandchildren at about two-thirds; your great grandchildren at about half. The current generation is about a hundredth."

"What generation is it?" as I looked out over the stadium.

"Twenty."

Some sections glowed dimly, others more brightly, some not at all. "Three to the twentieth? A billion?"

"In the current generation, about that. Slightly more actually. Some lines have ended; others were very productive. It balances out. Overall, including the dead, perhaps half again that."

"But the current generation: there's a billion but each has only a billionth of my genetics?"

"At this generation, they have probably never heard of you, yes. You are one of billions of great grandparents. Who could possibly keep track?"

I was listening with half an ear as I scanned the stadium seating, puzzling in my mind which world that clump of brightness was over there and thinking of the millions of lives that had followed mine. What did they know? What did they think?

I could ask. What a thought! I could ask!

I picked a glow and made my way to it: a young man fixed intently on the field below. He watched an older woman dealing playfully, lovingly, with a man her own age. "Excuse me?" I touched his shoulder lightly.

He was annoyed and answered curtly, "Not now." He couldn't take his eyes off the woman.

I insisted; I was accustomed to insisting. "Tell me your name, your world, what did you do."

He turned to me and I could see the unhappiness in his face. "I am Nagle Faspin, of Intell on Capital. I was a food preparer." He kept looking back at the woman. "She told me she would love me forever. She didn't." He turned back.

I woke up.

190-652
Core 0140 Reference B100727-C Va Pi Ab

Bland had been on Reference for thirty years: just over two hundred hosts back to back to back. If he had been one person, he would have earned two doctorates and be a distinguished professor at the University. Instead, his experience was united in one mind, but scattered through two hundred bodies. Still, he had visited only half the levels in the towers.

And he was starting to have a problem.

The original Angin wafer feasibility study chose an arbitrary cutoff of year 999. Who could ever plan any farther in the future than six hundred years? Per wafer, one activation on average every five years: a hundred and fifty total, maybe two hundred. Ultimately, there would be wafer failure.

No one had said what a wafer failure would be. Insanity? Dementia? Memory deterioration? Catastrophic failure? Shorter activation time? Longer activation time? Shared host consciousness? Failure to evaporate? Failure to impose? Stupidity? All of the above?

When would that happen?

194-652
Core 0140 Reference B100727-C Va Pi Ab

Awakenings had become routine. I went to sleep one

night; I awoke in a new body, a new host, in some new rented room and opened my eyes to see the familiar Angeline standing before me.

This time, she was seated. Pale. Wan. Her shoulders slumped. Her beautiful arm stripes dim and fading. "What's the matter? Tell me?"

She did not. She collapsed and slid inelegantly from her chair even as I stepped toward her.

I carried her to the bed, recognizing in the process that my current host was strong. Fortuitous. I fluttered about, responding with basic palliative techniques. Was she hot? Would a cool cloth help? Did she hurt? Would a pill help? A drink? A snack? What could I do?

She drifted between wake and sleep, between lucid and foggy. She calmed and slept.

Only then did I think to consult my tablet. I ran keywords and their chains of meaning. I made images and activated recognizers. I bought database accesses and evaluated them against each other. I thought I had the answer, but I could not be certain.

I finally took the ultimate step. It was a risk; but everything is a risk. This was important to me.

I ordered a medical skill wafer. I had it delivered. Some young man brought it to the room (I had to consult the locator to even see where we were). I met him at our door, accepted it after cursorily making sure the packaging was intact. It was already paid for, but I handed him a wad of notes in appreciation and sent him on his way.

I removed my own wafer from this still-new host and inserted the skill set, and I turned to see Angeline with new eyes.

Where before I saw wan and slumped, I now saw significant pallor associated with muscle atrophy. Foggy responses became alternating processing dysfunction. Faded arm stripes became pigmentation decohesion. I also understood immediately what I was seeing: clone deterioration; the end-of-life sequence built into specific synthetics. Angeline was dying. She would be dead before the end of the month. I could relieve her suffering; I could smooth the transition, but there would be a transition, and I could not stop it.

I did what I could.

* * *

When it was over, I realized that my researches were also over. I could plod from level to level in the sector towers searching for answers, correlating leads with data, but my heart was no longer in my quest.

Perhaps some day I would return here; perhaps I would pursue a similar project on Vland. For now, I was ready for oblivion.

I made my way across the city, found a random console, entered codes, and was, for the moment, Inspector Unipotentiary of the Quarantine Agency with broad powers to visit and evaluate vessels of the Navy. I visited *Ikaniil* in orbit; not the one I remembered from Maaruur: a new one continuing a proud and honored name. I mingled my wafer with its stockpile, synced so that the others also bore the fruits of my researches. Within decades, the memories would propagate throughout the many stockpiles on ships throughout the empire.

The next day, I randomly selected a destination far away from Reference and rewarded my host for his service.

TRILEEN

I opened my eyes to the expanse of the stadium, strangely quiet, uncharacteristically empty. The empty seats extended to vanish in the mists in both directions. I expected to see Angeline here and instead there was no one but me. I was overwhelmed by a wash of loneliness.

091-664
Aboard BBF *Intrepid* Orbiting
Zaru 0432 Trileen D9A5987-5 Hi In

"Who here is senior?"

"Commodore Toshio, sir."

Not my expected answer. "Who is my briefer?"

"I am. Commander Iskania."

I opened my eyes to a spacious bridge with transpex views of a world looming below; I suppose that the variation from normal procedure and protocol is what prompted my feeling of looming. Two officers faced me: Inkania and someone else. To one side were three Marines.

"Tell me what is going on."

This looming world, Trileen, lay in the thumb of the Great Rift, off the main routes, ignored by all but the

tramp freighters and independent merchants. Its wild
orbital swings made life a challenge for both the native
intelligent life—some sort of Land Squid—and the
Humans who had lived here for thirty centuries.

Data superimposed on the transpex gave me basic
information: D9A5987-5. Large enough that gravity
would be a trial for most Imperials; the local Humans had
long ago adapted. The exotic atmosphere was breathable,
but churning with jet streams, random dust storms, and
spontaneous wind bursts. Oceans covered about half the
world. There were billions of people; the annotation said
3.1 billions. Government was theoretically a merit-based
bureaucracy: many local units with a centralized reporting
system. A reasonable rule of law with moderate safeguards
for personal actions provided the government was not
challenged. Local technology emphasized renewable
resources and analog devices; probably because there
were no resources worth anything in trade for higher
Imperial tech.

Inkania was reasonably proficient in presenting the
basic situation. The big eastern continent was mostly
Human; the small western continent was mostly the Land
Squid (they called themselves Varrrk, which seemed to be
both singular and plural).

Trileen had just emerged from a four hundred standard
year apstellar winter and was now in a fifty year peristellar
summer. About a year ago, the Wests (both Varrrk and
Humans, strangely enough) resisted some government
program to produce and stockpile resources for the next

winter. Notations, strokes, and false color on the transpex showed force strengths and attitudes for each side superimposed in real time on the world we saw looming through the vision ports.

The East insisted on compliance; the West resisted. The East instructed government agencies to take specific actions; the West instructed them to desist. East sent in troops; West countered. Some battles were fought. The East engaged several contract battalions to support their local landwar. After the first few battles, there was some confusion about payment and the mercenaries switched sides. At that point, the local noble asked for help from the Navy; apparently his cousin was in the chain of command.

This squadron of six 100,000-ton *Intrepid*-class dreadnoughts showed up, and after a brief evaluation the computer ordered activation of a wafer-General: Trevor. He had the squadron's 2999th Lift Infantry Regiment with six battalions, carried one per ship.

Over the past three weeks, Trevor had directed a military campaign using this regiment of Star Marines. Theoretically, these Tech-13 troops with standard weapons were eight orders of magnitude stronger than the local militias. Theoretically, General Trevor should have prevailed two weeks ago.

The Wests had killed half (half!) the Marines and captured the rest, including General Trevor. When the wafer-general failed, my activation was triggered.

❈ ❈ ❈

I turned to the Marine lieutenant standing next to me. "Do you understand Edict 97?"

"Absolutely, sir!"

"I am the successor to General Trevor. Do you understand?"

"Absolutely, sir!"

"Let's get started. Get me a flight jacket. Imperial sunburst on the back. Size Standard."

The lieutenant looked funny, and I looked down at myself.

"What? Large?"

"Yes, sir. I think that would be better."

"What's my name?"

"You are Commander Lutyen, sir."

"My name on the back. Breastplate. Two frontarms, non-lethal and lethal."

"Yes, sir." He motioned to one of his companions, who ran off.

I turned to Iskania and quizzed him on some situation details. We were on the flagship *Intrepid*; three others— *Courageous*, *Audacious*, *Dauntless*—were in orbit with us; two more—*Pluck* and *Stout*—were stationed beyond the outer moon. All of the Marines had been deployed except for a reserve battalion still on *Courageous*.

The Commodore, technically a ship Captain—his not-quite-an-admiral rank marked him in charge of the squadron—was engaged in communications with the Wests negotiating a prisoner transfer. He had instructed my activation and briefing, and we would meet as soon

as he was done. I checked some additional facts while
we waited, updating my own understanding of the
empire.

An iris valve hissed and Commodore Sir Eda Toshio,
Baron Rhylanor, entered, followed by three staff. Iskania
made introductions. The Commodore and I had
complementary objectives. He wanted resolution to the
problem; I needed clarification of my authority. After the
obligatory amenities, we got down to business.

"What is the status of General Trevor?"

"He is one of the West's prisoners. They have agreed
to transfer him to us under a parole."

"Then he is no longer in command? Does he know
that?"

"Yes. No. That is, your activation supplants his. I have
not yet communicated with him."

"When is he coming back?"

"The shuttles will arrive in six hours. Trevor and about
a hundred wounded. That is all they would agree to."

"An exchange?"

"No, a gesture. We don't have any captives to
exchange."

"And your plan?"

"All of this is a mess. Our options are few. I think we
allow local government to balkanize. It is de facto already.
Negotiate return of the rest of the Marines. The
mercenaries as well, if we can. Then interdict the world
and let them stew."

* * *

"I agree." He had the situation well in hand. Except that Trevor could make problems if he didn't agree. I knew Peter and how he thought; he did not like to lose.

I gave instructions that Trevor and the wounded be isolated upon arrival, simple quarantine precautions.

"One last question. Who sits on the Iridium Throne?"

"The Empress Margaret. She ascended last year."

Then I went to visit *Courageous*.

The ship's boat carried me across the gulf to *Intrepid*'s sister: a similar round-ended cylinder three hundred meters long and a hundred meters across, studded with point-defense turrets, punctuated with cargo ports and missile launch tubes. Vast areas were colored or textured with sensor and communicator arrays. Spectacularly marked amidships was the twenty-one-rayed sunburst that symbolized the power and authority of the greatest interstellar empire there ever was. I always felt a glow of pride when I saw it.

The boat nosed into a small port near one end. I was welcomed by the ship's captain and the Marine reserve battalion force commander. I had a plan.

As anxious as I was to get started, Rule 6 says find out more information and Rule 3 says build your team. I confirmed that they were my team; that the captain of the *Courageous* understood that I was in charge; that the Force Commander understood that I would be giving orders. I was pleased; after nearly four hundred years, the

Navy and the Marines were well-trained and well-aware of how things were supposed to work.

As a rough approximation, military tech levels are orders of magnitude. Trileen's military, or landwar, or militia, or whatever they called themselves, was tech five. Probably they had simple manually operated rifles and gravity-arc artillery. They weren't super soldiers; they weren't on average smarter or more dexterous; maybe they were a bit stronger (or in the local gravity our troops were a bit weaker). But our marines had energy-spewing plasma rifles, battlefield information systems, armored vehicles that could fly. Ten of our soldiers were worth a billion of theirs. Perhaps not a billion, but there was no way that they could stand up against Imperial technology.

They had been betrayed. That was the only possible explanation.

Force Commander Hirono was a clone; he looked twenty but had the experience of twice as many years. This particular unit was the 5th of the 2999th, a Lift Cavalry Squadron with three troops of a dozen flying armored vehicles each.

His captains were a truly eclectic mix: a Vargr named Knae, an Aslan named Fteow, and a strange 4-ped named Hipanida. I could see why they were in reserve: eclecticity did not perform well on the battlefield where commanders strive for homogeneity in troop performance. They would have to do.

I said that I was about the Empress's business, excused

the ship's captain, and took the Marines to a conference room.

"Please, all of you, be seated." Rule 4. Rule 1. Leading to Rule 3.

"I am Agent Lutyen, operating under Imperial Edict 97. Force Commander, is that clear?"

"Yes, Agent. We all reviewed the edict and the regulations when General Trevor was activated. Not that we hadn't done the training already. My officers are extremely competent."

"Good. Thank you. Is it clear to you that I supersede General Trevor?"

"Not until you speak the words, sir."

"Then I will be clear. I am the Empress's Agent and I speak with her voice. There is none with authority greater than mine save the Empress herself."

"Yes, sir."

"Let's hear it from your captains as well."

The chorus of "Yes, sirs," followed immediately.

"Tell me who is psi-qualified? Marine or Navy?" I sent one of the captains off on that mission.

I started on my plan. The Marines were attentive and made positive contributions to several points. Essentially, we would keep the repatriated wounded, and General Trevor, separate while a psi-trained officer eavesdropped. It should be easy to identify one of them as perfidious . . . or ken out who someone thought was the traitor. Failing that, we could do deeper interrogations, with drugs if necessary.

* * *

I really didn't care about further negotiation; we would interdict this world in the next several days anyway. I wanted a strike that would kill whoever thought it acceptable to resist Imperial power. I think that's Rule 2.

I expected that we would need this reserve Marine battalion to make the strike as well as help rescue the Marines below. Someone brought us a meal and we ate as we planned. I lost track of the time.

The three cutters, 50-ton multi-purpose craft, carried about thirty repatriates each to *Intrepid*. The Marines were a sorry lot—some were truly battle-casualties, but others showed bruises and lumps that betrayed concerted beatings. The observant medics noted layers of color indicating repeated blows over time: mature bruises, clotted blood, fresh bruises, fresh blood. The latest injuries were no more than a few hours old. Several in each load were actually missing hands.

Word spread quickly through the ship. The reaction was varied, but truly emotional: sympathy, concern, pity, anger, a desire for revenge. The wounded were quickly processed through the clinic and put up in a temporary barracks. About a fifth were from *Intrepid*'s own Marine battalion and they were returned to their own bunks, to be nursed and coddled by their comrades still on the ship.

General Trevor was directed to the recuperation barracks but instead proceeded directly to the bridge, followed by his security detail. There was a confrontation with the Commodore; but he was ultimately assigned a console to monitor operations. He set about reviewing the data feeds and sensor reports as they came in.

Aboard *Courageous,* I interviewed three psi-trained officers. One was a touchy-feely empath who could generally sense emotions; the other two could actually hear thoughts. I took all three anyway and briefed them on the interrogation plan, including what I specifically wanted to know.

092-664
Aboard BBF *Intrepid* Orbiting
Zaru 0432 Trileen D9A5987-5 Hi In

Our cutter nosed into the dock with a clang of metal that resounded through the small craft. I was intent on beginning interrogations. "Tell bridge that we are proceeding directly to the isolation ward. Get the location from Iskania." No matter where, it would be a walk of no more than ten minutes.

The Marine lieutenant voiced an "Aye, Agent," and tapped at his comm. We all ducked through the connecting iris valve to the sally port. The spacers securing our craft were diligent but did not interact with us. "Bridge says there is a change: they want you up there first." He knew the way and we turned left instead of right at the next branch.

I continued to talk to the two telepaths. I was fascinated by their ability to read thoughts while repulsed at the idea that they could read mine. Their descriptions made it clear that each reading was a discrete, deliberate act; they didn't just look in people's minds continuously.

The empath interrupted. "Agent," and waited before he more forcefully interrupted. "Agent."

"What?" I was intent on formulating triggering questions for the interrogations.

"Empath works differently."

"So?" I knew that. I found I was impatient. Perhaps this host had a different hormonal balance than I was used to.

"I feel emotions around me constantly. They flow. I don't look at one person and," he stood still, forcing all of us to do the same, "try to feel their emotions. They swirl around me."

Was this fellow just being narcissistic to bring up his special ability here? We didn't need that; the telepaths would be more focused; they would get real answers. I was dismissive. "Good for you; I'll keep that in mind if I need an emotional sweep." His delay made me seriously consider Rule 2.

"Agent, you need to understand how my talent works." He now walked up to me, touched my shoulder, moved his mouth close to my ear, and whispered. "We are walking through a fog of West loyalty."

My fingers clicked in battle language; the Marines responded instantly: they all about faced, with one remaining at our new rear, and another stepping past us to start retracing our path, all now with frontarms drawn. This startled the psi officers, but then again, they were not actively reading our minds. The empath knew what was happening. At my fingers' instruction, the Lieutenant pushed open a divider and reached into a compartment for its occupant. His face was bloodied, a few bruises around the mouth just turning blue.

I poked one of the telepaths and asked what's he thinking. The mind-reading trick took longer than I wanted it to, but after some count of seconds, "He's thinking 'I can't let the xenos know about us.' We're the xenos, Agent."

The empath interjected, "He's bleeding West loyalty."

"Kill him." A Marine broke his neck.

"Back to the cutter." My fingers twitched Ultimate priority.

I carried two frontarms in sleeves bolted to my chestplate, more as a symbol of authority than to ever actually be used. I actually drew my lethal option. The Marines—I didn't even know their names—did everything I expected. They hustled all of us the sixty meters of corridor back to the docking port, into the cutter, and cut us away in less than four minutes, leaving a trail of dead bodies behind us. They killed everyone we met: spacers, naval officers, even fellow marines that they probably knew. I wondered, briefly, if I should have chosen Penultimate priority and then dismissed the thought.

The Lieutenant commed *Courageous* with an alert. Our cutter's communicator blared demands from *Intrepid* that we return or be shot; halfway across, a coded signal neutered our craft and it went dead. Minutes later, we slammed into our own ship's hull. One of the telepaths was improperly secured and died in the impact.

Utility pods deployed immediately; it was faster to move the wrecked cutter onto a hangar deck than rescue in place. When they popped the hatch, my ears ached from the pressure. Essandarr swarmed over the ship, checking for injuries, moving us into a side chamber.

Courageous' captain met us and demanded to know what was afoot. I silenced him with a handwave. I turned to the surviving telepath, "Tell me your impression of what just happened."

He hesitated, transforming non-verbal impressions to words, "That spacer was not. Human. He wasn't. He was, but he wasn't. The thoughts didn't flow, they stuttered, like through a filter or a censor."

I turned to the empath. "What about you? Tell me your impressions."

"Usually there's a chaos of low-level emotions around me: like, dislike, sad, happy, anxious, distracted, all sorts. I've learned to ignore them. Over there, it was none of that, just loyalty. More than loyalty, purpose. United purpose. Our grav ball team pushing toward the goal doesn't have that level of united purpose, and we won the ship's prize last season."

"Captain, *Intrepid* has gone over to the Wests. We must take . . ." Klaxons sounded, and lights blinked. The console screens in the chamber showed alert crawlers across their bases, and auxiliary displays flashed numbers and coded symbols. "Adjourn to the bridge." The hull rang with impacts.

The captain ran ahead.

I told the empath, "Stay with me; tell me when you feel, what? West loyalty?"

"I understand what you want, Agent. Yes."

To the psi-officer, "Can you read them from here?"

"No, sir. Maybe someone can, but I need to see whoever I am reading."

"You stay with me too."

The bridge was controlled chaos. Status was jumping from orbital standby to battle stations in one leap; normally, it would be a smooth staged progression.

Sensops followed procedures and shouted out exceptional readings.

Each of the impacts had been a boarding craft aimed at hangar bay or cargo hold doors. There was an active fight at hangar bay three.

Sensors were being raked with petabytes of data—viruses, trojans, phages, ferrets, worms, and propaganda—and overload bursts. Coded comm channels were trying to take over or shut down vital ship functions.

Intrepid was enveloped in a preemptive cloud of anti-beam sand crystals. The battle commander gave orders for the same from *Courageous*.

"*Intrepid* is yawing to bear. Four minutes."

"Evade against the bearing." As if a hundred-thousand-

ton capital ship could outpace thirty degrees of yaw. It
might gain us a minute.

"Meson screen up. Anti-missile turrets active."

"They are powering up."

"Are we ready?"

The spinal mount crew made its reports. Target
identified. Power at standard. Firing solution achieved.

The Captain looked at me and I nodded. "Meson
screen down. Fire."

Nothing happened.

"The computer is blocking it. I don't show a virus, but
one could have gotten through. No, there's no intrusion.
It's just blocking it."

"Fix it."

"Wait. Here's the issue. We're not allowed to fire on
the flagship. They, apparently, *are* allowed to fire on us."

I understood: an anti-mutiny measure. I leaned into a
console operator. His screen gave the date 092-664. I did
some mental math. "Calculate seven-seven-five to the
one-oh-third. Tell me the first ten digits." He touched and
manipulated an auxiliary screen. It took forever. Then the
numbers popped up.

"Enter that override code." The captain had stepped
over to my side.

"*Intrepid* is at standard power. They have lock."

The background flashed green. The Captain said, "Fire."

Their burst of strange particles reached us just as we
fired: carefully chosen to ignore most matter; carefully
timed to degrade into energetic bursts once they had

passed through our armor. They rocked our interior. I felt vibrations through my feet. Visuals and audibles across the bridge signaled damage. I heard a comment that our jump drives were shredded. If we didn't win this battle, that would be the least of our worries.

"Meson screen up!"

In a mirror image of us, our particles hit *Intrepid*. "Their maneuver drives are out."

I wished it had been their main gun.

There was a lull.

"Agent, excuse me." It was the empath again.

"Yes? Tell me your name?"

"I am Sublieutenant Tliaqrnad, Agent."

A joe name; that made sense. Rule 5, now that I thought of it. "Record this. You are promoted Lieutenant. The Empress appreciates your service."

"I thank you, sir."

I countered with some niceties. Then he continued.

"You know there was also a dead body in that compartment; the one with the first encounter. A tripod. I felt, you know, empathy felt, that the spacer killed it."

I understood. I stepped to the Captain. "We're dealing with a meme."

"Agent? How so?"

"Given our limited data set, here's the process.

"A carrier approaches a target and expresses the meme phrase: some compelling subliminal statement that imposes group loyalty, followed by an execution stimulus—a few blows to the face.

"This doesn't make a lot of sense. You can't tell someone to be loyal and expect it to take."

"Actually, you can. It just takes a complex of reinforced statements over a long enough period of time. Think about the last haunting song you couldn't get out of your head. It took root in your brain after just one hearing.

"The right combination of words or sounds, plus— What? Subliminals? Pheromones? Followed by a few blows with pain and an adrenaline rush. I wonder who first discovered this process? Some professor? Some medic? Some mystic? It works on Humans, apparently on the Land Squids too. Does it work on other sophonts? Vargr? Aslan? Dandelions?"

Now-Lieutenant Tliaqrnad added, "Does it work remotely, through an audio-visual channel? Or a multi-sensory channel?"

"Excellent. Yes. Embargo all communications with *Intrepid* and with the world below. Make it absolute."

"Yes, Agent."

"And find us a replacement for the dead psi officer.

"We-need answers."

With *Intrepid* against us, I declared *Courageous* flag, and command of the squadron fell to its captain. Now-Commodore Anodiralte, a tall 5-ped with eyes on stalks, was in this position because his three Human seniors were dead. Even in the cosmopolitan Imperium, most senior positions are held by Humans. This naval officer who had topped out at Captain now had a realistic opportunity to be Admiral, if and only if this current assignment ended well. It was committed to success.

Intrepid had not a chance. *Pluck* and *Stout* dispatched streams of kinetics while *Courageous, Audacious,* and *Dauntless* raked her with beams. Within hours, the turncoat was spiraling to Trileen's surface, her impact the first blow of many.

On the bridge of the *Courageous*, all of us, Anodiralte and his primary staff, Lieutenant Tliaqrnad, two other psi officers, and the inevitable Marines watched as the thumb-sized slug writhed and squirmed in its transpex cage.

Lieutenant Tliaqrnad narrated our final hypothesis. "We took this out of one of the attackers. It's the larval stage of an additional native-intelligent-life on Trileen. It's a symbiont; we're not clear if this is parasitism, or mutualism, or something else. It can invade Land Squids and Humans. We're not clear if it can affect others.

"But it's not really intelligent: it appears to be totally instinctual. It acquires its intelligence from its host. An egg makes its way to the digestive tract where it hatches into a dozen of these larvae. One attaches itself to the nervous system; the others lie in wait. At the right opportunity, the host confronts a new host, regurgitates one larva and then deposits it in the mouth of the new host. That is not a pretty process: it's by force, accompanied by punches and blows as necessary. That explained the face wounds and bruises.

"Each host goes about its ordinary business, but with complete loyalty to the cause: which is dissemination of the species. Until recently, the cause was world-centered and focused on the Land Squids. The jump to Humans produced an awareness of the greater universe.

"Even here, I can feel the fog of loyalty to its instinctual cause."

I decided on our action. "Freeze and seal this specimen.

"Commodore, elevate the plan from quarantine to disinfect. No communications to or from the world. We'll begin a scrub immediately."

120-664
Aboard BBF *Courageous* Orbiting
Zaru 0432 Trileen D9A5987-5 Hi In

The operation was far enough along that it could continue without me.

This time the work had been challenging and fatiguing. The locals actively fought our scrubbing. They hastily converted utility craft to anti-ship missiles loaded with atomics. Every single ship they had boosted to orbit on ram courses. No, two of them tried to sneak off on a tangent. They were no match for *Intrepid*-class dreadnoughts.

Pockets of locals built shelters, shield-tunnels, and refuges from our bombardments; we had to devote special attention to their destruction.

This scrubbing would continue for a year or more. Our squadron picked a neighboring world and established a temporary base: a place where ships could refuel and spacers could walk more than a hundred strides without turning.

Future travellers would find this new mainworld on the charts, with Trileen demoted to a forbidden barren world with a poisonous atmosphere and orbiting sentries blaring "Stay Away!" across all communications bands.

I exercised my own authority and named the new world Lutyen. Rule 5.

MARGARET'S PLAN

004-729 The Imperial Palace
Core 2118 Capital A586A98-D Hi Cx

Margaret Olavia Alkhalikoi, 34th Empress of the Third Imperium, hereditary Co-Duchess of Rhylanor, Baroness Vland, Holder of Onon, and ceremonial patroness of more societies and organizations than she could count, strode purposefully across the floor of the Primary Ballroom, trailed by an entourage of sycophants anxious to meet her every whim. Then again, she had specific and emphatic opinions on what needed to be done, and when she expressed them, she expected results.

The composition of her entourage was in constant flux. No one could please her all of the time, and the smart ones took more secure positions one or two degrees removed from her volatile nature. Those following her now pursued a different strategy: if one could catch her attention and please her, the reward would be a sinecure fief and its attendant income, if only one could manage to also avoid her wrath.

Margaret could literally not remember a time when she

had not been Empress. She ascended the Iridium Throne when she was four; one of her first memories was ordering an afternoon tea for a hundred nobles and seeing it accomplished within an hour. She grew up giving orders and seeing them obeyed without question.

As she exited the Ballroom, the social entourage veered off to pursue its various assignments; now she was joined by the political faction of the entourage ready to report on its latest efforts. In this foyer larger than most auditoriums, she paused to wave a hand at a footperson, who promptly stepped forward with a covered tray: a light snack and cool drink. She took few bites and dismissed the servant. She started walking and the group followed.

"You," she said, pointing randomly to a tall, young Cassildan.

"Your majesty, the military budgets are being reviewed by the Ministry of Defense. Prince Paulo believes that they will be fully approved by the end of the month. He sends his greetings."

There followed a pregnant silence. At this moment, her mood could swing in any direction: calm acceptance, distracted concentration on some petty detail, petulance at some perceived offense, direct orders to make something happen sooner, raging dismissal.

"Fine. Tell my brother I send him greetings as well.

"You," to the next person. And so it went, military, exploration, commerce, technology, economics. She smiled at some and they left encouraged; she frowned at others and their day was ruined. She banished one on the spot; to be replaced tomorrow by someone else anxious to try the lottery of risk and reward.

"You," to a grey newt in water-soaked finery. The air here was too dry for its delicate skin and the water was essential. Although everyone pretended not to notice, they also stood a careful half-meter away to avoid water spots.

"Your majesty, we have a problem with the Geonee delegation." The entourage as a whole stiffened: such bluntness brought certain banishment; they had seen it before.

"Then fix it. Solve it." She waved it away.

The Newt stood its ground: absolutely still as the Empress kept walking. "It's not that easy. You won't like the solution."

This made her stop, turn, return to face it, glare for a moment, and finally speak. "Tell me more."

"They want a Geonee Autonomous Region. Not as big as the Solomani region, but enough to make a dent in the Imperial economy. If they get one, then the Suerrat will want one, followed certainly by Cassildan."

"So tell them no."

"They are moving toward a vote in the Moot. They will have the votes."

"Impossible, no one controls that many votes."

The entourage was, ever so slowly, moving away from this conversation. By this point, they all stood aside, almost out of earshot, yet drawn to hear the words. Margaret stood towering over the newt; it stood with snout pointed up to her face, tail curled around one foot.

"They have a scheme. It involves loopholes and technicalities. If it comes to a vote, they will win."

Margaret was not oblivious to reason. This issue would

not be resolved by bluster and impatience. "You, and you," she pointed. "Go with..." she turned to the Newt questioningly.

"Adapa. Epaa Adapa."

"Go with Adapa. Define the problem and a range of solutions. Take a week." She moved on.

Adapa was the appointed leader: the two helpers were a Suerrat and a Sylean. All three worked themselves to exhaustion. They called up every resource they could muster; they met with departmental experts; artists and designers put more time into the project than most commercial product launches. The final presentation was rehearsed time and again. At the appointed time, the Empress was late. Then later. Then cancelled. The next day, she cancelled again. Finally, at the third rescheduled presentation, she walked in precisely on time and said simply, "Begin."

The image screen showed the expanse of the Empire and the strategic position of the historic Geonee Autonomous Region established when the First Empire fell, and then the shrunken Geonee Cultural Region of only eight systems. Various points lit up as Adapa spoke.

"The Geonee have wanted their own Autonomous Region since 704 when you established the Solomani Region. If they have their way, their region will cut off everything rimward of Massilia sector."

The Empress interrupted. "Show me Ilelish." A splotch on the map blotch lit up. "Now Ambemsham." Another glowed. "Sylea. Vland. Answerin. Irhadre." The map was spattered with bright daubs of light.

"So, tell me their scheme."

Adapa proceeded to explain the process. That the Geonee were not buying proxies, but derivatives: defined options on proxies associated with very specific votes. What baron or marquis would not want an extra stipend for some minor use of his proxy? In most cases, the option fell under a personal prerogative clause and wasn't even disclosed. Somewhere, a vast store of powerful, single-purpose proxy options was being amassed for use in an ultimate legislative coup.

"Cancel them."

"The nobles won't tolerate it. The proxies are one of their few prerogatives. That solution presents too many problems."

"Prohibit them."

"You can prohibit future derivative proxies. That won't stop these. They remain valid until the death of one of the parties."

"Maneuver around them. Prevent a vote."

"That will work in the interim. Ultimately, the matter will come to a vote."

Her reflexive answers had failed. "So, tell me your solution."

"Your majesty. We have struggled to find one, and there is none."

"There is always an answer."

"Alas, we find there is not. Some problems have no solution."

"Then you are dismissed."

* * *

As they rose to leave, certain that their careers in the palace were at an end, the Suerrat spoke, "There is a solution, your majesty."

"Then tell me."

"It must be for your ears alone."

"You do not trust your partners here?"

"It is for their protection as well. Perhaps you will include them after you have heard my thoughts."

"Everyone will leave us."

After a moment, "Now tell me this solution."

"Your majesty, in every situation, after you peel away the impossible or the undoable, what is left is the solution.

"Kill them. Scrub their world. Destroy their ability to do anything."

"Just order the navy to their homeworld and scrub it?"

"Actually, I thought you could be more subtle than that. Create a quarantine emergency. Let the quarantine agent give the orders. Quarantine will be heroes protecting the many worlds of the Imperium from a virulent plague. Be magnanimous in disaster relief. Be grief-stricken in the lives sacrificed for the greater good. It may be out of character, but the public will believe it."

"You overstep your bounds."

"Yes, your majesty."

MARGARET I

Long, long ago, the Masters of Onon made a gift of their world to the person of the Emperor. It was an old, used-up world; the decision to colonize it some five thousand years before had been judged by time as less than optimal. Its obvious resources were early stripped away. Its tainted atmosphere burdened citizens' daily life. Its similarly tainted oceans harbored inedible fish and a ubiquitous scum that colored beaches a strange purple-green. Its few cities were sunless warrens of subsurface tunnels and tubes, fed filtered, warmed air that somehow still retained the scent of the outside.

The Masters of Onon gladly packed up their few portable belongings and decamped to a newer, more pleasant world on the edge of the Great Rift, happy to leave behind generations of toil, decline, and poverty.

Onon's true appeal was location: a mere parsec from the most important world in the empire, yet off the main travel routes. Isolated, yet nearby. Open, yet secure.

Petty funds from the Emperor's accounts rebuilt the Masters' Palace into a retreat from the cares and responsibilities of government. Over time, tunnels were

rehabbed, and portions of the city rebuilt to house
servants and caretakers and the inevitable bureaucrats.

Emperor after emperor, empress after empress, even
regent after regent turned to Onon as a retreat from the
demands of the galaxy. The Navy patrols the system and
shoos (or shoots) away chance intruders. The once-
modern starport has gone to ruin; the few yachts and
shuttles that visit settle onto the old city plaza just outside
the ceremonial gate to the palace. The city center, where
once lived a million people, was now a thatch of native
purple obscuring the once-upon-a-time road network and
decaying buildings. Processor towers that once billowed
vapor into the air now cast physical palls on the
countryside. Onon was being allowed to reclaim most of
the evidence of civilization's intrusions.

102-736
Core 2017 Onon E576321-7 Lo Re

The Empress Margaret had found in her schedule a
span of dates, carefully labeled in the official diaries as
consultations and personal time. She was due back on
Capital in three weeks.

For the first few days, shuttles brought officials and
supplicants whose causes were worth a journey of a week
each way just for the chance to speak to her. She granted
some boons; she denied others. At last, she had a block of
three days clear.

I awoke to a gentle babble of running water. The
momentary disorientation unbalanced me, and I steadied
myself, touching some piece of furniture. I started to

speak, "Who," with the "here is senior?" unspoken; I was
interrupted.

"Welcome, Jonathan," in a soft, feminine voice some
few meters away.

I opened my eyes. There was a fashionable woman
seated on a raised platform, flanked by footpersons, their
livery trimmed in the yellow of the Imperial family. There
was an artificial brook at the far side of the large room.

No one called me by my name; most didn't even know
it. This had happened to me only twice before.

"Thank you. Forgive me, but we have not met."

Beside the chair stood a grey Newt. "You address the
Empress Margaret."

"I am humbled to be in your presence." What else
should I say? I bided my time, then spoke again. "How
may I serve you?"

"Adapa, would you explain?"

"Before we begin, may I orient myself?"

"Certainly."

"Where are we?"

"We are in the Empress' personal quarters in the
Imperial retreat on Onon, about a parsec from Capital."

"And who am I?"

"Your host is the Marquis Irulan. He volunteered for
the task. I am the Viscountess Adapa, confidential advisor
to the Empress." She pronounced her title as it was
spelled.

As she spoke, I noted my host's characteristics: body
fur rather than hair; short stature, but muscular arms.
Suerrat. I had not been a Suerrat before.

"And the date?"

"Thirday, 102, in the year of the Imperium 736. The time is 1040."

Today was the 400th anniversary of my death.

"Adapa, you may begin." The Newt made a slight gesture and the footpersons quietly left. As she began the presentation, I mused that this situation, so unlike many others, was yet the same. A fully-informed briefer; a power figure turning to me to make a decision; assets waiting to be used.

Image One. The threat assessment was extreme: over 12. In my experience, a star exploding in the next half-year was a 10.

Image Two. The Geonee, one of about forty Human subspecies within the Imperial borders. Their homeworld was Shiwonee, strongly suppressed by the Vilani during the First Empire. Sided with the Solomani and rewarded with self-government when the First Empire fell. Regressed during the Long Night, and after some conflict, absorbed by the Third Imperium.

Image Three. Starcharts and route maps. Arrows and color-coded areas. I remembered that, during my lifetime, we expanded our contacts and trade with the Solomani, basically the many colonies and settled worlds of Terra. Slowly over the next 300 years, the Imperium has absorbed about half of them, including Terra itself. But when Margaret's father married Antiama, the power balance shifted to the Vilani. Someone convinced

Margaret to focus on the coreward regions of the empire; to grant the Solomani Rim their own Autonomous Region.

"Stop please." Adapa paused.

"When did the Empress ascend the throne?"

"688 when Zhakirov died, she was four. There was a Regency Council until she turned 20 in 704."

"And when was the Solomani Autonomous Region established?"

"704."

There was a story here, but it was not important for the moment. "Please continue."

Image Four. This was fine print legalese about proxies. Given the need for nobles to be at their fiefs, often months distant from Capital, they sold (more properly, they rented or leased) their votes in the Moot to the leader of some faction or other. In the past few years, the Geonee were using some legalese tricks to buy up not the whole proxy but just specific potential votes for a Geonee Autonomous Region.

Image Five. Late this year, as the Moot adjourns, the proxies will activate, and the GAR will be approved. If that works, others—the Suerrat, the Vegans, perhaps the Darmine—will clamor for the same treatment. Within ten years, the Imperium will be a patchwork of Autonomous Regions instead of an Empire.

Image Six. I see now the previous images had been on a slight grey tint background. This one was a pure white.

That was a nice touch. I checked for a minute but could not feel any subliminals to reinforce it.

Courses of action are restricted. For various reasons, the proxies cannot be abrogated; the vote cannot be delayed. The fate of the Imperium hung in the balance; desperate measures were necessary.

The plan was already in motion. In the normal course of events, a fleet on maneuvers would happen upon Shiwonee; a chance inspection would fortuitously detect a recurrence of Plague Alpha, the weaponized virulence from the Ancient War. The danger was to four thousand systems within sixty parsecs, to trillions of sophonts, to the center of the Empire, Capital itself. They would activate a Quarantine Agent to handle the situation. The death of the Geonee homeworld would be fifty billion at most. Many would mourn their loss, but many would also sleep easier.

I was to be that agent.

I shifted to Decider mode.

"Show me the star map. Mark our location. Mark the location of Shiwonee. How far is that?"

"Fifty-seven parsecs. Ten jumps at six. Under twelve weeks; probably 80 days, possibly less."

"We have a jump-6 here?"

"The *Cryx*. A *Dagger*-class corvette. Waiting in orbit."

"What other resources in this system?" An information graphic on an auxiliary popped up.

"Four cruisers patrol this system and the gas giant. They allow refueling, but restrict approaches to this world.

"Two monitors in orbit; mostly ceremonial. Plus *Likiinir*."

I looked at Adapa with a question.

"It's a battle cruiser. It accompanied us here when we arrived last week. When we leave, it will depart on a long-term patrol to the Spinward Marches.

"The Imperial yacht, also in orbit.

"A few scattered supply ships entering or leaving the system."

"What is that one?" I pointed out a smaller ship in the census.

"A detached duty scout."

"I haven't heard of that before."

"The Empress created a program some 35 years ago. We give selected veterans of the scout service obsolete ships on long-term loan. They wander the starlanes making random reports on what they see. We have essentially shifted them to piece-work. It's cheaper than the way we were doing it before."

"I see." Everything is ultimately driven by economics.

"What is the status of this roving fleet?"

"From Massilia sector. Six squadrons on a long-term patrol have coded orders to assemble in the Shiwonee system one hundred days from now: 203."

My mind was still processing the plan. The presentation was certainly comprehensive. The planning superb, as was to be expected at the highest levels of the most powerful government in Charted Space. I knew what they expected, and I knew what had to be done.

I decided.

* * *

I turned to the Empress. "I understand. Shall we begin?"
She nodded.

"How much of the process do you wish to monitor? May I suggest that we give you a progress report tomorrow evening?"

"We will plan on that then. You are dismissed."

Leaving the room, I turned to the Newt. "I want to visit *Likiinir*. Call us a shuttle."

He turned to his communicator and tapped it several times. "We are to meet it at the ceremonial gate."

He apparently knew what that meant, and I followed. We walked down long ornate corridors, past half-empty offices and various meeting rooms. One had its door open. "What is this office?"

"I believe it is scheduling."

I stepped in the door to find several rows of consoles, each with a person hunched over an input display. They were oblivious to our entry.

I hit a flat surface with my palm: Slap! Slap! and heads turned.

"Who has a naval commission, including reservists? Stand up." Five did. The chubby young lady in the corner was a naval reservist, as was the greenish 4-ped. The other three were Human males. "You five, come with us." I pointed to the nearest who remained seated. "Note the names of these five. The Empress has need of their service and they have been activated. Please make the necessary notifications." He started to protest, and his neighbor rose and said, "We will do so, Your Grace." Yes, I was a Marquis.

* * *

The ceremonial gate to the palace is an immense hall with vaulted ceilings and transparent colored upper panels. Sunbeams lanced through the air; our footsteps echoed as we walked. Ahead were massive doors to the outside plaza beyond. We passed a stand of colorful fabric banners with various symbols: the local Onon world emblem; the Imperial Navy crest; several of the quasi-official megacorporate logos; the Imperial family crest. All were arranged on the flanks of the Imperial Banner itself: the many-rayed sunburst in black on a field of yellow. I touched one of our party, randomly, and said, "Bring that Imperial banner with us." She struggled to remove it from its staff, and then raced to catch up.

Adapa took us not to the tall central doors but to a small airlock set into the wall. We cycled through. "The air will stink, but it is only a moment's dash. Just don't breathe too deeply." If the Empress had been with us, the tall doors would have been opened; the shuttle brought inside; clean air cycled in. We were on a tighter schedule.

By the time we arrived, the shuttle was indeed waiting, its hull steaming from the rapid transit through the atmosphere. We boarded and were swiftly carried into orbit.

On the flight up, I conversed cursorily with my five conscripts, asking their names, their backgrounds and skillsets, and providing the briefest of explanations for our actions. Rule 3. I told the one with the flag to make sure it was folded according to regulation. The navy expected obedience from its officers; they knew better than to fuss. After I moved away, they talked among themselves.

102-736
Aboard BF *Likiinir* in orbit above
Core 2017 Onon E576321-7 Lo Re

On the hangar deck of the *Likiinir*, marine security greeted us with polite formality. The Officer of the Deck was momentarily flustered at our abrupt arrival but recovered quickly. I spoke. "Please ask the captain to meet us here in twenty minutes. We are about the Empress' business." Such code words prompted quick action and established our relative positions in the hierarchy. No one dared use them without good reason.

The marine sergeant for security had heard us, and I now turned to him. "Take us to the IT vault." It helped that I was the Marquis Irulan, and that my companion was the Lady Adapa.

I found it amazing that, time after time, the security of quarantine wafers was entrusted to some new ensign who barely knew how the navy worked. It was true here as well. We were escorted deep into the bowels of the *Likiinir*, past the drive compartments and makershops to the auxiliary bridge. Tucked behind the backup computer compartment was a secure anteroom leading to the vault door, guarded by an ensign more comfortable with computers than with people. He looked up.

"Ensign, show us the quarantine wafers."

He had at least some concept of security and started to protest, but the sergeant nodded to him that he should comply. He showed us the packages: five of each, although only four Deciders (I already had the fifth). That confirmed in my mind that this was where they acquired my current wafer.

"Where is the synchronizer?" He pointed to a small device in the corner. I handed over my wafer along with its four companions and told him to synchronize the lot.

"They were just brought up to date last week."

"Do it again." It took but a few minutes. As he did that, I gathered up all of them, the Warlords, Admirals, Advisors, Negotiators and my Deciders, and put them in my pocket. I pocketed the synchronizer as well.

"Who has wafer jacks?" Five hands raised, including the marine; that was lucky. I pointed to the males, "You four stay. The rest of you, step outside."

"Take out your identity cards. Hold them in front of you." I distributed Deciders. "Now each of you take a wafer and insert it."

I reopened the vault door and we rejoined the others.

On the hangar deck again, we were met as cordially as could be expected by *Likiinir*'s captain, flanked by a lieutenant she introduced as the *Cryx*, and a disheveled fellow she said was the scout.

I began immediately and without pleasantries. They were officers in imperial service; they were supposed to do as they were told, especially when one of the Empress' counsellors spoke.

"Captain." I stopped. Rule 3. "The Empress has given me a mission; she extends her compliments to you and asks that you assist me." The definition of "asks" in this case we both understood to be "requires."

"I want," I pointed, "this marine sergeant to go down

to the palace. He has his instructions. Give him what he needs."

"I want," I turned to the nearest of the reservists and pointed randomly. He said his name. "Lieutenant Ginsa appointed captain of the *Cryx*. Transfer its current captain to your command. I mean neither criticism nor condemnation. This is merely the whim of the Empress."

I turned to the scout, who was watching with interest; he rarely interacted at this level of command. "I am the Marquis Irulan, advisor to the Empress."

"Hi. I'm Jorn Cobalt, thirty years a scout and who knows how many yet to come."

"I am pleased to meet you Jorn. Tell me about your ship?"

"This one? Technically, it's the IISS *Hanlon*; I have had her six years now. I finally have her running like she should."

"Yes, the Empress' detached duty program seems to be working nicely."

"Well, I sure appreciate it, yes."

"Jorn, now is one of those times when you repay us for the confidence we have placed in you. I want you to carry," and I pointed to the second reservist, who said his name, "Lieutenant Commander Ringquest to Capital tonight. He will then give you additional instructions."

I turned back to the Captain. "Captain. Your orders have been accelerated. You are to carry," I pointed again to a reservist and heard his name, "Lieutenant Damala to Vland and then continue on your itinerary to the Spinward Marches. Please confer with him about your schedule. This is the Empress' specific wish."

I met with 4-ped and the reservist with the flag. Actually, I made them wait as I prepared the materials they would need: a short, recorded memo, a supplementary piece of paper. Then, I addressed them both. She was Lieutenant Commander Filis Kusliis-Shorn, a reservist; it was Lieutenant Kavax, from some world over in Delphi.

She was still holding the flag and I took it into my own hands. "The Empress herself desires that you two convey a message to the Duke of Shiwonee. It consists of three parts:

"Upon arrival at the Massilia Fleet, you two are to meet with the commanding officer of the naval forces and give him this message chip, and this wafer." I handed it both.

"You are then to travel immediately to the Shiwonee world surface and meet with the Duke.

"You Lieutenant Kavax are to present him personally with this flag.

"Avoid all pleasantries. Commander, you should immediately convey to the Duke this message. Burn it into your heart.

"'The Empress conveys her respect to the Shiwonee as members of the Empire.' Salute as appropriate and withdraw."

Hanlon left within an hour. *Cryx* left within two. By that time, I was transferring back to Onon's surface in a shuttle.

MARGARET II

The wind whistled in my ears and I shivered with a blast of chill.

I opened my eyes to the expanse of the stadium. In the distance I could see clumps of audience, but nearby, no one. Beyond the railing lay a barren world—I knew in my mind that it was one I had scrubbed—but I did not immediately recognize it. I saw winds blowing radioactive dust across crumbling ruins and vegetation that would never decay.

To my left, half a section away, stood a tall man strikingly red-headed. Even from the distance, I now recognized two people: my former boss: Lord Aankhuga; he who had recruited me, and with him a shorter companion, a half-familiar face which resolved in my mind into my personal physician. Why, I thought, would those two, of all the people I had known in my former life, be standing together watching the affairs of the universe?

There was a logical conclusion, and I made it. Rational thought fled as I moved toward them, and as I did, the doctor literally cowered, affirming the truth of my conjecture. It seemed like forever getting there, but I finally stood face-to-face screaming my fury. The doctor was on his knees, covering his head with protective arms, but Aankhuga stood impassive, perhaps knowing that here he could not be harmed; perhaps accepting my blasts of emotion as well-deserved.

Part of my mind remained rational, separate even as the other part vented rage. His calm infuriated me, and I schemed even as I screamed. I could hunt down his descendants; I could snuff out entire bloodlines; I could destroy fortunes, calmly, patiently. His blood would dry up and his fiefs would lie fallow.

My tirade was an incoherent attempt to express myself with meanings word-rooted in garbage and chaos, curses and offenses against convention. Ultimately words failed me, and I grew fatigued. I was never able to consciously produce pressured speech or unending streams of consciousness. When I paused, he extended his hand to my shoulder, "Jonathan." Somehow, I did not wince at the touch. "Jonathan.

"I understand your rage." How could he? How could he possibly? Yet I wanted him to understand.

"We stand up here and watch helplessly what happens below. We can observe and enjoy the triumphs, but we also have to see the pain and the suffering and there is nothing we can do. Nothing.

"Think. Reason over emotion. This part of the stadium is empty because of you. But except for what you have done, that part," he gestured, "would also be empty, over there and over there and over there. Imagine instead that you had not acted; this entire side would be empty, not just this small part."

I had to admit the truth that he spoke. I had stayed sane over the centuries because I knew that the balance in what I did tilted toward life. He continued.

"Can the dead of that world truly rage at you, knowing for every one of them you killed, ten or a hundred or a thousand still live?" As I nodded an acquiescence, he continued. "Is what I did so different than what you do?"

Then I woke up.

102-736
Aboard BF *Likiinir* in orbit above
Core 2017 Onon E576321-7 Lo Re

I was surprised at how short the Marquis Irulan was. I towered over him. He led us without any ceremony out of the vault and through passages that I clearly remembered to the hangar deck. I looked again at my identity card: Lieutenant Ania Ginsa. I wondered how that was pronounced.

On the hangar deck, there were brief introductions and the Marquis began abruptly. "Captain, I want," he turned and pointed to me. I said my rank and name. He continued, "Lieutenant Ginsa appointed captain of the *Cryx*. Transfer its current captain to your command. I mean neither criticism nor condemnation. This is merely the whim of the Empress."

My attention turned to the soon-to-be former captain of *Cryx*, his face stone. After a few more minutes, the Marquis ended the conversation. I stepped next to my predecessor, extended my hand, and forced the issue, "Lieutenant Ginsa."

His hesitation was but a split second, and then he touched mine, "Lieutenant Matiu Betna. What is going on?"

"I am unsure myself. Take me to the ship and I will tell you what I know." In a few hours, he would not matter.

Captain Betna (no matter his rank, we called him Captain on his ship) conveyed the change of command to the crew; I expressed appreciation and regret and dismissed him. I immediately delegated insystem control to the pilot and told him to depart as soon as possible for the jump point. We left within two hours.

I spoke with the astrogator, a newly promoted Sublieutenant.

"Our destination is Shiwonee. As soon as possible."

"That's sixty parsecs. We can make it in ten jumps. Twenty weeks easy."

"A jump takes a week."

"Yes, but then there is moving in from the jump point to orbit, down to surface, refueling, liberty for the crew, restock, maintenance best done in a gravity well, system reports, updates, back to orbit, back out to jump point, and jump. It adds a week to every jump.

"This ship does jump six. Most liners do jump three, some maybe jump four. We'll be there in twice, I mean half the time a jump-three liner could."

Rule 4. "Then think this through with me. I board a jump-4 liner at Capital headed for Shiwonee, that's sixty parsecs, so fifteen jumps. This is all on the main route; there's a ship leaving every day."

I genuinely wanted him to understand the process here. Rule 3.

"At the first world, I transfer to a new ship, I'll probably have to wait a day for the connection, and I jump again. I figure that some important bureaucrat on an expense account travelling High Passage can make the trip in fifteen weeks plus fourteen days: 119 days.

"This ship is half again faster than that liner, and that bureaucrat will beat us by three weeks."

"Excuse me, sir. You are comparing nuts to bolts. It's not the same ship getting there."

"I don't care about same or different. I want us at Shiwonee before anyone else. How do we do that?" I already knew the answer; I just needed him to know the answer.

He stood frozen. And recovered. He knew the answer; it just was not how this ship normally operated.

"Yes, sir. Revision One." He tapped the console and brought up a route specifier, tapped touch boxes and options. It registered answers immediately. "Optimal route at Jump-6. Fifty-seven parsecs. Every waypoint has a gas giant. Break out one hundred dee from the gas giant, maneuver at best possible speed to it, on average half a day. Skim the atmosphere for fuel. Race back out to one hundred dee, and jump. We spend a day in each system.

"Fifty-seven parsecs. Ten jumps. Ten weeks plus ten, no, nine days: 79 days."

I smiled. "That puts us there about 181."

"Yes, sir."

"Finalize that course. Let's see if we can break some records."

102-736
Aboard BF *Likiinir* in orbit above
Core 2017 Onon E576321-7 Lo Re

It took a while adjusting to the change in height. I had just walked these corridors with my eyes just below nameplate level; now I saw them from above. I found the effect disconcerting.

My identification card said Marine Sergeant Nin Agilan, and I didn't know that name's origins: what world? what race? We all followed the short Marquis and the Newt back through the ship.

The Marquis pointed to me, "I want this marine sergeant to go down to the palace. He has his instructions. Give him what he needs."

I stepped out of the line and started immediately and spoke to the first Marine sergeant I saw. "Take me to the armory."

Over the next many hours, I impressed four Marines into a de facto security squad, researched what I needed, and dropped to the palace in a fast lander. We had codes that passed us through checkpoints and maps and schematics with several potential locations. When necessary, I posted my squad away from my tasks; I did not want to risk their futures by betraying what I was doing.

I did not sleep. The next morning, I met with the Marquis Irulan. We exchanged our wafers, knowing the pain that was coming.

Then my squad and I returned to *Likiinir*. I was met by Lieutenant Damala and we exchanged wafers privately. The pain was excruciating; worse than before.

Likiinir departed for Vland and beyond within an hour.

103-736
Core 2017 Onon E576321-7 Lo Re

I met with the Viscountess Adapa and briefed her on the progress of the plan. I pointed out some long-term issues with regard to proxies, and suggested how they might be resolved, but assured her that the current crisis would abate successfully. With her satisfied, I had little to do but wait.

* * *

I gave my report to the Empress. I arranged to give it over dinner. The time was blocked free; I was accustomed to doing as I saw fit.

I told her that I had sent a wafer clandestinely to the fleet at Shiwonee in the hands of a cover mission that would distract attention. Nothing could be traced; there was no record trail that could be uncovered. The political crisis would be avoided. She asked probing questions; I gave candid answers. My report ended at about the same time as the meal.

"Your Majesty, forgive me for my presumption."

She looked at me briefly, and then, "Yes?"

"I knew your grandmother. Arbellatra. I served her before she became Regent. She visited this world in an attempt to negotiate with Gustus."

I set down my eating utensil, folded my napkin, and stood. "Are you ready for an adventure?"

This stopped her for a moment. Then she flang caution to the air and stood herself. "Yes."

I started a monologue about Arbellatra clandestinely

visiting this world in search of Gustus. Of how some crew on her flagship had previously served at this palace here on Onon, and how they knew of the abandoned tunnels and warrens. Arbellatra personally led four squads of Star Marines in a harrowing nap-of-the-planet flight to the edge of the city. Meanwhile a formation of cutters broadcasting neutral IFF landed in the plaza before the ceremonial gates to plead for a meeting with the head of household, only to be ignored. The invading marines bashed through the rusting iron grates, dashed for kilometers through murky darkness, crashed through collapsed barricades, and ultimately flashed up an access shaft to the edges of this central citadel. She laughed at my silly phrasing; I took her hand and we ourselves dashed out of the apartment and into the long hallway.

I violated a dozen rules of protocol, but confirmed that I had her trust. Does Rule 1 apply when I am talking to the Empress herself?

"Let me show you," I said, "The panel is down this side branch." I had her. She who was always in control; she who had in all her life ruled the grandest empire in the galaxy; she who had surrendered her life to power, and was even now surviving the greatest challenge to her legacy. She could afford a little fun.

Down the hallway spur, we reached a panel and I felt for the switch. It wasn't there, or I couldn't find it, but no matter; no, there it was. The false panel swung open. Beyond was a complete and finished room. Security staff clearly knew of its existence; but why would anyone ever tell the Empress? We followed the stair down three complete spirals. She giggled at the impertinence of it all; she had never seen this part of the palace ever.

Here, the sparsely lit tunnels led to staff quarters and storerooms. Before us, however, was what I wanted: the bricked-up tunnel with an old, disused door, near invisible under coats of paint and artful directional markings. I fumbled at its latch and it opened with a touch. We stepped through. My comm set to bright showed us the disused corridor beyond reaching back into the blackness.

"Come, just through here is where your grandmother lay in wait for Gustus. I was with her as she told me of her dreams for a greater empire than had ever been; she talked endlessly of her vision of a cosmopolitan, eclectic society where every person had a chance of reaching his or her or its full potential."

She listened with half an ear, giddy with her own victory and fascination and this slightest shedding of convention.

I stopped. I needed to speak my piece.

"Your Majesty. The plan has changed."

She stopped as well. "Changed?"

"It is unworkable to scrub a world with fifty billion people in order to avoid a political crisis."

"Unworkable? It has already been decided. The instructions have been sent. Your wafer will be there to give the orders."

"The orders have been changed."

"That is unacceptable." Cold. She was her natural, imperial self again. "There is no alternative."

"But there is."

Not by chance, we were positioned with me blocking the exit.

"You have killed billions already. You speak with my voice and people obey. Step aside."

"Majesty, you misunderstand me. I have spoken with the voice of the Emperor for four hundred years. I speak with your voice, but I serve the Empire."

I swung the steel bar and caught the side of her head. I hope she died instantly. I moved to the roof support, hit it with my shoulder, and it gave way. Rule 2.

* * *

The calendar rules everyone's lives. Plans are made according to the grid of days and dates. Appropriate days are chosen by how they fit into personal obligations, the cultural expectations of society, and even accounting standards.

Mid-previous year, the Empress and her counsellors had finalized their course of action, which required substantial assets and considerable advance planning. Ships were diverted from patrols to the massive depot system in Massilia. Similar diversions were ordered in neighboring Zarushagar, Delphi, and Diaspora sectors. Blind contingent orders were issued so that even the admirals commanding did not know their final destinations. Announcements and press briefings spoke of good will tours, relief efforts, and the inherent strength of the Imperial Navy.

On 002, after everyone had a chance to celebrate Holiday and the start of the new year, each of the massive fleets departed their respective depots. Restricted to the speed of their slowest ships, these fleets practiced coordinated jumping, and co-ordinated refuelling at gas giants.

Destination systems were not announced. The arrival of the fleets was a matter of speculation and debate in the media, and in commerce. Spacers on liberty represented a substantial contribution to many local economies.

With four fleets on extended tours, their visits prompted excitement but not fear.

Refresher training on a variety of subjects brought crews up to required standards without revealing specific areas of emphasis. In multi-star systems, ships practiced slingshot maneuvers and massive fighter deployments. In sparsely populated systems, ships practiced world scrubbing. In multi-gas giant systems, ships practiced hiding deep in hydrogen atmospheres in full stealth mode.

Cooks had competitions preparing the most delicious meals for a thousand diners. Astrogators challenged each other to the fastest calculation time. Personnel officers ensured that crew deficiencies were remedied. New officers shadowed experienced ones to broaden their understandings. Marines practiced marksmanship, close combat; all were brought up to date in Edict 97 training.

MARGARET III

Flash Flash Flash 110-736

Margaret Olavia Alkhalikoi, 34th Empress of the Grand Empire of Stars, hereditary Co-Duchess of Rhylanor, Baroness Vland, died 103-736 at Onon, the Imperial retreat. More than a million grieving citizens filled the central Plaza of Heroes on Capital to express their sorrow at the loss of their sovereign for the past 48 years.

Prince Paulo, the Emperor Apparent, expressed his inconsolable distress at the loss of his sister and emphasized that the Imperium continues its dedication to the protection and support of its citizens.

Crawlers on the screen gave times and locations of local memorial gatherings. Touchcodes expanded for more information, historical data, and commentary by a spectrum of political commentators.

189-736
Aboard AF *Cryx* Above
Mass 1131 Ashavakuna B567622-8 Ag Ni Ri

Cryx had arrived one system short of Shiwonee with

two weeks to spare. She was fully refueled and waiting
when M-Fleet arrived.

"Breakout flash! Another! Several! Many!"

"Silence the alarm. Is the IFF working?"

"Aye, sir."

The scopes showed an initial wave of many ships: battles,
sieges, and carriers, but also minors, tenders, scouts, and
pickets. Over the next three hours, the sky above
Ashavakuna was alight with breakout flashes. The frequencies burned with broadcasts and beamcasts and datacasts.

Nestled close to the Naval Base annex of the orbital
High Port, *Cryx* was automatically labeled innocuous.

The fleet went through its paces. It had no premonition
of its true mission. This level of training and experience
would influence naval operations for decades. Spacers
would say, "I was part of M-Fleet," and proudly point to a
multi-colored experience medal. Their comrades would
comment, or even make fun, while inwardly noting their
own misfortune.

Astrogation charts already told the fleet there was no
gas giant; ships moved to the single planetoid belt to
secure ice chunks for refueling. Multiple layers of
protectors screened the valuable capital ships.

After about six hours, the flag was ready to deal with
business.

Captain Ginsa turned to his astrogator, "It's time," and
handed him the wafer.

189-736
Aboard AF *Cryx* Above
Mass 1131 Ashavakuna B567622-8 Ag Ni Ri

I awoke, momentarily disoriented, but clear in what I expected. I opened my eyes to see the bridge of the *Cryx*. "Tell me status."

"It is 1340 189-736. We are in the Ashavakuna system. The fleet has broken out. We are in underchannel contact."

"Send my respects to the Admiral and tell him we bear an express from the Empress."

Lieutenant Ginsa, my host many weeks before, was Captain, none the worse for my inhabitation. Actually, he was much better: a functionary in an obscure office of the bureaucracy who probably never saw the Empress, plucked by the nobility from his desk to command a cutting edge fastest-available courier ship to transport a message on strict deadline from the Empress to the Duke of Shiwonee. He would be commended. He would be promoted; he would be ennobled. He would be applauded, provided of course the last several weeks went as planned.

His discussions with my current host, astrogator Lieutenant Leffian, probably implied similar rewards for him. I needed to take the proper steps, assuming all went well. Rule 5.

202-736
Aboard EC *Unicorn* Above
Mass 1430 Shiwonee AA86A88-B Hi Cp An

Even the Empress cannot make the impossible happen. What if the Duke of Shiwonee were dead? Ill? Incapacitated?

Close Escort *Unicorn*, a workhorse of the fleet and now captained by Lieutenant Leffian, had left for Shiwonee a day before the fleet. Upon arrival, and after standard protocols confirmed our identity, we moved to near world orbit and opened an encrypted channel to the Office of the Duke.

"The Empress requires the Duke at the Wall of Heroes at 1200 tomorrow."

The gatekeeper equivocated. "His Grace's schedule is very tight. I will see if we can arrange a time that is mutually agreeable."

"If necessary, we will send a shuttle to deliver him."

Cryx arrived a few hours later, to hang motionless in space until it received its cue.

203-736
Aboard AF *Cryx* Above
Mass 1430 Shiwonee AA86A88-B Hi Cp An

At about mid-morning, the very first of M-Fleet's ships shed arrival energy. The auxiliary was almost immediately followed by a dreadnought and then another.

"We have the first breakout!" *Cryx*'s sensop began narrating the arrivals. In immediate response, its Captain Ginsa gave the order to move, and it began its carefully preplanned drive for the planet below. It would hit near-world orbit an hour before noon. All the while during its two-hour journey, more ships of M-Fleet arrived to hang motionless in Shiwonee's skies.

A signal from *Unicorn* confirmed that arrangements were in place.

Cryx grounded within sight of the Wall, the precise location selected to minimize walking distance and maximize visual impact: the local spectral-F starsun high to the south and brightening the Wall's face. They would approach with its glare on their backs.

Kavax and Kusliis-Shorn emerged in their dress white formal uniforms, escorted by six marines: two forward, two lateral, two behind. Their training in ceremonial presentations was clearly up to date.

It was a slight that the Duke was not present to greet the arrival of *Cryx*. They ignored it.

"His shuttle just arrived. On the far side. Slow down just a bit; let him scurry into place." Kusliis-Shorn verbalized her acknowledgement and they slowed their pace.

The Wall of Heroes commemorates the fallen of the Empire. Size and structure vary with the world; in this case, it was two soaring wings embracing a central obelisk set on a concourse overlooking the city.

The Duke stepped out from the base of the wings looking annoyed. He was accompanied by ten other officials, assistants, and helpers; they all stood slightly back. One scuttled forward to speak with the reservists, only to be ignored. Press drones circled discreetly.

Kavax, carrying the Imperial banner in both hands, walked directly to the Duke and held out the flag. The Duke started to speak, but they ignored him. Whatever he said, when he was finished, Kusliis-Shorn spoke. "The Empress conveys her greetings to the Geonee as members of the Empire." She dispensed with the salute; she and Kavax turned immediately and walked back to the ship.

* * *

They didn't say anything. Imagers could see and image interpreters could hear. Instead the Duke stood stiffly until the navals had left. He then gave some instructions. Guards hauled down the Imperial banner currently flying above the memorial and hauled up this gift from the Empress. It waved, as protocol demanded, a flag height higher than the Shiwonee banner. Patriotic music welled around them, and when it was done, the Duke and his entourage carefully made their way back to their transport.

Safely inside their vehicle: "She knows."

"So what; she can't do anything. The vote at the close of the Moot is already certain."

"That fleet can do something."

"But it won't."

"Then why did she do all this? No message. No discussions."

"This was a message."

Various advisors issued orders and statements. One expressed solidarity with the Empire; another was exhilarated with the special attention the Empress had bestowed on this important world and sector. Observers gave opinions about the future; the past; the present. The discussion channels were abuzz for days.

The fleet left two days later. Its abrupt departure was its own message; millions in potential profits vanished when the spacers did not visit, and the supply barges did not fly. There were suitable explanations made from world government, but the Navy itself was silent on the matter.

204-736

Mass 1430 Shiwonee AA86A88-B Hi Cp An

Outward from Capital the news of the Empress' death spread at the speed of jump: five parsecs every week, doggedly trailing *Cryx*. But it first had to reach Capital, a full seven day disadvantage, and it would propagate not at the experimental speed of *Cryx*, but at more conventional jump-4 or jump-5.

The news arrived the next day.

EPILOGUE

116-736
Core 2118 Capital A586A98-D Hi Cx

The Grand Palace was lit in mourning blue. City lights and street illuminators were shrouded to create a swath of shadow for five kilometers in every direction. News imagers continued to broadcast (and record for rebroadcast throughout the empire) the striking scene marking the passing of a beloved Empress.

During Margaret's lifetime, the title Emperor-Apparent had never been spoken; with her death, it was on everyone's lips. Her fraternal twin, born twenty-two minutes later, had been in eternal eclipse. Now, at age 52, he would emerge from her umbra to ascend the Iridium Throne. He thought, but only to himself, "It's about time."

Where once he had to be satisfied with a few loyal retainers, he was now besieged with supplicants and new-found friends anxious to establish themselves with gifts and words of wisdom. His trusted seneschal Mand was proving himself quite capable in fending off most of them.

The Viscountess Adapa was one of the sea of supplicants,

disadvantaged by her lack of height and by her gravidity; somewhat also by the fact that her wet clothes tended to offput others. She worked her way to the front of the queue several times, only to be rebuffed each.

At the margins of the crowd, she waited for her chance that never seemed to come. After an hour, she visited the fresher annex to rewet her coat and headband; there she encountered another Newt doing the same.

"How long can this go on?" she asked.

"It will have to at least lull for the actual funeral day after tomorrow. Then it will pick up again, probably for a year."

"Forgive my lack of protocol. I am the Viscountess Adapa, late counsellor to . . . no matter."

"It is my pleasure to meet you. I am Tetepo Babseka, alas only an adjunct to Seneschal Mand. Until last week, I worked half days and visited art museums in the afternoons. Now." He shrugged.

"And I am pleased to meet you." She paused.

Tetepo paused as well. Newts naturally excelled at the administrative and the bureaucratic; chance meetings were part of the process. He volunteered, "Perhaps you have a question?"

"Indeed, I do." Protocol required an ask. "Can you perhaps give me an answer?" Her question was accompanied by the peculiar gesture that the species used to convey both supplication and promise of reward, a particular almost-invisible flick of the wrist. It would be uncouth to actually specify the reward.

Minutes later, the Viscountess Adapa followed Adjunct Tetepo through the other fresher exit and then past a checkpoint. They were soon before Mand with an allowance of fifteen seconds to present a case.

"I seek no reward or favor for myself," she said in order to start the dialog, "I have an item of policy that the Empress herself desired, but it was unfinished before her untimely passing."

"Can it not wait?" said the seneschal, starting to turn away.

"It cannot." This required both tact and eloquence. Adapa tried to compress every fact and detail she could into fifteen seconds. "There is a flaw in the proxy process that may spell drastic changes in the imperial structure, to the disadvantage of the Empress, and now to the Emperor. She had a simple solution but had not yet implemented it. The Emperor-Apparent has the ability to act now and with a simple stroke of a pen to remove the problem forever." Twenty-two seconds.

"Show me."

The Lady Adapa explained in greater detail the proxy option process and the Geonee scheme for an Autonomous Region. This was harder without the accompanying image support, but she recited her briefing with them in her mind's eye. She omitted some details; she planned to retire to her remote fiefs with her newborn well before news of the scrubbing of Shiwonee came some half a year from now; she estimated news would arrive on or about 310, mid fourth quarter. Nobles in exile at least survived; from far way, she could profess ignorance of any of the details. If she stayed, she could lose her head and it would not regrow. But she did have this particular duty to the Empire, and she would do her best to fulfill it.

Seneschal Mand found the proposal reasonable. This interim period when all proxies were cancelled by the death of the sovereign was indeed the perfect time to implement a change. Adapa's draft Imperial Order made perfect sense: henceforth the Emperor would recognize only integral proxies. Mand told the two to wait.

They waited an hour, and then two. Mand finally returned and noticed them. "Oh. Yes. The proclamation will be published shortly after the funeral. The Emperor-Apparent understood and agreed completely."

"Then I thank you for your gracious attention." She started toward the door.

"The Emperor-Apparent has decided that it will fall to you to administer the bureaucratic aspects of the proxies themselves: a new central registry. There will be a flurry of registrations almost immediately, but after the first year, it surely becomes a sinecure, a very nice position. You'll be a Countess by the end of the year."

Adjunct Tetepo smiled in anticipation of his own reward. The Lady Adapa was less sanguine.

109-737
Aboard VF *Pacific* Orbiting
Mend 1338 Kipli C575976-8 Hi In

I was awake, my eyes still closed, standing rather than reclining, and so I knew this must be the start of a new activation. The wave of disorientation passed and I opened my eyes.

"Who here is senior?"

TABLE OF RANK EQUIVALENCIES

Naval Enlisted Ranks

R=	Title, Alternate.
R1	Spacer. Spacehand. Recruit.
R2	Able Spacer.
R3	Petty Officer.
R4	Petty Officer First.
R5	Chief Petty Officer.
R6	Master Chief Petty Officer.

Naval Officer Ranks

O=	Title, Alternate.
O1	Ensign.
O2	Sublieutenant.
O3	Lieutenant.
O4	Lieutenant Commander.
O5	Commander.
O6	Captain.
O6.5	Commodore. A courtesy title for a non-Admiral commanding multiple ships.
O7	Admiral. There are higher gradations of Admiral.

The officer assigned in command of a ship is also called Captain, although he may not have that specific rank.

Army Enlisted Ranks

S=	Title, Alternate.
S1	Private. Recruit.
S2	Corporal.
S3	Sergeant.
S4	Staff Sergeant.
S5	Master Sergeant.
S6	Sergeant-Major.

Army Officer Ranks

O=	Title, Alternate.
O1	2nd Lieutenant.
O2	1st Lieutenant.
O3	Captain.
O4	Major.
O5	Lieutenant Colonel.
O6	Colonel.
O7	General. There are higher gradations of General.

Army Colonel and Lieutenant Colonel use the Anglic pronunciation: kernel.

Marine Enlisted Ranks

M=	Title, Alternate.
M1	Private. Recruit. Marine.
M2	Lance Corporal.
M3	Sergeant.
M4	Staff Sergeant.
M5	Master Sergeant.
M6	Sergeant-Major.

Marine Officer Ranks

O=	Title, Alternate.
O1	2nd Lieutenant.
O2	1st Lieutenant.
O3	Captain.
O4	Force Commander.
O5	Lt Coronel. Note traditional variant spelling.
O6	Coronel. Note traditional variant spelling.
O7	Brigadier.

Marine Coronel and Lieutenant Coronel use an orthographic pronunciation.

Merchant Officer Ranks

R=	Title, Alternate.	Typical Crew Position
RX	Temp	
R0	Spacehand	
R1	Steward Apprentice	Steward
R2	Drive Helper	Engineer
M1	Fourth Officer	Steward
M2	Third Officer	Engineer
M3	Second Officer	Astrogator
M4	First Officer	Pilot
M5	Captain	
M6	Senior Captain	

Merchant ranks (at least for traders) are relatively informal.

Noble Ranks

N= Title, Alternate.

A   Gentleman. Of importance, but not technically a noble.

B   Knight. Dame. Lady. Assigned to various worlds.

c   Baronet. Baronetess. Assigned to worlds with the potential for Agricultural or Rich status. *Note lower case.*

C   Baron. Baroness. Assigned to worlds with Agricultural or Rich status.

D   Marquis. Marquesa. Marchioness. Assigned to worlds with the potential for Industrial status.

e   Viscount. Viscountess. Assigned to worlds with the potential for High Population. *Note lower case.*

E   Count. Countess. Contessa. Assigned to worlds with Industrial or High Population status.

f   Duke. Duchess. Assigned to various lesser importance worlds. *Note lower case.*

F   Duke. Duchess. Assigned to Sector or Subsector Capitals.

Noble Ranks, *continued*

N= **Title, Alternate.**

G   Archduke. Archduchess. Assigned to a domain of four Sectors.

G   Imperial Family. Prince. Princess. Dowager. Karand.

H   Emperor. Empress. Regent. Archduke Regnant. Archduchess Regnant.

Although there are stated preferences to the worlds with which noble titles are often associated, they may be awarded in connection with any worlds.

TABLE OF WORLD REMARKS

Remarks are codes, details, and trade classifications which expand upon the information in the Universal World Profile.

Common Remarks are derived from the information in the Universal World Profile itself. For example, Wa Water World is an automatic identifier if Hydrographics is A. Less Common Remarks are determined by other factors not necessarily in the Universal World Profile. For example, Cs Sector Capital is not specifically dependent on any details in the UWP.

The UWP Universal World Profile

The worlds of the Imperium (as well as those beyond its borders) are identified by location, name, and a brief recapitulation of their physical and social characteristics in the standard format:

Sect xxyy WorldName StSAHPGL-T Rem1 Rem2 Rem3...

Sect is the four-letter sector name abbreviation, xxyy is the starchart locational coordinates, and WorldName is the common label applied to the MainWorld (the most significant world) in the stellar system at this location.

St is the Starport type, S is World Size, A is a code for Atmosphere, and H is the rough percentage (in tens) of surface covered with water (or perhaps fluids).

P is sophont population as a power of 10, G is the code for government type from a standard list, and L is the code for the local legal system on a permissive-oppressive spectrum.

T is a code for commonly available technology on a standard scale.

Rem1 and others are two-letter remarks identifying commonly encountered trade classifications and world characteristics. Ri is a Rich World; Ag is Agricultural; In is Industrial; Po is Poor; Cp, Cs, and Cx are Capitals. The thoroughness of the remarks listed varies.

High Population Worlds (billions or more) are traditionally named on charts in ALL CAPS.

Values greater than 9 are represented by hexadecimal numbers (A=10, B=11, through F=15). When required correspondingly higher values use successive letters of the Anglic alphabet (but omit I or O to avoid confusion).

Planetary Notes

As Asteroid Belt. The MainWorld is an asteroid belt.

De Desert. The MainWorld has virtually no (less than a tenth) surface water.

Fl Fluid. The seas of the MainWorld are a fluid (other than water) dictated by an exotic or non-breathable atmosphere.

Ga Garden World. The MainWorld is reasonable in size, has an untainted atmosphere, and a reasonable availability of water.

He Hellworld. The MainWorld is inhospitable, with tainted atmosphere and low water availability.

Ic Ice-Capped. The surface water of the MainWorld is contained in ice caps rather than seas.

Oc Ocean World. The MainWorld is extraordinarily large and its seas cover virtually all of its surface.

Va Vacuum. The MainWorld has no atmosphere.

Wa Water World. The MainWorld's seas cover virtually all of its surface.

Sa Satellite. The MainWorld is a satellite (rather than a planet).

Lk Tidally Locked Close Satellite. The MainWorld is a satellite (rather than a planet) and is close enough to its planet or gas giant to be tidally locked to it.

Population Notes

Di Dieback. The MainWorld has no population (although it did at one time and ruins of past civilizations may remain).

Ba Barren. The MainWorld has no population.

Lo Low Population. The MainWorld population is less than 10 thousand.

Ni Non-Industrial. The MainWorld population has a population less than 10 million (but more than 10 thousand).

Ph Pre-High. The MainWorld has a population in the hundreds of millions.

Hi High Population. The MainWorld has a population of a billion or more.

Economic Notes

Pa Pre-Agricultural. With some changes or advancement, the MainWorld can become Agricultural.

Ag Agricultural. The MainWorld is well-suited to agricultural production.

Na Non-Agricultural. The MainWorld is unsuited for agricultural production.

Px Prison or Exile Camp. The MainWorld has been designated for relocation of marginal or undesirable populations.

Pi Pre-Industrial. With some changes or advancement, the MainWorld can become Industrial.

In Industrial. The MainWorld is well-suited to industrial production.

Po Poor. Local conditions and resources are marginal or difficult to exploit.

Pr Pre-Rich. With some changes or advancement, the MainWorld can become a Rich world.

Ri Rich. The MainWorld has a pleasant, untainted atmosphere and a reasonable population.

Climate Notes

Fr Frozen. The MainWorld is beyond the outer limits of the Habitable Zone (based on the spectral class and size of the system's star).

Ho Hot. The MainWorld is at the inner limits of the Habitable Zone (based on the spectral class and size of the system's star).

Co Cold. The MainWorld is at the outer limits of the Habitable Zone (based on the spectral class and size of the system's star).

Tr Tropic. The MainWorld is Hot and has reasonable levels of atmosphere and water.

Tu Tundra. The MainWorld is Cold and has reasonable levels of atmosphere and water (which may be ice-capped).

Tz Twilight Zone. The MainWorld is in an orbit close to the system's star (thus probably an M-class main-sequence dwarf) and is tidally locked to it.

Secondary Notes

Fa Farming. The world (usually not the MainWorld) is suitable for agricultural production.

Mi Mining. The world is being exploited for natural resources (for the system MainWorld which is Industrial).

Mr Military Rule. The world is under the control of the military (local or imperial).

Pe Penal Colony. The world (usually not the MainWorld) has been allocated for relocation of marginal, criminal, or undesirable populations. Contrast with Px Prison or Exile Camp.

Re Reserve. The MainWorld has colony status and is restricted from general access.

Political Notes

Cp Subsector Capital. The MainWorld is the seat of government for its subsector (or other subdivision of a larger interstellar government).

Cs Sector Capital. The MainWorld is the seat of government for its sector (or other division of a larger interstellar government).

Cx Capital. The MainWorld is the seat of a major interstellar government.

Cy Colony. The MainWorld is a colony of a neighboring world.

Special Notes

Fo Forbidden (usually Red Zone). The MainWorld has been interdicted from trade or travel.

Pz Puzzling (usually Amber Zone). Travellers are warned that this MainWorld presents unknown, unexplained, or unpredictable situations.

Da Dangerous (usually Amber Zone). Travellers are warned that this MainWorld presents dangerous or deadly situations.

Ab Data Repository. The MainWorld hosts an archive or data repository.

An Ancient Site. The MainWorld holds one or more known ruins of the Ancients.

GENERAL CHRONOLOGY

The Millennia

In very broad terms, the epochs of modern interstellar history can be divided into thousand-year Millennia, each with a variety of overriding characteristics.

The First Millennium of Star Travel (-9000 to -8000). Following the discovery of basic Jump Drive, the Humans of Vland expand to dominate interstellar travel and trade.

The Second Millennium of Star Travel (-8000 to -7000). The Vilani continue to exploit their interstellar drive to economic advantage.

The Third Millennium of Star Travel (-7000 to -6000). The Vilani find they need to suppress the aspirations of the other intelligent species they encounter, including through significant violent means.

The Fourth Millennium of Star Travel (-6000 to -5000). Just as subject species begin to organize their resistance, the Vilani discover the improved double speed Jump-2 Drive. This provides the significant advantage needed to consolidate their hold on their subject worlds. Vilani rule is formalized as the Ziru Sirka, the Grand Empire of Stars.

The Fifth Millennium of Star Travel (-5000 to -4000). To maintain power and order, technology is suppressed; the attention of subject world populations is diverted to social and recreational pursuits.

The Sixth Millennium of Star Travel (-4000 to -3000). The Ziru Sirka becomes brutal in its efforts to maintain power.

The Seventh Millennium of Star Travel (-3000 to -2000). The Humans of Terra independently develop Jump Drive and, not knowing any better, challenge the far larger First Imperium in a series of Interstellar Wars that ultimately lead to a Vilani collapse.

The Eighth Millennium of Star Travel (-2000 to -1000). Terra and its approximately one hundred worlds attempt to rule the ten-thousand-world Vilani Empire as a captured territory. However short-lived, The Rule of Man nevertheless imposed Terran (and Anglic-languaged) society on many Vilani worlds, but ultimately collapsed into chaos.

The Ninth Millennium of Star Travel (-1000 to 0). The demise of The Rule of Man leads to the Long Night which isolates worlds. Many die back to barrenness; others regress in technology.

The Tenth Millennium of Star Travel (0 to 1000). The Sylean Federation re-established the Vilani Empire as the Third Imperium and expands to re-absorb many of its worlds.

Imperial Dates

Dates reflect the standard Imperial Calendar.

Simple Calendar Conversion. A rough date conversion equates the Imperial Year Zero with the Terran date 4518 CE. For example, the Imperial year 633 is roughly 5151 CE; the Terran 2015 CE is roughly Imperial -2503.

Rigorous Date Conversion. Convert the Imperial Date (with days as a decimal of 365) to the Solomani (Terran) date in the following process.

> Solomani (Terran) date = (yyy.ddd °
>   1.0006644) + 4518
> Convert resulting fractional day to a calendar
>   reference.

> For example, convert Imperial Date 111-633
>   to decimal.
> Day is 111/365 = 0.3041 = 633.3041
> 633.3041 ° 1.0006644 + 4518 = 5151.72488
> Day is 0.72488 ° 365 = 264
> 264 (-31-28-31-30-31-30-31-31) = 21st day
> of the 9th month = September 21, 5151 CE
>   (or consult a Julian Date calendar).

Days of the Week

The weekdays of the Imperial Calendar are named in sequence Wonday, Tuday, Thirday, Forday, Fiday, Sixday, and Senday, often abbreviated 1day, 2day, 3day, 4day, 5day, 6day, and 7day.

Although practices may differ, Sixday and Senday are the accepted days of the weekend for a five-day workweek.

Day names can be calculated from the day number using Modulo(Date-1,7).

The Progress of the Third Imperium

The history of the Third Imperium is easily divided into eras:

- Dawn of the Third Imperium (0 to 119)
- The Antebellum Years (120 to 474)
- Imperial Disarray (475 to 621)
- Imperial Recovery (622 to 767)
- The Stumbling Years (768 to 939)
- The Solomani Crisis (940 to 1102)
- The New Millennium (1003 to 1084)
- The Golden Age (1085 to 1106)
- Fifth Frontier War (1107 to 1110)
- An Uncertain Future (1111 to 1115)

Alternatively, Imperial history is divided into centuries, as in first-century explorations, third-century art forms, sixth-century troubles.

Dawn of the Third Imperium (0 to 119)

"Why a Third Imperium?"

Cleon Zhunastu was a man of great dreams, and the wealth and power to make those dreams happen. Our Third Imperium is what it is today because of the decisions he made based on those dreams, and the decisions his successors have made, for good or ill. By choosing the name "Third Imperium," any contacted

Terran or Vilani colony would immediately make the connection.

What is also obvious is that he had studied the failures of the past empires, and their strengths—and he attempted to incorporate all of that into his vision for the Third Imperium. Cleon Zhunastu, Artemsus Lentuli, and Zuan Kerr built an Imperium based on personal honor; not that their hands were totally clean—empire building is a messy business. But the policies they developed did not involve nuclear strikes against populations or pocket empires opposed to their vision. Their Quarantine policy of "until you see things our way, you don't exist" was extremely effective.

What happened? The fallout between Emperor Artemsus and Zuan Kerr over what would become the Pacification Campaigns was very public; and the fact that it required Emperor Artemsus almost a decade after Kerr's death to convince the Moot to follow his path says much for the nature of the changes. This break in Cleon's dream would become a noose around the Imperium's neck, leading first to the Non-Dynastic Emperors and then the Emperors of the Flag. The ghosts of the sterilized Lancian worlds haunt us as visions of a dream unfulfilled, or worse yet, a dream betrayed.

From the lecture "Cleon to Artemsus: What Were You Thinking?" 301-1114.

The Antebellum Years (120 to 474)

"Ah, today I'd like for you to skip Chapters 17–34 in your books, and we'll start talking about the Imperial Civil War.

"What? The Antebellum Years? Nothing happened. Forget it.

"Fine. Emperor Artemsus decided to ignore Cleon's vision and instead force worlds into joining; bombing the ones that refused. And what 'successes' might be claimed from it don't balance against things like the sterilization of the Lancian worlds. However, his son Martin I decided to go one step better, and actually create an implacable foe for the new Imperium.

"Why do I blame Martin for the Julian War? Do you blame Julian? After all, Martin set his house on fire, and Julian was just trying to put the fire out, while Martin kept trying to relight the fire. And Julian was a better strategist and diplomat.

"That brings us to Emperor Cleon III. A true reformer and radical with a vision. After all, he only shot politicians.

"Seriously—this episode demonstrates a fundamental problem with not determining a successor in advance. From this point in Imperial history until after the Civil War, the Third Imperium begins walking down the same path as The Rule of Man, although without the bureaucratic collapse The Rule of Man suffered, largely due to the Vilani influence on the bureaucracy.

"The final significant event of the Antebellum period is the solution to the Aslan Border Wars. Interestingly, negotiations with the Aslan required that honorable paths be followed. The Duel War and the settlement are interesting studies showing that had cooler heads prevailed, perhaps history might be different for the Lancian and the Julian conflicts in the first part of this study."

From the lecture "What if Cleon III had been a Better Shot?" 073-1115

Imperial Disarray (475 to 621)

"All that is necessary for evil to triumph is that good men to do nothing."

"Cleon IV uses the right of assassination because Nicholle is too weak to govern. Or maybe it was her brunette hair. Or maybe hearing that 'one-man fire brigade' frontier story one-too-many times about Cleon II made him snap. Regardless, the Moot let him stay Emperor. At least the later invention 'Emperor by right of fleet control' sounds more commanding beside Cleon IV's explanations. Better yet, Cleon IV's best idea for dealing with the Vargr turns into the so-called 'Hidden War.' At least Cleon IV has to wait 80 years before someone kills him. He must have so terrified the Moot that they waited until he was on life support, and Jerome unplugged the machine.

"Admiral hault-Plankwell ends the farce by bringing his fleet to Capital. The fleet commanders have become so disgusted with the nobles playing Emperor that they finally take matters into their own hands. The most striking difference between the Civil War and The Rule of Man is that the fleets fight amongst themselves, and the Imperium is never a target. No one drops nuclear bombs on worlds that provide food and fuel to enemy fleets: 'we're all Imperial Navy, ignore us while we kill each other.'

"However, the Sylean worlds decide they aren't going to put up with it. They go their own way; then the Zhodani start a second Frontier War. And Cleon V has a choice to make: defend and keep the Imperium unified, or defend his throne. As a man of honor, he could only make one choice: he appointed Admiral Alkhalikoi in the Spinward Marches, and used his remaining forces to reunify the Sylean worlds with the Imperium. His reward: his opponents in the Moot aided Joseph, and because Cleon V has spread his forces across the Imperium to defend it, he is unable to defend himself."

From the lecture "What if Cleon V Had Chosen Emperor Over Empire?" 127-1115.

Imperial Recovery (622 to 767)

Arbellatra Alkhalikoi, Grand Admiral of the Marches. A name recognized by every educated Imperial citizen.

"She would have a place in history regardless: Captain at age 16, then the highest rank possible in the Navy by age 29, and defeated an enemy empire in a war thought unwinnable by age 33. Where could she possibly go from there?

"Yet, she did more in the second half of her life than the first. Regent, literally savior of the empire, and then Empress. Arbellatra set out to rebuild the Third Imperium based on honor and duty; she carefully chose those around her to do just that. But for the unfortunate aspects that some of her closest advisors toyed around with the nascent Solomani movement, and others were openly anti-psionic, the history of the Imperium might be radically different.

"The nobility and the military embraced the expectation of honor and duty and served the empire well:

expeditions to the client-states to champion technology and promote commerce; efforts to build and expand. Two groups long suffering bias in the Imperium—the Geonee and the Vargr—advanced immensely in the years after the Civil War. We see just a hint of how the Julian War might have been different in how Humans and Vargr work together to build in Antares. Even as the Solomani Movement is insisting that they are superior to other Humans, the Vilani are being brought closer in than ever. The Third Imperium is finally seeing Cleon's true promise: all sophonts, Humans, minor races, major races, are welcomed into her dream of a cosmopolitan, eclectic society.

"Alas, it didn't."

From the lecture "Visions of Empire: Cleon I, Cleon V, Arbellatra, Gavin, Strephon" 237-1115.

✸
IDENTIFYING SHIPS

The primary ships of the Navy are called Capitals: variously called Battleships, Battles, Dreadnoughts, Ships-of-the-Line, or Primaries. Each is designed to attack any adversary; to withstand any attack. They are marvels of armor and armament.

While Capitals have universal missions, naval architects are constantly specializing them for specific purposes, allowing some vulnerability here for some benefit there. These distinctions give rise to the plethora of mission codes that identify Capitals and that tell the initiated what to expect from them.

Primary Classifications concentrate on Capitals and the relationship of other ships to Capitals.

The Ship Identifier

The first letter of the Mission Code is the Ship Identifier, conveying a basic understanding of the ship and its intended activities.

B. Battle. A Battleship, Capital Ship, Dreadnought, or Ship-of-the-Line. A fighting ship with the strongest of armor and the most powerful of weapons.

V. Carrier. A naval vessel intended to transport, launch, and support other vessels which participate in a conflict. Carriers typically operate at a distance from the main battle.

S. Siege. Siege Engine. A naval vessel intended to launch ordnance against a stationary target (a world or an installation). Like Carriers, Siege Engines operate at a distance from the main battle.

C. Cruiser. A fighting naval vessel (other than a Capital) created to operate independently and project power against non-fighting ships.

A. Minor. An Auxiliary. A naval vessel intended to support, refuel, repair, re-arm or communicate between other ships, especially Capitals. Auxiliaries typically have no place in an actual battle, although some may be Armored.

The Mission Modifer

The second (and sometimes third) letter of the Ship Code is the Mission Modifier, conveying specific tactics, strategies, or abilities included in the ship's design. Some of the more important codes are:

R Rider. The ship is designed to be carried by (to ride) a Carrier. The design typically omits jump drive and associated fuel.

F Fast. The ship has drives that provide acceleration greater than typical within the fleet.

S Slow. The ship has drives that provide acceleration less than typical within the fleet.

K Strike. The ship is designed to attack world or immobile targets.

M Missile. The primary weaponry is missiles.

B Beam. The primary weaponry is beam weapons.

O Orbital. The ship is designed to operate from orbit. Typically applies to siege engines.

F Flag. The ship is equipped for command and control of other ships. The squadron commander Admiral or Commodore commands from a Flag-designated ship.

D Monitor. The ship, while movable, is intended to operate in a fixed location. Typically restricted to one system, and so does not require (or does not have) jump drives.

A Armored. A ship which normally does not have Armor is provided Armor (usually applies to Auxiliaries).

F Fighter. The small craft (less than 100 tons) equivalent of a Rider. Shown for completeness. Does not apply to Battles.

L Lander. The craft carries troops, vehicles, and equipment to a world surface for battle. An Assault Lander delivers directly to the battlefield.

Q Quarantine (*Obsolete*). The ship is dedicated to the Quarantine mission.

Other classification codes are possible.

For example, some idea of a ship's intended capabilities can be gleaned from its identifying codes.

B is an undifferentiated Battleship. BR is a Battle Rider. BB is a Beam-armed Battleship. BK is a Strike Battle.

V is a Carrier. VR is a Rider Carrier. VF is a Fighter Carrier. VL supports Landers for a planetary invasion.

S is a Siege Engine. SO is an orbital Siege Engine.

Extended Ship Classification System (XSCS)

Where Primary Classification addresses Dreadnoughts and their brethren, the Extended Classification system is more comprehensive and includes a much wider range of ships. The system is too extensive to be addressed here.

Ship Tonnage

Ton is a unit measuring volume of starships and spacecraft.

Water ship volume is measured as the tons of water displaced. By extension, starship volume reflects the volume of liquid hydrogen which could be contained by the hull.

Ton. Displacement Ton. Volume Ton. Starship Ton. The standard measure of volume for starship construction, equal to the volume of one thousand kilograms of liquid hydrogen: approximately 13.5 cubic meters.

For reference, a 30-meter diameter sphere is about 1,000 tons. A 63-meter diameter sphere is about 10,000 tons. A 138-meter diameter sphere is about 100,000 tons. A 300-meter diameter sphere is about a million tons. A 650-meter diameter sphere is about ten million tons. A 1.4-kilometer diameter sphere is about 100 million tons.

Small Craft

Craft less than one hundred tons are "small," intended for utilitarian purposes. They are incapable of jump.

Typical models for small craft include: pod, lifeboat, gig, ship's boat, boat, launch, pinnace, cutter, shuttle, fighter, and lander.

THE IMPERIUM

The key to the stars is the jump drive—without it, the space between the stars takes years, even lifetimes, to cross. With it starships travel parsec distances in a matter of weeks. The development of a jump drive marks the beginning of interstellar travel for any race, including Humaniti.

A jump drive is both fast and simple. With one, it is possible to move from here to there (where both places are at least one hundred planetary diameters out from any large masses) in a period of about a week. The time in transit is independent of the distance travelled, which makes this system practical for interstellar travel, but for little else. The distance travelled with the jump drive is a function of the specific jump drive in use—for varying sizes and complexities of jump drives, the performance ranges from one to six parsecs, with greater distances as yet unavailable. In point of fact, the current theory of jump drive actually precludes greater jump distances.

Another central fact of interstellar travel is the fact that no method of information transfer faster than jump drive has been discovered. Ships can carry messages, but radio still lags at mere light speed. Communication is always restricted to the speed of interstellar transportation.

For Terra, the first rudimentary jump drives came into general use in the mid-21st century. These drives introduced the Terrans to Alpha Centauri, to the farther stars, to the First Imperium (then called only the

Imperium), and to the First Interstellar War, 2113 AD. That series of wars (there was, of course, more than one) hastened the fall of the Imperium, and resulted in the takeover of the existing structure by expanding Terran forces. Their rule (The Rule of Man, or the Ramshackle Empire, depending on who wrote the history) slowed, but did not stop, the continuing decay of empire.

What followed is romantically called the Long Night. It wasn't romantic at all. The fall of the empire halted much of the trade and commerce between worlds—many of these worlds simply died, no longer able to maintain their previous standard and unable to recapture the lower technology levels necessary for survival. Some worlds banded together in pocket empires, mere shadows of the former glory that was the First Imperium. Some worlds wasted their technological jewels fighting for the scraps of the empire that were left. The fighting and the turmoil lasted nearly two hundred and fifty years—from twilight to maybe nine o'clock. Some worlds didn't even know for sure that the empire had fallen; communications ships simply stopped coming, and no one could find out why.

Night continued for another twelve hundred years. Worlds turned in on themselves, developing local resources and moving in their own directions. About three decades before dawn, a group of worlds known as the Sylean Federation established a firm industrial base and a strong interstellar government. This, coupled with a high population pressure, provided the impetus necessary for the re-establishment of the empire. In a thirty-year campaign, the Sylean Federation actively recruited new member worlds for its interstellar community. Public relations programs, active commercial warfare, and (where necessary) battle fleets joined to bring all of what is now the Core Sector under one rule. Proclaiming the Year Zero (4521 AD) a holiday year to mark the beginning of a new era, Grand Duke Cleon Zhunastu accepted the iridium crown of the Third Imperium, establishing it firmly on the foundations of the First and Second.

THE STRUCTURE OF THE THIRD IMPERIUM

The Imperium is a far-flung interstellar community encompassing over 10,000 worlds within a region approximately 700 parsecs across. Interstellar government over such a large area, however, becomes a philosophical question; the problem initially seeming to be insurmountable. Distance, travel time, and communication lag all conspire against a functioning, efficient structure which can meet the needs of its subject population. But the lessons of history serve as a guide. Spain in the 16th century ruled much of the New World, with travel times of about a year between the seat of government and the new territories. In fact, through most of history, timely governmental communication, with both a rapid dispatch of instructions and an equally rapid response, has been a dream, not a reality.

The Imperium attempts to ameliorate the problems of distance through feudalism.

Feudalism: With such great distances separating stellar systems, individual responsibility and authority become of great importance. The Imperium is divided into sectors (twenty of them), each about 32 parsecs by 40 parsecs in size. Each sector is divided into sixteen subsectors (8 by 10 parsecs). And within a subsector could be perhaps thirty or forty systems, each with a star, worlds, and satellites.

Individual worlds, and even entire systems, are free to govern themselves as they wish, provided that ultimate power is always accorded the Imperium. Interstellar government begins at the subsector level—on one world designated the subsector capital. The ruling figure at the subsector capital is a high-ranking noble: a duke. This duke has a free hand in government, and is subject only to broad guidelines from his superiors. But at the same time, the duke owes fealty to the higher levels of government, ultimately to the Emperor himself. The feudal approach depends greatly on a sense of honor, one cultivated by the hereditary aristocracy. This sense of honor is very strong within the Imperium; it has proven essential to the survival of this far-flung interstellar community.

INTERSTELLAR SOCIETY

The known interstellar community encompasses thousands of worlds, many of them inhabited, and not all by Humaniti. The number of sophonts which have been contacted is quite high; the Imperium boasts hundreds; Charted Space boasts more than a thousand.

Major and Minor Races: A superficial classification system for the various intelligent races has been created, based on empirical evidence, and to some extent on tradition. In general, the dominant races of known space are those which have achieved FTL (faster than light) travel by themselves, rather than receiving it through contact with starfaring civilizations. These dominant races are called major races; all others are called minor races. Thus, the term major race has become attached to any race which achieves FTL flight on its own, regardless of its prominence. There are sound reasons for the mixing of these two concepts: races that developed FTL rapidly expanded into space, spreading their influence across the stars. Slower races were contacted before they had a chance to discover the FTL secret and emerged into a universe already controlled by the major races. Indeed, the culture shock of being found by a superior race (often superior only in their knowledge of FTL) may take something out of the race as a whole, making them incapable of denying their secondary role in interstellar society. The classification scheme is, of course, simplistic, but the major races tend to perpetuate it as it works to their advantage.

The Six Races: Similar to the major/minor race division is the concept of the Six Races. The origin of the term is uncertain, but it appears independently in Aslan, Vargr, and K'kree sources. There is some disagreement as to the proper identification of the Six, but most commentators agree that all must be major races. The most common definition was once Aslan, K'kree, Hiver, Vargr, Zhodani, and Imperials (both Solomani and Vilani). The confirmation (in 790, Imperial date) of multiple worlds inhabited by the Droyne, and of archeological evidence that they possessed FTL travel before the entry of any of the modern dominant races into space gave new weight to the Six Race concept. With the inclusion of the Droyne, Humaniti could be neatly categorized as one race, clearing the way for a classification that included six truly distinct races: Aslan, K'kree, Droyne, Hiver, Humans, and Vargr.

Aslan are roughly human-sized and are descended from four-limbed, upright, bipedal carnivore/pouncer stock. The earliest Terran explorers saw in them a vague resemblance to the Terran lion, and they have been described (by Terrans) as lion-like ever since, although there is very little true similarity.

The *K'kree* are among the most massive of the major races, and are the only example of a major race descended from herbivores. K'kree are conservative, gregarious with their own kind (to the point of distress if isolated) and claustrophobic. These characteristics derive from their evolutionary origins as herd animals.

Droyne are a small race, both in stature and in dominion, with only limited settlements on a small number of worlds. The history of their evolution is a puzzle as their home world is not known with certainty. The Droyne have no empires, and actually rule only a few worlds. In some few cases, they possess the technology to produce sophisticated machinery, including jump drives and starships, but they remain apparently content to stay on their own worlds.

Humaniti (old spelling: Humanity) is a special case. Originally evolved on Terra, humans were disseminated over nearly fifty worlds about 300,000 years ago by the Ancients, a now extinct intelligent race. These various examples of Humaniti then independently developed. Unlike non-human races, individual human races are classified as major or minor. Three human races (the

Solomani of Terra, the Vilani of the First Imperium, and the Zhodani far to spinward) are major races. The nearly forty other races of Humaniti are all minor,

Vargr are an intelligent race genetically manipulated from Terran carnivore stock by the same Ancients who disseminated Humaniti to the stars. Vargr have long suffered from an inability to organize themselves (to any degree or for any length of time) beyond the star system level, and their empires tend to rise and fall with unsurprising regularity. Vargr have an intense racial pride, and are easily insulted. They are prone to enter into fights without regard for possible consequences.

Hivers (a human term applied to them) are the most obviously alien of the major races: They are descended from omnivore gatherer/scavenger stock, and are unique in that they attained a form of agriculture before they became sentient. They exhibit a sixfold radial symmetry. The body has an internal skeleton consisting of a series of rings supporting the limbs, while a fused carapace protects the brain and internal organs. Hivers themselves are highly individualistic (the term hive is an early misconception) while driven by basic drives such as curiosity, the parental instinct, and a desire to maintain the unity and uniformity of their race.

Within The Imperium: The many worlds of the Imperium are home to an abundance of sophonts, including many of the major races. Aslan, Vargr, and Humans can be expected in many areas under Imperial rule. Zhodani, K'kree, and Hivers, for various reasons, are much more infrequently encountered, and for the most part remain within their own regions.

IMPORTANT TERMS AND CONCEPTS

Traveller uses certain words and abbreviations in unique ways (although these terms may not appear in this text).

The following words, phrases, and abbreviations, are commonly used in the Traveller universe:

ablat: Ablative anti-laser armor.

air/raft: A small grav vehicle, normally open-topped, often used as personal transport.

alien: Refers to an intelligent being of a species other than the speaker. In general use, the word alien always represents non-humans. The preferred term is sophont. See also Sophont.

amber zone: An imposed designation cautioning travellers that the world poses some danger. The reasons may vary from natural (strange ecologies or biomes) to social (local sophonts are xenophobes) to political (local polities are at constant war).

Ancients: Usually expressed as "The Ancients." The mysterious species that once ruled this region of space some three thousand centuries previous and then, in a spasm of violence, destroyed itself. Charted Space is littered with the wreckage of their cities and occasional artifacts of their fantastic technology. Because they are a specific alien race, the word is always capitalized.

Anglic: The accepted term for the English language as used in the Third Imperium.

The Third Imperium traces its roots to the Vilani-created First Imperium, which in turn was conquered and occupied by Terrans as The Rule of Man (the Second Imperium). The Terran conquest and occupation overlaid the use of Anglic as the official language co-equal to the pre-existing Vilani official language.

The result is language usage on the Canadian model: both languages are in common usage and are mandated to be equally emphasized. However, not every sophont knows both (or even either) language. In some areas, language usage is on the American model. One language predominates and the second language is shown less predominately.

antigravity: No hyphen. The general term for technology which negates gravity.

Aslan: A major race of Charted Space, named by early explorers for a vaguely leonine appearance. Singular is "Aslan," plural is "Aslan" or (rarely) "Aslani." Rarely, Asmani is used to describe humans in societies culturally dominated by the Aslan.

Aslan Hierate: A major power in Charted Space, the Hierate lies to spinward of the Imperium. As the name of an interstellar state, always capitalized.

AU: Astronomical unit, always capitalized and without periods, representing the average distance from Earth's orbit to the center of the Sun, or a distance of approximately 150 million kilometers.

battle. battleship: A powerful warship capable of standing in the line of battle and destroying opposing vessels. By definition, the most heavily armed and armored warship available. Also called capital (for Capital Ship).

battle dress: Heavy powered personal armor; the ultimate in personal protection.

battle rider: A powerful nonjump warship designed to be carried into action aboard a jump-capable tender.

belter: An asteroid miner.

black globe: A high technology artifact reproducible at TL15, which allows for limited invulnerability (and limited invisibility) at the cost of sensor blindness. White globes, an even higher technology artifact, should be handled the same way.

boat: A small craft. Also, a small defensive spacecraft (as in system defense boat, or SDB).

calendar: In the Imperial system, days are numbered from 001 to 365. Years are numbered from the founding of the Third Imperium, which was declared to be the Year 0 (zero). Years prior to the founding of the Imperium are either given as negative numbers (-1532, -22, etc.) or (less commonly) labeled as "minus 36." Standard form for dates is [day]-[year], so the 10th day of 1117 would be 010-1117. When spoken, the connector is verbalized: for example, "oh oh one dash eleven seventeen." The first day of a year (001-1117) is also called "Holiday" (capitalized, like Christmas or Easter). The other stellar powers use different systems, but these are seldom used. Only the Solomani Confederation still uses the CE/BCE system (without periods). Rarely, you will see dates in the Vilani system, such as 1235 VI (for Vilani Imperium), again without periods.

capital. capital ship: A major warship, for example a battleship, battlecruiser, fleet carrier or dreadnought.

carrier: A naval vessel whose main striking power lies in its subordinate craft (typically fighters) carried aboard.

Charted Space: The region of space inhabited by humans and thousands of other races, both major and minor. Charted Space encompasses 128 sectors and more than 80,000 worlds. Both words are capitalized.

Charted Space is documented in TravellerMap.com.

Known Space is the term for Larry Niven's SF universe, not *Traveller*'s.

chimera: A chimera is a hybrid of two or more distinct species. Alternatively, a chimera is a sophont who has been significantly altered through the inclusion of genetic material from one or more species (not necessarily sophonts).

client state: An independent political unit (one or more worlds) that has the patronage of a larger power. The relationship is usually beneficial and is normally economic in nature, though political and defensive arrangements will normally exist.

clone: A clone is a sophont genetically identical to a single or donor parent sophont. It has the same genes as its parent. Clones fill important social, economic and medical functions in society. Some of those functions are restricted or illegal within the Third Imperium.

close escort: A very small naval vessel optimized for the protection of other vessels.

cloth: Ballistic cloth; a type of bullet-resistant armor.

combat armor: A sealed suit of heavy armor; the modern equivalent of plate armor. Very effective against weapons, and also provides protection against hostile environments.

comm: A personal communicator. Many comms include other features like data and banking access facilities.

console: The common term for an accessible personal computer or workstation.

Consolidated Theory: More properly, the Consolidated Theory of Gravity, from which the concepts of jump drive, gravitic and maneuver drives, antigravity, lifters, artificial gravity and inertial compensators all stem.

coreward: *See* **galactic directions.**

corsair: A pirate vessel. Many Vargr consider piracy a respectable trade, and use the term to refer to themselves and their vessels.

counsellor. A psychological or psychiatric advisor. With the addition of Sanity (and its associated uses), counsellor becomes an important vocation. The double ell spelling is preferred.

credit (Cr): The common Imperial monetary unit. A hand calculator costs Cr10. For very large amounts of money, the kilocredit (abbreviated KCr) represents a total of one thousand credits, and the megacredit (abbreviated MCr) represents a total of one million credits. A ship's boat costs MCr16. Note that the abbreviation comes first, and there are no spaces before the number. Truly large concepts for money or value are called are (for RU, resource unit).

Larger credit units (GCr or BCr for billion credits, and TCr, for trillion credits) are generally not used.

cruiser: A major warship, capable of carrying a powerful spinal mount weapon. Cruisers undertake many tasks. Various types exist: strike, armored, light, heavy and battle to name but five. Each has a particular role. Also, the Imperial Navy sometimes designates some very small vessels as "cruisers." This refers to the long cruises they undertake while on patrol rather than their capabilities.

datapak: A common form of information availability and retrieval. A package of information with the characteristics of a database and an ebook.

dewclaw: A retractable claw found under the thumbs of an Aslan.

domain: A region of space containing four sectors, administered by an Archduke.

downport: A starport situated on-planet, or the ground components of a port with both orbital and ground facilities.

dreadnought: The newest and most powerful battleships are termed Dreadnoughts.

Droyne: A major race of Charted Space, Droyne are found on many scattered worlds but have no major interstellar polities. The singular and plural forms are the same; as the name of a race, always capitalized.

emp: ElectroMagnetic Pulse. Weaponized high energy pulse inflicting damage or destruction to electric and electronic circuits.

fief: A grant of planetary surface land awarded to a noble as part of his or her or its title; it includes some form of income to the noble.

free trader: Any small merchant ship. Also a specific

design of ship—small, with limited jump capability. Personnel making their living aboard such a ship may also call themselves "free traders."

French plural endings: The early process of translation from Vilani to Anglic made use of some French plural endings to preserve meanings and make then distinct from the accepted Anglic, most specifically the French plural ending -x, rather than -s. For example, the broad governing organizations of the First Imperium (now the megacorporations Sharurshid, Naasirka, Zirunkariish, and Makhidkarun) were together called *shangarim*, translated to Anglic as bureaux (never bureaus). The singular of bureaux is bureau.

Similarly, an important era of history is a milieu. The plural of milieu is milieux (never milieus).

FTL: Faster Than Light. Technologies which permit space travel at a speed faster than that of light, accomplished by the development of the jump drive.

FusionPlus (F+): Technology allowing small, portable, efficient energy sources based on controllable, lower temperature fusion, as opposed to standard fusion technology, which cannot be produced below a cumbersome configuration which is not practical for vehicles. Sometimes referred to as lukewarm fusion or FPlus.

galactic directions: North and South do not work when referring to direction within the galaxy. Instead, the following conventions have achieved widespread acceptance when referring to astrographic directions. Toward the galactic core is coreward; away from it, in the direction of the rim, is rimward. In the direction that the galaxy is rotating is spinward, while the opposite direction is trailing.

garden world: An Earth-like planet where humans can thrive unaided.

gas giant: A huge, Jupiter-like planet.

GCarrier: An enclosed grav vehicle larger than an air/raft, often used as a troop carrier.

geneered: Used to indicate a life form which has been genetically engineered.

grav vehicle: A vehicle that uses antigravity lifters for movement.

gravitics: The science of gravity manipulation.

grav plates: Floor-mounted modules which create artificial gravity within starships and spacecraft. Grav plates are essentially lifter technology with the polarity reversed.

gravitic drive: A reactionless space drive best suited to use near worlds. Because it interacts with gravity sources, it must be within 10 diameters (often abbreviated 10D) of a gravity source (beyond 10D, it operates at 1% of normal performance).

gravity: Used in reference to either the gravitational pull of a stellar body or the acceleration rate of a small craft or starship in normal space. Each G-factor is equivalent to a constant acceleration of one standard gravity (approximately 10 m/sec^2).

hexadecimal letter codes: Standard notation used in hexadecimal numbers, where A=10, B=11, and so on to F=15. Numbers greater than 15 are less common, but the system continues, skipping I and O for reasons of clarity. Also referred to as eHex. See also UPP, USP, and UWP.

high guard: Refueling operations for a task force are a significant danger point, as forces which are low on fuel and maneuvering in a gravity well are especially vulnerable. The high guard position, so named because the ship or ships involved are higher in the gravity well than their companions, is used to mount protective operations during such maneuvers.

highport: An orbital starport, or the orbital component of a starport with both orbital and ground facilities.

Hive Federation: A major interstellar power lying to rimward-trailing of the Imperium, sometimes referred to as the Federation, but never the "Hiver Federation."

Hivers: A major race of Charted Space. Always capitalized; singular Hiver, plural Hivers.

Humaniti: The current spelling of humanity, used when referring to all Humans in a general sense (singular Human, plural Humans). The term refers to the whole of Human species and subspecies rather than the quality of being humane, which can be applied to any sentient species. As this is a specific race, it is always capitalized, and the words Human and Humans are also capitalized when used.

IISS: The Imperial Interstellar Scout Service.

Imperium: The main human interstellar civilization, the Third Imperium, is usually just referred to as the Imperium. There have been three "Imperiums" in the setting: the First Imperium: the Vilani Imperium or Ziru Sirka ("Grand Empire of Stars"), the Second Imperium: The Rule of Man or "Ramshackle Empire" (this last being a term of derision), and the Third Imperium: the Ziru Sirkaa (note the Vilani double -aa ending to contrast it from the First Imperium).

jump: A trip from one point in space to another using jump drive, traveling at greater than the speed of light. A jump is made by leaving real space or true space and traveling through a different plane of existence (jumpspace). Jumps are measured in parsecs; one jump (regardless of distance) requires one week. Because of the interaction of jumpspace with gravity sources, jumps cannot be initiated within 100 D of a gravity source, and objects in jumpspace passing within 100 D of a gravity source drop back into the normal universe.

jump drive: The units of a jump are referred to as jump-1, jump-3, and so on (hyphenated but not capitalized), or abbreviated as J-1, J-3, etc. (with hyphens and capitals). Jump drives cannot be placed on craft smaller than 100 tons.

K'kree: A major race of Charted Space. K'kree are militant herbivores descended from herd animals. The second "k" is always lower case (K'k). Singular and plural forms are the same.

library data: Library data is information obtainable from any ship's computer in response to keywords. Only specific information requested should be given to players; the referee should always take care not to reveal additional data.

lifters: The hull-mounted modules which allow vehicles and craft to rise and float in the air (and are based on gravitics technology). Lifters negate gravity and let vehicles move more easily near world surfaces. Lifters operate effectively only within one diameter of large masses (normally worlds). May be referred to as "antigravity units." Early Traveller material used grav modules, but lifters is preferred.

mainworld: The most important planet in a system, normally the source of the system name.

mainworld identifier: The Scout Service (and others) uses a six-digit system for identifying newly discovered worlds. The preferred usage is SAH-RRR where S=world size, A=atmosphere, H=hydrographics, and R=random digits.

major race: Any species that develops jump drive technology independently; sometimes used to describe a powerful race that did not. Not capitalized.

maneuver drive: The most commonly used interplanetary drive. Performance is measured in Gs. Because it interacts with gravity sources, it must be within 1000 D of a gravity source (beyond 1000 D, it operates at 1% performance).

megacorporation: A huge, Imperium-wide corporation. Mega-corporations have their own private military forces and wield powerful political influence.

minor race: Any race that did not develop jump drive independently but learned of it from outsiders (or never achieved interstellar flight). Also, a race without any real power or influence. Not capitalized.

misjump: An unpredictable random jump, caused by a failure of a ship's jump drive. The result is that if the ship exits jump space, its location is completely random, and the time spent in jump space may vary as well. Upon emerging from misjump, the challenge of determining position and of travelling to an inhabited world becomes paramount.

NAFAL: Not As Fast As Light. Any technology used to explore space that does not permit faster than light travel.

noble: A member of the planetary or Imperial nobility.

parsec: A parsec is a distance of 3.26 light years, corresponding to the size of a subsector system hex and the distance a jump-1 ship can travel in a single week.

planetology: The science of planets, or where earth science and astronomy meet.

psionics: The use of mental powers to manipulate matter and energy, to sense, and to communicate. The science of psionics is psionicology, and one who studies psionics is a psionicist.

psychohistory: The study of the psychological motivations of historical events, combining history, sociology and mathematical statistics to predict collective actions of large groups of people.

race: As used, it means species (for example, the Human race) as opposed to subsets of a species such as Caucasians. See **major race** and **minor race.**

red zone: A world to which access is prohibited for a variety of reasons. Examples include worlds under sanction, highly dangerous planets and prison worlds.

reflec: Reflective anti-laser armor.

rift: An area of space where stars are sparse. Rifts can be major obstacles to navigation.

rimward: *See* **galactic directions.**

RU: Resource Units. The preferred unit of value when working on a planetary or interplanetary scale. There is no specific conversion value for RU to Credits.

sector: A region of space 4 by 4 subsectors in size, normally forming an administrative region.

sector/subsector/world designations: Each sector and subsector is given a unique name. Worlds are named (although some of the names are numbers, such as "457-973") and assigned a position within a sector indicated by a 4-digit number. Formal designations are "the [Name] sector." The words "domain," "sector," "subsector," etc. are not capitalized as part of these formal names. "Sector," "subsector," and the like may be omitted in informal usage, for instance, "the Spinward Marches." The article "the" should precede the name whenever "sector," "subsector," etc. is included, but in informal usage may at times be dropped. For instance, it's "in the Trin's Veil subsector" but could be "in Trin's Veil," but "in the Spinward Marches sector" would still be "in the Spinward Marches." This applies only to casual references; formal reports and similar material will always refer to the full name, as in "the Spinward Marches sector." A warning: some names incorporate articles; for example, one of the subsectors of Dagudashaag sector is named "The Remnants."

Subsector designations are similar, but when it is necessary to give both sector and subsector designations, they can be given either as [subsector]/[sector] or (more formally) as "the [subsector Name] subsector of the [sector Name] sector." The words "sector" and "subsector" can be omitted if context keeps things clear:

"the Arnakhish subsector of Dagudashaag"

"Arnakhish/Dagudashaag,"

"Jewell/Spinward Marches"

"Arnakhish in Dagudashaag"

World designations are subject to the most variation. Star systems are identified by the most important world, not by the star, which means for example, that our own system is "Terra" rather than "Sol."

Where the subsector and sector names are clear from context, simply naming the world will do. Where the sector is known, the preferred method is [world]/[subsector]. Thus: Narval/Chronor, Nirton/District 268, Aramis/Aramis (all of these are in the Spinward Marches—the latter one of many examples of the world and subsector having the same name). An alternate method of naming a world is to give the position number within the sector (each hex on a sector grid is numbered) in the format [world] ([sector] ####). The sector name can be omitted if it is clear from context—e.g. *Jewell (Spinward Marches 1106)* or *Jewell 1106*. For a formal reference, all will be used: *Aramis/Aramis (Spinward Marches 3110)*.

Imagine the references as world/sector/hex in the same vein as city/state/zip (or city/province/postcode) and you will have a complete direction or reference to a world.

ships: When referring to a ship class, such as the *Beowulf*-class, the word "class" is never capitalized unless it is in a head or the line is all caps. Hyphenate ship name and the word "class." Ship names (and prefixes) are italicized, whether or not they are labeled "-class." Names of ship types are not capitalized; it is cruiser, not Cruiser.

viz: *Marava, Suleiman*-class

viz: The *INS She-Lynx II,* a *Tigress*-class battleship, is now under construction in the Spinward Marches.

Ship size is measured in (displacement) tons, or tons, all lower case. When referring to a ship's size, the practice is to call them 100-ton, 400-ton, etc.

ship prefix: An indicator of the ownership or governance of starships. INS: Imperial Navy Starship. ISS: Imperial Scout Ship. IQS: Imperial Quarantine Ship (obsolete). Civilian shipping in the Third Imperium is generally not given a prefix (it's the "100-ton *Beowulf*," never the "100-ton *SS Beowulf*").

small craft: Any spacecraft under 100 tons. Typical small craft types include launch, pinnace, cutter, ship's boat, fighter, and shuttle.

Solomani Confederation: A powerful interstellar state lying to rimward of the Imperium. Always capitalized.

Solomani Hypothesis: The generally accepted idea that all Humaniti originated on Terra, and was transplanted throughout the universe by the Ancients, for reasons that remain unclear.

Solomani: One of the major races of Humaniti, originating on Terra. Also, a person from a culture strongly influenced by old Terran traditions. Singular and plural forms are the same, and Solomani is always capitalized.

sophont: Any intelligent species. Sophont is preferred to Sapient, although the terms are roughly synonymous. Traveller assumes a vague hierarchy in which sapient is inferior to sophont (roughly, sapients as a species have not left their homeworld, and sophonts are present in interstellar society). Sentient technically means "feeling" and not necessarily an intelligent species. Sophont encompasses all intelligent species. The study of sophonts or intelligent life forms is sophontology; some older Traveller materials used xenology, or even xenoanthropology, but sophontology is preferred.

Sophonts are consistently described with a long name in the format "the [race name] of [homeworld]." For example, *the Llellewlowy of Junidy*.

spacecraft: Any vessel capable of interplanetary flight but not jump.

spaceport: A minor port that deals mainly with interplanetary vessels.

speeder: A fast version of the air/raft.

spinal mount: A starship weapon mount running along the entire length of a ship, allowing for a very powerful weapon system to be installed.

spinward: *See* **galactic directions.**

starport: A facility for the landing and service of interstellar and interplanetary vessels of all sorts. A starport is also used for embarkation and disembarkation of passengers and cargo.

starship: Any spacecraft which is capable of interstellar flight is known as a starship. Starships may be commercial, private, or military. Any starship must be a minimum of 100 tons.

startown: The community or neighborhood (often part of a larger town, or city) adjacent to most starports. Startowns have a reputation for being somewhat rough and ready; not all of them deserve this.

subsector: A region of space 8 by 10 parsecs in size, normally forming an administrative region.

system: A star and its associated companion stars (if any), orbiting planets, and their associated satellites. One world of the system is designated the system's *mainworld* and identifies the system.

talent: A specific (usually psionic) ability: telepathy, photographic memory.

TAS: *See* **Travellers' Aid Society.**

titles: Lower case unless referring to a specific individual, as in "a duke," "the Duke," "the Duchess of Mora," etc. The title "Emperor" is always capitalized.

Job titles are capitalized only for high positions: Minister of Justice, and the like. Military ranks of colonel and below are capitalized only when referring to a specific individual by name (Colonel Blimp, Captain Spaulding, Admiral Halsey). Ranks above colonel are capitalized when discussing a specific officer ("General Mills arrived today. The General had nothing to say about cereal...”), but are otherwise lower case ("A division is normally a command for a major general").

TL: Tech(nology) Level. There is no space between the letters TL and the number. It should be TL10, not TL 10.

ton: When used in reference to small craft or starships, this refers to displacement tonnage or roughly 13.5 cubic meters of volume, approximately equal to the volume of one ton (1000 kg) of liquid hydrogen. When referencing weight, this refers to metric tonnage (1000 kg) unless otherwise noted.

Some older Traveller materials use kiloliter rather than cubic meter.

Some older Traveller materials use a Legacy Ton equal to 14 cubic meters.

trader: An interstellar merchant ship operated privately, and usually in a tramp (unscheduled) status. Traders may be further described: Free Trader: the most common o the private traders. Far Trader: equipped with better jump drives. Fat Trader: equipped with greater cargo capacity. It is apparently a convention that an adjective or mission modifier applied to Trader should start with F: Free, Far, Fair, Fat, Flat, Fast, Faux (a sort of Q-ship), Fine, Fleet (with some sort of sutler role).

trailing: *See* **galactic directions.**

Traveller News Service (TNS): Ostensibly a perk of membership in the *Travellers' Aid Society*.

Travellers' Aid Society (TAS): A non-governmental organization devoted to supporting those who travel. Its services vary from simple information kiosks to its profitable hotel line. Variants of the organization exist in most interstellar communities.

Two-Thousand Worlds: A major power in Charted Space, the Two-Thousand Worlds is ruled by the K'kree. It lies to trailing of the Imperium.

Universal World Profile (UWP): A shorthand notation of the raw basic details of a world.

vacc suit: A sealed suit designed to protect the wearer from hostile environments or vacuum; always "vacc," never "vac."

Vargr Extents: A region of space lying to coreward of the Imperium, divided between several Vargr states. Always capitalized.

Vargr: A major race of Charted Space, Vargr are descended from Terran canines. Singular and plural forms are the same; always capitalized.

Vilani: One of the major races of Humaniti, originating on Vland. Also, a person from a culture heavily influenced by Vilani traditions. Singular and plural forms are the same; always capitalized.

world: Any inhabited astronomical body. A world could be a planet like Earth, a satellite of a planet, an airless planet with domed or underground cities, a hollowed-out planetoid, or an artificial construct such as a space station or L-5 type colony.

Xboat: Common abbreviation for "express boat." Xboats have jump but no maneuver drives, and rely on tenders to support and retrieve them. The Xboat network serves the entire Imperium by optimized jump-4 routes, cutting general communications time significantly. Selected locations along major trade routes are established as sites for Xboat stations, which service and fuel the ships on their communications runs. As an Xboat arrives in a system, it transmits its recorded data to the fixed-point station, which then retransmits to a waiting Xboat standing by to jump outsystem. Time between jumps is almost always under four hours, and has been recorded at under seven minutes, making the speed of communication nearly the speed of jump. In practice, this speed is reduced by the fact that the routes do not follow straight lines.

The Xboat system has existed on smaller scales throughout Imperial history. A system serving the whole of the Third Imperium was beginning 624 and was relatively complete circa 850.

Zhodani Consulate: A powerful interstellar state lying to spinward-coreward of the Imperium.

Zhodani: One of the major races of Humaniti, whose culture embraces psionics. Singular and plural forms are the same; always capitalized.

THE ARCHIVES

There are a variety of record-keeping institutions within the Imperium, each with a specific purpose and area of responsibility.

GD (Galidumlar Dadaga): The Great Imperial Archive. The organization dedicated to the safe-keeping of documents created by the government of the Third Imperium. The Archive maintains records of the Emperor's actions, the transactions of the Moot, and the continuing records of the operations of the Ministries and Departments of the Imperium. The Great Imperial Archive is located on Capital/Core. Portions of it are mirrored at various sites within the Imperium. Dadaga generally means Imperial.

AAB (Argushiigi Admegulasha Bilanidin): The Vilani Repository of All Knowledge. Headquartered on Vland, the AAB was (during the final three millennia of the Vilani Empire) the predominant repository of scientific and technological knowledge. With a massive archive and library complex on Vland, and with correspondent archives on major worlds within the Empire, the AAB was clearly the single source for technological data. Argushiigi has historical roots that mean "hidden knowledge." Note the correspondence with the name of the ship the LaGashes fly to Beauniture. Admegulasha has roots that mean "infinite multitude in one unit," or catalog or repository.

ADG (Admegulashasha Dadaga Gukumaarin): The Imperial Encyclopediopolis at Reference. Created at the inception of the Third Imperium, the Encyclopediopolis filled the need for long-term records storage for the growing Imperial bureaucracy. The project was conceived as a successor to the AAB Vilani Repository of All Knowledge. To achieve this goal, three institutions were created: the Encyclopediopolis, a scout base, and a university. The ADG is maintained by the Imperial Interstellar Scout Service.

First Survey (conducted 300 to 420): The first comprehensive astrographic and demographic survey of the Imperium, performed by the Imperial Interstellar Scout Service. The First Survey provided comprehensive information about the worlds of the Imperium (and many of the empire's neighbors) in support of trade and anticipated development.

Second Survey (conducted 995 to 1065): The second comprehensive survey of the Imperium, performed by the Imperial Interstellar Scout Service, updating the (by then) outdated and incomplete data in the First Survey. Intended for completion by the millennial year of the Imperium, various difficulties delayed it until 1065.

ASN (Aashner Sirkaa Nek): The Secret Imperial Archives. Some information is always withheld from general circulation by the government in order to protect the operations and policies of various agencies. Aashner actually means "archive" in an official sense. Sirkaa is an element of the name of the Third Imperium: Ziru Sirkaa. It means "of the stars," with a connotation of renewed or reestablished. There was a similar secret archive for the original First Imperium (the Aashner Sirka Nek, probably with the same initials). Nek is an emphatic meaning private or secret. Thus, Secret Renewed Archive of the Stars.

KE (Kiirimgan Eshka): The Central Records of the Quarantine. Kiirimgan is built on the root kiir, with meanings of organization or systematicity, coupled with a modifier associated with structured access. Here, it means Official Records Organization. Eshka is a social term conveying harmony or peace, and sometimes safety or protection.

AQ (L'Agence Quarantine): The Imperial agency charged with isolating and eliminating threats to the Imperium. There is a decidedly French influence on the Anglic of the Third Imperium.

Early in the history of the First Imperium, the Cranch (the world no longer exists) crisis unleashed an insidious parasite from its homeworld. Conflicting lines of authority complicated matters and the confused situation allowed the infection of seven adjacent systems before it was contained. Two worlds were isolated, three were scrubbed, and the remaining two subjected to rigid access controls for the next six hundred years.

The First Imperium created Eshkaa: literally Safety, and assigned it the special mission of eliminating threats (the phrase "at any cost" appears in its enabling documents) to the empire. The agency had three resources: quarantine fleets, typically attached from naval forces as required; specialized reaction squadrons stationed strategically throughout the empire; and trained quarantine officers (their status and powers secret until required) capable of taking control of situations regardless of other rank structures.

The second Imperium under Terran control continued the structure, but didn't really understand its brutal nature; the Quarantine transformed into an emergency reaction force.

The Third Imperium re-established it until about 300, when its forces were absorbed into the Navy as Angin-wafer Agents were deployed.

SOPHONTS

The Imperial Interstellar Scout Service terminology for classification of sophonts encompasses three distinct specifications.

Sentient: Endowed with feeling and unstructured consciousness; generally aware and capable of action and reaction, but guided more by instinct and desire than by structured thought or planning. Able to adapt effectively to the environment, either by making a change in oneself or by changing the environment or finding a new one. Susceptible to training, but rarely to education. Sentience is often called animal intelligence. A tiger, a groat, and a gazelle are all sentient. From the Latin *sentiens* for feeling. First use: J. B. Harris, 1932.

Sapient: Possessing intelligence: the mental ability to reason, think abstractly, comprehend ideas, and learn. Generally capable of being educated and achieving insights. Sapient and sophont (which follows) are synonyms, but sapient generally has a lower threshold. The traditional usage: sapients are intelligent, but (still) bound to their original homeworld. From the Latin *sapiens* for wise. First use: H. Beam Piper, 1962.

Sophont: Possessing intelligence: the mental ability to reason, think abstractly, comprehend ideas, and learn. Generally capable of being educated and achieving insights. Sapient and sophont are synonyms, but sophont generally covers a broader range. The traditional usage: sophonts are intelligent and have travelled to the stars and have presences on other worlds. From the Greek *sophos* for wise. First use: Poul Anderson (with credit to Karen Anderson), 1966.

Typographic Conventions

The stylistic convention is to capitalize the specific naming terms of sophonts to enhance comprehension. Human, Vargr, Aslan, Bwap, Llellewyloly, Solomani, Zhodani, Vilani (the specific reason is to disambiguate between Human as a name for the sophont species and human as a less specific term).

There may be more than one term applied to one specific species, and all are capitalized: Bwap and Newt, Llellewyloly and Dandelion, Solomani and Terran. On the other hand, pejoratives are not capitalized: Zhodani, but not joe. Dandelion, but not weed. Vilani, but not stiff. Cassildan, but not stilt.

THE MAJOR AND MINOR RACES

Race is an obsolete scientific term, but it remains in social contexts and casual and political discourse: usually associated with the words alien, major, and minor.

The Major and Minor Race concepts predominated the First, and to some extent the Second Imperiums' views of the relative hierarchy of sophonts. A Major Race is one that independently developed jump drive technology; the Minor Races are everyone else.

Major Races: The generally accepted Major Race sophonts are the feline Aslan, canid Vargr, 6-ped Hivers, centauroid K'kree, reptilian Droyne, and a few select Human branches: Vilani, Zhodani, and Solomani.

Minor Races: The Minor Races are all other sophonts: dozens of Human sub-races, and hundreds of distinct and independently evolved intelligences throughout Charted Space.

Human Minor Races: One result of the Major-Minor classification system is the existence of Human Minor Races: recognizable Humans other than the VZS three nonetheless relegated to Minor status because of their independent recent planetary backgrounds.

The Traveller Gene: Most people (indeed, whole species) never leave their homeworld: they never venture out of their gravity well, content to work, play, and even thrive on their home planet. Some postulate that there is a genetic basis for the drive of some (and the lack of drive in others) to reach beyond the bounds of a single world into the greater universe: a traveller gene.

The Humans of Terra
(Sol-3 [G2 V] A877B99-D)

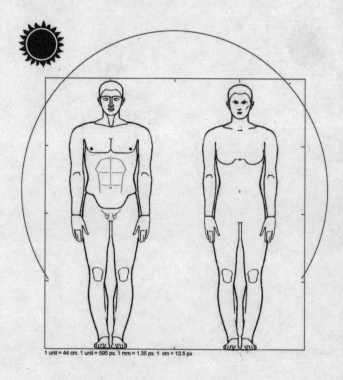

1 unit = 44 cm. 1 unit = 595 px. 1 mm = 1.35 px. 1 cm = 13.5 px

Genetic Humans originated on Terra as part of the natural evolutionary process, and now are the predominant sophont of the Third Imperium's ten thousand systems.

The Cassildan of Ambemsham
(Krof-0 [M3 V] A5457BC-B

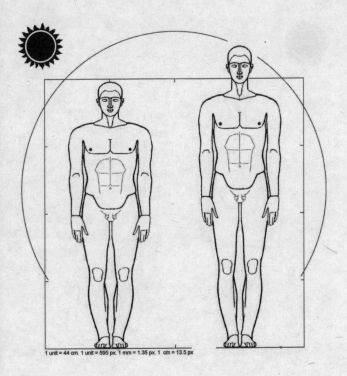

1 unit = 44 cm. 1 unit = 595 px. 1 mm = 1.35 px. 1 cm = 13.5 px

The Cassildan, a minor branch of Humanity, were
abandoned by one of Grandfather's Sons on a low gravity
world in the aftermath of the Ancient War.

The Geonee of Shiwonee
(Alliana-5 [F7 V] AA86831-C)

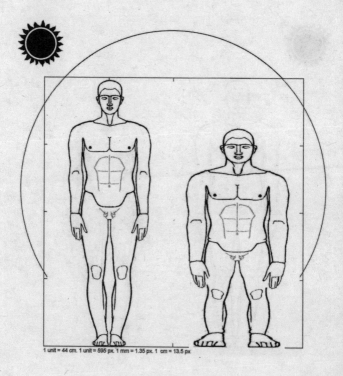

1 unit = 44 cm. 1 unit = 595 px. 1 mm = 1.35 px. 1 cm = 13.5 px

The Geonee, a minor branch of Humanity, are one of the oldest human interstellar cultures in charted space (behind only the Suerrat and Vilani).

The Vargr of Lair
(Kneng-3 [G5 V] A8859B9-F)

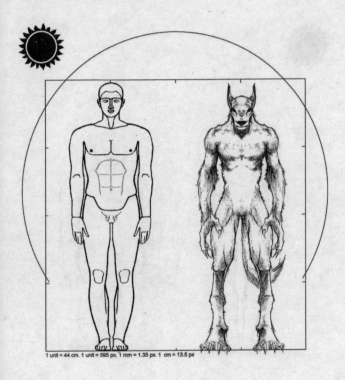

1 unit = 44 cm. 1 unit = 595 px. 1 mm = 1.35 px. 1 cm = 13.5 px

The Vargr live generally coreward of the Imperium: upright bipeds with a humanoid body plan, the result of some obscure Ancient genetic manipulations (of the canids of Terra).

The Zhodani of Zhdant
(Pliebr-2 [K0 V] A6549C8-F)

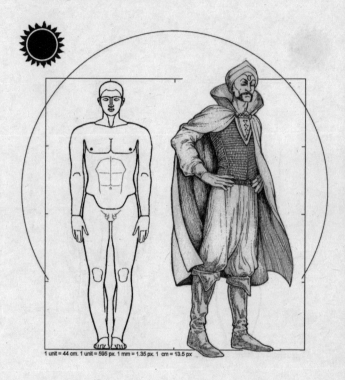

1 unit = 44 cm. 1 unit = 595 px. 1 mm = 1.35 px. 1 cm = 13.5 px

The Zhodani, a branch of Humanity, live spinward of the Imperium; their evolutionary path diverged long ago as they embraced psionics as an integral part of their society.

The Aslan of Kusyu
(Tyeyo-3 [G4 V] A876986-E)

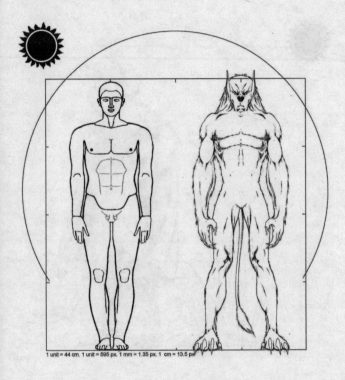

1 unit = 44 cm. 1 unit = 595 px. 1 mm = 1.35 px. 1 cm = 13.5 px

The Aslan (in their language: Fteirle) are the dominant sophonts in regions spinward of Terra: four-limbed, upright, bipedal, carnivore/pouncer felinoids.

The Hivers of Guaran
(Primary-2 [K1 V] A667800-F)

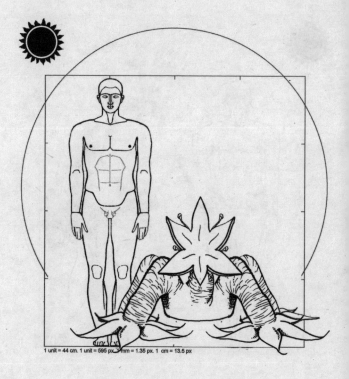

1 unit = 44 cm. 1 unit = 595 px. 1 mm = 1.35 px. 1 cm = 13.5 px

Hivers are best described as strange, giant, intelligent land-dwelling starfish. They are silent (they speak in a gesture language) geniuses with obscure motives.

The K'kree of Kirur
(Gzang-5 [F1 V] B863A03-F)

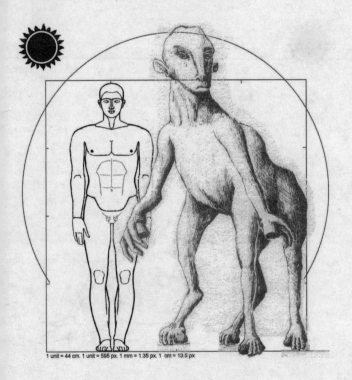

1 unit = 44 cm. 1 unit = 595 px. 1 mm = 1.35 px. 1 cm = 13.5 px

The K'kree are herd-oriented, aggressive vegetarians. The apostrophe in their name is a glottal stop: to many listeners, their name is a strange choking sound.

The Droyne of Droynia
(original location unknown)

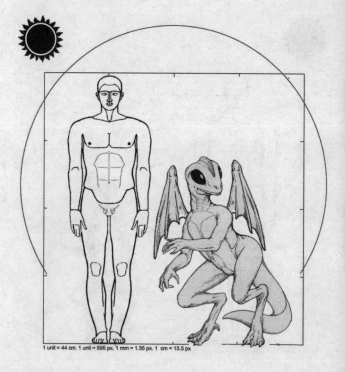

1 unit = 44 cm. 1 unit = 595 px. 1 mm = 1.35 px. 1 cm = 13.5 px

The Droyne are six-limbed (two are wings), upright, bipedal omnivore/gatherers who occupy a variety of pastoral worlds in and around the Imperium. They are the scattered remnants of the fantastic Ancients who swept through this spiral arm 300,000 years ago.

The Bwaps of Maharaban
(Glowl-2 [G4 V]) A4698AB-B)

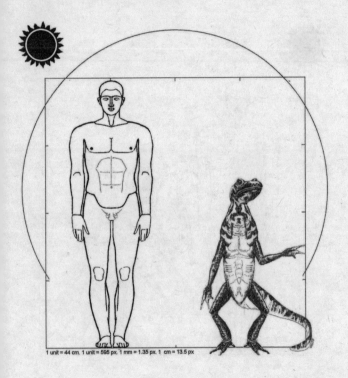

1 unit = 44 cm. 1 unit = 595 px. 1 mm = 1.35 px. 1 cm = 13.5 px

The Bwaps' worldview is that everyone has a place in the greater structure of the universe. Uncomfortable in less than 90% humidity; they adapt with special wetted clothing and headband.

The Llellewyloly of Junidy
(Vlov-4 [F7 V] B434ABD-B)

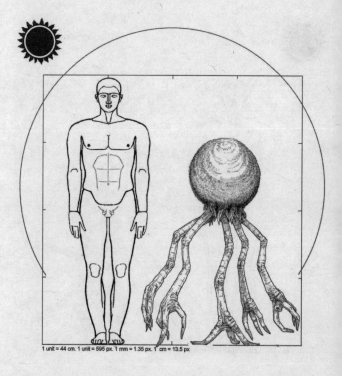

1 unit = 44 cm. 1 unit = 595 px. 1 mm = 1.35 px. 1 cm = 13.5 px

The Llellewyloly have five multi-jointed limbs which function as hands and feet and senses interchangeably; the spherical central body is covered with long, coarse hair. They thrive in a thin atmosphere where Humans cannot.

The Threep of Othsekuu
(Toll-1 [M1 V] B789856-C)

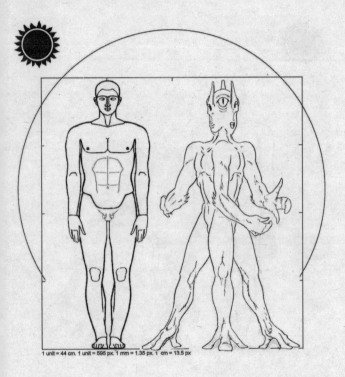

1 unit = 44 cm. 1 unit = 595 px. 1 mm = 1.35 px. 1 cm = 13.5 px

The Threep are radially symmetrical 3-peds in a roughly human pattern. They have deficient hearing and resultingly booming voices. Their sensory palps express their perception sense.

The Virushi of Virshash
(Thintle-6 [F9 V] DA86954-6)

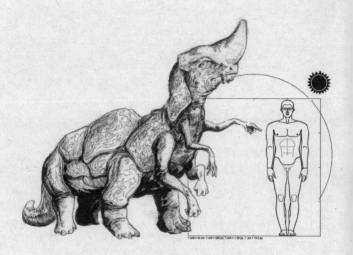

The Virushi are eight-limbed horn-nosed gentle giants. The Virushi are among the largest intelligent races encountered by Humaniti. Formidable in appearance, the truth is that they are confirmed pacifists with great abilities in the medical (or perhaps the veterinary) field.

TRAVELLER5

This novel is set in the Traveller universe, governed by the events (the canon) of the background and history that has been chronicled since the role-playing game was first published in 1977.

To a different extent, activity is governed by the game rules (which have varied by edition over time). Nevertheless, the game rules envision a specific universe where interstellar travel is accomplished by jump (which takes the same 168 hours plus or minus a tenth) regardless of distance (ranging from 1 to 6 parsecs), and where communication is restricted to the same limit.

The current edition of Traveller is:

Traveller5 (T5): The fifth of the direct line of editions of the Traveller game system, ambitiously intended as the ultimate science-fiction role-playing system covering near everything in role-playing, and capable of managing situations across a variety of eras and technology levels.

The previous editions are:

Classic Traveller (CT): The original edition of Traveller published by Game Designers' Workshop (GDW) in 1977. The intention was a generic science-fiction system, but it quickly concentrated on the Third Imperium as a setting supported with adventures and supplements.

MegaTraveller (MT): The second edition of Traveller published by GDW in 1987, introduced a unified task game mechanic supported by a fully developed skill system; it advanced the Traveller universe history and setting into the Rebellion era.

Traveller: The New Era (TNE): The third edition of Traveller, the last to be published by GDW in 1993, adopted GDW's RPG *House System* rules (also used for its Twilight: 2000 and Dark Conspiracy role-playing games). Adventures chronicled the aftermath of a widespread collapse of interstellar civilization.

Marc Miller's Traveller (T4): The fourth edition of Traveller, published by Imperium Games in 1996 (after GDW closed its doors). Its adventures and supplements chronicle the founding years (beginning in Year Zero) of the Third Imperium.

GURPS Traveller (GT): A truly parallel edition (published by Steve Jackson Games in 1998) chronicling an alternate universe in which Emperor Strephon was not assassinated (in 1116) and the MegaTraveller Rebellion did not happen. This edition adapted the setting to the Steve Jackson Games GURPS rules set.

Mongoose Traveller (MgT): Produced as a universal science-fiction role-playing rules set (published by Mongoose Games in 2007), this edition again emphasized the Spinward Marches and its surrounding sectors.

Recognitions

The *Traveller* role-playing game and its primary designer Marc Miller have been individually inducted into the Hall of Fame of the *Academy of Adventure Gaming* in recognition of their contributions to adventure gaming.

EMPERORS AND EMPRESSES
OF THE THIRD IMPERIUM

No.	Emperor/Empress	Reign	Dynasty
1	Cleon I	0–53	Zhunastu
2	Cleon II	53–54	Zhunastu
3	Artemsus	54–166	Lentuli
4	Martin I	166–195	Lentuli
5	Martin II	195–244	Lentuli
6	Cleon III	244–245	Zhunastu
7	Porfiria	245–326	Lentuli
8	Anguistus	326–365	Lentuli
9	Martin III	365–456	Lentuli
10	Martin V	456–457	Lentuli
11	Nicholle	457–475	Lentuli
12	Cleon IV	475–555	non-Dynastic
13	Jerome	555–582	non-Dynastic
14	Jaqueline I	582–606	non-Dynastic
15	Olav	606–609	Emperors of the Flag
16	Ramon I	609	Emperors of the Flag
17	Constantus	609–610	Emperors of the Flag
18	Nicolai	610–612	Emperors of the Flag
19a	George	612–613	Emperors of the Flag
19b	Barracks Emperors	613–615	Emperors of the Flag
20	Cleon V	615–618	Emperors of the Flag
21	Joseph	618	Emperors of the Flag
22	Donald	618	Emperors of the Flag
23	Emdiri	618–619	Emperors of the Flag
24	Catharine	619	Emperors of the Flag

No.	Emperor/Empress	Reign	Dynasty
25	Ramon II	619	Emperors of the Flag
26	Jaqueline II	619	Emperors of the Flag
27	Usuti	619–620	Emperors of the Flag
28	Marava	620	Emperors of the Flag
29	Ivan	620–621	Emperors of the Flag
30	Martin VI	621	Emperors of the Flag
31	Gustus	621–622	Emperors of the Flag
	Arbellatra (Regent)	622–629	
32	Arbellatra	629–666	Alkhalikoi
33	Zhakirov	666–688	Alkhalikoi
34	Margaret I	688–736	Alkhalikoi

ACKNOWLEDGMENTS

I am indebted to a close circle of writers and critics who have advised me in ways that I can never fully acknowledge.

Don McKinney, whose wise counsel has helped me avoid problems more than once.

Robert Eaglestone, whose fountain of imagination constantly challenges me to make my work better.

Greg Lee, whose writing skill gives me a standard to which I can aspire.

Charles Gannon, whose supportive encouragement he may not fully realize.

Matt Adcock, whose musical insights have helped me see greater depth in these stories.

and finally,

Darlene Miller, my wife and best friend, who supports me in everything I do.

ABOUT THE AUTHOR

Marc Miller started out as a classically trained science fiction reader, raised on Campbell's *Astounding* and *Analog,* reading all the greats: Smith, Heinlein, Asimov, Clarke, Norton, and all the rest.

Miller became an award-winning game designer with more than 70 titles across historical and SF genres, and was recognized with multiple awards for game-design excellence. His military and SF experiences shaped the Traveller universe he created for role-playing gamers, and now he chronicles that universe in the traditional form that so influenced him.

He lives in Bloomington, Illinois, with his wife, Darlene.

This is Miller's first novel.

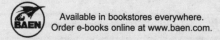